DEEP KILL

Michael Kilian

BERKLEY BOOKS, NEW YORK

THE BERKLEY PUBLISHING GROUP
Published by the Penguin Group
Penguin Group (USA) Inc.
375 Hudson Street, New York, New York 10014, USA
Penguin Group (Canada), 10 Alcorn Avenue, Toronto, Ontario M4V 3B2, Canada
(a division of Pearson Penguin Canada Inc.)
Penguin Books Ltd., 80 Strand, London WC2R 0RL, England
Penguin Group Ireland, 25 St. Stephen's Green, Dublin 2, Ireland (a division of Penguin Books Ltd.)
Penguin Group (Australia), 250 Camberwell Road, Camberwell, Victoria 3124, Australia
(a division of Pearson Australia Group Pty. Ltd.)
Penguin Books India Pvt. Ltd., 11 Community Centre, Panchsheel Park, New Delhi—110 017, India
Penguin Group (NZ), Cnr. Airborne and Rosedale Roads, Albany, Auckland 1310, New Zealand
(a division of Pearson New Zealand Ltd.)
Penguin Books (South Africa) (Pty.) Ltd., 24 Sturdee Avenue, Rosebank, Johannesburg 2196,
South Africa

Penguin Books Ltd., Registered Offices: 80 Strand, London WC2R 0RL, England

This is a work of fiction. Names, characters, places, and incidents either are the product of the author's imagination or are used fictitiously, and any resemblance to actual persons, living or dead, business establishments, events, or locales is entirely coincidental.

DEEPKILL

A Berkley Book / published by arrangement with the author

PRINTING HISTORY
Berkley edition / June 2005

Copyright © 2005 by Michael Kilian.
Cover illustration by Gallucci Imaging Inc.
Cover design by Rich Hasselberger.
Interior text design by Stacy Irwin.

ISBN: 0-425-20351-4

BERKLEY®
Berkley Books are published by The Berkley Publishing Group,
a division of Penguin Group (USA) Inc.,
375 Hudson Street, New York, New York 10014.
BERKLEY is a registered trademark of Penguin Group (USA) Inc.
The "B" design is a trademark belonging to Penguin Group (USA) Inc.

PRINTED IN THE UNITED STATES OF AMERICA

10 9 8 7 6 5 4 3 2 1

Author's Note

This is a work of fiction. Though there are some references to a few actual persons of public note, all of the characters are fictional and imagined and bear no resemblance to any actual persons, living or dead. The author has nothing but the highest respect for the many federal agencies involved in homeland security, including most especially the Coast Guard and the Coast Guard Investigative Service.

For my father, Frederick Kilian,
U.S. Coast Guard, World War II; and
for Col. Chris Branch (U.S.A.F.)
and Lt. Kara Hultgreen (U.S.N.),
among the heroes at Arlington

Acknowledgments

I am indebted to Dr. Robert Ballard, the legendary deep-sea explorer who discovered the wreck of the *Titanic,* for contributing immensely to my knowledge of the sea. I am grateful also to Steve Shlopac, onetime swordfish boat skipper and now proprietor of the Greenwich Village literary saloon Chumley's, and to Morris Kohler and Tom Haley of the *Keena Dale IV,* for adding similarly to my maritime knowledge. I want to thank Special Agent Marty Martinez of the Coast Guard Investigative Service for educating me on the workings of one of the least known but most valuable law enforcement, intelligence, and defense agencies in the federal service, and to thank my good friend and former Air Force test pilot Richard Locher for instructing me on military cargo aircraft. Thanks, too, to my editor, Gail Fortune, and literary representative, Dominick Abel, for their years of splendid service. I am grateful to my wife, Pamela, and sons, Eric and Colin, as only they can know.

Chapter 1

It was a half hour past the agreed-upon time and yet the bomb had not been detonated.

The parades of headlights and taillights moving over the great Chesapeake Bay Bridge in the summer twilight continued unabated—the traffic bound for the Eastern Shore and the Atlantic beaches as heavy as the westbound flow heading home for Washington and Baltimore and the workweek to come.

Somewhere in that westbound ribbon of red—if actuality was conforming to plan—was the White House Homeland Security adviser, riding with his wife in a government car driven by an Executive Protection Service officer and accompanied by an escort vehicle containing two other protectors.

Gabor Turko wondered why this target had been selected. The American Secretaries of Defense and State were much more desirable victims. But, inconveniently, neither of those more prominent officials had weekend beach houses on the Delaware shore. They were also nearly as well protected as the President and the Vice President. The Pakistanis in

Turko's crew were not up to a challenge that formidable.

Jozip Pec, Turko's boss in this enterprise, had decided on the Homeland Security aide as the most acceptable alternate choice and the easiest to bring down. A man of habits, the adviser left his oceanfront house in Rehoboth Beach, Delaware, around seven P.M. on Sunday evenings, returning to his suburban Chevy Chase, Maryland, home about three hours later.

Passing over the Bay Bridge at about nine-fifteen.

The bridge was the major component of the plan. Its destruction would spread fear and confusion throughout the country like a virulent disease. Who would willingly drive across the Golden Gate or the George Washington Bridge or through the Holland Tunnel if this mighty span was dropped in the water? New York would strangle this time. It might even die.

Turko had arrived early at the waterfront restaurant so that he might assure himself of a table on its outside deck. The establishment was situated on the western shore of Kent Island, just at the eastern end of the great bridge. The spectacular water view provided an excuse to be sitting there, but not forever. He'd been there for nearly an hour and a half, his meal long finished.

It was fully dark now. Turko was lingering over his third cup of coffee. The overweight waitress had put down his check and had come near twice, looking at him pointedly. Turko guessed she was about to go off duty and was irritated by his keeping her this long.

He laid a credit card down. It had been issued to him as Anthony Bertolucci. Turko was dark, and counted on being taken for Italian. He assumed that the waitress would pay more attention to the credit card and the generous tip he would leave than she would to his face and appearance.

He wore the kind of clothes favored by the other customers—khaki trousers, a short-sleeved knit shirt, running shoes. He'd worn sunglasses into the place, but had taken them off when the light had left the sky.

He could not remain there much longer.

Once again, he carefully removed his slim cell phone from his pocket and made certain it was still on and that there were no messages. The lack of word bothered him almost as much as the lack of an explosion.

They had worked on this operation for several months and had rehearsed it a half-dozen times, using Turko's rental Ford as the target vehicle for the drill. It had gone as planned every time in these exercises.

It was a simple plan, employing a chase car that was to fall in behind the Homeland Security adviser's as it turned from Highway 404 onto Highway 50. The slow-moving truck and the blocking car would then move onto the Bay Bridge just ahead of the target vehicle. When they reached the towers of the high suspension portion of the span, the final phase of the operation would be executed.

Turko trusted the men in his attack group, but only because he had been told he must. Their cell had been organized and trained by someone else and he had never met any of the men before picking them up at the assigned collection point in Oxon Hill, Maryland, a few weeks before. He had to assume they would carry out his instructions. He had made it very clear they were to notify him by cell phone the instant anything went awry.

There was another of his instructions he'd been counting on them to obey—though his confidence in their doing so may have been misplaced. In executing the climax of the plan, they were to blow up themselves along with the truck. It was not too much to ask of men of faith. Others had done it with enthusiasm, and to great effect. Many Chechen women had given their lives this way in the war against Mother Russia. These Pakistanis had all sworn to commit this selfless act. It was the one great advantage of their enterprise.

But it was nothing Turko wished to do himself. He worried that they might not be much different than he.

Mary Ann Ryan was driving well over the speed limit. She had her two youngest children in the backseat and her oldest beside her, but her need for haste was compelling. She had promised her husband she would be back from the beach by ten. It was nearly that, and she was still an hour from home. He was always angry when she was late.

She was tired, a little sunburned, and had her own job to go to early in the morning. Her children were crabby and the two in back were punching each other with increasing frequency, while the one beside her continued to make annoying noises. She had shouted at them, effectively at first, but no longer. Were the traffic not moving along so well, she would have pulled off the highway on Kent Island and administered a couple of roadside spankings.

Instead she endured, willing the miles ahead to vanish. There had been construction blocking one or more of the three lanes on the westbound span of the bridge for more than a year, but they'd finally finished the project. Despite the Sunday night volume, she was able to maintain fifty to sixty miles an hour, even in the center lane.

Her youngest began kicking the back of her seat. She reached behind it to grab his ankle, but missed and was struck in her elbow by the heel of his shoe, the numbing pain running all the way down the bone of her arm. She shouted again, and swore—as she almost never did in front of the children.

"Stop it! All of you stop it! Or we'll never go to the beach again!"

That silenced them—for about a minute. Her middle child, in the right rear seat, began calling the youngest names. The punching resumed.

Mary Ann rubbed her still-stinging elbow, holding the

steering wheel loosely. The cars ahead were slowing. There was a rental truck in the right-hand lane, moving slowly, compelling the vehicles behind it to pull out in front of her to get around it. Then a car from the lane to the left moved into hers and slowed down abruptly. She tried to switch to the fast lane herself, but there were other cars coming up swiftly on the left.

Hitting the brakes, she waited for them to pass. Two other vehicles were coming up behind her on the right—a dark sedan and then a large SUV with high bright lights. The car in front of her was slowing still more, as was the truck. Seeing a break to her left, Mary Ann jerked the wheel and hit the accelerator, sliding into place.

There was steel grating in the pavement here, causing the tires to slip from side to side and make an irritating whining noise. She gripped the wheel tightly with both hands, but then her youngest let fly another kick against the back of her seat. She tried to whack him, taking her right hand and her attention from the wheel. Her left front tire struck something and, before she could do anything about it, her car skidded sideways into the bridge railing, bouncing off it like the bumper cars at Funland on the Rehoboth Beach boardwalk. She tried desperately to correct, but so violently that the skid only increased. Spinning sideways, she was struck by the front end of the car behind her.

That auto and the following SUV then collided and careened off to the right, jammed together against the bridge. The driver of the truck in the right-hand lane now hit his brakes. She saw the red taillights get larger and larger. She stood on her own brakes, but it was too late. Her car crunched into the left rear corner of the truck.

The air bag in her steering-wheel column explosively inflated. She felt as though she'd been head-tackled by some huge football player. As it collapsed, she saw that the bag beside her had inflated as well, enveloping her oldest child. The two kids in the back were screaming.

A man got out of the driver's side of the truck. Another man joined him, and then a third. She thought they were rushing to help her, but they hurried past her car and kept on running.

The explosion came just as Turko was signing the credit card slip, causing his hand to jump. He looked up to see a flare of orange that illuminated the four towers of the two bridge spans, but it was much smaller than it should have been. He rose, the scraping of his chair suddenly the only sound in the restaurant. The other diners had all fallen silent, and were staring gape-mouthed toward the bridge.

Turko went to the railing. All of the traffic on both spans had stopped. Horns were honking, pointlessly. Boats out on the water stopped. Somewhere in the night, a tug whistle sounded.

He waited. The orange light flared again and then rapidly began to diminish. According to the plan, the towers by now should have been beginning to crumple, the bridge twisting and falling into the darkness of the bay, spewing hundreds of headlights and taillights into the night and the water below.

But there was only the rapidly vanishing orange light. Nothing more. And then it was gone.

Turko quickly took his copy of the credit card bill and, easing his way through the crowd that was gathering on the deck, went first to the men's room and then out to his car, keeping his pace slow.

He'd go no farther along Highway 50 than the nearest bar. He needed to watch the television reports. That was a wonderful thing about America. Everything was on television.

Chapter 2

Lieutenant Timothy Dewey was nearing the end of his tour as the skipper of the 110-foot Island Class cutter *Manteo,* having happily been reassigned to the larger, Puerto Rico-based U.S. Coast Guard cutter *Sentinel*. The *Sentinel*'s captain was retiring at the end of the year and Dewey had been told he would likely be replacing him.

He would be assuming a considerable responsibility. The *Sentinel* was one of the big new blue-water cutters taking part in the ongoing "Operation New Frontier," the Coast Guard's weapon against the drug smugglers who for years had been operating with near-impunity on the high seas because of their high-speed, fifty-eight-knots-an-hour go-fast boats.

The *Sentinel* carried one of the new MH-68A attack helicopters, capable of two hundred miles an hour and armed with an MK-40 machine gun and a special .50-caliber sniper rifle that could blow apart a boat engine with a single shot. On the same aft deck, the *Sentinel* also carried a twenty-six-foot, thirty-knot-an-hour, high-speed interdiction inflatable intended to put boarding parties aboard suspect vessels fast. And the mother ship was amply armed with cannon and machine guns as well.

There were New Frontier "packages" working both Atlantic and Pacific waters, and they were enjoying an extraordinary success rate. Before their advent, the Coast Guard had been able to apprehend only about ten percent of the drug-smuggling craft it located. With the cutter-helicopter-interdiction boat package, the apprehension rate had gone up to ninety percent.

The reassignment would mean long patrols in the Caribbean and time away from Sally, his bride of six months. But at twenty-nine, Dewey was not about to decline an opportunity for action. He'd done a couple of tours as a junior officer on icebreakers in the Great Lakes, a stint at the Coast Guard's national headquarters in Washington as an operations officer, and a year in his present job, performing mostly search-and-rescue operations out of Cape May, New Jersey. If he was ever going to make admiral, as his Naval officer father had done, he needed to mix it up with the bad guys sometime in his career. The Caribbean was awash with bad guys.

In the meantime, the *Manteo* was all his. For the last month, his boat had been doing port security duty at Baltimore Harbor, and was now relieved of that mission to go back on station at Cape May, New Jersey.

He was at that hour heading for the upper reaches of Chesapeake Bay and the Chesapeake and Delaware Canal that cut across the narrows of the Delmarva Peninsula and connected Chesapeake and Delaware Bays. The *Manteo*'s base at the Cape May Coast Guard station was directly across the mouth of Delaware Bay from Cape Henlopen and the Delaware town of Lewes. Every ship headed for Philadelphia and the other upriver ports passed through Dewey's jurisdiction. He was their guardian, and these were nervous times.

He and Sally had a rented apartment in an old Victorian Cape May house a block off the beach. The *Manteo* would be tying up there by noon the next day. He was counting the hours.

"Port twenty degrees, Bill," Dewey said to the bos'n's mate as he peered down at the computerized chart on the video screen of the bridge console. They had cleared Baltimore's outer harbor and were rounding Sparrows Point.

"Port twenty degrees it is," said the bos'n's mate, a red-haired, ruddy-faced man named McKeon.

Someone had once asked Dewey if one said "Aye, aye" or "Yes, sir" in the Coast Guard. Dewey was viewed as a straight-arrow, by-the-book officer, but he'd replied, "Either—and often neither."

On the *Manteo*, at least when there were no high-ranking superior officers aboard, the rule was "neither."

The lights of Fort Howard were visible on the port side of the *Manteo* and those of Bayside Beach on the starboard. Dead ahead, the Eastern Shore was a dark, distant band separating the dark, blue-gray sky and the silvery, moonlit waters of the Chesapeake.

Dewey moved to the starboard side of the bridge, standing at one of the windows. There were two large coal ships steaming in toward Baltimore, almost side by side. They'd be dropping anchor soon, to wait for a harbor berth. It could be a long wait, as the dockside moorings were full and they'd not be allowed in the Baltimore harbor until there was clearance. South, down the bay, were the lights of a large vessel identified on the radar as a tanker.

Chief Petty Officer Hugo DeGroot, the quartermaster on the *Manteo*, came up the companionway. He was officer of the deck the next watch, but had arrived early.

The bos'n's mate at the helm acknowledged him first; then Dewey gave him a nod. DeGroot had twenty years on the lieutenant, and the relationship was more one of father and son than superior and subordinate. The Coast Guard was not much of a stickler for formality, at all events.

"Got a bay full of boats, I see," said DeGroot.

"I was just thinking how long it would take to search 'em all," Dewey said. "If we ever go back to doing that."

"It would take all damn week."

DeGroot went to the computer console and punched up a magnified view of the chart. They'd be passing by Pooles Island, which was part of the Army's Aberdeen Proving Ground. There was little to stop intruders from making landfall there—except that sooner or later they'd run into a lot of Army.

The computer displayed a continuous projection of the *Manteo*'s position on the electronic chart. After they had passed the Sparrows Point shoals, Dewey called out a new course, resulting in a tighter turn to port. The three vertical white lights of a safe-water channel marker appeared directly off the bow.

"It's all yours, Chief," Dewey said. "But I think I'll hang out here a while."

DeGroot grunted. The crew called him "the Dutchman," and sometimes "the Flying Dutchman" when he had the *Manteo* up to full speed. Dewey was "the Admiral," not because of his father or his ambitions, but after the Spanish-American War Naval hero, to whom he was distantly related. Dewey hoped that sometime in his career he'd be assigned a WEPS officer named Gridley.

Two of the bridge windows had been partially opened to admit the summer night air. Hearing a thud of thunder to the south, Dewey looked up, surprised. The sky was clear. There was still moonlight. He clicked on the weather radar. There was no precipitation for a hundred miles, and not much out there.

He went outside onto the small bridge deck. The southern horizon was clear of cloud. But there was a strange orange light off the stern quarter.

The radio began crackling with alarm. Annapolis was reporting a major accident on the Chesapeake Bay Bridge. De-Groot had already called for a 180-degree turn by the time orders came for them to proceed down to Kent Island and stand by to assist.

Dewey returned to the helm. The strange orange light was soon dead ahead. The turn completed, he ordered full speed.

"That's not an automobile accident, Hugo," he said.

"Maybe somebody hit a tanker truck."

"Maybe. But I wonder." Dewey watched the light flare and then diminish. Then he went to the intercom and summoned all hands to their duty stations.

His No. 2, Lieutenant J.G. Bob Kelleter, was on the bridge within a minute, coffee cup in hand.

"What's up?" he asked.

"Big trouble on the Bay Bridge," said Dewey.

"Station Annapolis patrols that area," DeGroot said. "They're supposed to check out the bridge base."

"They can't patrol the roadway," replied Dewey. He noticed something awry on the foredeck. "Where's the fifty-caliber?"

"Second officer had it stowed below," DeGroot said.

"SOP transiting to duty station," Kelleter explained.

"Get it back on the mount, Hugo."

"You think we're going to need heavy weapons?"

"I don't know what to think."

Coast Guard Investigative Service Special Agent Erik Westman was at the tiller of his small sailboat, heading downstream from Alexandria and the Wilson Bridge toward his mooring at Belle Haven Marina. He had sailed up to Washington for dinner and was returning after dark, but he knew the Potomac well and there was a moon.

With his prematurely white hair, deep tan, Navy polo shirt, white shorts, and Sperry Topsiders, he looked more a yachtsman than a federal agent. There were times when that proved useful on undercover missions.

Westman was from Bristol, Rhode Island, and had grown up with boats. He had quit college at the University of Rhode Island after only two years and joined the Coast Guard as a lark, thinking he'd spend a little time doing something he truly enjoyed while he figured out what he wanted to do with his life. When it had come time to reenlist, he'd realized the service was it, though his parents hadn't been very happy with his choice of a career.

His architect father had hoped he'd become one too, or perhaps an artist, for Westman had shown talent as an amateur painter. But the Coast Guard made him happy, and even lowly petty officers made more than most artists.

Four years after signing up with the Coast Guard, Westman had been selected for the warrant officers program. Two years after that, having earned admission to the Coast Guard Investigative Service, he'd been promoted to chief warrant officer four, the top grade before you got into the regular officers' caste. Westman had no interest in that, because the Investigative Service accepted no one in its special agent ranks above the rank of warrant officer. He'd been with the CGIS, mostly as an intelligence operative, for nine years. Westman could not imagine himself doing anything else.

As always, he was returning to his marina reluctantly. He loved sailing this river, night or day. He was put in mind of an afternoon he'd spent on it years before with a woman from Rhode Island—a lady who might have become his wife, had he not been inconveniently and unfortunately involved with someone in the Coast Guard.

She had brought a picnic lunch and wine and after they had finished it he had kissed her knee. That was all there was to it that day, but it was a memory never far from his mind. He wondered what might have happened had they gone on more such sails—especially on soft summer nights like this one.

Instead, the lady had married a fighter pilot friend of his. The Coast Guard lady friend had abandoned him for higher rank. There had never been anyone else, though he'd come close.

The wind was light and from the east. Raising the centerboard of his nineteen-foot Flying Scot, he crossed directly over the sandbar that ran just off the river's western shore. Reaching the deeper water of the harbor, he lowered the board again, turning away from his mooring and heading for the dock. Tying up there, he'd just stowed his jib when his cell phone rang.

He'd been thinking of his small town house on the west end of Alexandria's Old Town, and the pleasant prospect of a glass of wine and a book. He thought he'd revisit Nicholas Monsarrat's *The Cruel Sea*.

"Westman," he said.

"This is Admiral dePayse."

Her voice this evening was very sharp. Usually she was much gentler with him. The lady was deputy assistant Coast Guard commandant for operations—a world above mere warrant officers, though theirs was a less-than-formal relationship.

"Yes, ma'am."

"There's been some kind of explosion on the Bay Bridge. Early reports are confusing, but there's a possibility it's a terrorist act. I wonder if you'd mind going out and showing the flag. Under the memorandum of agreement, the FBI will be running the show, but I'd like us on stage."

"Any particular reason to believe it's terrorism?"

"A better term might be attempted assassination. The Homeland Security adviser was on the bridge at the time."

"Is he all right?"

"I haven't heard otherwise."

"Traffic'll be backed up from Annapolis all the way to the District line."

"There's a helicopter en route from Activities Baltimore—

an HH-60 Jayhawk. Go to your office on Telegraph Road and
I'll have it waiting for you."

"To whom do I report?"

"You're probably the only chief warrant officer in the
Coasties who says 'whom.' "

"Yes, ma'am. Who then?"

"The usual channels. And to me."

From the air, Highway 50 and the roads running to it looked
like a weave of sparkling, illuminated snakes. Traffic
seemed to have halted throughout Anne Arundel County and
all along the bridge beyond. Around the near end was a large
cluster of whirling red-and-blue police car lights.

"I don't see anyplace where we can set down," said the
pilot over the intercom.

Westman leaned to the left, pressing his head against the
Plexiglas. He could see boat lights all along the line of
bridge supports. Nearer was the familiar outline of Sandy
Point State Park.

"How about that parking lot on Sandy Point?" he said.

The chopper pilot had no view of that section. Slowly, he
turned the machine until he could see the bayside park from
his side.

"They've got some emergency vehicles down there—and
it looks like light poles and other obstructions."

"And the beach?"

"I might try that in an emergency—if the alternative was
death. Night landings, Erik. Hard on the equipment." He began turning the machine to face the open bay again.

"You're right," said Westman. He looked forward. "An
awful lot of boat activity. What resources do we have on the
scene?"

"I'll check." The pilot clicked on his radio microphone.
The response was immediate. "Got the *Manteo*—Island

Class cutter—plus a couple of forty-sevens out of Station Annapolis."

"Call the skipper of the *Manteo*. I know him—a lieutenant named Dewey. Tell him you've got me aboard and I want to transfer to his deck."

"That's a hundred-ten-footer, Mr. Westman. Not a two-ten. There is no helo pad." There were other helicopters in the night sky, hovering around the bridge like fireflies.

"I know that. I'll use the basket hoist."

Dewey returned the radio microphone to its holder. "Prepare to receive a passenger."

DeGroot frowned. The *Manteo* had two inflatables in the water, searching for victims from the bridge incident. One of the Annapolis forty-seven-footers was working the other side of the span while the second was busy shooing away gawkers in motorboats.

"Who is it, some brass hat from headquarters who thinks the situation requires flag rank?"

"A mere warrant officer. Erik Westman, from CGIS."

DeGroot grunted—his form of approval.

The Jayhawk pilot approached the *Manteo* by the bow. The vessel had a derrick-style mast that rose three stories above the deck and bristled with antennae. The pilot apparently wanted to have it fully in sight while he hovered.

Leaving DeGroot in charge on the bridge, Dewey went forward to receive his guest, standing by the starboard rail to keep his footing in the rotor wash. The helicopter began lowering its basket with great care.

The basket was swinging in a gentle arc. Two crewmen rushed forward to take hold of its sides when it was low enough to reach. Westman waited until it was perhaps a foot above the deck, then stood up and swung over the basket rail, landing on the *Manteo* with a slight thump. He backed away from the basket, watching to make sure it was retrieved without fouling on the cutter. Then he turned and joined Dewey.

"Permission to come aboard, sir," he said after the helicopter had lifted away and its roar diminished.

"You got it, Erik," Dewey said. "I'm glad to have you on the *Manteo,* but why aren't you working with the FBI? They're all over the place."

"I haven't reported to them yet. It would take me forever to get out onto that bridge. Anyway, I doubt they'll have much use for me on this one."

"Their mistake."

"What's the situation?" Westman said.

Dewey looked to the bridge span above, and the rectangular gap in its flooring. "Couldn't get much out of the Bureau boys, but the Maryland State Police gave me a report. Exploding truck. Surprisingly little damage. A number of casualties."

Westman studied the bridge flooring as well. "They're certain it was a bomb?"

"Pretty sure. First report was it was a tanker truck, but witnesses said it was a rental stake truck. The explosion blew out the bridge railing and damaged a section of the roadway. A couple of vehicles went into the water, including the truck."

"How many casualties?"

"No idea how many."

"The White House Homeland Security adviser?"

"He's alive. Maybe a little singed. They walked him off the bridge. It'll be a while before they get that traffic moving again."

"And you're doing SAR?"

"Search and rescue. Victims and survivors. Haven't found either yet."

"Perpetrators?"

"Witnesses said they saw men running along the bridge back toward the Eastern Shore, but they could have been motorists just trying to get away."

DeGroot blew the *Manteo*'s horn in five quick blasts—a signal to an approaching motorboat to stand off.

As the last blast trailed off into a faint echo, another sound was heard—a hail from one of the cutter's inflatables, which was returning on the *Manteo*'s port side. Westman and Dewey went to the rail.

"Find something?" Dewey said, calling down to the crewman at the helm of the inflatable.

"Yeah, Cap. Nothing good."

"What do you mean?"

The crewman flashed his light at the center of the craft, where a canvas cover had been thrown over a small human form. Westman could see a small foot protruding.

"A little girl," said the crewman. "What's left of her."

"Here we go again," said Dewey. "The bastards."

Chapter 3

It had been a routine nighttime takeoff, just like hundreds Burt Schilling had done since he'd joined the Air Force shortly before the Vietnam War.

And it had proceeded routinely that cold March night nearly forty years before, at least in the beginning. He had lifted the big C-130 Hercules cargo plane off the main runway of Dover Air Force Base without incident and was climbing to altitude in the usual laborious but steady fashion.

Ahead and to the left were the bright lights of Cape May, New Jersey. Off to the right were those of Lewes, Delaware. Beneath his lumbering airplane, the flat blackness of Delaware Bay stretched between the two. Beyond its mouth, a vastness of dark that was the Atlantic Ocean, and beyond it their eventual destination of Frankfurt, Germany. The four big turboprop engines were throbbing and thrumming in their usual harmony.

And then suddenly they weren't.

Burt looked to his instrument panel. The needles were

showing normal readings. But the airspeed was falling. Burt detected the anomaly first as a subtle change in engine noise. Then it finally registered on the indicator—a jiggle, then a slight movement in the wrong direction. The altimeter was still holding steady. Or was it?

They were clean—gear up, flaps retracted. He'd throttled back a little as the C-130 had gained height over the bay. Now he jammed all four throttles to the wall and checked the engine gauges again. Two of the needles were falling back. Engines one and two. Fewer and fewer RPMs.

"We got a serious problem," said Olssen, his copilot. The man's pale eyes took on a maniacal cast from the red glow of the instrument lights.

"Yep."

Burt heard Sergeant Mikulski, his flight engineer, swearing behind him.

"Number one and two goin' out, Captain," the sergeant said.

Burt looked out his cockpit window to the left. A few licks of blue flame and sparks from the outboard engine on that side; the other was dead and dark.

The left wing was beginning to drop. Gripping the controls tightly, Schilling put in some compensatory aileron and rudder.

Altitude was 3,800 feet and slipping. Airspeed was two-twenty. Then less.

"No fire indicated," Olssen said.

"Three and four still normal," said Mikulski.

Schilling looked to the left. No exhaust flames.

"Try to restart?" said Olssen.

That could risk a fire. "Negative. Cut the throttle and feather props on one and two."

A drop of sweat slid into Burt's eye. Was he that nervous? Or was the word "scared"?

"What are you going to do, Cap? We can't fly very long like this."

Right. What the hell was a pilot in command to do here? Was he out of options already?

Altitude 3,600 feet. Airspeed two-fifteen. Burt had to act fast. Somehow get back to Dover. There was another, smaller field nearer, just to the right, at Milford, Delaware. He could almost see the lights. But he'd have to go far over land to line up with the too-short runway. They'd probably end up in the dirt and trees, digging their own grave with a C-130. Ocean City had an airport with a long runway, but it was too far down the shore.

No, it had to be Dover. Dover or death.

A younger pilot might panic here, as Burt had often done himself as a beginner. The impulse was to throw the aircraft into a tight 180-degree and head for home—Hell or high water. But a steep turn like that with faltering power and the heavy cargo they were carrying would cost them precious altitude fast—or even bring on a stall. They'd be in the drink before they saw the Dover approach lights.

There was still time for everyone to get chutes on and plenty of altitude yet to jump. But this was night. It was March. The dark water below was dangerously cold. There was a Coast Guard station at Cape May, but there was no telling how long it would take for a rescue.

Schilling could try to ditch in the bay close to the shore. But the chances of a successful night-water landing in a clumsy aircraft like this were essentially nil. The plane wouldn't float for more than a moment. Not with what they had aboard. The very full belly might well rip apart on impact.

There were fifteen other men aboard.

They had only one chance. He had to make the ship lighter. Flight occurred when lift overcame gravity and thrust overcame drag. They'd lost too much thrust and were losing lift. He had to decrease the pull of gravity. Fast.

Burt called in a Mayday. The origin of the term was French: *"M'aidez."* "Help me." But there was no help. Not outside this aircraft. He gave the Dover tower his situation, position, and intention, then looked to Olssen.

"We've got to jettison the cargo."

"Cap! We can't do that! Not what we've got!"

"It all has to go."

He clicked on the intercom, and told the rest of the crew. He explained the seriousness of their plight as swiftly as possible—telling them their safe return depended entirely on how fast they could move. Then he gripped the controls, ordering Olssen to go below and help with the cargo.

"The main cargo, Burt? You mean it?"

"Go!"

"President Johnson isn't going to like this."

Burt was sweating all over now. He could feel it running cold down his back. He and a couple of pilot pals had hit some bars in Baltimore the previous night. Hit them too hard. His eyes were burning from the perspiration.

Olssen was barely out of the cockpit when the rear hatch opened. The ship jerked downward a bit, as though a gigantic hook had caught it. Straight ahead now, through the windshield, there was only blackness. To the side, the lights of Rehoboth Beach were at an odd angle.

The altimeter was unwinding at a rapid rate.

"How're we doing down there?" Schilling said into the intercom, as though asking God.

"Still working on it, Cap," came a desperate voice.

"Joe," said Schilling to Mikulski. "Get down there and help them—quick!"

The engineer hurled himself aft. Schilling could hear his feet clanging down the ladder to the cargo deck.

Fighting the pull to the left, Schilling leaned to the right, hooking his arm through the control wheel.

"Hurry up! Damn it, you guys! Get those things out!"

Altimeter twenty-two hundred. Airspeed close to three hundred, and rising. Schilling could measure his life now in passing seconds, in the unwindings of a needle. He hadn't thought much about his life, about what he would do with the rest of it. Now, suddenly, here he was at the end.

There was little he could remember about the night before this flight—after his fourth drink.

He rubbed his eyes. He couldn't keep the perspiration out of them. Once, years before, he'd heard men in a doomed, plummeting aircraft screaming their last over the radio. They'd shouted obscenities. No dignity. No faith. Just rage.

There was a sudden lurch.

Burt heard a sharp bang, and then a thump and the groan of metal, something heavy rolling, and then another thump. The pull to the left abruptly increased. His arm, lodged in the control wheel, felt near to breaking. He had his landing lights on. He could see the water ahead.

"Are they clear?" He shouted this.

"Last one's hung up! Mikulski's working on it!" He heard screams, profanities, rage.

"Goddamn it!" Schilling said. "Get that thing out of the airplane!"

A dreadful banging. He heard more shouts and swearing over the earphones. Something jarred the aircraft again.

The Dover tower was calling him, but he ignored it. His landing approach at that moment was in the realm of fantasy. More wrenching sounds. He felt the plane shudder again.

"It's gone!" someone yelled.

"Pull up, Skip! Up!"

He could hear and feel the loading hatch being retracted, the plane lifting. With his arm still hooked in the wheel, Schilling pulled back as hard as he could, centering the rudder as he sensed the nose and left wing come up. His eyes were now on the airspeed, which was decreasing rapidly as they came out of the dive. A stall would be fatal now.

Life so short and death so long. Just half an hour before, they'd been standing around the hangar, drinking coffee, talking, killing time. Waiting for maintenance to finish with some small problem.

About five knots above stall speed, he pushed the control forward again, seeking level flight. When he achieved and sustained it, only then did he look again to the altimeter.

Two hundred feet.

His arm was numb. He clicked his microphone back on, holding the control wheel with his knee.

"Crew report!" he said.

They were flying again. The altitude held steady. Losing six tons had done it. Schilling began a long, slow, agonizingly shallow turn back toward Dover.

"Report!" he repeated.

There was a long pause; then Olssen could be heard, but not coherently.

"Jim! What's the situation?"

"Fuckin' terrible, Cap." The copilot sounded a little crazed.

"Cargo clear?"

"Yes, sir. Cap?"

"What?"

"We lost Mikulski."

"Lost Mikulski? He was just . . ."

"He went out with the load."

Schilling stared down at the sea, until tears turned all into a blur.

When he awoke from this terrible, recurring memory—nearly four decades later—there were tears in his eyes again.

Chapter 4

Schilling sat up in a sudden rush. He was in his bed, and covered in sweat. His mouth was as dirt-dry as it had been on that long-ago flight. His head was spinning and there was a pain in his side.

He hadn't been dreaming. Merely remembering.

Again.

There was a pint bottle of whiskey on his night table—to his surprise, still nearly half-full. Burt uncapped it, eyeing the round opening in the faint, gloomy light as he might the barrel of a loaded pistol. Then he drank—hard. As he lowered the bottle again, he heard the breeze gently stir the bushes on the dune opposite his house. In the storm of the night before last there'd been a furious wind and pounding waves on the bay. Now everything was at peace.

Except him.

He had to go to the bathroom—the curse of his age. He'd be seventy-three in the fall. He thought upon that as he stood before the toilet. He could not comprehend how he had come to be this old—how his battered, chemically assaulted tissues could have survived this incredibly long.

But they were now clearly giving up. The pain in his side ebbed and waned, but no longer completely went away. He'd made a doctor's appointment at the VA Hospital in Maryland, but he knew what the medical men would say. They'd been saying it for some time, but now their prophecy was coming true.

All prophecies came true, if you waited long enough. The world was coming to an end. Someday, some millennium, some billion years to come, there would no longer be an Earth. No bay, no breeze. No toilets.

Burt washed his hands and face. He'd slept in a pair of cut-off denim shorts. Leaving them in place, he pulled on an old white T-shirt and, with some clumsiness in the dark, went downstairs. Without turning on any lights, he found his cigarettes and matches, fetched a bottle of whiskey and a glass from the kitchen, then quietly went out onto his screened-in front porch.

The air was cool and fragrant. Though he had a view of the bay from the upstairs windows, all he could see from the porch was the shadowy back side of the small dune across from his house and the sand-tracked narrow street that ran in front of it. His rusting old Chevrolet pickup truck was parked in front of his wooden steps. Just to the other side was his pretty blond neighbor's Jeep Wrangler, its worn white paint a faint gleam in the lingering night.

Burt set his things on an old, listing table and sank into a creaking, ancient wicker chair drawn up beside it. He managed to light and inhale from his cigarette and then take a drink of whiskey without coughing. A major accomplishment. Perhaps a sign of a promising day.

He finished his smoke and then another before finally draining his glass of whiskey. Tilting the chair back against the clapboard wall of the house, he closed his eyes. He could sleep now. This was the only time and place where sleep came easy.

But not for long. He heard the sound of a screen door opening with a noisy spring, and then a gentle click as it was carefully closed. Burt opened his eyes, but otherwise didn't move except to glance at the luminescent face of his watch. It was a little shy of five A.M., with only the barest, faintest hint of the morning light detectable above the dune.

As Schilling had discovered just a few weeks before, Catherine McGrath customarily left her house next door to cross to the beach at this lonely, early hour so she could swim in the nude. She had inherited her beach place from her uncle, a former Navy pilot who'd been a friend of Schilling's. Cat had been a Navy pilot too—though her career had been cut short.

She had been born in Delaware, but had spent much of her early life in Key West, Pensacola, and the Caribbean, becoming quite used to swimming naked in the reef-sheltered waters there. She'd told Burt about that, but not about these predawn slippings into the sea here at grungy old Lewes, Delaware. He'd discovered this penchant of hers all on his own.

Usually, she crossed to the beach with her towel wrapped around her, but sometimes it slipped—and sometimes, when she reached the top of the dune and thought no one was about, she removed it altogether.

Burt kept absolutely still. He was sure she had no idea he was often up at this ghostly hour as well, lurking in the shadows of his screened-in porch.

The path over the dune began just opposite Burt's house. He held his breath as she crossed the street before him and started up the sandy slope. A few steps from the top, the towel fell away. There was light enough from the streetlamp down the block to limn the curves and edges of her tall, slender figure. Her blond hair was gathered into a loose ponytail that swung a little as she walked. Her legs were very long.

She looked more like a sailing lady than a pilot. Burt liked her either way.

She was thirty—if that. He was more than twice her age. He sighed.

Cat reached the top of the dune and, descending, vanished. Only then did Burt Schilling allow himself another bout of violent coughing.

The water was very cool at this hour. Not quite cold this far into the summer, not as chilly as New England's, but still far removed from the deliciously warm, clear waters of the Caribbean.

When she'd lived down there as a teenager, Cat had come to think of herself as one of the sea's own creatures, a natural denizen of the reefs. Here in Lewes, she had felt herself a stranger. But she was becoming used to it.

It had been two years since her uncle had died and left her this place; nearly one since her general discharge from the service as a Navy lieutenant.

Wading into the watery darkness till she could barely touch toes and keep her chin above the gentle swells, she took a very deep breath, then slowly, gracefully, curved her body forward and slid headfirst into the deep—turning and rolling in odd, disorienting tumbles, her eyes wide open but seeing only blackness, above and below and all around, her body gently pushed and lifted by the movement of the bay. There was something almost rapturous in this fixtureless moment. She clung to it until her heart began to pound and her lungs became anxious. Straightening, exhilarated, she let the float of her body whoosh her to the top, opening her mouth to the cool air as she broke the surface.

Tilting her head back, looking to the gauzy dark above, she treaded water a moment, then turned till she was facing back toward the few dim lights and murky shadows of the land.

Cat had been living here on the Delaware shore ever

since her discharge from the Navy, working on her case for reinstatement and sounding out airlines for pilot jobs—without much success on either front.

She wasn't giving up. She was a good pilot. Damned good. They'd had no right to do what they did.

In the meantime, she had become fond of the funny old town of Lewes—the oldest in Delaware—and the sea was still the sea, rough and dirty or no.

After her discharge, she'd worked for a few weeks taking tourists for seaplane rides out of Atlantic City. But the pay was low, and the commute from Lewes long and difficult. Cat also hated the place and the kind of people it attracted. Flying seaplanes in the Caribbean was another matter, but she needed to stay in the States to press her case with the Navy.

As it turned out, the New Jersey seaplane operation went out of business a month after she'd joined it.

She now had a different but equally unrewarding flying job, hauling skyborne advertising banners back and forth along the beach between Rehoboth and Ocean City. Occasionally, she helped her neighbor Burt Schilling with his big pay-by-the-head fishing boat, though he didn't always have money to pay her.

More or less, she got by, but little by little her savings were slipping away. She doubted she could last until winter if something didn't turn up.

Turning again in the water, she looked to the east, past the end of the breakwater by the Lewes-Cape May ferry dock and out toward the open ocean. The red light of a channel marker buoy winked at her. She could hear a buoy bell off to the distance, and farther out, a horn.

Cat swam a few strokes until her feet could touch bottom again, then kept moving until her breasts were exposed to the air. If she didn't stop this dawn nude swimming of hers, she'd one day get herself pinched by the local coppers.

Lewes would lose its charm in a hurry if she found herself in the Sussex County jail charged with indecent exposure.

Another quick plunge beneath the surface. At the touch of a fish or some other cold-skinned creature against her leg, she quickly rose again, then started wading back toward the shore. Halting on the sand where she had left her towel, she dried her hair a bit, glanced up and down the beach, then wrapped her torso carefully. There was getting to be too much light.

She'd heard Schilling coughing earlier, as she had so many nights—presuming he was in bed and the sound was coming through an open window. But now, crossing the road to her house, she spied the red glow of a cigarette in the shadows of his porch and a patch of white she took to be a T-shirt.

How long had he been there? Damn well long enough, no doubt. Perhaps he'd been there other nights, even every night.

Cat could forgive him that, as she had his booze and other failings. He was an old guy, and a pretty decent one. This had been a hard and lonely year for her, and he'd been a good friend and good neighbor.

And Burt was a pilot. Some might say "had been a pilot," but once a flyer, always a flyer. All pilots were brothers—and sisters. All pilots were different from everyone else. That she knew above all other things.

On impulse, she paused, then turned and walked boldly over to his porch, leaning close to the screen.

"You'll catch a cold there, Captain."

"Morning, Cat."

"A cold is what you deserve, sitting out here trying to cop a peek of a poor girl taking the waters in solitude."

"Didn't see a thing, Catherine."

"Well, your loss then." She could smell the whiskey, even from there. "You taking the boat out today?"

"I am. Got a few customers signed up. Maybe we'll get some more." She could hear the booze in his voice. This was happening too often. "I could use a hand," he said. "Only got Amy and the boy for crew. You by any chance free?"

She knew what he was saying. Cat had been out with him on fishing runs quite a few times—at first for pleasure; then when she needed a few extra bucks; more recently, because they were both worried about his ability to manage the boat. It was a large one—a "head boat" that could carry sixty or more paying passengers. Lewes's river, more properly known as the Lewes & Rehoboth Canal, had a narrow channel, and was crowded with boats, many of them very big.

"Maybe later in the week," she said.

"You're flying advertising banners today?"

"That's what I do now."

"They don't pay you much, do they?"

"They've got too many green pilots who'd fly for nothing just to rack up the hours."

"It's a waste of your talent."

"It's a job." She took a step away. "Maybe I'll get off early. I'll stop by the dock and see if you're there. You're doing half-day trips, right?"

"Right."

"You still have time to get a little sleep."

He waved the hand holding the cigarette. "Sleep enough when I'm dead."

Cat could think of nothing useful to say to that. Back in her own house, she pulled off the clammy towel and went into her bathroom, taking her time in the lovely, very hot shower. She brushed her teeth, pulled on a pair of khaki shorts and a short-sleeve knit shirt, and went into the kitchen to make breakfast.

Then she turned on the radio. She had just sat down to a bowl of cereal when the news came on.

Her stomach clenched and a chill came over her. She sat there motionless, staring at the silly animal on the front of the cereal box as though it held some secret meaning, some explanation for this madness.

Then she picked up her spoon and threw it at the wall. The bastards had done it again. They were relentless, like some kind of vermin that resisted extermination.

Cat had flown F-14 Tomcats before her grounding. There'd been women pilots flying missions in Afghanistan, Iraq, and the Sudan. She wished she was now.

They kept talking on the radio. The Bay Bridge was closed. The Coast Guard had doubled patrols. Washington's Reagan National Airport and the Baltimore-Washington Airport were closed. The Air National Guard was flying combat air patrols over the Capital area. A ban had been ordered on all general aviation flights within a 150-mile radius of Washington.

That, of course, included beach runs hauling advertising banners for Frisky's Shrimp and Suds.

Maybe she'd join Burt on his fishing boat anyway—though she'd be hard put to keep from joining him in his damned whiskey.

Chapter 5

Once he was finally free of Kent Island, Turko drove south on Highway 50 to the rich man's town of Easton, Maryland, then cut east across the Choptank River and up the county road to Denton and beyond to the small farmhouse that his team had used as a meeting place and a staging point.

He turned off his headlights a mile away, steering by the dim gray dawn. Approaching a stand of trees just shy of the farm, he slowed and turned off up a narrow lane that led into the woods. Parking where he was sure his car could not be seen, he quietly shut the door and started toward the house on foot.

The news report on his car radio had said that men had been seen running from the truck before it exploded, though it was unclear how many there had been. If they had made it off the bridge and onto the Eastern Shore, Turko was sure they'd come here—doubtless in the hope that he would join them at this house and tell them what to do next.

The Pakistanis had come into the United States relatively recently and would have few friends or resources. As their mission had been to sacrifice their lives in the name of Allah and Jihad—and they had not done so—they would not know what to do. Even without him, they'd likely try to hide here.

There were no lights on that Turko could see. He moved from the trees, crossing the neighboring bean field obliquely to come up on the house from the rear. The kitchen door was unlocked. Pausing, he pulled it open and stepped into the darkness within. Standing still, he listened to the sounds of the house for a time—a humming, grumbling refrigerator, a ticking clock—then moved into the hall and repeated the precaution.

The group had not yet arrived. They'd have come off the bridge on foot. He wasn't certain if they had the wit to steal a vehicle without being detected. They easily could have been picked up by the police as simple car thieves. But if there was a chance they could get here, Turko had no choice but to wait for them.

He went into the living room, choosing a chair off to the side that had a view out the front window but could not be seen by anyone unless they entered the room. It was a distinctly uncomfortable piece of furniture, but as he had done so many times in this ill-considered operation, Turko made do.

In its hours of searching, the *Manteo* had recovered three bodies—the small child's, a woman's, and a man's. The crew laid them in a row on the foredeck and covered them with foul-weather gear. At sea, they would have been taken below, but Dewey fully expected one of the police agencies on shore to come out and collect them.

Finally, in the rising light of morning, that happened. A police marine unit approached from the Sandy Point area at some speed, heading straight for the Coast Guard vessel. As it drew nearer, Westman took note of two men in sport coats standing at the bow. He recognized one of them as the police boat drew alongside.

"The FBI is full of first-rate people who could work this investigation," he said to Dewey. "Look who they chose instead."

"Don't know him."

"Special Agent Payne. Spell it as you like."

Dewey ordered a ladder lowered. The wind was stirring and there were choppy waves rocking the cutter. The other federal agent made the ascent easily, but Payne slipped twice before finally gaining the deck.

"Hello, Westman. What're you doing here?"

"This is a federal waterway. We have jurisdiction, just like you."

That wasn't entirely true. The Coast Guard Investigative Service was usually the first responder when crimes occurred on the water, but the memorandum of agreement between the two agencies required CGIS agents to defer to the FBI and let them take precedence if they wished. Coast Guard units had beaten the FBI to this chaotic scene, but as search-and-rescue teams, not investigators. The bridge blowup would be an FBI case from the git-go.

"I'm informed you've recovered some victims," Payne said. He was losing his hair and wore an FBI baseball cap with his jacket and open-collared shirt.

Lieutenant Dewey nodded toward the stiff forms under the orange slickers. "The last one about half an hour ago."

"I'd like to take a look at them."

"Sure," said Dewey.

A deckhand obligingly turned back the coverings as Payne went from one body to the next, oddly resembling a general reviewing his troops. His expression was set and grim, but became more so when he came to the child.

Westman followed. He had looked at each of the victims as they'd been hauled aboard the *Manteo,* but his interest then had been compassionate, not investigatory. Now, in brighter light, he paid closer attention, keeping his observations and conclusions to himself. Payne was not much interested in assistance from the Coast Guard.

When the FBI agent had finished, he took out a small notebook and jotted down a few lines. Then he closed it with a snap, signaling finality.

"You don't want to examine them more closely?" Westman asked.

"I'll leave that to forensics. A car got blown off the bridge—a minivan with a family in it. This must be them. We'll need to make a positive identification."

"There could be more than these three."

"Not many. And only a dozen injured." Payne looked up at the bridge, where the damaged flooring gaped like a missing tooth. "We're lucky. Reminds me of the World Trade Center."

"Reminds you of *what*?"

"The first time. In 1993. The sons of bitches tried to blow the one tower into the other when both buildings were full of people, top to bottom. Instead, they screwed up—caused a little structural damage but only killed six people. Put their truck bomb in the wrong part of the garage." He turned toward one of the huge support towers. "If they had done this one right, they might have knocked down the bridge. It's funny they didn't try it from the water."

"We maintain patrols here," Dewey said. "They would have been noticed."

Payne drew their attention back to the bridge span. "Whatever they had in mind up there, they sure blew it. The truck bomb was placed the wrong way. The force of the explosion went lateral—straight out the side of the truck. It blew the truck and that minivan off the bridge, but most of the blast went into the air."

"Terrorism is losing its touch."

"You making a joke, Westman?"

"I'm making an observation, Special Agent Payne."

Payne looked to what seemed a junk pile on the forward deck. "What's that?"

"Recovered debris," said Dewey. "We've fished out all we could find."

Payne went over to it, gingerly retrieving a license plate. "Why didn't this sink?"

"It was caught in some flotsam—some floating rubbish."

"Maybe it was there in the first place."

- "There are scorch marks," said Westman.

Payne studied the plate more carefully. "It's a rental plate. Probably from the truck."

"Then you have a piece of evidence," Westman said.

"Right." Payne looked to his associate, who stepped forward, producing a large, clear plastic bag. He carefully but efficiently put the plate inside it.

Payne started toward the ladder.

"What about the rest of it?" Westman asked.

The FBI man halted, turning to Dewey. "Can your crew bag those items for us?"

"We have some kitchen garbage bags in the galley. Will that do?"

"Sure. You know the procedure, don't you, Westman?"

"Something about not contaminating the evidence."

"Make sure you don't."

"Very well. What about the bodies?"

Payne halted again. "Can you take them into shore for us, Lieutenant? We're going to check out all the other boats who've been working out here."

"Where do you want them?" Dewey asked.

"Annapolis. Municipal dock."

"I'll have to transfer them to one of the forty-seven-footers," Dewey said. "We're too big for that mooring."

"Okay, okay. Thanks." Payne disappeared over the side. A moment later, the police boat was under way, heading out to the middle of the ship channel.

Westman went to the dead man lying on the deck. He was

missing most of his shirt and his left arm was burned, but the body was otherwise intact. Carefully, Westman started searching him. Rolling the body over, he reached into the man's left rear pocket, removing a wallet.

"What're you doing, Erik?" Dewey asked.

"Whoever he is," Westman said, opening the wallet and taking out what looked to be a very new driver's license, "I doubt very much he is married to this woman. I think he may have been with the truck."

The wallet also contained a passport and a thousand dollars in hundred-dollar bills. Nothing else.

"This was no family man," Westman said.

"What are you going to do with that stuff?" Dewey asked.

"Put it back. But I'd like to photograph the driver's license and passport first. Do you have an evidence camera aboard?"

"Sure. Regulations." He sent a seaman to fetch it from his cabin. "Shouldn't we call Agent Payne back to look at these things?"

"He didn't seem very interested."

"You're going to piss him off."

"Did that a long time ago."

Turko's comrades, as they considered themselves, liked to rage against Americans, denouncing them as Zionists and infidels and worshippers of Satan who deserved death by any means. But Turko was actually fond of the U.S. and its people, and the life he had been leading here. There was an exuberant rapaciousness in the way Americans went about their business, much as people did back home in Chechnya. Also as in Chechnya, the criminal class was well entrenched at the higher end of society and enjoyed distinct freedoms and privileges. Though they could be obstreperously patriotic if pushed, Americans seemed to value self-indulgent pleasures and the making of money above all other things. Turko thought of them as kindred spirits.

For the Pakistanis, the attack on the bridge had been part of Jihad. They could not understand Turko's doing his part solely for the money.

But there was of course more to it than that. Turko hated the Russians who had killed his wife and brother. In their war on Islamic fundamentalism, the Americans had made common cause with Moscow. The Russians committed atrocities every day in Chechnya. The Americans said nothing. It was altogether logical for him to be fighting them.

Jozip Pec, the Kosovar who was running this show, understood Turko. Because Turko had undertaken the assignment for money, Pec trusted him to do his job. Turko trusted the Pakistanis to do their jobs because of faith, but faith had failed them.

The goal of these attacks was not simply to kill Americans but to provoke them, to make them turn the full force of national fury on Islam, and thus cause millions of Moslems to rise up in a massive rebellion as the dervishes had done under the Mahdi more than a century before in the Sudan, as modern-day Moslems had come close to doing several times now. In the face of such an overwhelming uprising, the Russians would be compelled to release their death grip on Chechnya.

Not that it really mattered to Turko now. His wife was gone. He had nothing waiting for him in Chechnya. He'd been paid well. He hoped to remain in the United States, and be paid again. There was a lot of money behind what was going on.

His future would be up to Pec, a man motivated by neither faith nor money but a fierce and unyielding hatred—directed at perhaps the entire human race. Pec was no more religious than Turko, but had killed relentlessly in the 1999 Kosovo war simply because his victims were Serbs and Orthodox Christians. He'd lost a brother too, to an American bomb that had gone astray. He'd lost his parents when the

Serbs had first come through his village. When the war turned the other way, he'd sought out the Serbs who had done the killing. But when he tried to shoot them, the Americans arrested him and locked him up. This was called peacekeeping. Pec had fled to Albania the moment he had a chance to escape.

Turko did not trust Pec.

The television news reports Turko watched were calling the bridge bombing a major terrorist attack. The authorities were certainly taking it seriously. Both spans of the Bay Bridge had been sealed off. The nation had gone on "red alert"—the highest threat level. Police checkpoints were in place at key points everywhere and the Air Force had doubled the combat air patrols over America's major cities. The vice president had been flown to "an undisclosed location" and cordons had been put around the Capitol and the White House. Politicians were talking war once again.

But they weren't yet fighting one. There'd been no waves of cruise missiles or air strikes against yet another foreign nation. An investigation had been launched. The results were awaited.

Pec would not be satisfied with that. He wanted the United States raging mad again, lunging about the planet.

There was the sound of tires on gravel. Turko leaned forward slightly to look out the window, fearful that it might be a police vehicle. Instead, he saw a pickup truck with three men in the front, talking excitedly.

They continued talking as they entered the house, coming through the door without noticing Turko—the result he had hoped for in positioning his chair. He waited until the third man was inside and had closed the door behind him. He then shot that man first, firing at the next two in order. It took three shots to fell the man closest to him, who died at his feet.

The house was wooden, had a gas stove, and burned easily. Flames were visible in his rearview mirror as Turko drove out of the trees into the road. He'd set up a safe house for himself over in Ocean City that no one knew about. He was not ready to talk to Jozip Pec yet.

Chapter 6

Clothed now in an old, faded polo shirt emblazoned on the chest with a Naval aviator's insignia, a pair of khaki shorts, and some beat-up L.L. Bean boat shoes, Cat McGrath walked to the wharf on the river where Burt Schilling moored his big head boat, the *Roberta June*. It was a little past seven-thirty A.M. Amy Costa was aboard, on the big aft deck, cutting pieces of squid as bait and putting them into plastic cups for the customers. Joe Whalleys, the other deckhand, was on the wharf, preparing the fishing rods for the day trip.

Amy was small, dark, and a bundle of muscles, her skin so deeply brown from sun it seemed a permanent stain. A local girl from the Delaware farm country just to the west, she was very bright, but woefully uneducated. Cat had felt a kind of angry sympathy for her from the start. She deserved better than a life of bean fields and chopping bait, but nothing much else seemed in prospect—especially if she ended up marrying someone like Joe Whalleys.

He was a very good-looking boy. Dressed up, with his

wild hair combed and presentable, he could pass for an Ivy League college student. But he was dumb as a brick and had no ambition. One could imagine him as old and grizzled as Burt Schilling, still working head boats—on them, not owning them.

"Where's Burt?" said Cat, making a little jump of the step off the gangplank onto the *Roberta June*.

"Said he'd be late," said Amy, with a quick look up that did not halt her slicing of squid. "You coming out with us?"

"Thought I would. If you're going out."

"Why wouldn't we?"

"Didn't you hear about the Bay Bridge? Somebody tried to blow it up last night."

Amy simply stared.

"They didn't succeed, but the government's closing things down," Cat said. "Maybe even this river. I'm not sure any tourists are going to show up."

"Maybe that's just as well," Amy said, "if Burt's having another one of his 'late' days. But I hope not. I need the day's work."

Cat gave her a quick and, she hoped, reassuring smile. "Maybe someone will turn up."

It looked to be a good weather day. There was an abundance of sunshine among the piles of cumulus clouds. The breeze was enough to cool their passengers in the summer heat, but hadn't kicked up much chop out on the bay.

There were only three customers on the dock by eight and Burt still had not appeared. He needed to do better than this. He'd only just paid off the boat, which he'd had for sixteen years. The *Roberta June* was shabbier than the tourist boats moored farther upriver by the Savannah Avenue bridge. Unlike them, she'd been built as a commercial fishing boat—a trawler—with a wide aft deck. Burt had removed most of the gear, installing an awning and some stadium seats he'd bolted to the deck flooring along each side, but she still looked like a vessel of labor, not fun.

Cat climbed the ladder to the flying bridge Burt had constructed above the wheelhouse, noting unhappily the grimy bait bucket and soiled rags left in a corner. She opened a small storage locker, fearing she'd find a bottle of whiskey or vodka. Happily, there were only charts. After so many years at this, Burt needed no underwater maps. He doubtless knew every reef and shoal by name. But Cat had no such intimate familiarity, and would need a chart's guidance as long as she had the helm.

She pulled out the plastic-coated section for south Delaware Bay and its inlets, flattening it down over the control console.

The course to the fishing grounds was simple enough. She'd follow the river northwest from the wharf out to where it entered the sea through the cut at Roosevelt Inlet. After that, a heading toward the buoy at Starsite Reef and then around Cape Henlopen into the ocean fishing grounds, unless Burt wanted to go first to an underwater valley called Deepkill and the adjoining shoal that bore the same name.

Which, for the last few months, he always did.

Delaware Bay had some depth to it—seventy-four feet in the main channel between Cape May and Cape Henlopen and 150 feet or more in its wider reaches. But there were shoals and reefs scattered all across the bay and out into the ocean beyond.

In Cat's time here, the Deepkill shoal had never proved much of a fishing ground, but Burt usually made straight for it, working the territory over in zigzag fashion before going on to richer beds worked by the other boats. It was a ritual.

Schilling appeared a few minutes after eight. She could tell he'd continued with his drinking, but not enough yet to spook the customers, who numbered seven by the time Amy was ready with the bowline.

He came up the ladder slowly, nodded to Cat, then settled himself onto the chair mounted on the other side of the bridge.

"I sure appreciate your comin' along, Cat. Really not my-self today."

"I can't fly. The federal government shut down all the general-aviation fields on the Eastern Shore. Might as well help you out. You're lucky to have any customers at all."

She started the engines, then shouted to Whalleys to cast off the aft line. When he'd done so, she spun the wheel to port and eased the throttle into reverse, causing the big stern to swing out into the channel. Holding the *Roberta June* there a moment, she waited as the brightly white head boat *Kenna Dale* burbled by, then called to Amy to release the bowline. The girl, as always, was ahead of her. As Cat throt-tled forward, the bow came about smartly and the *Roberta June* headed downriver in train with the *Kenna Dale*.

"You sure you want me to do this?" she said to Burt.

"Shit, Cat. I'd trust you with an aircraft carrier."

Cat knew boats as well as airplanes. Both her uncle and father had been sailing men as well as pilots and she'd been crew for one or the other from the time she was eight. The Lewes river was tricky, but she'd always managed it. Her qualms arose from something else.

"That's not what I mean," she said. "You ought to have Amy up here. She could run this boat in her sleep."

He shook his head, not looking at her. "She's too small. Looks too young. Might spook the customers."

As Cat steered the *Roberta June* down the middle of the river, Burt took up the loudspeaker mike, pulling himself to-gether sufficiently to welcome and instruct the passengers, and sounding very much like the airline pilot he'd been after his truncated Air Force career.

Done, he put down the microphone and slumped back, looking drained.

"How many more of these trips are you good for, Burt?"

She meant it as a joke, but his reply was quite serious.

"Not many, Cat. Hardly enough to count."

There was a yellow look to his cheeks. His eyes were caves. "Are you okay?"

He lighted a cigarette. "Sure. Just got a few things on my mind."

Cat moved the helm to starboard a little. The excursion boat *Lewes Princess* was coming upstream.

"You know, I may not be around to help you anymore," she said.

"Every man's luck runs out. I've been lucky to have a year of you."

"Burt, I've got a shot at a job."

"Back with the government?"

"No. Airline."

"Pilot?"

"Right seat, not left. Twin-engine turboprop. Little feeder commuter line for one of the trunk carriers."

"Where?"

"Iowa. I guess there are a few flights into Illinois and Wisconsin."

"Not exactly your speed." His eyes were on the approaching excursion boat.

"It's a job. I need one."

"Girl's gotta eat, don't she?"

"Girl's gotta get on with her life."

"Give up on the Navy?"

"No, but . . ." She shrugged.

"I'll miss you big-time, honey."

He looked extremely old. As she studied him, he began coughing, and she turned away. With the *Lewes Princess* finally past them, Cat edged back into the middle of the channel and increased their speed slightly.

There was a small Coast Guard patrol boat standing off Roosevelt Inlet in Delaware Bay. The boat had its machine gun mounted and the crew looked vigilant, but they let the *Roberta June* pass unmolested.

Once they were clear of the inlet, Cat churned on steadily north toward the New Jersey shore, just to see if he'd let it pass this time.

Sooner would he go a day without whiskey. She wasn't a quarter mile off the edge of the shoreline shallows when Burt took a long squint at the horizon and called out: "Mind your helm, Cat. Our course is east by southeast."

"Steer toward Deepkill."

"Yep."

"The shoal this side of the Kill runs mighty shallow in places, you know."

"I know."

"At low tide, a big boat like this might run aground if the current's been playing games with the bottom—like it always does."

"Hasn't happened yet."

"Why do you work that area at all? You almost never pull up a fish."

"Couple of sea robins last week—when you weren't around."

"I mean real fish—keepers. What people make the trip for."

"Workin' Deepkill is just something I like to do. They get their money's worth. I give them more time out here than the other boats."

Hand still on the wheel, she leaned a little closer to him, bracing herself as the *Roberta June* took an unexpectedly large swell on the quarter. She sought his eyes, but they stayed on the horizon.

"What's down there, Burt?" she said.

He took the longest time to reply, but not with any useful answer.

"You ever kill anyone in the Navy, Cat?"

The question hit her sharply.

"Is that what's down there? Someone you killed?" she asked.

His gaze continued unaltered. "Just mind the helm," he said.

Westman used his cell phone to call his Alexandria office, where one of his fellow special agents should have been on duty. But three tries got him only one-sided chats with the office voice mail. Calling CGIS headquarters in Arlington proved more productive. The director himself responded.

"Did you get the faxes I sent?" Westman asked.

"Affirmative. You turned those personal items over to the Bureau?"

"I returned them to the gentleman who owned them."

"The dead man?"

"Right. We put all three remains on a forty-seven and transferred them to the Annapolis wharf. Those were Payne's instructions."

"That evidence should be at the center of the investigation. Ought to be moving faster than this."

"The Bureau's primary. What can we do?"

"I'll take it up with headquarters."

"Should I come in?"

"You still aboard the *Manteo*?"

"Yes. We're just off Sandy Point."

"When it's convenient, have the skipper drop you off. You're wanted at Buzzard's Point yourself."

"What for, sir?"

"Request from Admiral dePayse. I guess she wants a fill on the situation—in person."

Westman looked at his watch. "How soon do I have to be there?"

"No rush. Seven o'clock."

"In the evening?"

"That's what she said."

* * *

Westman rejoined Dewey on the bridge. The younger man was on the radio, talking to Activities Baltimore—the conversation not dissimilar to the one Westman had just had with his director.

While he waited, Westman went to the forward windows, looking up at the wounded Bay Bridge. The state police appeared to have gotten all the vehicles off the westbound span except for those involved in the wreck and explosion. There were men crawling around the support girders. Westman couldn't tell whether they were repair crew or evidence technicians. In either case, they were very brave.

"I've been ordered to get under way," said Dewey, hanging up his microphone. "They're going to send some auxiliarists and a couple of patrol boats from Baltimore to flesh out security here. They want the *Manteo* at Cape May, to help cover Delaware Bay."

"I have to go ashore. Washington."

Dewey leaned back against the control console, rubbing his eyes. "I'll drop you at the Naval Academy. You can get transport there, can't you?"

"Think so."

"We're going to be putting in a lot of duty hours before this thing is done."

"They saw three men running off the bridge," Westman said. "It would be nice to get those bastards."

Dewey reached into a drawer and took out his Coast Guard issue Sig Sauer 9mm automatic and holster, hooking it to his web belt. Then he looked to DeGroot. "Prepare to get under way, Master Chief."

Chapter 7

The new safe house Turko had chosen for himself was a second-floor rear apartment in a wooden, walk-up building in one of Ocean City's seediest sections, just a few blocks from the frowsy resort town's aging amusement park in a neighborhood currently crawling with every variety of inebriated, stoned, and strung-out youth—of male, female, and indeterminate gender.

Turko had been a lawyer once, back in Chechnya. Most of his clients had been people just like these miscreants.

The police here were tough on shoplifters, but otherwise tolerant of behavior good for commerce. Turko had little fear of being picked up for looking suspicious. In these surroundings, he was noticeable mostly for being too well dressed.

Once inside his little three-room apartment, he immediately set about altering his appearance, changing into a pale-blue T-shirt with a dolphin on the front, baggy yellow shorts, and the flip-flop sandals that so many Americans favored as beach wear—though Turko thought them silly. He'd bought the clothing at a nearby Sun and Fun store, one of many along the shore. They had such an infinite variety of this unseemly garb, he figured he could disguise himself many times over without having to go to any other place.

He had selected this apartment because it had both front and rear doors, as well as a small balcony that overlooked the dingy, sandy alley where he had parked his car. There were chain locks on both doors, which he augmented with wooden wedges on the bottom. They weren't an absolute bar to intruders, but could give him time to use the balcony and make his escape with a short drop to the ground.

He'd told no one of this little retreat, informing Pec only of another apartment he had rented in Wilmington.

The advance rent in Ocean City he'd paid for in cash. He'd stocked the place with groceries, so there was no need to leave the apartment for days—or even a week or more if necessary.

But now he discovered he'd neglected one thing.

Turko was a Moslem more by circumstance of birth and family than inclination. His abstinence in America was due more to the need for a clear head than any fervent faith.

Now he needed to put such temperance aside. His nerves had held throughout this enterprise, even as he'd waited in the farmhouse for his team to return. Here, where he was at last safe, they'd begun to fray.

He'd turned on the apartment's barely functioning television set and, as he watched the aftermath of the bridge explosion replayed seemingly continuously, his anxiety began to overwhelm him like a swiftly spreading fever.

Pec should have been satisfied with the turn of events. The United States Department of Homeland Security had ordered the highest level of alert. The Congress had adjourned. The U.S. military was at its highest state of readiness, and large numbers of National Guard and Reserves had been activated.

The stock market had dropped more than five hundred

points before trading had been ordered stopped and the exchanges closed. Air travel had been shut down for more than a day and access had been at least temporarily halted to all major bridges and tunnels. According to the television, National Guard troops were riding subways and Amtrak passenger trains again.

It wouldn't last forever, but the American nation was once more in a state of officially ordained chaos. Once again, it had been shown to be weak and vulnerable.

But Pec, Turko knew, would not be happy. There had been an almost rapturous glow in his eyes when he'd told Turko his plan to knock down the Bay Bridge and kill a White House official. That glow would now be extinguished. The President, joined by the Homeland Security adviser, had gone on television to assure the nation all was still well. The bridge still stood. There had been only six fatalities—a woman and her three children, a state policeman who had fallen from the bridge into the bay, and Amin Sandar, one of Turko's cowardly crew.

Pec had dreamed of hundreds if not thousands of deaths. He wanted massive slaughter.

Turko needed a drink.

He went out the back door of the apartment, locking it behind him. Pausing on the stairs that led down to the wide, sandy alley, he calmed himself as best he could. There was a dog below, poking its nose between two garbage cans, and a fat blond girl in a bathing suit who was sprawled snoring on a lawn chair on the balcony opposite. Neither took note of him. No one else was to be seen.

Turko had his pistol at his back in his belt, hidden by his overlarge T-shirt but reached easily. He waited a minute more, then continued down the stairs.

It was only three blocks to the nearest liquor store and he decided to leave his car and walk. He passed a bar on the corner—filled with noisy drinkers, most of them young and many of them already tipsy or worse. He had an impulse to stop for a drink right then and there, but restrained himself. There was nothing more unpredictable than a drunk, and he could ill afford to be accosted by one. He did pause at the Sun and Fun store a few doors on to buy a pair of oversized sunglasses and a stupid-looking beach hat. Continuing to the liquor store, he bought two half-gallon bottles of vodka— nothing remarkably cheap or expensive—and then returned to his apartment by a different, longer route, coming down the alley from the other end.

The dog had vanished. The blond woman was still on her chair, in much the same position.

With the wind out of the northeast, the warmth of the bright sunlight was tempered by a cooling breeze, but Turko continued to sweat. His flat had no air-conditioning, yet he was reluctant to open his windows.

Closing and locking his back door, setting chain and wedges in place, Turko went to the small kitchen, putting one of the bottles of vodka in the freezer. Opening the other, he filled a tall glass halfway, added ice, and then Coca-Cola from a can. Stirring the mixture with his finger, he returned to his living room and the television, which he'd left on. Seating himself, he took a large swallow of his drink, rejoicing in the spreading, soothing warmth that followed.

They were now showing a picture of the pretty woman who'd been killed on the bridge. Turko's wife had been pretty. She'd been blown to bits by a Russian artillery shell fired into their apartment building.

He had tried to persuade himself that the Russian gun crew had no particular intention of killing her. As he sat there now, he contemplated the fact that he'd had no intention of killing the woman smiling at him from the television screen. Her death had been a random matter—as much a matter of chance as a traffic accident. He felt no remorse for her, nor anger for what she represented. He'd been doing his job, carrying out his mission. He'd done what he did because it had been asked of him—just as the members of the Russian gun crew had likely done.

Turko had never found out which Russians fired that shell into his building. He'd had to settle for killing several soldiers who simply belonged to the artillery service. He'd shot most of them. One he'd strangled to death.

He wished there were Russians here.

His nervousness and fear were abating. He took another large swallow.

Turko had been careful, as always, to cock his pistol and place it within easy reach on the table beside him. Unfortunately, it was the drink and not the gun that was in his hand when a dark figure appeared in the bedroom doorway.

Dropping the glass, Turko snatched at the pistol as he flung himself forward onto the carpet. He was very good with guns. Firing by instinct without aiming, he hit the man in the belly as he came forward—the force of the bullet lifting the intruder from the floor.

The gunshot was amazingly loud, ringing in his ears. As he waited for that to subside, he looked furtively all about him. Seeing no other sign of movement or presence, he returned his focus to the open bedroom door.

The wounded man gave out a series of small, gasping whimpers, then fell silent. Waiting a moment more, Turko slowly rose, his automatic to the fore. Giving a quick glance to the window facing the alley, he saw that the woman in the bathing suit was standing at her balcony's railing, staring wide-eyed at his apartment. Not a second later, a red circle appeared in her forehead and she collapsed with a thud he could hear across the alley.

Then came a sharp, paralyzing pain at the back of his head. He too was falling. As he lost consciousness, he thought he heard his name.

Chapter 8

Westman arrived at Buzzard's Point, the Coast Guard's national headquarters on the Anacostia River, having stopped at his Alexandria office to retrieve his car and at his nearby town house to shower, shave, and change into a blue dress shirt, a pair of old white duck trousers, and a Navy blazer. He kept on the boat shoes and decided to forgo a tie.

At the drab government-architecture headquarters building, he showed his ID to the lobby security guards, proceeded through the metal detector, and then took the elevator to the admiral's floor. The receptionist, a third-class petty officer, asked him to take a seat and wait. It wasn't for long.

Joan dePayse emerged quickly from her office and strode forward to greet Westman with a firm handshake. Special agents in the investigative service were not required to observe the tribal niceties of rank, even with admirals, but she would not have treated him formally in any case.

She had dark hair, gray eyes, and a tan that was surprising for someone who spent so much time in an office. Her hand lingered in his a moment, then fell away as she led him into her large office, with its commanding view of the river. She sat back on the edge of her desk and smiled, but only fleetingly—in recognition of the gravity of the moment.

"How is it out there?"

"Grim. We recovered three of the victims when I was aboard the *Manteo*. One was a child."

"You're certain another of them was one of the terrorist team? I hope so, because that's what I've told the White House, based on your initial report."

"Yes, ma'am."

She smiled again. "I wish we had more people to put on this, but I'm afraid you'll have to do for now. Try to work with the Bureau as much as you can. If that doesn't fly, go wherever you think best. I want you to report directly to me. I'll clear it with your director."

Westman looked away, to the murky Anacostia below. "I think the perpetrators are still on the Eastern Shore."

"The Delaware and Maryland state police have put road-blocks up at all the Chesapeake and Delaware Canal crossings. The bridge at the mouth of Chesapeake Bay has been closed."

"They may have boats."

"We have boats."

Westman watched a small working vessel chuff down the greasy channel. The Coast Guard was the country's principal enforcer of federal marine environmental laws, but had placed its headquarters beside one of the most polluted waterways on the Eastern Seaboard.

"The big targets are on this side of the bay, of course," she said. "You've noticed the security."

"Certainly have."

She stood up straight, looking at her watch. "I think we're both entitled to a dinner break. You want to try one of those places along the Washington Channel?"

"Is that, uh, prudent, Admiral?"

"No fraternization, Special Agent Westman. A working dinner."

"Yes, ma'am."

"Erik, please don't call me 'ma'am.'"

Sitting in a favorite old chair by her living room window, Cat had all but fallen asleep when Burt's pickup truck noisily pulled up at his house a little past ten in the evening. Letting the book she'd been attempting to read fall to the floor, she got to her feet and then went outside, reaching Burt's driver's-side window just as he was turning off the engine.

He looked so very old, but brightened at seeing her.

"Like a drink?" he asked, grinning.

"Sure."

There was a grocery bag full of liquor in the cab and a case of beer in the back of the truck. He winced getting out of the vehicle and swore lifting the beer, but insisted on doing it himself and managed to heft it into his house without calamity.

Cat brought in the hard hootch, setting the bag on a clear space on the otherwise-cluttered counter beside his kitchen sink. He'd not done his dishes for a bit. Ignoring that, she took out the bottles, finding bourbon, scotch, and gin. After neatly folding the grocery bag, she turned to face him.

"Where've you been?" she asked.

Burt opened a beer and nodded toward the liquor. "What's your pleasure?"

"Scotch, please."

He reached for the bottle of Johnnie Walker, pouring a little carelessly. It was a nervous night.

"I was running some errands," he said. "Tending to some business. You want to go sit outside?"

"Been there."

"We could walk on the beach."

"Maybe later."

"Okay."

They sat at his kitchen table. The breeze off the bay stirred the curtains of the windows.

"You look kinda down, Cat."

"I am, a little. I don't want to work for an airline in Iowa, but if I don't get reinstated in the Navy, I don't know what else I can do."

"You could hang around here a while."

She gave him a small, wry smile, then shook her head. "What will I do for a job in the winter?"

He took a swig, tilting back his head, then set the beer bottle down on the table. "I guess I'm not thinking that far ahead."

"I want to keep flying, but . . ."

"But not haulin' hayheads around the prairies. Like I used to do after I left the Air Force."

Cat sipped, making no response. She wondered how late this night would go. They'd had more than a couple of dawners, she and Burt, in her time in Lewes, sitting at this table, drinking beer or whiskey, telling pilot stories, swapping lies.

"So are you going to fly tomorrow?" He reached for another beer.

"They still have the airports shut down, and they have the Air National Guard flying CAP."

"Can you help me out on the boat again?"

"I'd be surprised if you had any customers." She looked at him, noting no change in his expression. "But that doesn't seem to matter, does it?"

She had a more compelling question.

"Burt, why do you keep taking the *Roberta June* to Deepkill Shoal?"

His eyes retreated.

"If you're going to stay my friend, Burt, you'd better tell me."

"You'll think I'm crazy. The Air Force does."

"No, I won't."

"Long story," he said hesitantly. "Only, now I've got to turn it into a short one."

They both drank. Then he lighted a cigarette. Someone in a car with the windows open and the radio blaring heavy metal rock music moved slowly down the street outside, the bass notes thumping.

He'd said something to her about a doctor's appointment—days before.

"Burt, have you been to the doctor?"

"Yeah. I went."

"What did he say? Do you need an operation or something?"

"No, Cat. I don't need any goddamned operation. I've got nothing inside worth fixing."

The mere mention of his internal organs provoked a cough. He was a long time finishing it.

"Maybe I'd better switch tanks," he said. It was his way of saying he was moving on to hard liquor. He filled a small glass with bourbon, then returned to his chair, leaning it back a little. A puff of smoke.

"What's at Deepkill, Burt?"

He exhaled from his cigarette, then put it out in his ashtray and got to his feet—unsteadily, and with something of a grimace.

"Okay," he said. "Come with me."

Schilling led her upstairs, past an open door that revealed a rumpled, unkempt bedroom and on down to a closed door at the other end of the hall.

"My little museum," he said, opening the door and turning on a lamp.

In contrast to the rest of the house, this room was very neat and orderly, though crowded with objects.

The walls were half-covered with old framed photographs, most of them military, many of them pictures of aircrews standing and kneeling in front of their aircraft. Here and there were odd pieces of memorabilia: a blue Air Force officer's cap, much crumpled; a glass-topped box containing insignia and a few medals; a stack of ancient pilots' logbooks; a painting of a giant cargo plane. Burt said it had been done by Dick Tracy comic-strip artist Dick Locher, who'd been in the Air Force a few years before Burt and had flown the aircraft.

There was also an old ball compass that had once belonged in an instrument panel, a survival knife, and an old-fashioned .45 automatic, once standard issue for officers before the advent of the modern 9mm model. Cat had a 9mm in her bedroom she had taken with her out of the Navy, but it was no souvenir.

Burt went to a wide, battered old desk set against the room's lone window and turned on another lamp. Half the top surface was covered with stacks of bulging file folders and binders. There were framed black-and-white photographs standing at either end of the desk. That on the left was of a man in Air Force uniform whom Cat took to be one of Burt's military flying buddies. He was young, broad-faced, and had very light, friendly eyes. He'd autographed the photo for Burt.

The picture on the right was of a woman, also rather young, with dark hair worn in an old-fashioned early 1960's style. There was no signature. Her eyes were dark, very open and frank, but not communicating much affection.

Cat peered more closely at the woman's picture, noting small lines around the eyes, and other signs of strain. Then she turned back to face Burt.

"Who are these people?" she asked.

"People I lost," he said.

"Lost? You mean they're dead?"

"One is."

He plucked a mounted scale model of a multiengined aircraft from a shelf, removed it from its stand, and then handed it to her. It was a big cargo plane just like the one in the photograph, and very complex in its detail work. There were actually tiny pilot figures visible behind the little plastic canopy windows.

"Ever fly anything this big?" he asked, leaning back against a table.

Holding it by the bottom of the fuselage, she examined it carefully, tilting its wings as though banking in flight.

"No," she said. "A Gulfstream jet once. Never anything like this."

"In some ways, it was like flying a house," he said. "Parked on the ramp with the gear down, the pilot's seat was a good two stories off the ground."

She squinted at it. "You could get a truck into one of these."

"Yup. Trucks. Armored personnel carriers. Did that. Used to fly to Germany with 'em in the belly."

He'd brought his glass and his cigarettes up with him. He found an ashtray and once more lighted up. She guessed he hadn't changed a single one of his habits since the 1960's.

She nodded to the pictures on the desk. "Is that your copilot?"

He shook his head. "That's Joe Mikulski, the flight engineer on my last 130. Hell of a guy. Always did the right thing, followed all the rules. A straight arrow, but he was never a jerk about it. One of the guys. Real nice. Safest man I ever had in an airplane."

"What happened to him?"

Burt gestured with his glass toward the other photograph.

"That's Roberta June. She went by June. Hated Roberta."

"Your wife?" He'd never told her for whom the boat was named.

"She was, until 1968."

"Did she die?"

"No. She's living in California. Married some guy. But I lost her. Lost Mikulski. In different ways, but both because of that flight. It was my last flight—last time I flew an airplane for the Air Force. Took off just up the coast from here, Dover Air Force Base. Night flight to England, then a hop over to Germany. I'd done a couple dozen of these trips out of Dover. All routine. The ship had been down for maintenance, but everything in the preflight and run-up showed perfect. You want another drink?"

"I'm fine, Burt."

"Never had a problem before that, not in all my time in the service. Never had anything go wrong with that aircraft. Nothing big-time anyway. But just as we were climbing out of four thousand, right by the mouth of that bay out there, both port engines died on me. Turned out to be a blockage in the fuel line—a minor fuckup that went major, some valve that was put in backward. Did I ever tell you about the real Murphy's Law?"

She shook her head.

"The real Murphy was a colonel in charge of the Army rocket sled project in the late forties. Remember Paul Stapp, the test pilot they had riding the sled?"

Cat shook her head again.

"It was in the movie newsreels—his face all flattened and distorted when the rocket sled hit speed. The project was a test of G-forces on pilots. The first run damn near killed Stapp, but the G-meter showed zero. Colonel Murphy took a look at it and discovered somebody had wired in the telemetry sensors backwards. And so he uttered the immortal words 'If there's a way to fuck something up, somebody will find it.' Later on, it got kinda cleaned up for public consumption."

Cat snapped off the lamp on the desk. "You know, Burt, I think I'll take you up on the offer of a walk on the beach."

She again declined another drink, giving him something of a dark look at the renewed suggestion. He ignored the implied reproach, and brought the bottle of bourbon with him.

Pausing first to drop her shoes in her Jeep, she led Burt in a trudge over the dune, happy in the coolness of the sand on her bare feet as she came down the other side. The daylight was gone from the sky in the east, but there was still a pastel wash of blue and pink in the west. Delaware Bay was turquoise fading to dark blue, with only a light chop showing, though the breeze to weather was increasing.

Cat walked out into the water, till it came up nearly to her knees. Burt stood at the edge of the sand, just behind her.

"You're not going swimming?" he asked.

"No such luck, old man."

She looked back. He was lifting the bottle. She waded back onto the beach.

"Let's walk," she said.

"I was telling you about that flight."

The click and yellow flame of a cigarette lighter.

"You're supposed to be telling me about Deepkill," she said, looking straight ahead. In the distance, she could see the evening party boat coming out of the Roosevelt Inlet, its lights twinkling and merry. Whoever they were, those people weren't worrying about terrorists.

"You know, except for bombing missions during the big war, I never heard of anyone losing two engines like that," Burt said. "Two at once. On the same side. I had a hell of a time. Couldn't keep the wing up. Couldn't hold altitude. We started flying like a brick. It was night. End of winter. I was over the ocean. Not far off the shore, but not near enough."

He stopped to point to a place in the sky.

"You might have died in the water," Cat said. "Hypothermia comes on pretty quick."

"That's the truth. I figured there was only one way out. Dump cargo. It was the only chance we had."

They started walking again.

"I had two big pieces of cargo—weighing more than two tons apiece."

"Armored personnel carriers?"

He stopped again, looking at her. "I was never supposed to say anything to anyone about this. Top secret. Talk and you go to jail. All these years."

"I won't rat on you."

"They were nuclear weapons."

She stared at him, blinking, not quite comprehending.

"Missiles?"

"This was 1967. They were bombs."

"You dropped two atomic bombs off the Delaware shore?"

She gazed out over the darkening water, imagining it, imagining weirdly the bombs detonating, evaporating everything in view.

"Hydrogen bombs. Mark 28's. They contained a lot of HE—high explosive. But that was just to ignite the nuclear stuff inside. Nothing happened when they hit the water."

"Are the bombs still there? In the water?"

"Yeah. They sure as hell are." He stared out to sea as though one more good hard look might reveal the exact location. "Somewhere a little south of here, other side of Cape Henlopen. Near the Deepkill shoal. Maybe in the Deepkill Slough that runs along the shoal. As soon as we jettisoned them and stabilized flight, I returned to Dover. I was low. Skimmin' the waves. I don't know how we made it."

"No one did anything about them? The bombs?"

"You're Navy, Cat. Didn't you ever hear of Palomares? In Spain?"

"Something about a B-52 crash?"

"A B-52 collided with its refueling tanker over Palomares. It was carrying Mark 28 nuclear weapons and three of them hit the ground. They didn't explode, but spewed radioactive debris all over the place. The fourth one went into the drink. It took them weeks to find it. The Navy came in with a couple of submersible underwater vehicles—one of them called 'Alvin'—and finally found it by following a track it left in the sea bottom after it hit. The whole recovery project cost the U.S. government eighty million dollars and a hell of a lot of ill will all over the world. The Air Force didn't want another."

"They just ignored it?"

"Publicly. On the quiet, they had the Navy poke around out there for a while, but they didn't find anything. They never called in the varsity team—which was Bob Ballard."

"The undersea explorer?"

"He was Navy then. A sub hunter. Sunken submarines. Ours and the Russians. But they never went to him. They'd gone through the motions, and that was enough. The Air Force debriefed me and my crew, then told my CO they'd take care of everything. They assured me there was no problem. The Mark 28's had three stages, not counting the uranium—high explosive, the plutonium core, and the triggering mechanism. You had to have the plutonium core and the trigger mechanism installed before they could go off. They contained maybe a couple kilos of plutonium. The bombs on my plane weren't supposed to have the triggering mechanism in them while in transit. They installed that in Europe at the bomber bases. So there wasn't any real problem with their going into the sea. That's what they said. Nothing to worry about."

"You said they never told anyone."

"Oh, they put out some cover statement to the local papers that some 'general cargo' had been jettisoned because of the emergency. They ordered us to keep our mouths shut. Olssen, my copilot, he raised a little hell about it, and got himself transferred out to Guam for his troubles."

The slope of sand was somewhat steep where they were. Cat sat down on its incline, leaning forward, hugging her knees as she gazed out over the water. The party boat was crossing the bay. To the north, a large ship was coming down toward the sea, out of Wilmington or Philadelphia or maybe the Delaware Canal. The lights of Cape May directly opposite were brightly visible now. How many people lived in that town year-round? Or in Lewes?

"We had some trouble with one of the bombs," Burt said, sitting down beside her. "That's how I lost Mikulski. He went out with it. Right into the sea. They never found his body. I think he may have gone all the way down to the bottom with it."

"Dear God."

"The bomb had gotten hung up somehow. Mikulski, he got himself down on the cargo ramp and was working on the nose of the damn thing. The bomb came free, and he went with it."

Yet another cigarette. More whiskey. Leaving the cap off, he offered her the bottle. This time she took it.

"When they debriefed Olssen, they didn't like what he insisted had happened. They sent him to the Pentagon, then shipped him out to the Pacific. They must have really put the fear into him because I never heard from him again. He did his tour and then left the service. Moved out to Montana."

Another swig of whiskey.

"He died last year," Burt continued. "His wife sent me a letter he'd written me toward the end but hadn't sent. It said that the last bomb had the plutonium core and the trigger in it. Mikulski discovered that when they were getting the thing ready to jettison. Olssen was afraid to mess with it. The bomb was about to break free. But Mikulski crawled down there and was trying to remove the trigger device when the bomb went out."

Burt took a deep breath, then coughed.

"So I dropped at least four kilos of plutonium 239 and I don't know how much uranium into the ocean out there, along with a device to set it off. Along with my friend."

Four kilograms. About the size of a couple of softballs. Maybe a little larger. Enough to kill a city.

"But it's been all these years," she said. "Nothing's happened."

"Everything corrodes in the sea," Burt replied. "Sometimes you get concretions. Rocky lumps that form around rusting metal. But mostly things rust through, and break up—ships, airplanes, bombs, whatever."

"Didn't you tell the Air Force about your copilot's last letter? Surely they'd want to do something about it."

In the dim light, she could see his bitter grin. "I've written 'em three times since I got that letter from Olssen. I only got one letter back, and they didn't say very much useful. They must have just checked the files. Same as before. No problem. Nothing to worry about."

"And you believe Olssen over the Air Force?"

"Any fucking day of the week."

Yet another cigarette—and another swig of bourbon. It was as though he had some quota of them to consume before he left this life, and was hurrying.

"There was an official report on all this," he said. "It was declassified in 1989 but they didn't get it into circulation until 1996. I got a copy from an outfit called Save Our Shores. 'Narrative Summaries of Accidents Involving U.S. Nuclear Weapons, 1950–1980.' It's upstairs. There were some other incidents like mine. In '57, a cargo plane dropped a couple of unprimed Mark 17's into the Atlantic off the Jersey Coast, and nobody knew a damn thing about it until this report came out." He smoked. "The difference is that one of mine has plutonium and a trigger in it."

"If it's in an official report, then they ought to be doing something about it."

"No, ma'am." Another swallow of whiskey. "The report says the 'devices present no hazard.' And the location? That's 'defense information.' They say they'll neither 'confirm nor deny the presence of nuclear weapons at any specific place.' You know what that means? That means they don't know where these damn things are and don't give a shit about finding out."

He started coughing again, and then doubled over, almost retching. To her amazement, when he was able to sit upright again, he took another drink of whiskey. Who said drunks had no willpower?

Cat got to her feet, brushing off her shorts and looking

skyward, where the lights of a high-flying jet were visible as it passed from southwest to northeast. Had to be a fighter, moving that fast—someone flying a combat air patrol.

The breeze was really brisking up now. She was getting a little cold.

Burt tried to get up himself, but slipped back. She leaned over and offered her hand. He took it, seeming surprised at how easily she was able to pull him up.

"I didn't want to tell you this, Cat. I'm goin' to die, honey."

"We're all going to do that."

"For me, it's pretty damn soon."

"How soon?"

"A year maybe. Not much more than that."

She swallowed. Now she was cold all over. She knew he didn't want her to say anything. She took his hand, squeezing hard. Sick and old as he might be, it was like squeezing mahogany.

"I thought about dying a lot, last few years," he said. "I always thought that at the end, I'd just go down to New Orleans or up to Atlantic City or someplace and spend my last days eatin' fine meals and drinking good whiskey and renting myself some dangerous woman." He coughed again. "But that's all out the window. I've gotta do this, Cat. Find the damn bombs. This is what I want to do with what time I've got left. Trouble is, I need some money to do it."

"Burt, I'd help you out, but . . ." she said.

"That's not necessary, and I wouldn't ask you anyway. I'm going to sell the *Roberta June*. It ought to bring more than enough to hire an underwater salvage outfit. I found one up in Wilmington. The guy seems to know his stuff. But first I've got to figure out where the bomb is."

"There are two bombs—and only one is the problem. And you've been looking for them with what, a fish finder?"

"It's more elaborate than that. I bought some stuff. Magnetometer. A handheld GPS."

"This outfit says it can recover it for you?"

"If I give them a good location. Otherwise, they'll just wander around down there wasting my money."

"I don't know, Burt. Selling your boat . . ."

"They've got to know what they're doing. The guy who runs it used to be a Navy SEAL."

Chapter 9

Ned Gergen, better known as "Bear," didn't think of himself as a thief, grifter, or smuggler—not professionally anyway. His main source of livelihood was maritime salvage. He was the owner/captain of a very serviceable, nearly paid-for, and large oceangoing salvage tug and liked to think of himself as a mariner—the master of a seagoing vessel—with a certificate to prove it.

But he was not a man to pass up opportunities, whatever they were, whenever they presented themselves. He hated leaving them to the next guy in line. On the open sea, there were always opportunities. And there was always a next guy.

If he showed occasional disrespect for U.S. maritime statutes and customs laws in pursuing these opportunities, Gergen had been administered a sizable dose of disrespect himself from that body of federal law called the Uniform Code of Military Justice.

He'd been kicked out of the SEALs and dishonorably discharged from the Navy—after serving six months in Do Right City—because of a sexual assault charge that an en-

listed woman had brought against him. He'd only been out
for a little fun, as the woman told him she was. Consensual
sex. Happened all the time. But Gergen had been a
lieutenant—her superior officer. The disciplinary board had
been out to get both of them for breaking the officer/enlisted
taboo, and the sexual assault charge had been her out. She'd
found a willing ally in an uptight commander who'd long
been looking for a way to nail Gergen to the wall.

Gergen had killed for the U.S. Navy. He'd had some very
bad, nasty people trying to do the same to him on a number
of occasions, including one involving war with Iraq. But the
Navy had done a number on him anyway, just because he'd
grabbed some enlisted snatch instead of a whore while on
liberty, prostitution being a practice of which the Pentagon
tacitly approved. So much for gratitude and loyalty. So much
for Gergen's regard for the law.

Ned was called "Bear" Gergen because of his muscular
bulk, reddish-blond beard, overlong hair, gorilla chest, and
six-foot-two-inch height. His cousin, Leonard Ruger, who
ran a boat and personal watercraft rental operation at Ocean
City with his wife, Mary Lou, somewhat resembled Bear
and had the same color hair. But no one would ever have
thought to call him Bear. Maybe Snake was better.

Leonard was much shorter and rail-thin, a man to use a
knife or gun instead of brute strength, a smoker who carried
a pack of cigarettes rolled up in the sleeve of his T-shirt, in
James Dean 1950s style. He often helped Bear on his
jobs—legal and otherwise. He was with him on the water
that day.

Sometimes Leonard brought his wife, Mary Lou, along.
That always made Bear Gergen happy, but she was not with
him this time.

Gergen and his blunt-bowed salvage tug were several
miles off Fenwick Island, Delaware, heading north toward
Delaware Bay and Gergen's home port of Wilmington. They
had a small coastal freighter in tow they had pulled from the

wreck-strewn shoals off Assateague Island, where it had foundered in heavy weather the week before. A maritime court would decide the freighter's disposition and the amount the insurance company would have to pay him.

It wouldn't be enough. Never was, what with the payroll and loan payments Bear had to meet. So when they came upon a big drifting sailboat about twelve miles due east of Indian River, it struck him that maybe he'd been handed another interesting opportunity.

The stricken yacht was a motor-sailor—sloop-rigged and about sixty-five feet long. Her mainmast was knocked down, she was trailing sail and rigging, and she appeared to have taken on a lot of water, listing as she was to starboard. Not a sign of passenger or crew on board.

There was a Coast Guard station at Indian River Inlet almost due west of them. It had been two days since the storm. A distress call should have been answered long before this.

Gergen picked up the microphone of his seagoing tug's radio. Cousin Leonard gave him a look.

"Who you callin'?"

Contrary to first impressions, Bear had all the smarts of the two. Leonard had his uses, but thinking was not one of them.

"I'm calling the Coast Guard to report that motor-sailor."

"Why the fuck you want to do that?"

"Because I'm supposed to. This close to Indian River, I'm going to do what I'm supposed to do."

"You think that wreck's worth stopping for?"

"I want to find out. It's sure as hell a rich man's boat."

The Coast Guardsman on duty at Indian River said there'd been no distress signal from any sailing vessel during the storm, but added, after a "Notice to Mariners" check, that a large yacht of similar description had been stolen two weeks before from a harbor in South Carolina. Gergen said he would investigate the derelict, and asked and received permission to take it under tow if circumstances permitted. All very neat and by the book. Nobody would come out to bother him. Widespread port security duties and the new terrorist alert had put a big crimp in the Coast Guard's resources.

Using his portable two-way, Gergen radioed his man at the helm of the freighter on tow that he was going to heave to and take a look at the sailboat. Then he had his crew lower his sixteen-foot inflatable. Despite its small size, it was almost as seaworthy as his big oceangoing tug, and powered by an eighty-horsepower outboard. Though the swells were substantial, Gergen was able to get to the side of the drifting yacht in three minutes.

He made a slow circle around her first, noting the name *Breezee B* and the degree of list, which seemed constant. He guessed she had stopped shipping water.

Was this a legitimate wreck? The incidence of boat theft was on the increase on the Atlantic Coast, but many cases were suspect. Insurance fraud was becoming a common scam. Owners who couldn't unload their tubs at anything like their book value often took their boats out and deliberately scuttled them or fired them, filing claims for more than they'd ever get on the market. Others would report their boats stolen, but have the hull and superstructure altered and repainted for sale in some foreign port.

The *Breezee B* looked a case of honest theft—as the Coast Guard had said—and the abandonment a genuine response to dangerous weather. No man could have broken the mast that way.

But why head up here from the Carolinas with a stolen vessel this distinctive? The Caribbean or Mexico was a hell of a better idea. That's where Bear Gergen sold the boats he occasionally stole.

Coming around to the leeward side of the yacht, he found its starboard rail still a foot or two above the sea, and no dinghy or life raft visible on deck. The forward hatches were closed, but the main one was gaping open and the cockpit area was awash.

He made fast a line from his inflatable to the big boat's rail, then, getting a knee onto its decking, heaved himself aboard, sloshing through the cockpit to the hatch and peering down inside. He called out. No response.

There didn't seem to be enough water down there to drown in—two or three feet max. Easing his bulk down the ladder, he clicked on the flashlight he'd taken with him and held it high as he carefully waded aft.

Gergen found three staterooms back that way, the main one and two smaller. Finding no passengers in the small chambers, he moved on to the main, making a discovery that explained a lot. Two drawers had come loose or been pulled out from the bulkhead storage cabinets. Inside one was a large plastic bag. Bear squeezed it, suspicious. Taking the rigging knife he wore on his belt, he cut it open.

Marijuana. He sniffed and tasted a sample. Very high grade.

Opening more bins and cupboards, he found a treasure of similar bags. Returning to the other staterooms, he found more there. This was a Florida thing—stealing yachts, taking them out to sea, loading them up with dope, then making a fast night run ashore at some isolated place and transferring the cargo to cars or trucks, leaving the boat as carcass for the DEA or local cops to pick over. Whoever had grabbed this boat in the Carolinas had probably been planning to make such a drop at some point on the Delaware or Jersey shore, but instead had gotten caught in the storm and abandoned ship. They might be drifting in a raft or dinghy now in the northerly current.

A boatload of good weed. No wonder they hadn't radioed for help.

Making his way forward now, Gergen came upon two cabins beyond the main salon. The door to the one on the starboard side opened easily, despite the water in it. The one port side was shut fast, either locked or jammed by something.

Bracing his foot against the bulkhead, Bear heaved himself at the door. Its uppermost portion gave slightly but the latch held fast. He tried again with the same result.

The door was locked, and from the inside.

This time he kicked, directly above the latch handle. With bits and splinters of wood flying, the door edged free.

There was quiet, then a sound he couldn't place for a moment.

It came again, familiar now. Someone vomiting.

Gergen flashed his light to the side of the chamber. Hanging over the side of the bunk was a nearly naked young woman, clutching the sodden, filth-stained sheets with both hands to keep from sliding into the water that had flooded the cabin. Even at two feet, it would mean her death if she tumbled in. She looked so weak he imagined she could drown in a washtub.

He waded to the bunk and rolled her over onto her back, shining the flashlight into her face. She was wearing a T-shirt as filthy as the sheets, but nothing else. He guessed she might be a looker, if she wasn't such a pukey mess. She stared back at him now, her eyes showing as much madness as fear and sickness. A word burbled out of her lips.

"Carl."

She said it angrily.

Bear brought the girl back to his salvage vessel to be cleaned up and put in his little cabin, then returned to the yacht with Leonard and two crew members. Securing a towline from the tug to the sailboat's bow, they brought her slowly into train until she'd been pulled alongside the freighter.

"If you're going to take the dope off the sailboat, why put it on the freighter?" Leonard said. "That's a lot of fuckin' work for nothin'."

Bear replied slowly, giving Leonard time to understand each word. "I've got a salvage claim on the freighter and nobody's gonna look in her until we get back to Wilmington and the court puts a seal on her. We'll have hours and a half-dozen places along the river to unload her before that. I don't know what the deal's gonna be with the yacht, but she's reported stolen and the Coast Guard has an open case on her. If there's any trouble, we can cut the yacht loose, and not lose a fucking thing. If we can't unload the freighter in time and law enforcement finds the dope in it, we can say we didn't know the stuff was there. Okay?"

"But why not just scuttle the sailboat now?"

"Leonard. That boat's worth a good hundred thousand or more repaired and refitted. Why turn our backs on a piece of that if the Coast Guard lets us? How many fucking Jet Skis you gotta rent to make the money you could get from your cut of the salvage?"

"How much we gonna get for the marijuana?"

Bear shrugged. "Depends. I don't know. Maybe twenty, twenty-five thousand. Could be twice that. Depends on where we sell it."

"Where you want to offload?"

"Delaware Point. Maybe stick it in that old half-sunk barge by Cedar Swamp. Don't want to get any closer than that to the Reedy Point Patrol Station."

"What kind of split?"

"Don't worry about it. We'll all make some money. But you gotta do some work for it."

Leonard looked the derelict over, bow to stern. It still seemed to be holding above water, but was making some ominous noises—creaks and some slurping and gurgling sounds coming from belowdecks.

"I think she's okay," Gergen said. "She's not taking on any more water. But let's work fast anyway, okay?"

* * *

They got all the plastic bags they could find out of the yacht and into the forward hold of the freighter. Bear had just lowered himself into the inflatable when one of his men on the salvage tug called him on the handheld two-way.

"Hey, Bear. Spotted what looks like a life raft off the port bow."

"You sure?"

"Yeah."

"Anyone aboard?"

"One or two. Hard to tell. You want to check it out or should I send someone in the skiff?"

"I'll do it."

Bear throttled back the inflatable's outboard as he approached. There were two men aboard the raft—one alert and looking at him, the other lolling with his head over the side. Bear steered his own craft to keep that one between him and the wide-awake guy.

"Glad to see you, man," said the alert one. "Thought we were fuckin' goners."

"You off the *Breezee B*?"

The other hesitated. "Yeah."

"Are you Carl?"

The man scowled. Bear had told him too much by asking that.

"She okay?"

"Why'd you leave her on the boat, Carl? You thought it was going to sink, right? That's why you're in this raft."

"She didn't want to leave. Wouldn't come out of her cabin. Locked the fucking door. She was scared, man."

He moved as though to come nearer Gergen's inflatable. Gergen revved the outboard to move it out of reach.

"You could have made her come. Dragged her out. You left her to die."

"She was stoned—crazier 'n shit." He paused, squinting

at Bear, sitting up straighter, preparing himself. "Everything okay on the sailboat?"

"You mean with all that marijuana you had aboard? It's fine. Got it stowed safe in the hold of that freighter."

"My marijuana?"

"Yours. Whoever's. It's in the freighter."

"You can't take anything off that boat! It belongs to me!"

"Sure it does. You got it as a present when you graduated from Yale. You better learn something about sea law, pal. When I put a line aboard a stricken vessel, she's mine."

Bear moved the inflatable again, standing off from the raft another six feet. He wondered if Carl had a gun. There was nothing like that visible. Neither were there life jackets on that raft. Carl and his unconscious friend must have panicked, fleeing the *Breezee B* without any other thought than to get the hell off before she went down.

Gergen had a gun in his belt—a big eleven-millimeter Glock automatic, one he had stolen while still in the Navy. He took it out.

"Hey, man, what're you gonna do? Shoot us?"

"Wouldn't do that," Bear said. "That'd be murder."

He aimed the automatic at the raft's inflated rim, waited for an intervening swell to pass, then fired quickly, twice. The airtight material burst with a sharp report, opening a big hole. Carl began swearing at him. As he motored away, not looking back, Bear heard the man begin to scream.

"Please! Please!"

Gergen returned to the salvage tug at high speed, alone.

"What're you gonna do about them?" said the member of his crew who had first sighted the raft.

"Wait a couple minutes. Then we won't have to do anything."

The girl was sleeping peacefully in his cabin, on his bunk, now completely naked but under a sheet. Bear considered keeping her. But that would be dumb, something Leonard would do. Whoever had put that dope on the yacht in Carl's care would be looking for it. This girl might be a friend of the gentleman. Complications.

Bear carefully gathered her up in his arms. Carrying her effortlessly back to the stern of the tug, he looked at her young, sleeping face a moment. He didn't want to do this. He wasn't that kind of guy.

But she likely had other friends—or employers. Bear didn't want them to know what kind of guy he was. Or who.

No. He couldn't do this.

He'd killed people. All kinds. But on the job. Not like this. This wasn't just killing. This really was fucking murder. Not at all the same as whacking some Commie Latin American greaser or Middle Eastern rag-head. Not like what he'd just done to those two scumbags he'd found in the inflatable. They'd left her to die.

She opened her eyes. They filled with terror as swiftly as they did with light. He began to turn back toward the deck, lifting the girl high to clear the safety line along the top of the rail, but her foot caught in it.

"It's okay," he said. "Be cool."

She turned her head, looking at the ocean, then screamed. Her knee came up, hitting him under the chin. She was in his arms and then she wasn't.

His last sight of her was as she went into the water, staring at him with widened, crazy eyes.

Then the sea folded over her and she was lost in the tug's heavy wake.

Chapter 10

Westman awakened after less than four hours' sleep to the insistent beeping of his alarm. Silencing it, he lay still a moment, watching the wind flutter the leaves of the tree outside his window. He tried to keep his mind from serious thoughts—especially of the work that awaited him and the reason for it.

But they were unavoidable.

Joan dePayse was one of the bravest and smartest Coast Guard officers he'd ever known. He had been under fire with her in a dustup with a particularly nasty bunch of druggies in the La Perla section of San Juan years before, and she had been far cooler than he, except for one particularly unpleasant moment.

But this quality of hers sometimes bordered on recklessness, and the previous night she'd crossed that line, oblivious to the ruin it portended for both of their careers. Years before, when they were young and new to the Coast Guard, that hadn't mattered so much. Now it meant everything, especially to her. What she meant to him now was mostly frustration, aggravated by their inequality of rank.

He reminded himself of the concerns of the day—all of them of infinitely more consequence than his relationship with Joan. The enemy was still out there. Maybe the worst bad guys they'd ever been up against.

While his coffee was brewing, he watched the morning television news. They were running video footage from the day before. There was nothing new.

He wondered if he'd be allowed to drive across the undamaged span of the Bay Bridge.

His Coast Guard ID and Investigative Service badge sufficed. They waved him onto the southern span as though he were somebody important.

Erik kept his speed at forty miles an hour on the bridge, slowing as he went past the crime scene.

They'd removed what wreckage there'd been on the westbound span, but he could see yellow police tape marking off a large section of the bridge. No work appeared to have started on repairs. Looking below, he saw a dredging barge moored near the base of one of the bridge towers. Near it were two Coast Guard forty-sevens and some police patrol boats. There was no sign of the *Manteo*. He assumed Tim Dewey had taken the cutter on into Delaware Bay, as ordered.

Driving across long suspension bridges had never bothered Erik before. He was glad when he reached dry land.

Special Agent Payne had established a command post in a motel on Kent Island, not far from the eastern end of the bridge. A task force had been hurriedly formed—led, of course, by the FBI, and including investigative units of the Maryland State Police as well as uniformed cops from Annapolis and the local sheriff's office. Erik was the only one there with any military authority.

This assemblage of law enforcement filled a large corner suite and several rooms along the hall. Payne was busy on the phone in the main room of the suite. Another agent, Leon Kelly, an old friend, motioned to two chairs in the corner. They had worked a number of cases together over the years. Erik liked the man.

"My admiral said I was to report here," Erik said. "Provide whatever help we can."

Kelly nodded. "Not much stirring yet, Erik. Waiting on the medical examiner. And the forensics report. We have a lot of people interviewing witnesses."

"Anything I can do."

"Sure. I'll tell Payne you're here."

If nothing was stirring, there was still a lot of coming and going, and the telephones were constantly ringing, punctuating the chatter coming from several radio receivers. But it was obvious little was being accomplished. There wasn't the sharpness, the urgency there should have been this far into a very major case. Except for the numbers of law enforcement involved, it was more like the second day of a routine murder.

Erik got himself a cup of coffee and moved to another chair near a table piled with reports. He began to leaf through them as he listened to Payne's men proceed with their work.

FBI agents and police had fanned out all over Kent Island. Payne had made the sensible presumption that this operation had been mounted from the Eastern Shore, a logical conclusion, given that the Homeland Security adviser had been heading west.

Little of consequence had thus far been turned up. There were reports of dark-complexioned men getting in and out of cars up and down Highway 50. A waitress at a shore-side restaurant at the foot of the bridge recalled serving a man who had lingered an inordinate time after getting his check and then left immediately after the explosion. Mysterious boats had been seen operating without running lights. A teenage girl had run out of a shopping mall, screaming. There'd been an unusually obstreperous barking of dogs in Easton, Maryland. A cabin cruiser on the Severn River had had Middle Eastern music playing on its stereo.

"What are you looking at?" said Payne, looming over the armchair where Westman had taken a seat.

Erik held out one of the computer printouts to the agent. "You've probably seen this one. A waitress in a restaurant at the east end of the bridge says there was something funny about a customer who was there before the explosion."

"She says he kept looking at the bridge," Payne said, reading from the printout. He looked to Westman. "I know that restaurant. It's got a wide deck in back overlooking the water. People sit there to watch the sunset."

"This was after sunset."

Payne said nothing more.

Westman gently took the paper back. "The name on his credit card was Anthony Bertolucci."

"Not an Arab."

"Not an Arabic name," said Westman.

Payne snatched back the printout and put it with the others. "If you're suggesting we check this out," he said, "I can tell you that of course we're going to check it out. We're going to check everything out—like we always do. That's the whole point of the Federal Bureau of Investigation. We're big enough to do that."

His not-so-oblique reference was to the Coast Guard Investigative Service—a miniscule outfit compared to the mammoth Bureau.

Westman leaned back in his chair, clasping his hands behind his head. "Is there anything you'd like me to do?"

"Just observe. For now."

Erik knew and had worked with some very fine and intrepid FBI agents in his time. Leon Kelly was certainly that. He knew a female special agent in New York who was as tough, smart, and effective as she was pretty and blond. She could have been a poster girl for law enforcement.

But Payne was hard to bear.

Erik finished his coffee and stood. He waited a moment, then walked out of the room. No one paid him any attention.

The waitress seemed anxious to speak to him, perhaps wondering why no one else had asked to talk to her. She was in her mid-twenties, a bit overweight—a real blond with sickly-looking pale skin to match. Erik could tell she was bright, but probably ill-educated. She was also scared.

"I never would have expected it," she said. "That bridge has been there like forever. I'm still scared."

They were seated in a corner table on the restaurant's rear deck. Erik's view was of the bridge. She was happy enough to be looking away from it.

"No one from the FBI has contacted you?" he asked.

"No sir. Just state police. A detective. Named Roger Poricky."

"Tell me about this man you saw."

She looked about nervously, as though he might be watching her.

"Well, he just kept looking."

"Looking?"

"At the bridge."

"Not just at the water."

"No, sir. People who sit out here, they look around. At the boats going by. At the bridge. At each other. He just kept staring at the bridge. He was looking out there for a long time—even after the sun went down."

"And then? After the explosion?"

"He kept looking a little while longer. Then he left."

"What did he look like?"

Her face went blank. She thought about the question for a long time. For a moment, Erik feared he'd been wasting his time.

"I don't know. Dark. Foreign. Something about him made me nervous."

Erik waited. He'd long before learned to push in interrogation, but not lead or steer. That's what produced testimony that was later recanted.

"Did you feel threatened by him?"

"A little. I think maybe it was his voice. He was real polite. More polite than what we usually get. But he wasn't friendly. His voice was kinda cold. Like an undertaker or something. You've been to funerals?" Erik nodded. "Well, it was like that. His voice was cold—like an undertaker's at a funeral. Very polite. But cold."

"And this is what scared you?"

"His eyes too. He had sunglasses on part of the time he was here. He kept them on even after the sun went down. Then he took them off when the bomb went off. His eyes were like his voice. Cold. Kinda hard. My sister's married to a cop in Baltimore. He's got eyes like that."

Erik leaned back. A sailboat was approaching the bridge. One of the Coast Guard forty-sevens moved out to intercept it.

"You get a lot of people in here," he said. "How can you remember so much about him?"

"I remember him because of the bomb."

"But the restaurant must have been full of people. No one else attracted your attention? Acted strangely?"

"Some people were scared. Some jumped up. One woman tried to jump off the deck. This guy just stared."

Erik made a lengthy entry in his notebook.

"Anything else?"

"His voice."

"You've already told me about that."

"No. He had a sort of accent. He didn't sound American."

"Middle Eastern?"

"I don't know what that would be like. Anyway, I don't think so. He sounded Polish."

"Polish? As in Warsaw?"

"Something like that. Over on the beach—Rehoboth, Bethany—they've got a lot of Eastern Europeans working there. Young people mostly—from Bosnia, Romania, Russia, places like that. Working jobs like mine. That's what he sounded like. Maybe Polish."

"You didn't tell the FBI about this?"

"I talked to the detective from the state cops. He didn't let me say very much. He was talking to everybody who works here. Talked to the manager here the longest."

"Did the manager see what happened?"

"No. He didn't see anything. He was in the kitchen, arguing with a chef."

"He didn't see your customer—the hard, cold one?"

She was fishing out a pack of cigarettes from her bag. "No."

"Would you be willing to talk to a sketch artist about this guy? They use computers now. It won't take long."

She lighted her cigarette. "Okay."

Erik had already take her name, address, and phone number.

"The FBI will take care of it," he said, uncertain if that was true. "I'll have somebody call you."

"They won't use my name or anything, will they? I mean, I'm not going to be on television or anything?"

He could tell she very much did not want to be. "The FBI doesn't do that."

"But you're in the Coast Guard? I didn't know the Coast Guard had detectives."

"Just a few of us. For things like this."

"Are we done?"

"I'd like a beer. Do you have Mousel?"

She shook her head.

"Okay, a Heineken's."

*　*　*

Erik had forgetfully left his cell phone in his car. It rang the instant he turned it on. He had two messages, one from Joan dePayse, the other from Leon Kelly. The cop in Erik was interested most in talking to Kelly. The military man in him commanded otherwise. Chain of command.

It took a while to contact her. She was in a meeting, but had left instructions to be informed if he called. Erik wondered what the admirals and captains thought of being interrupted by a warrant officer.

"Admiral dePayse," she said formally.

"Westman," he replied, trying to sound less formal.

"Anything new?" she asked.

"They're still casting their nets." He paused. "I did some independent investigating. I think I found someone who saw one of the suspects. Got a name on him. I'm sure it's an alias, but it's on a credit card."

"Terrific! Did you tell the FBI?"

"I've only just left the witness. The Bureau had a report on her, but didn't follow it up."

"Send them a memo and send me the copy. You have your laptop?"

"Yes, ma'am."

"Soon as you can."

"Right."

"They treating you all right?"

He sighed. "Not really."

"We're hearing that some members of Congress may try to blame us for this."

"Blame the Coast Guard? Did they expect we'd have a cutter patrolling Highway 50?"

"The bridge is marine infrastructure—which we're supposed to be protecting."

"We did. No terrorist vessel got near it on the water."

"Erik. I just want us to be doing everything we can."

"Well, I'd like them to talk to my witness."

"I'll bring it up—with Intel."

"Okay."

A pause, and then a continuing silence. He supposed it did for words. Talking about the previous night was as dangerous as the night itself had been.

"Erik?"

"Yes?"

"Do what you want. Do what you can. But watch out for sharks. They're not all in the sea."

"Yes, ma'am."

"And keep me informed."

"Of course."

Another pause. She was contemplating saying something else, but then thought better of it.

"Take care." She clicked off.

Erik called the number Kelly had left. It was the agent's cell phone. He was in a car, heading east on Highway 404 in a hurry.

"Things are moving, Erik. Moving fast. They found the wreckage of the truck. There's a recovery barge on scene. And the medical examiner came through on the male victim you brought into Annapolis. They got an ID. It's a phony, but he sure wasn't the lady's husband. Most likely one of the perps off the bomb truck."

"That's great news."

"There's better news. There was a fire in a farmhouse south of Denton. Three victims. All male. Pickup truck, stolen from Kent Island shortly after the event. It's got to be them, Erik."

"What's the location?"

Kelly gave him the particulars. "I'm heading there now. Payne thinks we've got them all."

"May I join you?"

"Sure. You're part of the task force."

"Thanks, Leon."

* * *

Erik had been based in the Washington area for many years and knew the Eastern Shore roads well. He arrived at what was left of the farmhouse not long after Kelly. There were at least a dozen marked state police cars, plus nearly half that many of Bureau vehicles, identified solely by their "U.S. Government" plates.

Special Agent Payne welcomed Erik with a boast. "We got 'em all, Westman! There were four men seen on the bridge and they're all accounted for."

"Any names?"

"Working on it. But it's got to be all of them—with these three and the one you guys fished out of the bay. We got a positive on the truck. Witnesses to their stealing it."

"Congratulations," Erik said.

"We've got a lot of work still to do. Tie all this together."

"Where are the bodies?"

Payne pointed to the ashy ruin. "Right there in the middle. Don't contaminate the crime scene."

"Wouldn't think of it," Erik said.

He walked toward the remains of the house. Payne followed. The FBI agent kept just behind Westman as they stepped gingerly through the ash to where they could closely view the three corpses.

"You think this wraps it up?" Payne said to Erik. "I mean, we've got them all. One was blown off the bridge. The other three ran off and now we've found them."

Erik took a step closer. "Cause of death?"

"Unknown. Until we get an examination."

"Not fire."

"How do you know that?"

"Too relaxed. Burn victims writhe. You find a lot of them in a fetal position."

Payne shrugged.

"What if they were shot?" Erik asked.

"What if?"

"It would mean there were at least five," said Kelly, who had joined them. "Counting the guy who did the shooting."

Payne looked at the corpses thoughtfully, then moved away, saying nothing. Erik went to his car and activated his laptop, using the satellite phone he'd been issued for the first time. He typed and then filed his report on the waitress, sending an e-mail copy to Admiral dePayse.

He was driving back to Kent Island when his cell phone rang. He pulled off to the side of the highway to answer it. The bean fields stretched to a tree line. Off to the right were the lights of a house.

"Westman."

"It's Leon Kelly."

"Long day."

"Gonna be shorter for you. How close did you get to the farmhouse?"

"I don't know. Close enough to see the bodies."

"Payne says you disturbed and contaminated the crime scene. He put a request through to Washington asking the Coast Guard to reassign you."

"You're kidding."

"Sorry, Erik. I'm not."

"Okay. I'll go independent. I'm authorized."

"Just steer clear of him."

"That'll be easy."

"How's that?"

"I mean to find this fifth guy."

Kelly waited before answering, perhaps moving to a more discreet location. "Let me know."

"Sure."

"Erik?"

"Yes?"

"I'll be talking to you soon."

* * *

Westman reached the intersection with Highway 404 and pulled off to the side. Behind him, to the west, was Highway 50, Kent Island, the Bay Bridge, Annapolis, Washington, D.C., and his base. To the east was the rest of the Delmarva Peninsula.

He took out his cell phone again and called Joan de-Payse's office number.

She wasn't there. He waited to leave a message.

"Ground effort not working out," he said. "Am going to sea."

Chapter 11

Turko was still alive. He didn't understand why. He supposed it was not going to be for long. Pec would be trying to arrange the most unpleasant death for him he could. The Kosovar knew of many from his years of murdering Serbs.

They had put him in the trunk of a car, with Sandor's body for company. His hands and ankles were tightly bound and they'd put duct tape over his mouth. He could breathe well enough, and almost wished he couldn't. He'd shot Sandor in the belly and the bullet had torn open much of his digestive tract.

There had been three of them, including Sandor. He could hear the other two talking up in the front seat. Both were ethnic Albanians from Kosovo, like Pec, and Turko didn't understand the language, but it struck him they were just chatting—about sports or women. They might have been furniture movers.

They had efficiently cleaned out Turko's Ocean City apartment in about five minutes—removing groceries along with Sandor, but performing only a minimal cleaning up. He had no idea what had happened to the fat blond woman across the alley. It would be a terrible mistake to leave her where she fell. The Ocean City police might not have had a lot of experience with homicides, but the FBI was out on the Eastern Shore in force. Any violent death in the area was going to be thoroughly investigated by the best the Americans had.

Wherever they were taking him, it was taking a long time. To occupy his mind, and distract him from the unpleasantness of his deceased companion, Turko tried to calculate their eventual destination.

It was certain they'd left Ocean City by the causeway and bridge to the mainland. There'd been a long rumble across the span. Not too far beyond, they'd made a right turn onto a major highway used by heavy trucks. Traffic moved fairly fast, but there were many stoplights. Turko guessed it was Highway 113, and was sure they were traveling north. He had no useful idea of the passage of time, though they were consuming a lot of it. But when their speed picked up, and the interruptions from traffic lights ceased, he figured they had moved onto Delaware's only limited-access north-south road—Highway 1. The possible destinations were many: Baltimore, Wilmington, Philadelphia, Atlantic City—or some farmer's field in New Jersey where his body would not be readily discovered.

He tried thinking about something else. His wife's face. His wife's voice. The touch of her hand on the back of his neck.

He'd been promised Paradise, where the clerics said she'd be waiting. This required of him only a martyr's death. He wasn't sure if being tortured and executed by a wrathful Pec qualified.

The car stopped. Turko frantically tried to produce one last desperate idea that might effect his escape. The trunk lid was opened quickly and he was pulled halfway out, head down. As he attempted to see where he was, one of the men hit him with something heavy. The other then pulled a bag down over his head and he was lifted completely out and set tottering on his feet.

Fighting to stay conscious, he stumbled along as they dragged and pulled him up a flight of wooden stairs and across a porch, then through a doorway. The door that was slammed behind him made a sound that indicated it had a glass window in it. Then he was held up against a large metal object he quickly realized from the motor vibrations was a refrigerator. He was in a kitchen—on a second floor. Houses had kitchens on the first floor. This was an apartment. The wooden stairs and porch would belong to an old building, probably in a run-down neighborhood, judging from the smell. They must have parked in the alley.

One man held him against the refrigerator. He could hear the other one moving away—walking on a wooden floor. There was an exchange of words in the Albanian language Turko didn't understand. Then a sharp command. He was yanked away from the refrigerator, pushed along a hallway, then made to turn into a room, whereupon he was kicked from behind and sent sprawling on the floor. He swore—in Chechen, in Russian, and in English. One of his escorts then rolled him over on his back and yanked off the hood. Blinking, Turko found himself staring up at Pec, who sat in an armchair not six feet from him, holding a gun.

Westman had called ahead to the Lewes-Cape May ferry, discovering that it was still not operating. This meant he'd have to take the long way around, driving up to Wilmington and taking Interstate 95 over the Delaware Memorial Bridge to New Jersey, then heading south to Cape May.

Tim Dewey was expecting him. The *Manteo* was on 24/7 duty, but was authorized to return to the Coast Guard station at Cape May as necessary. This included refueling and dinner breaks.

Westman drove fast. When he finally reached the Coast Guard station at Cape May, he stowed his gear aboard the cutter, then joined Dewey for the walk to his apartment. To his amazement, Sally Dewey had a piping hot dinner waiting for them.

"It's just macaroni and cheese," she said. "Had it warming in the oven."

She was a sweet-faced and trimly athletic young woman who worked when she could as a substitute teacher, though Dewey's postings often prevented it. She accepted this, as she did his absences. It bothered Dewey that she didn't have more of a life for herself, and he tried to compensate her whenever possible. Westman liked them both. He envied them their marriage.

As they ate, Erik related the details of the investigation so far, leaving out nothing, knowing he could count on Sally's discretion absolutely. Dewey took a last bite of dinner, then leaned back in his chair.

"A cutter on port security patrols makes kind of a poor base for someone working a homicide investigation," he said.

"This is more than a homicide investigation."

"Exactly. You need a lot more resources than you'll have sitting on the *Manteo*. And I'm under separate orders."

"What I need is a place to work from that's total Coast Guard and where no one's going to interfere with me."

"Sounds like your office over in Alexandria."

"I think this bastard is still on the Eastern Shore, Tim. Don't worry, if we have to be in different places, I'll jump ship and get out of the way. But if we get a break on this, I'd like knowing I can call on you for backup."

"That's standard operational procedure." He grinned, then stood up. "Got to get back to the ship. You want to sleep aboard or in some Cape May bed-and-breakfast?"

"You'll be monitoring all the emergency and police channels?"

"Operational procedure from the git-go."

"I'll sleep aboard."

Sally produced a thermos full of coffee and a bag of brownies. "See you both for breakfast," she said, proceeding to give her husband the kind of kiss and hug usually reserved for much longer voyages.

Erik had gone too many years without that kind of life. Someday he'd have to do something about that.

But not this day.

"You killed Sandor before he could speak," said Pec. "You did not let him speak." He rested his gun hand on his knee, almost casually pointing it at Turko's midsection, preparing to shoot him where he had shot Sandor. The Kosovar was a small man of striking countenance, with sharp, dark, narrow features, cold blue eyes, and very short hair. His problem was that he looked like exactly what he was. He had none of the chameleon qualities that Turko and some of the others had mastered.

"I thought he had come to kill me." Turko was still lying on his back, his arms bent painfully beneath him.

"If he had come to do that, it would have been on my orders, which means you would have died. For Allah."

Turko said nothing. He had not thought of Pec being particularly religious. The two other men in the room had taken seats. He still had no plan, no hope to grasp for. All that kept him alive was the tension of the trigger of Pec's automatic. A slight contraction of Pec's index finger and Turko's world would vanish.

"Why did you kill your three Pakistanis?" Pec asked, almost idly, as though asking the time. His gun hand relaxed, the barrel dropping slightly.

"Because they were incompetent, cowardly, and might have revealed things to the Americans."

"Exactly," said Pec, smiling. The expression looked odd on him.

"Exactly?"

"Exactly why I sent Sandor to kill you."

"You should have sent someone else."

"Yes. You're better than he was. Not smarter, but quicker. Unfortunately, I had no one else. Our resources here are not unlimited. Which is why I am going to allow you to live."

"You are?"

"You saved your life twice by shooting Sandor. Once then. And now. I need you to replace him." He nodded to one of the others. In a moment, Turko's bonds were removed, and he was allowed to sit up. He made no further move.

"How replace him?"

"We are going to do another operation. Yours was a cock-up. We will try again. Sandor was to do it. Now you will."

"But there are police and federal agents everywhere."

"Soldiers too. All getting in each other's way. We have picked a good place. Near, but not where they expect."

"Another bridge?"

"No."

Turko rubbed his wrists. The skin was raw in many places. He waited, looking away from Pec. This displeased the Kosovar.

"Face me," said the Kosovar. Turko quickly did so. The two men, never friendly, stared at each other. Finally, Pec spoke again. "The Americans will be worried about Washington. That's where their attention will stay focused. We will strike nearby, but in the other direction. Just across the Delaware River."

Turko wasn't certain of his location. "Are we in Wilmington, Delaware?" he asked.

"Maybe you are smarter than Sandor," he said. "Yes. We are. And to do what you must do, you must cross the Delaware River."

"To New Jersey?"

Pec nodded.

"What's there?"

"Something to make me very happy. If you can blow it up."

Chapter 12

Erik awoke the next morning to a message broadcast over the intercom he had not heard in years.

"Mr. Westman. Lay to on the quarterdeck."

He'd brought only civilian clothes. Pulling on shorts, knit shirt, and boat shoes, he hurried up the stairs to the bridge. Master Chief DeGroot was at the con, and Skipper Dewey was at the chart table. The main computer screen was showing a chart of the Delaware coast extending down to Maryland and Ocean City.

"We've got an ops order," said Dewey. "I thought it might interest you."

"Everything interests me now," Westman said.

Dewey drew him closer to the electronic chart. "Some bodies have washed up," he said. His finger moved down the Delaware shoreline from Henlopen to a long stretch of Delaware State Seashore near Bethany Beach. "One's here. A young woman." His finger moved slightly down the shoreline. "Two others here. Young men. They look to be American."

"Not terrorists?"

"Not the guy you're after, for sure. Not Middle Eastern. Probably drowning victims. We had a pretty bad storm kick up off the capes couple days ago."

"Can't the Indian River station handle this?"

"They're on the scene in a forty-seven. They alerted us in because of the terrorist watch—dead bodies being suspicious activity."

"Anyone else on it?"

"A salvage tug out of Wilmington hauled in a motor-sailor yesterday. It had been adrift. Maybe these people were off it."

"I'll be happy to join you for a look-see, but it doesn't sound like it's linked to the bridge incident."

"You never know until you know." Dewey turned to the con. "Mr. DeGroot, let's get under way."

The master chief gave a command to the helmsman, then stepped out on the bridge wing and began giving orders to the deck crew. Within three minutes, the lines were slipped and the *Manteo* was heading out into the Cape May Channel.

Erik kept out of the way. There was a danger area in the shoal waters directly off the mouth of the channel. Once into the bay, DeGroot called a course of south-southeast.

Standing off to avoid an incoming Lewes ferry, the *Manteo* then increased speed, shifting course to due south to clear Prissy Wicks Shoal and then angling southwest with a bearing on the Cape Henlopen Light, the cutter's wide bow spreading the deep blue water aside with ease. Gulls swept in to follow, perhaps taking them for a fishing boat.

"Kill" was the old Dutch word for stream or channel, and some of the deep underwater ravines that cut between the Delaware Bay and Atlantic shoals still bore the name in a number of variations. Broadkill was just up the coast from Lewes, Deepkill to the south of Cape Henlopen. Erik's favorite was a tidal river up Delaware Bay actually called Murderkill. It was not far from the bayside Slaughter Beach.

Coffee was brought up and they stood drinking it. Westman noticed that the cover had been removed from the
twenty-five-millimeter deck gun.

"Cleared for action?"

"Orders. They've issued me an extra machine gun too—
and another one of those engine-killing .50-caliber sniper
rifles."

Westman had his nine-millimeter automatic in his duffel.
He noted that Dewey and DeGroot had theirs in holsters.
"Any news this morning?"

"CNN is on down in the galley, if you want to watch it,"
Dewey said. "Nothing new beyond what you told me last
night, except there's something about sources in the Justice
Department saying they've now accounted for the entire
gang. All four of 'em."

"How can they possibly know that's all? Did they ask the
four dead guys? And did they kill each other? Or do you suppose there might possibly be a fifth guy out there who had
something to do with it? Maybe even a sixth."

"I guess the Justice Department wants to put this down as
a success. The bridge is intact. No important U.S. official
among the victims. The perpetrators all killed. Plot foiled."

Westman smiled. "If that's the official line, how come
we're not standing down?"

"Admiral's orders. We're not part of the Justice Department."

"We are blessed."

As they passed Cape Henlopen, the helmsman altered
course, bearing off to starboard to move around a large fishing boat anchored dead ahead.

"That boat was here yesterday," DeGroot said.

"I remember," Dewey said. "Let's pass a little nearer."

DeGroot gave the order and the bos'n's mate turned the
Manteo toward the stern of the head boat.

"A little less speed, Hugo," Dewey said.

Westman went to a forward window and took a pair of

binoculars from the hook where they were hanging. *"Roberta June,"* he called out.

"Lewes boat," said DeGroot.

Signaling their intention with two blasts of their ship's horn, and receiving two in reply, they passed around the fishing boat by the stern, moving along its starboard side. Westman went to the port side of the bridge to get a good look at the craft. It was dirty, with rust stains at the scuppers.

There were only a few people visible, two of them women. One, a long-haired blond, was at the controls on the boat's flying bridge. She seemed to be staring at them. He lowered the binoculars.

"No one's fishing."

"Maybe they're not biting," Dewey said.

"Maybe he converted to whale watching," DeGroot said. "That's a swindle. No whales in these waters. Just dolphins."

"No one aboard is watching whales—or dolphins," said Westman. "Just us."

The radio crackled. The skipper of the forty-seven on the scene south of Rehoboth, a bos'n's mate, reported that the Delaware State Police wanted to remove the girl's body. A big crowd had gathered, he said, most of them young people, some of them drunk. They were trampling the crime scene.

"Negative," said Westman. "She's our case if she came off that motor-sailor. Tell the state cops to deal with the crowd. We'll take care of the victim."

Cat McGrath watched the Coast Guard cutter cross the *Roberta June*'s stern—much too closely for a vessel just passing by. She hoped they weren't going to be hassled. Burt had been drinking again and, as master of the *Roberta June,* he could be in for serious trouble if the Coasties wanted to make an issue of it—which they undoubtedly would.

When she was in the Navy, Cat hadn't really thought of the Coast Guard as a military service. More like oceangoing narcs and immigration agents—and lifeguards. But now, with creeps running around America knocking down and blowing up things, they were the ones on the front line on the water. It was the Navy that was backup.

There was a very tan, gray-haired man on the bridge of the cutter, watching her. She might have thought him the captain, were it not for his wearing civilian boating clothes instead of the regulation blue uniform. Whoever he was, he was definitely curious about them.

She waved. He didn't wave back, but turned away. The cutter kept on going, heading south.

"Burt," she said. "Maybe we ought to call it a day."

"It's still morning. I want to move out to the shoal and see what we find with this magnetometer."

Cat went to the control console, waiting for Burt to prepare his little sensing device. Flying for a puddle-jump little airline in Iowa was beginning to seem attractive.

The dead girl had been sampled by the denizens of the deep, but her face was still intact, her eyes wide and bulging. Westman had brought his digital camera ashore, and he now took three pictures—one of the entire body, a close-up of her face for identification purposes, and another of her right hand, which was badly scratched. He then knelt in the sand to examine the body, paying particular attention to the inside of her arms and the skin between her toes.

"User," he said, rising.

"Let's hope she was high when she went under," Dewey said, looking on.

Erik looked down at the tortured face. "I don't think so."

"You're the Investigative Service," Dewey said. "Why don't you take charge of this?"

Westman nodded, then took out his cell phone, calling a now-familiar number.

"Special Agent Payne, this is Special Agent Westman."

"What do you want, Westman?" came the reply. "I thought you were transferred out of this case."

"I'm just following the memorandum of agreement. We have three DOA here on the Delaware shore. Apparent drowning victims, but I think narcotics may be involved. Salvage tug brought in an abandoned motor-sailor yesterday. They're probably off of that. I've examined one body, a white female approximately twenty years of age. The fingerprints should be run through your—"

Payne had heard enough. "We have every agent working the bridge case, Westman. Why don't you guys keep this one?"

"You're not interested in any possible connection?"

"If you find one, let us know."

"Very well."

"You have time for this, with all your port security duty?"

"It's called 'the new normalcy.' Two-hundred-percent use of one-hundred-percent resources."

"Well, the case is all yours." Payne hung up.

Westman clicked off his phone and looked past Dewey to one of the Delaware state troopers. "Bag the hands, bag the head, bag the body. Tell your medical examiner we want fingerprints and a thorough look-over."

"Yes, sir."

Westman stepped away, looking up and down the shore. People were still gathered around, watching intently, though there was little for them to see.

"Let's go deal with the other two," he said to Dewey.

The two youths had come ashore about a hundred yards apart, making the job of crowd control all the harder, especially with the arrival of television cameras. Worse, the news media people had somehow gotten the idea these drowning victims were possibly linked to the bridge bomb plot. Running up to Westman as he approached, several peppered him with questions along that line—until the Delaware state cops intervened.

Westman took his time with each body. One of the young men had an athletic build and seemed to have been in reasonably good health except for a couple of nasty old scars. The other was a lardy lump of a fellow with large, tubular eyes and several days' growth of beard. Westman pegged him as an alcoholic or junkie—probably both.

"The medical examiner may find otherwise," he said, rising, "but they look like drownings to me."

"Off that motor-sailor," Dewey said. "They abandoned ship too soon."

One of the youths had been wearing a pair of cut-off jeans and a T-shirt out of the Sun and Fun shops. The other was in a pair of cheap khaki shorts and a short-sleeved print shirt with crocodiles on it.

"They don't have the look of yachtsmen, do they?" Westman said.

"I doubt they could have gotten jobs as deckhands on that yacht," Dewey observed.

"Where did that salvage tug take her?"

"Wilmington."

Westman nodded. "Well, they're not Middle Eastern."

"You done?"

"We can wait on the ME's report and a fingerprint match with the FBI's data bank, but I doubt they're anything more than some freelance drug smugglers who took on more than they bargained for when they got caught in that storm." He looked south, where there was some dark sky building. "You want to continue on patrol?"

"I'll check with the District in Portsmouth, but I'm guessing they'll send us back. They're more worried about the Delaware River than this beach."

"Suits me."

*   *   *

The head boat was working waters much farther out than where they'd left it.

"You say you know them?" Westman asked DeGroot.

He lowered his binoculars. The fishing vessel had slowed. The breeze was stiffening and the chop had increased.

"I know the boat. It works this area, right up to the demarcation line of the Henlopen wildlife refuge. The captain likes to make sure every one of his customers gets a fish."

Westman took another look through the binoculars. The blond woman was still at the helm of the boat. "There are no customers today," he said.

"You want to board her? Orders are to investigate any suspicious activity. In this case, suspicious inactivity."

Westman lowered the field glasses. "Yes."

Cat knew the Coast Guardsmen would be paying a visit the instant she noted their reduction in speed. There was no way to avoid them, but there was something that had to be done if their visit wasn't to lead to disaster.

"Burt," she said. "I want you to go below and find a bunk and get in it. Wrap yourself in a blanket and pretend you're asleep."

He looked to the cutter, watching as it lowered a rigid-hulled inflatable. "Aw, it's all right, Cat. I know these Coasties."

"Get below now," she said, "or I'll never come out here with you again."

"Cat . . ."

"Amy!" The girl had been ignoring all this, or pretending to.

"Yes?"

"Get Burt down the ladder and into a bunk. If you find any booze lying around, stow it quick."

"Okay."

Burt turned meek and allowed himself to be led below. Cat guessed he really wasn't feeling very well.

Three men were coming toward them in the inflatable from the cutter—an officer, an older enlisted man, and the man with gray hair, dressed in civilian shirt and shorts. She calmed herself, sitting back in the captain's chair as she waited for them to come near. What could they do to her? She had no master's certificate for them to take away. As they drew near, she turned again and waved—smiling this time—and climbed down from the flying bridge.

The Coast Guard inflatable was small, less than twenty feet long. It had a machine gun mounted forward.

The officer had a battery-powered bullhorn. "We'd like to inspect your vessel, ma'am," he said as he brought the inflatable near. "We're going to come aboard."

"Suit yourself," Cat said.

The enlisted man, an older, muscular specimen with master chief's insignia on his sleeve, tied the boarding boat to the *Roberta June*'s rail. The officer and the white-haired man came quickly up onto the *Roberta June*'s deck, the master chief following after.

"Sorry to bother you, ma'am," said the young officer, a lieutenant whose name tag said "Dewey." "This whole coastline's a control zone now, and checking out vessels is part of that."

"I understand."

"Won't take long." He nodded to the master chief, who started moving aft, poking at the rows of stowed life jackets.

The lieutenant was a boyishly good-looking young man, about her own age, but much like a thousand junior officers she had encountered in the service—eager, bright, with the program—though he seemed a little more gee-whizzy than most.

He started forward, leaving Cat with the gray-haired man, who introduced himself as Erik Westman. He was as tall as the young lieutenant, but a bit more muscular. His face was tanned and weathered, a little hard, but pleasant.

"Are you in the Coast Guard?" she asked.

He was studying her. He had light brown eyes about the same shade as his tan.

"CGIS," he said.

She gave him a blank look.

"Coast Guard Investigative Service."

"You're a civilian then?"

"Chief warrant officer four."

"A couple of years ago, I would have outranked you." It was a stupid thing to say. He'd have every right to be offended.

"Navy?" he asked.

"Tomcat pilot. Used to be."

"You're a little young to have retired."

"I didn't retire." She said that a little too defiantly, but she wasn't very good at hiding her feelings on that issue.

"Lieutenant then, right?"

"Was. Now I'm a civilian."

He grinned. "Then you outrank us all."

Dewey returned from a rather cursory look at the forward anchor gear. "May I see your vessel's papers, please?"

Cat went to a small compartment in the bulkhead near the main control station, taking out the plastic bag containing the documents. She had no idea whether they were in order.

The young lieutenant went through them quickly, pausing at one. "The only master's certificate here is for a Burton Schilling. Where's yours?"

She smiled sweetly. "I don't have one. You can see my pilot's license if you like."

"Miss, this is a commercial vessel. You carry passengers. You need . . ."

"The master—Mr. Schilling—is below, not feeling well. I'm just taking over for him."

"What are you doing here?" He looked back along the rail. "Fishing? I don't see any lines out."

"We're just checking out the fishing grounds—for when the tourists come back, if they ever do."

"I didn't know Deepkill Shoal was that good for fish."

"Burt thinks it is."

Dewey looked to the hatchway leading to the main cabin, then turned to the master chief, as though about to order him below. Westman intervened.

"Unless there's something you need to see, Lieutenant Dewey," he said. "I don't think we need to bother these people anymore."

Dewey smiled. "Fine with me." He took a notebook from his pocket that looked like the ticket books traffic cops carried, made a few entries, then pulled a yellow carbon from it and handed it to her. She knew what it was, and was grateful. A yellow copy meant the boat had somehow passed inspection. If he had given her a white citation, it would have meant corrections were called for, and an appearance in court. She didn't need that, with her reinstatement still a possibility.

Westman started toward the rail, then turned and stepped close to her. "May I see that pilot's license, please."

She dug her wallet out of the pocket of her too-tight shorts. She'd lost the medical certificate that went with the license, but she didn't suppose he'd notice. At all events, it wasn't his business.

Westman studied it, turned it over, then handed it back. "Where do you moor this vessel"

"A little downriver from the Lighthouse Restaurant in Lewes."

"Thank you." He gave her an odd, two-fingered, casual salute. "If you see anything suspicious, remember to call the Coast Guard."

Before concluding their patrol, they stopped two other boats, both in Delaware Bay, and made a circle around a Liberian-flag container ship bound upriver for Philadelphia. With its limited resources, the Coast Guard was able to search only about five percent of the container ship traffic inbound for the United States, and these searches were often cursory at best. But it was well to show the flag—and the deck gun.

After they tied up at Cape May, Westman lingered on the dock. Dewey had to stop at the office to make a report, but Westman was free to go where he wished.

"Will you be here for a while?" Westman asked.

"Yup. Dinner break. Sally and I are going out for seafood."

Westman looked out across the bay. "Any chance of using one of your inflatables?"

"Sure. Part of the investigation. Where do you want to go?"

"Lewes."

Dewey frowned. The wind was loudly flapping the American flag flying above the harbor. "Pretty big chop kicking up."

"I've been wet before."

"What're you after in Lewes?"

"I thought I'd troll the fishermen's bars, see what's the catch of the day in the way of loose talk."

"You wouldn't be trolling in waters where the catch might be blond?"

"You never know what you're going to catch," Westman said.

Chapter 13

They'd driven to a state park on the Delaware side of the river, pulling to the edge of a small parking area that had a view of the hulk of old Fort Delaware on its low island out in the middle. The former Civil War prison was not what interested Pec, however. Rising from the New Jersey horizon in the distance were the gigantic, tapered chimneys of a nuclear power plant.

Turko was sitting in the front passenger seat. Behind the wheel next to him was one of the well-armed men who had come for him in his Ocean City apartment. Pec was in the backseat just behind him. Turko presumed the Kosovar had his gun in hand, but it didn't matter. He was not fool enough to attempt an escape under these circumstances. Not with these people.

The radio was tuned to an all-news station. There was much less about the bridge attack than Turko would have expected. During the "top of the hour" news roundup they had quoted Justice Department officials as saying it appeared all the perpetrators involved were now dead, though they had identified only the man pulled out of the bay. The name they cited had been on a State Department "watch" list. The news report concluded with a member of Congress calling for public hearings into another FBI and CIA security lapse.

After a commercial for a furniture store, a woman came on with the weather report. It would be sunny the next day.

"What do you expect me to do with something like that?" Turko said finally, nodding to the plant across the river.

"Not 'with.' 'To.'"

"If you are observed even taking photographs within a mile of such a place, they arrest you. I have watched this happen. We examined these facilities when I first came over. They're very difficult. Maybe impossible."

Pec took something from the seat beside him and reached over the seat to drop it on Turko's lap.

It was a computer printout— the pages stapled together to make a sort of book. "What's this?"

"Read the cover page."

Turko stared at it. " 'Nuclear Insecurity: A Special Report.' " He began thumbing through it.

"A private organization put that out," Pec said. "It's their second report about nuclear power plant security this year. It says the security guard forces at these plants have been tripled in size but are still not sufficient for what they must protect. It says they are poorly paid. Receive insufficient training. Are weakly armed. At many plants, they carry only pistols and need special permission to draw automatic weapons. When they have mock exercises, the guard forces are informed beforehand and the intruders always come from only one direction."

"Surely they have made changes."

"What you have is the second report. Most of these complaints were in the first report. Several members of their Congress made speeches asking for changes, but nothing came of it. The White House was not interested. The nuclear power industry doesn't want to spend more money on security. The guards at this plant are paid less than the janitors there. It's called the Farmingdale plant. I want you to attack it."

"I am one man."

"No. There will be four of you. I am bringing down the last crew I have left besides my own group."

"From where?"

"You don't need to know."

"No four men ever made are going to be able to break into that place and blow up a reactor."

"You could. It would be hard. Very, very difficult. But possible. What I want is probable. You may forget reactors. Your target will be one of the spent-fuel pools. They're well covered, but situated out in the open, away from the major structures. You get close to one, blow it open, and the spent fuel they have stored inside will flow out and catch fire. This will be a catastrophic fire, filling the air with radioactivity for fifty miles, depending on the wind. It says so in this report. With a wind from the south, you could reach Wilmington and Philadelphia with it. There would be incredible panic, and all that means."

Turko imagined this. The image did not please him. "With four men."

"As I said, these people are trained for only one group of intruders, coming from one direction. Your group will come from two. One by land, the other from the river."

"They patrol the river."

"The Coast Guard goes up and down it, but they never stop here. There's a state police marine unit at the plant most of the time. Sometimes they are not there."

"Double fence," Turko said.

"A good-sized truck could break through it."

"Hmmm." He meant that to be noncommittal.

A tugboat was passing by, heading upriver without a tow.

"It can be done, Turko."

"What about escape?"

"That will be up to you. But it can be done and you will do it. Otherwise, I will not let you live. Do you have any doubt about that?"

"No."

Pec dropped something else on Turko's lap—an envelope thick with its contents. "Here is fifty thousand dollars. It is not really enough for this kind of operation, but it must suffice, and cover all costs. Our resources are now very limited. Your failure was my failure—do you understand? I dare not ask for more."

Turko put the envelope in his pocket. "How soon?"

"You have one week."

"A week!" It was the same as saying, "Today."

"I am promising them a week. If I make it longer, they will send people to kill us all. Our leaders are impatient—and unforgiving."

"That's not very wise. It should be a long while before the next strike. Two years, maybe more."

"Such waits are no longer countenanced. They wanted something big. The way it turned out, the bridge was not big."

"Why big?"

Pec answered obliquely. "That nuclear plant is big."

They both gazed it, as though it held all the secrets of the earth.

"Why do you do this, Pec?"

"Because I need to do something and this is the best thing to do."

"No. I mean, why do you do what you do?"

The Kosovar shifted in his seat. "I hate them. And I enjoy the work."

"I don't. . . ."

"Yes, you do. That much is clear. You enjoy it. I wish you were better at it."

"Sorry." Turko did not like saying that. He did not feel apologetic.

"It stirs things up, what we do. Our countries cannot sustain themselves otherwise. The Americans and the Russians will just trample over us. But if we stir things up, so there is chaos and confusion and fear, then there is a chance for us. Then maybe we can prevail."

"Are you avenging your people?"

"I am killing Americans. They are the ones who let the Serbs do what they did and they are the ones who left the Serbs in place when the fighting was over. They and their friends the Russians. They order the world as it pleases them. Together, the Russians and the Americans, they are the new Soviets. They think everything is for them. They take everything from the world and give back nothing. I hate them. I want to make trouble for them. I want to teach them there is a price they must pay for what they do."

Turko did not hate the Americans. But it was true they were becoming the same thing as the Russians. As far as Chechnya was concerned, they were as good as the same. With America's blessing, the Russians were waging their "war on terrorism" against Chechnya. The Americans at the same time had Afghanistan and Iraq, the Philippines, the Sudan, Indonesia. More to come.

"I agree with you," he said.

Pec reached around Turko's other side, and unlocked the door. Then he handed the Chechen a folded piece of paper. "When you are ready for your new crew, call this number, and they will come. If they don't answer, keep calling. Once you have talked to them, don't call it again. Now get out."

Turko did so. He still wasn't sure if he was going to be shot. He tried to remember how long a walk it was back to the highway, and how he would get from there to where he needed to go.

Pec lowered his window. "Over in the corner by those pine trees is a gray Dodge automobile. It was stolen yesterday in West Virginia, but has another license plate. There are more license plates in the trunk. If you need another vehicle, steal one. The truck you use, the boat you use, they should be stolen. Don't rent or buy anything. Stolen vehicles can be traced only to their owners."

"Very well," said Turko.

Pec's driver started the van. "I will see you in a week," Pec said. "If you fail, we will not meet again—ever."

"I understand," said Turko.

"So do I."

Westman tied up just aft of the *Roberta June* in the darkness, at a dock extension that offered ample mooring for the small inflatable. The waves in the bay were running two feet when he crossed, compelling him to put on an orange Coast Guard float coat to keep dry. He removed it now that he was at the dock, rejoicing in the coolness that followed. The stiff wind that had been blowing up the bay was only a soft, caressing breeze here in this sheltered anchorage. He stood a moment, savoring it, then reminded himself of the task at hand.

Returning the flotation jacket to its locker just forward of the inflatable's big outboard engine, he stepped up onto the dock and stood a moment, looking about, and listening.

There was some laughter coming from a boat across the river, and a dog barking somewhere on Westman's side of the waterway. The other sounds were also normal—air-conditioning, voices from a television set, frogs and insects, and the call of some night birds. Nothing from the *Roberta June*.

He approached the boat carefully. He had deliberately left his pistol in a pocket of the float coat. He wasn't expecting trouble, let alone gunplay. What he was fearful of was simply being caught aboard the head boat without a warrant. The director of the CGIS was as straight an arrow as could be found in Washington.

Walking a few steps more, pausing to look up at the starry

heavens, he waited by the entryway at the boat's port-side railing. No one was near, or coming near.

Stepping quietly onto the boat's deck, he slipped quickly into the main cabin, taking out his flashlight and shielding the beam from view from the shore. It looked much as it had on his earlier visit, though some of the junk and gear had been stowed.

Descending to the next deck, he found a storage area, filled with fishing equipment, and some cabins, two to each side. Three of them were empty but for gear and supplies, but the fourth contained a bunk, a metal desk, and a chair—all bolted to the flooring.

He searched the cabin quickly, finding nothing of interest. Opening the hatch to the engine compartment, he found things tidier than he had expected. There was little oil and almost no fumes in the bilge. This was hardly a first-class operation, but the boat was entitled to pass inspection. The whiskey bottle he'd seen on the floor of one of the cabins was another matter, but not one to deal with this night.

There was absolutely nothing to implicate the *Roberta June* in whatever it was the bridge bombers had been or might be up to here on the Delmarva Peninsula—or in any kind of wrongdoing, save some minor neglect of maritime regulations.

Clicking off his flashlight, Westman returned to the dock. Checking his watch, he decided to declare himself off duty. He started walking along the roadway that led to the Lighthouse Restaurant.

It was a warmly lit and friendly place. Taking a small table in the bar, he ordered a glass of cold white wine and a plate of fried scallops, with double tartar sauce.

There was music playing—bad soft rock. Westman tried to ignore it. His taste was wide-ranging and eclectic—Maurice Ravel and Erik Satie; Johnny Cash and Willie Nelson; Ramon Bermudez and Nokai; Django Reinhardt and Chet Baker. And Moondog, not to speak of Maxine Sullivan and Peggy Lee and Jane Monheit. But he could not fathom the processed pap and jittery noise that passed for popular music of the present era. He wondered how bar owners could think it a worthwhile investment to have it playing for customers.

But he hadn't come to this place for the music. He had hoped the bartender would know her and be able to tell him where she lived. As it turned out, he didn't need to. The blond lady off the *Roberta June* was there at the bar. She was staring down into her glass, paying him and the world about her no mind whatsoever.

Westman sipped his wine, taking the opportunity to note the lovely shape of her long legs, which were as tan as the rest of her.

His food came. Asking for a check only a second or two after his plate was set before him, he gobbled the meal down as decorously as he could manage. Wiping his mouth carefully with a napkin, he left enough money to cover the bill and provide a twenty-percent tip, then rose.

Her glass was nearly empty.

"Buy you a drink, sailor?" he said, standing just behind her.

Her head whipped around, but, recognizing him, she relaxed, and even smiled.

"I think that's supposed to be my line," she said.

"Consider it said."

"All right. One more."

"Have you eaten?" he asked.

"Yes. One of their fabulous cheeseburgers."

"May I join you?"

"I guess you have."

He settled himself on the stool next to hers. She had changed clothes, but was dressed much as before—khaki shorts and a light-blue polo shirt that matched the color of her eyes.

"You exercise," he said.

"You're observant."

"I'm a professional investigator."

"I swim. It's the best exercise there is. In cadet training, we had to swim ten laps in this circular pool in full flight gear."

"You made it."

"I lapped all the guys." She drank the last of her glass. "It's true."

The bartender came. Westman ordered scotch for her and a glass of red wine for himself.

"What brings you here?" she asked.

"I'm paid to check things out."

"Including me."

"Tonight. Yes."

"Do I check out?"

"I guess you do." That afternoon, he had run a computer search of the DOD database from the *Manteo*'s communications center. She'd been a Navy lieutenant—three pay grades above him—and a carrier combat pilot aboard the USS *Abraham Lincoln* until grounded because of a mishap. After that, she'd served as a base recreation officer. On the recommendation of her CO, she'd subsequently been separated from the Navy with a general discharge—though that was under appeal. There'd been an incident.

"You looked me up?" she said.

"Yes I did. Also your friend Captain Schilling."

"In the line of duty, or something else?"

"Curiosity, most of it official."

"I don't need any more trouble."

"You won't get any from me."

Their drinks came. Westman sipped his wine, wishing they'd turn down the music. She took a healthy swallow of her whiskey.

"You want to know why I'm no longer in the Navy," she said. A statement of fact, not a question.

"That was the reason for my curiosity. There was something about insubordination."

"Did you ever hear of Kara Hultgreen?"

The name was familiar, but he couldn't quite recall why.

"She was the Navy's first carrier combat pilot. A Texas girl, out of San Antonio—call sign 'Revlon.' A looker, as you guys would say. But with balls. As you guys would say. Terrific pilot. Afraid of nothing. I saw a tape once of her landing an EA-6 Prowler with one of the landing gear jammed in the up position. Landed it as gently as a butterfly. The wing barely brushed the ground when she brought it to a stop."

She lifted her glass again, this time taking only a sip. "You're not a pilot, by any chance?" she asked.

"Used to be. After a fashion. Sailplanes. Schweizer 1-26's."

He thought she'd respond with an odious comparison of flimsy toys with gigantic war machines, full of thrust and weaponry. He was wrong.

"Sailplanes," she said. "No engines. Then you are a flier."

"Was. Only sailboats now."

She stared down at her glass. "Kara Hultgreen was about the best goddamn flier I ever heard of. But she was a woman, so she got a ration of brown stuff all the way down the line. She hated EA-6's. Thought she was better than that—an attitude not exactly appreciated by the male Prowler pilots. When Bill Clinton became President, he opened the combat slots to women, and Hultgreen leapt at it. Some say she got special dispensation—that she was hurried along through the program because she was a woman during an administration that was obsessed with political correctness. And maybe that's true. But she qualified for a boat nevertheless. Had something like fifty traps, day and night."

She rubbed at her eye, and then drank again.

"Her boat was the *Lincoln* too. Some of the men they had in the squadron back then never really accepted her. I don't know if you ever met any carrier jocks, but the fact that theirs is the most dangerous and difficult form of military aviation is not lost on them. They think of themselves as superhuman—the ultimate macho. And maybe that's true too. But when a mere girl came along and did what they can do—well, it must have been devastating. Hultgreen did what they did, and not a few of them hated it."

"Did you know her?"

"I never heard of her until she was killed. But, yes, I know her. I learned everything I could about her. She's why I joined Naval aviation." Another sip. "She was a fully qualified F-14 pilot. Tomcats, just like I got to fly later. They were doing daylight traps, in good weather, when things went wrong. She made a bad approach, I'll concede that. No neat ninety-degree turn on final, but that wasn't the cause. Her port engine stalled. She kept trying to fly the plane in anyway. It was like she was willing it to land. But it was no go. She had lost control and was rolling to the left when her RIO—the guy in the backseat—decided they had only milliseconds to live and punched them out. His ejection fired first, shooting him out parallel to the sea at about two hundred feet. The plane had completely inverted by the time her ejection fired. She was shot directly into the water like from a cannon. It's funny. Her flight jacket had only one tiny tear. But when they got her body out of the water she had no face left."

Westman signaled the bartender for two more drinks.

"They spent a lot of money to recover that aircraft," she said. "It was three thousand feet down. They wouldn't have done it for a male pilot. You knew from the git-go they were trying to determine if a female aviator had screwed up big-time—and if so, whether the idea of call signs like 'Revlon' wasn't a big mistake."

She rubbed her eye again. Westman had an impulse to put his hand on her shoulder as a gesture of reassurance, but restrained himself. It would be taken badly. And he was on the job here—if working it a little self-indulgently.

"The official report was that it was engine failure—and it was. Some Pentagon reporter broke the story, and it was carved in marble ever after. But there was an unofficial preliminary report—where they take comments from everyone within miles and then sift through it all until they find something hard. Well, guess what all the macho types had to say? She wasn't qualified. She was rammed through the program just to suit Navy political correctness. All those right-wing talk shows picked it up. There was even a documentary on PBS to the same effect. Women couldn't cut it. They were a danger to American national security. Shit."

"I had a woman CO once," Westman said. "She was first-rate. Now she's a rear admiral."

"They grounded a number of women pilots after that," Cat said. "But guess what? They've got females in pretty much every squadron now—with no problems. They had dainty little ladies dropping precision bombs in Iraq and Afghanistan. They're doing it now in Africa."

Her voice sounded as though it were about to crack. He admitted to himself that he had never encountered this sort of attitude among male members of the Coast Guard.

"What happened to you?" he asked.

"The same thing as Kara," Cat said. "Only it was my backseat guy who didn't get out in time. They blamed the engine stall on my approach. Claimed I was in an excessive crab that cut off the air to the engine, causing a compressor stall."

"Those F-14's were notoriously underpowered."

"They lost a whole bunch of them to engine failures. There was a refit program in the eighties, but it got canceled."

The new drinks came. She quickly finished her old one.

"He was a sweet guy, my No. 2," she said. "He shouldn't have had to die that way. Just because of a shift in procurement priorities."

"Why did you leave the service?"

"I gather you read my 201 file."

"Not completely."

"I'll put it simply. They wouldn't let me fly anymore.

And then my flight leader made a pass at me. More than a pass. An all-out assault. I hit him. Broke his nose. I got hit with insubordination, striking a superior officer, conduct unbecoming, the whole fucking thing. They didn't buy the sexual assault charge I filed. So I had to walk out with a general discharge."

"I'm sorry. Wouldn't have happened in the Coast Guard."

"The Coast Guard doesn't have male carrier jocks. It's not the real military."

Working out of the Puerto Rico office, Westman had followed a crew of drug smugglers into a Yucatan jungle. He had shot one of them to death—after a DEA guy on their team had taken a burst of Uzi bullets in the belly.

"Just a bunch of lifeguards," he said.

"Sorry. I didn't mean that. Service rivalry getting to me, I guess."

"And what do you do now?"

"I fly advertising banners along the beach—when the federal government lets us—and work on Burt's head boat."

"Until you get reinstated."

"I don't know that that's going to happen. I just feel I owe it to myself to give it a shot. I have a job offer. A feeder airline in Iowa. Little turboprops. You know, my father and uncle were Navy—both pilots. I don't think this is what they expected of me."

"I'd like to see you fly."

"I'm no national aerobatics champion, like Patty Wagstaff. But I get by."

She took another very large swallow of whiskey.

"Easy there. You don't want to end up like your next-door neighbor."

"That's right. You said you checked Burt out too."

"He got bounced from the airlines for drinking."

"He had reason."

Westman reminded himself of his job. "Getting crocked isn't any more acceptable on the water than it is in the air."

"I'm working on that."

"What's his problem?"

She turned on her stool to look at him, her right knee close to his thigh. Her eyes were speculative. They remained fixed on him, even as she took another sip.

"He dropped two nuclear bombs."

Westman could think of nothing to say. He saw that she was deadly serious.

"You're confusing him with Paul Tibbets, who dropped the bomb on Hiroshima."

"It wasn't on Japan. He's not that old. He was a C-130 pilot. One night about forty years ago he lost two engines and had to dump cargo. The cargo was two hydrogen bombs. He says they're still there. Offshore, southeast of Cape Henlopen."

"Hydrogen bombs?"

"Yes, sir. Are Coast Guard warrant officers called 'sir'?"

"They're called 'mister.' But it doesn't matter to me. Is that what you were doing out by Deepkill Shoal, looking for his bombs?"

"Yes. With a metal detector."

"He didn't go to the Air Force?"

"He's been writing letters to Dover Air Force Base for weeks. They don't care. Burt thinks one of the bombs is harmless. But the other one definitely isn't. He's old and sick—possibly terminal. He wants to find it. Get it out of the water."

"It was such a long time ago."

"They both contain fissionable uranium. One has a pluto-nium core. That stuff has a half-life of five hundred thou-sand years, but the casing—the weapon itself—it deteriorates. A few decades and it deforms. That's why they're constantly testing the stockpile at Los Alamos."

Westman felt a little dazed. He had no doubt whatsoever she was telling the truth. But it was more than his mind could hold at the moment. He thought of the attack on the Bay

Bridge, and what that might have been like if it had been a nuclear device that the bastards had exploded.

She finished her scotch. "Buy me a drink, sailor?"

"Why don't I take you home?"

"Do you have a car?"

"In Cape May."

She stared at her empty glass. "I live just up the road—on the bay. You want to walk?"

"Sure."

Turko's abductors had taken his extra clothes with him from the apartment, and Pec had left them for him in the trunk of the gray Dodge in a sort of duffel bag. Digging through it, Turko had found something more dignified than his beach outfit—running shoes, khaki trousers, white shirt, and a blue windbreaker.

The rest of his possessions were in there too—though not his vodka and, pointedly, not his gun.

This might have been simple precaution on the Kosovar's part, or it might have been spite. For all Pec's unexpected and unusual talkativeness, he was still angry. But then, Pec was a man who had been angry for years.

What Turko knew now was that Pec was also scared. He was answerable to someone for what Turko did and did not do. For the week he'd been given to succeed at this new task, Turko would not be completely powerless.

He drove the Dodge up to Philadelphia, left it at a downtown parking garage with fingerprints wiped clean, walked to 30th Street Station, and bought an unreserved one-way ticket to Baltimore, paying cash.

Buying a copy of the local paper, he turned first to the sports pages, only afterward returning to the front page and the bridge-bombing stories.

The quotes the main story had from the FBI were much the same that had been on television earlier, but the newspaper reporter had gotten more information elsewhere—probably from the Maryland State Police.

He wrote that the three men supposedly found burned to death in the Eastern Shore house had been shot before the fire, an indication that there might have been others involved in the plot. This was elementary police work of the most basic kind. It was surprising that the FBI had withheld the fact. Assuming they were not so stupid as to have overlooked the possibility of shooting as the cause of death, he could only presume they were playing games—keeping their prey from finding out or even guessing how much they knew.

There was nothing Turko could do about that. What he could do was keep them from knowing anything more.

He found no mention in the paper whatsoever of the heavy blond woman on the balcony who'd been eliminated as a witness by the team Pec had sent to his Ocean City apartment to get him. Obviously, no connection had been made—unless the FBI was trying to keep that quiet too.

The train to Baltimore had few passengers, with only a dozen or so drowsy, nondescript people in Turko's coach. He kept reading his paper, ignoring all.

In Baltimore, he walked from the depot to the Inner Harbor Waterfront, a festively crowded public amusement area that included a half-dozen museums, all manner of shops and restaurants, an early 19th-century warship, and moorings for numerous boats and yachts. There was a throng despite the late hour. Turko moved through it, trying to keep his duffel inconspicuous, turning off finally to cross the street and enter a parking garage a block away.

He had just gotten the engine started in a small Honda station wagon when he realized his error. He had no parking stub to hand the cashier.

After a moment's thought, he decided to go through with the theft.

"Lost my ticket," he told the sleepy black man in the booth. "Guess I'll have to pay the full day rate."

"Yep."

The cashier made a notation, studied the computerized device before him, then hit a button, which showed that Turko owed twelve dollars. He gave the man the amount in exact change.

The gate flew up. As Turko turned into the street, he thought he heard a woman's voice cry out. Realizing it could be the car's owner, he headed west and north into the worst neighborhood Baltimore possessed, halting in a side street beneath a streetlamp with a burned-out or shot-out bulb. He changed the license plates in darkness, tightening the nut with some difficulty.

He froze. There was someone behind him. He had no pistol. He would have to get very close to these people if he was to protect himself.

There were two black youths, one of normal height, one quite short.

"What you doin' there?" said the short one.

"My license plate was coming off."

"You knows where you is?"

"Yes."

"You got any money?"

The taller one had a gun. Turko stood up, studying him.

"Ah acks you if you got any money?"

"Yes. Yes, I do."

"Give it here."

Turko took a step closer to the youth as he reached into his pants pocket, then took another, circling, closer step as he pretended to struggle nervously getting the wallet out. Opening it, he started to take the money out, but the short one leapt forth and snatched it away.

Seizing upon the moment, Turko lunged to within the taller one's reach, took hold of both gun and forearm, cracked the latter on his knee with enough force to break it, then grabbed up the pistol in time to get off one well-placed shot at the shorter robber, who cried out and fell backward, still clutching the wallet.

Taking that back, Turko fired a final shot into the boy's head. The tall one, watching all this, started backing away.

Turko killed him with one round, then got into the Honda and drove away fast.

He ditched the small Japanese sedan at a parking lot at one of the plazas along the Interstate, stealing a Volvo station wagon and driving it north and east. There were police cars at the Susquehanna River bridge, but they weren't stopping anyone. He proceeded on into Wilmington, left the car at the railroad station parking lot, and then walked along the Christiana River until he came to a sort of dump bordered by weeds and trees. There he lay down for the night, using his duffel for a pillow.

Westman and Cat walked up Savannah Road, stopped at the Diary Queen for a couple of cones, then continued on to the little town beach that faced Delaware Bay. The view was pretty. Westman could see all the way across the bay to the light off the Cape May channel.

She led him back to a sand-strewn road. Her house was a few blocks down.

They heard gunfire, but it proved to be from a television set.

"Burt's found himself a war movie," she said. "He's a frustrated would-be combat pilot. If they played these things continuously, he'd never go to bed. I can't tell you how tired I am of hearing John Wayne make patriotic speeches."

"We're at war now," Westman said.

"Not a war like World War II. Nothing so competent." She started up the steps to her screened-in porch, then turned. "Would you like to come in? I have some wine, if that's what you're drinking."

"I would—but I won't. I have a small inflatable I have to get across the bay by morning."

She looked over the dune to the darkness beyond. "Okay. Good night then."

"I'd like to help you," Westman said.

"What did you say?"

"Help you with what you're trying to do—as long as it doesn't cross regulations."

"There's not much about Burt Schilling that's regulation."

They stood looking at each other a long moment. Somewhere out in the bay, a gull called. Another answered.

"Good night then," he said.

The lights of Cape May across the bay seemed festive, as though a great and wonderful party was in progress. As he headed the inflatable out Roosevelt Inlet into the open water, Erik found his own mood much the same.

The waves were following, from time to time striking Westman's inflatable abeam as he kept the throttle forward. He was getting wet, but that didn't matter. He gave the wind no thought.

His cell phone was ringing. He let it.

Chapter 14

Bear Gergen had set a six-pack of Budweiser, a book, and a rusty lawn chair on the deck of his salvage tug, putting it in a position that afforded him an ample view of the aft deck, where cousin Leonard's wife Mary Lou was sunbathing. For whatever reason, she didn't much like tan lines, and was exposing herself to the hazy morning sunshine without benefit of bathing suit, lying bottoms-up on a towel and leafing through a copy of a mindless movie magazine.

Gergen was always interested in Mary Lou, and the geography of her all-over suntan, but he was not stupid. Mary Lou didn't seem to like her husband Leonard much. She certainly enjoyed provoking him, which, Gergen was sure, was why she'd traipsed out on deck wearing only the towel her very flat belly was now lying on. Gergen had no great fondness for Leonard either. But his cousin was quick to anger and very violent when he got that way. Also, Leonard had been an honest partner to Gergen, if to no one else. Gergen had enough trouble in his life without inviting in more.

They were tied up at the dock in Wilmington hard by Interstate 495—not in some sneak motel somewhere. Bear Gergen contented himself with looking.

She glanced up. Gergen kept his eyes where they were, but slipped her a wink, wanting her to be certain he knew what was what. Mary Lou apparently got the idea, but upped the ante of the game anyway. She rolled over on her back, exposing the only portion of her anatomy that had escaped a tan.

He and Mary Lou were alone on the tug. His crew was off getting drunk, laid, or stoned—or all three. Leonard had taken his motorcycle over to New Jersey to score a little something. His boat and personal watercraft business down in Maryland had been left in the charge of one of the idiot teenagers who worked for him.

No. It still wasn't a good idea. Gergen turned his chair more to the side. Mary Lou was distracting him from a problem. They'd taken nearly forty of those great big bags of marijuana off the *Breezee B*. A Philadelphia drug dealer had offered fifty thousand for the lot and sent one of his thugs with five thousand as a down payment. Gergen had immediately had second thoughts, and tried to give the five large back, but the bastard had insisted on completing the deal, threatening to blow Gergen's head off if it didn't happen. Bear didn't do a lot of drug business, but figured this was high-quality weed. He could probably do a lot better elsewhere—like maybe especially New York, just a couple hours away.

Unfortunately, he no longer had the five thousand. His crew hadn't been paid for a couple of weeks and he'd been compelled to give them something on account. What he had to do was get his stash to New York, do a deal, and find a way to get five thousand back to the Philly dealer, whose name was Enrique Diller.

Maybe he should have had his mind on something other than drugs. Three men were coming toward him along the dock. One of them wore a Coast Guard uniform; a second a sport coat and tie; and the third was in boating clothes—looking like he had just stepped off one of those America's Cup boats.

Gergen recognized the man in the sport coat—U.S. Customs Agent Paul Elward, a longtime acquaintance, though certainly no friend. The other two were strangers to him, though he knew a lot of Coasties.

"Mary Lou," said Gergen, his eyes still on the approaching men. "We got visitors."

He glanced to see her gather the towel around her middle, then return to her recline.

"Mr. Gergen," said Elward, stepping onto the deck, without invitation.

"Howyadoin'?" said Gergen, setting down his beer can. "This an official visit?"

Elward looked about the tug, pretending to pay scant attention to Gergen's comely cousin-in-law.

"This is Special Agent Erik Westman of the Coast Guard Investigative Service," Elward said. "And Lieutenant Tim Dewey of the cutter *Manteo*."

"Shouldn't you guys be looking for bridge bombers?" Gergen asked.

They were not amused. "We are," said the one named Westman.

Gergen tried to keep his eyebrows from upward movement. "You got some problem with me?"

Elward leaned back against a capstan. "That motor-sailor you brought in, the *Breezee B*?"

"I'm still waiting to hear on the salvage award."

"They put her in dry dock and pumped out the bilges."

"Right. Check for hull damage and like that."

"They found like maybe a million dollars street-value of cocaine and heroin down there. In waterproof sacks."

Gergen whistled. His mind was full of unspoken profanities.

"You didn't know about that?"

"No, sir."

"You didn't look down there?"

"The main cabin had three feet of seawater in her, Mr. El-ward. I stayed below only long enough to make sure there wasn't anyone aboard, and that she wasn't taking on more water." He stared down at the deck, thinking. "Cocaine and heroin, you say? Not marijuana?"

"There were a couple sacks of weed here and there, but it was mostly hard stuff," Elward said.

"Three bodies washed up down on the Delaware shore," Westman said.

"Yeah?"

"You saw no survivors, Gergen?" said the customs agent. "No sign of anyone?"

"She was abandoned when I took her in tow," Gergen said. "I radioed that information to the Indian River Coast Guard Station. Three bodies, you say. Who were they?"

"They haven't been identified. The girl wasn't wearing any clothes."

Elward treated himself to a glimpse of Mary Lou. Gergen merely shrugged.

"There was no naked lady when I went aboard her. I went through every cabin. My bet is they abandoned ship in a hell of a hurry when it looked like that boat was going to capsize—which from the looks of her she almost did."

"A lot of the storage drawers were pulled out. The drawers were hanging out in every cabin."

Mary Lou rolled over back onto her stomach, dislodging some of the towel. Elward's attention followed this distraction.

"When we came into port, Mr. Elward, I made a search for valuables. Everything I found I entered on the manifest. Wasn't much. Couple of cameras, binoculars, stereo. If you want to search my vessel here, or my office, go ahead. Anytime."

"I don't doubt your honesty, Mr. Gergen. If you were a

thief, you wouldn't have left a million bucks in hard narcotics aboard that boat."

"You got that right," Gergen said.

Elward was now openly staring at Mary Lou. She rolled over, sat up, and stared back.

"We just wanted to talk to you about it," said Elward. "If you think of anything, or hear about anything, let us know."

"Sure. Always do."

"I'm afraid you can't count on salvage money from the sailing yacht any time soon," said Elward. "Use in the commission of a crime—narcotics trafficking. That complicates things."

Gergen gazed at him bleakly. "You mean I'm not going to get anything?"

"Sure. Your costs. But it'll take a while for the courts to work it all out."

"Why? Do they think that dope belonged to the owner of the boat?"

"They've got to work it all out. Meantime, you've got something coming for that rust-bucket freighter."

"A little something. Do you know how much it costs to run this outfit—how much it cost to haul that hulk in?"

"You're in a high-risk business, Mr. Gergen," Elward said. He turned to go.

"Here's my card," said Westman. "If you hear anything about those three, or remember something, anything, give me a call. They'll find me."

Gergen pocketed it. He had quite a collection of these snitch cards. Sometimes he made some extra money that way. What the government chumps hadn't figured out was that the only time he passed on information about the criminal activities of others was when he wanted to distract authorities from his own criminal activities. It was useful to have a Coast Guard cutter headed upriver when he was doing business downstream.

As he watched the Feds depart, it occurred to him exactly what he and Leonard should do with the part of the sailboat cargo they'd hidden away in a half-sunk barge south of the Delaware Memorial Bridge. Nothing. That rusty old wreck had been lying in the shallows there for years—ignored because it presented no hazard to navigation. Gergen would just leave the stuff there.

For now.

Meantime, he needed some more money. It would have to come from legitimate business. A guy had come by with a kind of odd job. Recovery of some World War II relic or something on the sea bottom off of Cape Henlopen. Gergen hadn't heard from him since. He'd call the man back that night.

Mary Lou stood up, leaving the towel on the deck.

"I'm going below," she said.

"Suit yourself."

"What about yourself?"

"I'm happy where I am."

"Yeah? How happy?"

"You'd be surprised."

He picked up his beer, drank, then turned to his book—a paperback copy of Richard Marcinko's *Rogue Warrior: Task Force Blue*. Marcinko had been a Navy SEAL too. Knew his MagSafe Plus-P frangible SWAT loads and his Mad Dog DSU-2 serrated-blade knives to a T. Gergen loved his stuff. Tom Clancy's too. But his favorite book ever was Ernest Hemingway's *To Have and Have Not*. That rummy sonofabitch knew his ocean. Knew boats. Knew what hard times could be like. Knew that you had to do what you had to do.

Bear Gergen had discovered Hemingway in college. He was the only member of his family ever to go to one, though it was only a community college in North Jersey. According to the Navy, he had an IQ of 138.

"You got all the brains there is in this family," his mother had told him. "You got no excuse being a fuckup like the rest of 'em."

He set down his book and finished his beer. Maybe you didn't always have to be smart. Not every single minute of every single day.

Gergen stood up and stretched, giving the dockside area a casual but careful surveillance.

Then he went below.

Burt Schilling sat atop the dune across the street from his house, idle that day because the weather was too rough for either fishing or searching for the bombs. Sipping from a sixteen-ounce bottle of Coca-Cola that he'd half-filled with rum, he watched the ships in the bay. The nearest was an inbound container vessel running low in the water dangerously close to a reef known as the Shears. Burt wondered who the ship's pilot might be and what sort of conversation they might be having on the bridge, so far off the safer course. Beyond the freighter, several ships lay up to the northwest in Big Stony Anchorage, likely coal ships or tankers waiting for a pilot out of Lewes or their turn at Delaware River docks.

An altogether typical day on the bay. The sky to seaward was patchy blue, while that overhead was dulled by high cirrus clouds. Cumulus were building north over Jersey and the wind was increasing. Didn't have the look of rain, though. Didn't have the feel.

He took a long pull from the bottle. Instead of spreading warmth, the alcohol, oddly, increased the chill he felt. Lighting another cigarette changed nothing, though he was glad for it. Exhaling a cloud of smoke that was caught by the wind, he looked up and down the beach, surprised at how few people were out. Closest to him, no more than fifty yards along the shore, were a mother and two children—a toddler of a boy and an older girl, perhaps five or six.

Schilling had no children. Not that he wouldn't have minded some. Or grandchildren. Especially now.

The VA doctors hadn't told him anything he hadn't known or guessed, but the fact of their saying it had come as a hit in the gut anyhow. No more the stuff of fearful dreams and sad imaginings, but hard, irrevocable, inescapable truth—as inescapable as what happened when you lost all power in an airplane. You might auger in, you might glide, but you were going in.

This was his last year. He wouldn't have another summer. That's why he had come out here to sit instead of skulking inside his screened-in porch. For all his time on these waters, for all the time he'd lived on this stretch of coastline, he'd been seldom on this beach. There were a hundred things he'd not noticed before about this shoreline, including the driftwood sculpture some unknown artist had stuck in the sand at the foot of the little dune and the sandbars that were cau ig waves to break far out in the Broadkill.

There was a wreck out there—in some fifty feet of water. It was marked on all the charts, known to every mariner. But the bay bottom was littered with wrecks and pieces of junk identified simply as "obstruction." Some weren't marked on any chart at all.

With a happy squeal, the little boy tottered off his mother's blanket and headed for the water as though on bird's legs. The mother rose and followed, but allowed him his freedom. Burt was cheered a little by the boy's happy splashing.

Burt had telephoned the Air Force again, just as he had done a month before, calling one more time before setting about what he had to do. As with the doctor, he'd known exactly what they would say.

The bastards.

●

Westman was sitting out on the bridge wing, making observations of the river and bayside shoreline with binoculars. In an hour he'd seen nothing of particular interest. Once again the absurdity of their mission was impressed upon him, trying to protect every inch of the thousands and thousands of miles of United States coastline.

He leaned back, letting his mind drift from duty to pleasanter thoughts. He felt very different this day—almost as young as Dewey.

The lieutenant stepped out on the open bridge deck. "Just got a call on the radio."

"I heard," said Westman, raising the glasses again.

"Were you listening?"

"Not entirely. Sorry."

"There's a homicide. A woman down near Ocean City. Found her washed up in the St. Martin's River down in Maryland by some golf course. Blond in a bathing suit, with a bullet in her head."

"Blond?"

"I don't think she's anyone you know, Erik."

"Where's the St. Martin's River?"

"Empties into Assawoman Bay, due west of Ocean City, just north of the Highway 50 causeway."

Westman sighed. "Doesn't sound anything to do with what we're after."

"Probably not. I can't go there anyway. The waters of that bay are too shallow for the *Manteo*'s draft. And I've orders not to go south of the Delaware-Maryland line."

"That's all right. I'll drive."

"I'll stop off at Cape May Station. We'll be a while, though."

"She'll keep."

Westman's cell phone began ringing. "*She* won't," Dewey thought, but he said nothing.

The realization occurred to Gergen with such sudden swiftness that it shattered his concentration on the nice thing

Mary Lou was doing for him as he sat on the edge of the bunk in his cabin.

"Shit!"

"Bear?"

He sat up, pushing her aside, reaching for his pants. "Forgot something. Something I gotta check. Fast. Tell Leonard I'll be back tonight."

"Tell Leonard?"

Gergen left her kneeling. He hurried up the companionway as fast as he could manage, buckling his belt. The gas tank in the inflatable was full. He had it in the river in a minute.

Elward had said the Feds had found some marijuana with all the high-priced stuff in the bilge. Only some. A few bags. Gergen had examined the contents of just one of the bags he'd found in the main salon of the *Breezee B*. If he had looked in some of the other bags, what might he have found? Elward had discovered a big haul of heroin in the bilge. Why not in the main saloon too—in all those drawers? The boat had been stolen for a drug run. A big-money run. Had to be. How could he have been so incredibly stupid?

He might have actually scored ten or twenty times worth what he thought he had in those bags in the barge. Maybe a hundred times. Coming upon that sailboat could turn out to be the opportunity he'd been looking for all the years he'd been looking for big opportunities.

When he finally hove to abreast of the scuttled barge downriver, more than an hour later, he idled the engine a moment, watching the boat traffic out in the river channel. Nobody seemed to be paying him the slightest attention.

He waited a while longer anyway, trying to look like a fisherman. The sun was going down when he finally turned the craft toward the rusty hulk of the barge, which was barely visible lying there by the overhanging shore weeds.

As he climbed aboard, everything looked as it had when they'd left it. They'd stashed the bags in what had been the barge's anchor well, and in a big bin beside it. The covers to both were secured tightly.

But now they weren't. There'd been big iron pins through the hasps. Both were gone. One hasp was bent back. Gergen tried the metal cover. It was loose. He lifted it and flung it back.

He peered into the darkness of the well, unable to see any bags.

Of course, the plastic bags were dark too. The sunlight was nearly gone. It was hard to see much of anything down there.

He returned to the inflatable and retrieved a flashlight from the equipment box. Back on the barge, he clicked on the light, took a deep breath, and then looked into the anchor locker again.

Nothing but rusty chain. He turned in forlorn hope to the bin.

There was only a rat. It stared back at him.

Chapter 15

With the wait for the Cape May-Lewes auto ferry and the crossing itself, Westman took some three hours to reach the Ocean City police station, only to be informed he had come to the wrong place.

As the woman's body had been found in waters belonging to Worcester County, the county sheriff's office had primary jurisdiction. The OC cops directed Westman across Assawoman Bay to the county authorities, who were not overjoyed to see him but permitted him to view the body, which had been taken to a local hospital.

She had been shot with a small-caliber weapon about three inches above the bridge of her nose. The round had likely been a soft-nose bullet, for it had made quite a mess of what lay behind the point of impact. Studying her face, he tried to imagine what sort of person she had been. The ring at her left nostril and the tattoos on her arms and ankles indicated she was probably no debutante.

Though she had been wearing a bathing suit, her body did

not look as though it had recently benefited from the cleansing effects of the ocean waters—or any waters.

"Did you check for needle marks?" Erik asked the sheriff's deputy who'd been escorting him.

The man shrugged. Westman went ahead and performed the unpleasant task, surprised to find none.

"This kind of stuff interest the Coast Guard?" the deputy asked.

"This week, everything interests us."

Another call came just as Erik was returning to his car. A young man had come into the Ocean City police station, inquiring after a missing friend and, as an afterthought, mentioning he'd found blood on the balcony of the apartment they'd shared.

Erik got an address, and drove directly to the place, deciding not to wait for the young man to come out and identify the woman's body. Erik had little doubt that the ID would be positive.

Ocean City and Maryland State Police detectives were abundantly on the scene at the apartment by the time he arrived, thoroughly combing through the rooms and amassing a first-rate collection of cultural artifacts emblematic of twenty-first-century American youth. A forensics specialist had taken samples of the blood and other gore on the balcony. The misshapen, expended bullet had been found in the wooden building wall, about five and a half feet above the balcony floor.

Erik was an interloper here, and stayed on the periphery of activity, finally going out to the alley. He walked up and down it, looking to the woman's balcony from different points. Finally, he went to the apartment building directly opposite hers, climbing the wooden stairs to the second floor.

This was the most logical firing position. She'd been hit by someone shooting directly at her from the same level as her apartment's deck. The other balconies along the alley were too far away for an accurate handgun shot and would have required an oblique line of fire. Erik imagined the woman staring intently at something happening on this side of the alley, something very compelling. Her assailant must have fired reflexively and quickly—and accurately.

Not some angry boyfriend. Not some druggie settling a business score. The word came uncomfortably to Erik's consideration. The shooter was a professional; someone very well trained.

The rear door to the apartment Westman was standing before was locked, but the sliding one fronting its balcony was open a crack. He thought of swinging over to it, but quickly recalled what Payne had been able to do to him for having taken a few steps too close to the burned remains at that farmhouse.

Leaning back against the stair railing, he got out his cellular phone and called Leon Kelly. The agent answered on the second ring. Erik could hear traffic in the background.

"It's Westman. I'm working a homicide in Ocean City."

"White female, twenty-five to thirty, fatal gunshot wound to the head. We saw it on the flash. But I hope you're not trying to lag it to us. We've got our hands full. Headquarters thinks the farmhouse guys were whacked by accomplices. We're working that crime scene pretty hard."

"I would detail someone to come look at this, if I were you," Erik said. "I think the victim was a bystander who saw something she shouldn't have. The perpetrator was a pro. There's an apartment here that looks pretty suspicious and ought to be gone over by your best forensics people."

"Have you gone into it?"

"Negative. If I did that, I'm afraid your Mr. Payne would try to have me reassigned to Point Barrow, Alaska."

"How good is the local law enforcement there?"

"Routine homicide, they'd be fine. The needs here are pretty sophisticated. There are some tire prints in the sand. I've no idea what might be in the apartment."

"We're at least an hour from Ocean City."

"Not by helicopter."

"You really think this is worth it?"

"I think everything's worth it."

"I'd have to take the matter to Payne."

"Just leave me out of it."

"You don't want to look at that apartment?"

"Negative."

"We need to seal the apartment."

"You'll have to go through the OC police."

"I'll talk to Payne."

"I'll go sit at the bottom of the stairs and pretend to be resting my weary bones."

"Okay. And Erik . . ."

"Yes?"

"Thanks."

•

Bear Gergen spent a fruitless few hours prowling the Delaware River in his inflatable, looking for the odd twenty-pound bag of marijuana someone might have left afloat. The exercise wasn't entirely pointless. He found a half-dozen new places he could stash bulky valuables in the future—if he should ever again be so fortunate.

In the meantime, he had to find some other means of cash flow. The old pilot's undersea recovery now seemed very interesting. Bear could probably con the guy out of many thousands before he was done.

Tying up the inflatable, he mounted the ladder and went aboard his tug. Finding no one topside, he came noisily down to the main cabin, and was hit on the top of the head with something heavy enough to knock him to his knees.

Raising his arm to fend off another blow, he blinked, trying to comprehend who would be doing this to him, and why.

The next strike came against his ribs, below his upraised arm.

He brought the arm down, squirming and swiveling on his knees, keeping his head tucked defensively but trying desperately to see his attacker.

Thump. Another hit, this on his right shoulder. A wasted effort, as Bear's muscles there were as armor on a tank.

"You goddamn sonofabitch!"

It was Leonard. He had never done anything like this to Bear in all his life. Groping, Gergen reached out as the weapon came again. A baseball bat. It stung his hand but he was able to snatch it away, flinging it into a corner as he got to his feet. It was one of several bats Bear kept on the tug— mostly for dealing with competing salvage outfits.

His cousin, wide-eyed and stoned out of his mind, now seemed a very small man indeed. Without deliberating long upon the matter, Gergen decided he didn't need this many relatives. He quickly had one huge hand around Leonard's throat. Propelling his cousin across the cabin and against the bulkhead, he raised his right fist, preparing to transform Leonard's James Dean good looks into something more re- sembling a character in one of those gooey-alien science- fiction movies.

"Don't kill him!"

Mary Lou had somehow pushed herself between them. She was still as naked as she'd been the night before and had a reddish purple bruise on her cheekbone, and some scrapes on the shapely arm she thrust up before Gergen's face.

Bear stepped back. "Why not?"

"He thinks you were fucking me!"

Thinks. A stretch for Leonard, but better, in the circum- stance, than "knows."

Gergen lifted Leonard off his feet, prompting gurgling sounds and drool.

"Get his gun," Gergen said.

Mary Lou pulled up Leonard's T-shirt and reached be- hind his back, as space allowed, pulling out Leonard's short- barreled .38.

"And his knife."

She knelt down and lifted Leonard's pants leg, pulling forth a six-inch-blade buck knife from his black leather motorcycle boots.

"Now get outa here until I get his head back on straight."

She fled. Still holding Leonard high above the floor, Gergen leaned close—so near that his beard was brushing Leonard's face.

"You shit-for-brains junkie moron!" he said. "I wasn't fucking your wife!"

Gergen had heard the term "intellectual dishonesty," and supposed this was it. But it had been good enough for a U.S. senator who'd been caught getting a naked rubdown from a beauty queen, not to speak of a U.S. President and a White House intern. No penetration. No sex. No infidelity. No technical justification for getting his hair combed with a Louisville slugger.

He stared hard into Leonard's now-frightened eyes.

"If she'd been a virgin," Gergen said, marveling at that ludicrous notion, "she still would be! Understand?"

It finally dawned on Leonard how he could get his feet back on the deck and air in his lungs again.

"Okay," he burbled.

Gergen let him down slowly, pleased that Leonard kept on sliding down the wall, ending up in something of a crumpled heap.

"Then how come she was naked when I came back?" Leonard said weakly—his words cut off by a fit of coughing.

"You tell me! She prances around here like she was getting paid for it. She was lying out on the deck, bare ass to the world, when three Feds came on board!"

Leonard raised his head, a little more sanity in his expression. "Feds?"

"Elward from Customs and two Coast Guard guys. You know what was in the bilges of that motor-sailor? A million bucks in heroin and cocaine!"

Now Leonard sat up—all thoughts of Mary Lou gone.

"Heroin and coke?"

"In a bunch of bags we didn't know about. In the bilges."

"A million?"

"Million easy. In the bilges. It's all your fault."

"What're you sayin', Bear? The bilges were under a lot of water. That boat was fixin' to go down."

"I told you to make one more check below."

"Fuck you."

The relationship was back to normal. Gergen went to Leonard, offered his hand, and pulled him to his feet. His cousin, rubbing his throat, managed to stay erect.

"I was on deck, not down here with Mary Lou. I was talking to the Feds. When they left, I went downriver to check on the barge," Gergen said.

Leonard's eyes lost their focus. "Yeah?"

"So I've got bad news."

"Bad?"

"The stash is missing."

"What're you sayin'?"

"It's gone. I don't know whether we were seen by somebody or we picked somebody else's hidey-hole with that barge or the Feds got it staked out, or what. But the shit is gone."

Leonard was staring blankly. "Gone?"

"Gone! Ripped off!"

"But we got a customer."

"Yeah. Too bad."

"Bear, the guy gave us a down payment. We gotta deliver."

"Right. So get up there and take care of it."

"Huh?"

"Tell that Enrique in Philly what happened."

"Me?"

"Have Roy drive you in the truck."

Roy Creed was the largest of Bear's crew members.

"You want me to go to Philly?"

"Yes! Now. Tonight. Before they get too antsy. Tell 'em we've been ripped off and the Feds have the heat on heavy and if they don't want any trouble they should stay the fuck away from us. Tell him he'll get his five large back as soon as I can scratch it up."

"He won't like that."

"No, he won't. But too bad."

"Why me?"

" 'Cause you got diplomatic skills."

Leonard didn't comprehend.

" 'Cause I'll beat your brains out with that baseball bat if you don't."

This Leonard understood. He started toward the stairs to the deck.

"Wait a minute," Gergen said. "Did you smack Mary Lou in the face? That how she got that cheek?"

"Yeah. Why not?"

It occurred to Bear this would be a good occasion to retrieve the ball bat and give Leonard the whack across the top of the skull he deserved. But he wanted his cousin out of there—and on the Interstate to Philly. He didn't want to have to deal with Enrique Diller himself.

"You don't do that to a woman."

"Shit, Bear. You threw that girl from the sailboat into the ocean!"

"That was business. And I didn't hit her! And it was an accident! And she wasn't my wife!"

Leonard just stood there, swallowing.

"Move out," Gergen said. "Be back before morning."

"Don't know where to find him."

"Roy will."

"Come on, Bear. I feel like . . ."

Gergen had picked up the bat and was holding it fondly.

Leonard departed, very much revived.

Bear waited until the echoes from Roy's truck had dwindled to nothing, and then waited fifteen minutes more. Then he went to the cabin Mary Lou and Leonard used when they were aboard the tug.

She had put on shorts and a T-shirt.

"Get naked," Bear said. "I'd like a little payback for my troubles."

Westman drove up the shore to Bethany Beach in Delaware, stopping at a restaurant there for soup and a sandwich. There was little he could do until some results from the Ocean City crime scene investigation were processed.

He reminded himself that an investigator's most serious weakness was the conceit of belief in his or her own theory. The inclination was to pursue the theory to its ultimate conclusion, instead of applying skepticism and measuring it against all available contrary evidence. It was altogether possible—even probable—that he was wrong to link the Ocean City woman's murder to the terrorist plot. Her death could be explained in a number of criminal ways. For all he knew, it might very well have been a jealous husband who'd been lying in wait.

But he didn't think so. He was more convinced than ever that there were still dangerous people on the Delmarva Peninsula, and that the Bay Bridge bombing was not the last they would hear from them. All theories were to be encouraged. They all had to be pursued to their ultimate conclusion. No idea could be rejected, just as nothing suspicious could be ignored.

After his meal, he drove up Highway 1 to the Indian River Bridge, which crossed the channel that linked the ocean to Rehoboth and Indian River Bays. Turning off into the parking lot there, he chose a space that faced the sea. The tide was coming in, creating a small wall of surf where the channel met the sea. It was breezing up. Westman wished he were out there sailing.

He turned off his engine. Reaching into his pocket, he took out his cell phone. He didn't have to look up the number.

"Admiral dePayse," she said.

"It's Erik. I want to report."

"Very well. Go ahead."

He took his time, trying to leave out nothing. She was more interested in the murder of the Ocean City woman than he had expected.

"I'm going to call the Bureau and ask that we be kept fully informed of all aspects of this investigation," she said. "It sounds like Special Agent Payne needs some closer supervision."

"That's fine with me."

"You've done good work here, Erik. But you shouldn't have left that last crime scene."

"When Leon Kelly's guy showed up, I thought it best if I made myself scarce."

"We're not going to let ourselves be pushed around."

"No, ma'am."

"Where have you been?"

"I just told you."

"I mean last night."

"Believe it or not, I was working waterfront bars in Lewes, Delaware."

"What for?"

"I wanted to learn what the boatmen might have been seeing out on the water."

"And?"

"Nothing of interest yet."

She paused. "I'd rather you were more accessible. Your cell phone's off too much."

"Yes, ma'am."

"We'll talk soon."

Westman drove to the nearby Indian River Coast Guard Station, calling Dewey on the radio. He was still operating up in Delaware Bay, checking major infrastructure on both the Delaware and New Jersey sides.

They arranged a rendezvous at the Lewes pilot boat station in an hour and a half.

"You want to join Sally and me for dinner break?"

"Sure. My treat."

"See you then."

"Tim?"

"Yeah?"

"Was that head boat out again? The *Roberta June*?"

"I didn't come across it. But I never got south of Cape Henlopen today. With the winds this high, not a lot of fishing boats out."

"Very well. Just curious."

Cat had slept late and then spent much of the afternoon and evening on her computer, using the Internet to expand her knowledge of deep-sea exploration, maritime navigation, and elementary physics—as in the effects of gravity and momentum on falling objects.

When her brain could take no more, she made herself a dinner of microwaved Lean Cuisine macaroni and cheese, washed down with a glass of Almaden Mountain Burgundy, then went for a walk.

It took her to the Lighthouse Restaurant and its bar. She nursed two whiskeys late into the evening, but the Coast Guardsman never showed. Weary now, she paid her bill and headed back for her house. She was sad, lonely, and not a little irritated, but the time had not been wasted. She had hit upon an idea.

Chapter 16

Once again it was near dawn, and once again Burt Schilling was on his screened-in porch, smoking and drinking.

He'd had the four hours of uninterrupted sleep that was about the maximum any long-term alcoholic could hope for. The doctors had explained all this—how the nervous system reacted to the anesthesia of ethanol with wild reciprocal swings in the other direction that over time would eventually lead to delirium tremens and death.

So fucking what, he had thought. In the meantime, it was manageable. Four hours of sleep, a couple hours of fighting off those wild swings with shots of hootch and cigarettes, and then a few more hours of sleep. Then the day, whatever that was worth.

Cat had come home late without stopping by and her up-stairs light had gone out almost immediately after she'd turned it on. Burt thought of her on her bed. A girl who took nude swims at dawn assuredly must sleep naked—certainly during the summer.

There was a night during his time in the Air Force when he and an Air Force buddy had gone into a San Antonio bar and flipped a coin for the blond they spotted sitting in a corner booth with another woman. Burt had lost the toss and ended up with the other lady, a brunette almost as attractive—Roberta June. It had been a story with a happy ending. His buddy had married the blond and Burt had hitched up with Junie. But life had gone on beyond the happy ending.

For years he'd wondered what would have happened if he'd won the toss and gotten the blond. Now he wished he'd won and that the blond somehow could have been Cat.

What a gyp life could be. He meets the girl of his dreams at an age when even hard-up middle-aged divorcees wouldn't look at him.

She had promised to help him find his bombs. She wasn't going to take the Iowa flying job until then. He would have to be content with that. It was more than he had a right to expect, though he wasn't certain what had prompted her to make the promise.

Throughout his life, Burt had continued to read *Air Force* magazine and other military publications. He'd followed the retrieval of the wreckage from the TWA Flight 800 disaster off Long Island in 1996 every inch of the way. He knew that, once the bombs were located, recovery should be fairly easy—with the right equipment.

But what was really needed was underwater side-seeing sonar, submersible video cameras, scanners that could produce an underwater topographical map of the bottom and the objects upon it, grapplers strong enough to pull up the weight involved—maybe a dredge for undersea digging.

Only the military could provide that, and the military had told him thanks but no, thanks.

But if they located the bombs, then the Air Force would have to listen. Hell, more than listen, they'd have to act.

The sky was getting lighter. It was time and then some for

her morning swim. But she wasn't stirring. Something in her life had changed.

The sound of a screen door loudly closing snapped him wide awake. He looked to see Cat, fully clothed in shorts, shirt, and boating shoes, walking across his sandy patch of lawn.

"Up early again, I see," she said. "Good. Go brush your teeth and wash up a little, then come get in my Jeep."

"Where are we going?"

"Ocean City Airport."

"Mr. Westman, lay to on the quarterdeck."

Erik reflexively sat up in his bunk, swinging his legs over the side. He rubbed his eyes a moment, feeling the engine vibrations and the gentle rise and fall of a vessel under way. He stood up and got dressed. When aboard ship, you did as instructed.

"What's up?" he said to Master Chief DeGroot.

"You got a radio message from Ops." He nodded toward a notepad on the chart table.

It was from Special Agent Kelly. He was to call at once. Taking out his cell phone, he did so.

"Wait a minute," the FBI man said. He took more than a minute going from one place to another. When he came back on, the background noise had changed. Westman heard a truck's horn. "We scored big," Kelly said.

"Great. How?"

"Recovered blood and fingerprints from that apartment."

"Not the woman's."

"No, the other one across the alley. Several sets of prints. Thirty-two-caliber bullet found in a wall. It looks like a second homicide. The body removed, just like hers. Maybe dumped in Assawoman Bay, just like hers."

"She probably saw it happen and they eliminated her as a witness."

"Sounds probable. Listen, Erik. The dumb bastards left a car. They cleaned out that apartment and left a vehicle behind. A rental car."

"Are you sure it's connected to the apartment?"

"No. But the rental car company has a driver's license and a signature on the contract. What did that waitress of yours say was the name on that guy's credit card?"

"Bertolucci."

"Bingo."

"What state issued the license?"

"New Jersey."

"You'll have a photo."

"Trenton's e-mailing us the image, but I don't think headquarters is interested in disseminating it. Something about not wanting to spook the terrorists until we can grab the whole ring."

"That's ridiculous. You could end up grabbing the whole ring after they've made another strike. The bridge bombing came very close to succeeding."

"Not my call, Erik."

"Can you send me a bootleg copy to the *Manteo*?"

"What will you do with it?"

"Assist in the investigation."

"Payne doesn't know about your involvement—with the Ocean City case."

"I'm aboard a cutter. I don't think we're going to run into each other."

"It's my ass if he finds out."

"I'm sensitive to that."

"We'll stay in touch."

Westman clicked off. DeGroot was heading the *Manteo* into Delaware Bay again.

"You're not going out into deep water today?"

"Orders are to patrol the bay."

They were passing the beach that lay at the end of

Lewes's Savannah Road. Somewhere on the other side of the low dunes was Catherine McGrath's house.

Westman poured himself a cup of coffee.

Cat sat holding the Cessna's control wheel with one hand while peering up at the sky above her. It was overcast with some scattered clouds and occasional rain showers, but the ceiling otherwise was a good ten thousand feet and visibility in most places good. She could see patches of sunlight both up and down the coast in the distance.

She'd noticed no other aircraft aloft, not even the combat air patrol that was supposed to be in the area. Her worry was radar, which is why she was flying some twenty feet above the watery deck.

No one was pursuing her. The Ocean City airport had been deserted. There were two Air National Guard C-130's parked on the ramp—transports that had been used to bring some reinforcements to the National Guard camp at Bethany Beach after the bridge attack. Otherwise, there wasn't a sign of the military.

"You sure we're going to be able to pull this off?" said Burt, in the seat beside her.

"The hard part is going to be getting close to Dover."

"You won't need to go as far as the outer marker."

"If I get that close, they'll fire a missile at me."

"I remember our altitude crossing the shoreline at Kitts Hummock. It was always the same. About three hundred feet. Anything much different, I was worried."

She adjusted her throttle and trim. They were flying along the row of nine-story-high apartment buildings at Bethany Beach called Sea Colony, and the structures were causing disruptions of the wind. Looking left, she could see people on balconies watching her. At this early hour, though, the beach was largely deserted.

A puff of updraft lifted the starboard wing. She corrected.

"You're sure this is all right with your boss?" Burt said.

"He gave me permission weeks ago to use it as long as we weren't flying streamers and I paid for the avgas."

Burt squinted at her. "What about the CAP?"

"I'll tell him I forgot about it."

"They won't accept that as an excuse."

"What're they going to do, court-martial me?"

There were two fishing boats coming out of the Indian River channel as she flew by the Highway 1 bridge. The ribbon of land ahead between the inland bays and the sea was largely free of houses and buildings—Rehoboth Bay oddly sparkling in hazy sun on the left, the surf breaking along the wide breach on the right side of the roadway.

Sweeping along the town of Rehoboth just off its long boardwalk, Cat switched frequencies of her radio to learn if anyone was calling her. She'd switched off the plane's transponder, which was illegal. So was flying at twenty feet.

The dunes of Henlopen loomed ahead. Bearing off a little, she passed them to the right of the lighthouse, then banked hard left, heading up Delaware Bay, passing within sight of their two houses. Leveling off, she looked right and saw two ships—one the Cape May-Lewes ferry, steaming toward New Jersey; the other the Coast Guard cutter that had visited them.

"They could shoot us," she said. "They've got a twenty-five-millimeter deck gun."

"They can sure as hell report us."

She had let the aircraft rise to a hundred feet rounding the Cape. Using the throttle, she brought it back down until it seemed she could troll the water with her hand.

The landmarks swept by—Broadkill Beach, the Prime Hook Wildlife Refuge, Slaughter Beach, the mouth of the Mispillion River, and Big Stone Beach.

Kitts Hummock and the Little Creek Wildlife Area were just ahead.

"Okay, Burt," she said. "Stay alert now. I'm going to circle over that marsh and recross the shoreline at three hundred feet on a heading of one-six-five degrees. Stay with me now."

"I'm with you."

She was at ninety feet when she reached the Wildlife Area, high enough to see the strobe lights marking the end of the runway at Dover Air Force Base. If any aircraft were being scrambled, she couldn't tell. She couldn't bother about that now anyway. They had to concentrate on their flight.

Banking slowly to the right, her eyes on the altimeter, she pushed the throttle steadily forward until she reached the desired height, then eased it back as she tightened her turn. When the compass reached 165 degrees, she leveled the wings and headed out to sea.

"Feet wet at three hundred," she said, using the Navy term for crossing from land to sea.

Burt was staring at the instrument panel.

"Rate of climb's too slow," he said. "We were on four engines at this point."

She increased the throttle again. "I thought you said flying those C-130's was like flying a house," she said.

"A pretty fast house. A house with four humongous engines."

"Did you reach three thousand before or after you passed Cape Henlopen?"

"Before. My copilot could see it out his window."

"Well, we're not going to manage that in this little Tinkertoy. I'll have to circle until we do."

The skies were still clear of airplanes, but for hers. Someone was calling her on the radio, addressing her as "unidentified aircraft." She switched off the receiver.

"Three thousand," she said.

Schilling leaned close to her to look out the window on her side. "Straight and level," he said.

"That's what I'm doing."

"Just keep on."

"Okay." She was trying to figure out how she'd make this little Cessna 150 behave like Burt's old cargo behemoth on two engines.

"Now," he said.

She pulled back on the throttle. The engine slowed and the nose dropped a little.

"It was night, but the lights marked Cape May clearly. I remember it pretty good. Never forgot that sight. I thought it was going to be my last."

"Now what?"

"Just keep on steady, losing power."

"I don't want to stall. That'll screw everything up."

"Don't stall. Make a slow turn to the right, then fly parallel to the shore."

She dropped the nose more, decreasing the power. The altimeter was unwinding steadily.

"Now what?"

His eyes were on the beach to the right. "In a minute, I want you to start a turn to the left. I'll call out the altitude I want."

"We're almost to Rehoboth."

"That's right. I remember the lights of the boardwalk."

"You know where we are?"

"Turn now! And we're too high. Lose a few hundred."

She fiddled with the throttle, pushing the control column forward. He kept giving her new commands. Struggling to keep up with him, she found this worse than her most frustrating Navy check ride. But Burt had come fully alive. He was all but flying the plane himself.

"This is it!" he said. "Circle here."

They were almost in the water. Pushing the throttle to the wall, she banked hard. She could see the ocean straight out her window. Burt was craning to see the shore.

"You're sure?" she said.

"Yes. I could see that old World War II machine gun tower."

These old, odd concrete monuments to a long-ago Atlantic threat could still be found all along the Delaware shore from Henlopen to Fenwick Island—five-story-high cylindrical towers with curving slits cut into their walls at the top for machine guns and light cannon. Put there to resist a German invader who never arrived, they had a 180-degree field of fire. Now pointless and useless except as tourist curiosities—their entrances bricked up and lower walls covered with graffiti—they stood as silent sentinels, much like the famous stone heads of Easter Island.

"You can see them from a lot of angles."

"I know. I forgot about that. But now I remember."

"You trust your memory?"

"On this."

"Mark the chart."

"I just did."

She pulled harder on the control column and eased the bank, causing the Cessna to climb. At a hundred feet, she leveled and headed south.

"You're absolutely sure?" she asked.

"Yes."

"Well, you've been wasting your time," she said. "We're south of Deepkill Shoal. By several hundred yards."

He considered this, not happily. "I guess you're right."

"I'm little Miss Navy, remember? I was first in my class in navigation."

He swore, then put it behind him. "I'm going to take the *Roberta June* out today. This afternoon. Can you come out?"

"Not sure, Burt. I'm a little beat. We need to think about what we want to do."

"What we're going to do is find those damn bombs." He stared ahead, impatient.

Once past Bethany Beach, she cut in over the highway

and flew cross-country the rest of the way, keeping just above the trees and power lines.

Turning on final just south of Ocean City Airport, she set the Cessna down quietly and rolled to stop near one of the hangars.

It was then that she noticed the police cars.

Chapter 17

Once again Westman was compelled to make a laborious journey via the Cape May-Lewes ferry down to Ocean City. He was recognized at the police station and treated collegially, but there was a terrific mess to sort out.

Both Catherine McGrath and Burt Schilling were in the lockup. Before asking to see them, Erik sat down with the lieutenant on duty as watch commander.

"What are you holding them on?"

"You know them?"

"Yes. She's ex-Navy."

The policeman consulted the sheet on his desk before him. "Theft of aircraft."

"That all?"

"That's all we have on them. I'm not even sure the aircraft owner is going to press charges. The woman claimed she had his permission to fly the airplane as long as she paid for the fuel. He said he didn't give her permission to fly in violation of a federal shutdown of the airport."

"Her trouble ought to be with the FAA then—not local

law enforcement," Erik argued. "As for Schilling, all he did was sit passenger, right?"

"That case could be made."

"Schilling runs a head boat out of Lewes. They've been helping us with an investigation." This was a mammoth exaggeration, but Erik thought it worth the risk.

"Investigation?"

"The Bay Bridge."

"You came all the way down here again to spring these two?" the police commander asked.

"Yes, I did. She'll be in big trouble with the FAA as it is. I imagine she'll lose her pilot's license. But that's not a matter for the moment."

"I'll call the aircraft owner. It shouldn't be a problem. But there'll have to be paperwork, and I'll have to hang it on you."

Westman nodded. "Okay."

The lieutenant picked up his phone.

Cat was surprised to see him. Rewarding him with a tentative little smile and a quick handshake, she turned to assist her friend Schilling, who looked as though he had crawled out of a culvert.

"Would you like to get something to eat?" Erik asked as they exited the police station.

She looked to Burt. "I'd better get him home. He needs about a year's sleep."

"I'm all right," Burt said.

"A cup of coffee," she said. "We can do that."

Erik followed her Jeep Wrangler to the restaurant, which sat across the highway from a miniature golf course decorated with cheesy-looking dinosaur figures. She hopped out. Schilling remained in the Jeep.

"I'm going to catch some Zs here," Schilling said. "You go on in."

Westman talked her into some breakfast, and ordered a grilled-cheese sandwich and a cup of coffee for himself.

"How did you pull off that miracle?" she asked.

He responded honestly. "I lied."

"About me?"

"I said you and your friend were helping us with an investigation."

"And which one is that?"

"We're looking for suspicious vessels after the Bay Bridge explosion. You've been helping with that."

"How so?"

He grinned. "You were a suspicious vessel. We checked you out. Now you're not."

She cradled her face in her hands. "Whatever you told them, I'm grateful. I knew I'd get into trouble, but I didn't think I'd end up in the brig."

"You've ended up in a restaurant."

Cat lifted her head, her eyes seeking his. "Yes. Well, thanks."

"Down the line, you could be in some trouble. I'm afraid you might lose your pilot's license. And not just for operating out of a closed airport. The regs call for a thousand feet out from the beach and a thousand feet minimum altitude. You were observed at about fifty—over the sand."

"Twenty feet actually."

"And you violated restricted airspace—on the perimeter of Dover Air Force Base. It's a wonder they didn't try to bring you down. It's a jumpy time."

She sipped her coffee, then leaned back as the waitress set her ham and eggs before her.

"Why did you do it?" Westman asked.

"The low-level flying? I wasn't hotdogging. We were attempting to reenact Burt's flight—the one where he dropped the bombs. I stayed low to avoid radar detection so we'd have a chance to pull it off."

"Did you succeed?"

She shrugged. "I'll succeed if we can find the bombs. We were able to determine that they probably went in a lot farther south than Burt had thought. All these years, I think he's been working the wrong end of Deepkill Shoal."

"And now you really have a chance to find them?"

"A chance, yes. A better chance. But not a very big one." Another small smile, then she went back to eating.

"I believe you about your abandoned bombs—after the risk you took today."

"You didn't believe me before?"

"I wasn't sure I believed Mr. Schilling."

She made a face. "All we need to do is locate them. Then we'll turn everything over to the Air Force. They'll have no choice but to come get them."

"I meant what I said about helping you."

"I'm not sure what you can do."

"Just let me know."

"Can you provide us with a search vessel and some diving equipment?"

He shook his head. "I'm merely an investigator—and a warrant officer at that. The service is pretty hard-pressed right now. And . . ."

She put her hand on his—briefly. "I was just kidding. Burt's been trying to get the federal government to do something about this for years. No one's going to listen to us until we come up with something tangible."

"I'll listen. I'll bring it up with my superiors. I know an admiral."

She looked away, down at the floor. "Burt's so dead set on this."

"You two seem very close."

"He and my uncle were pals as well as neighbors. I've come to like him a lot. He's had a rough time of it. He surely got the shaft from the Air Force, and now he's just trying to do what's right."

Westman made some calculations. "There's forty, fifty feet of water out there—running five miles out."

"Twenty-seven feet along the shoal at mean tide. Maybe less."

"Have you any idea how much that bottom's been re-arranged after all these years? The bombs could be buried deep by now."

"Or uncovered. They wouldn't have moved. No more than those wrecks on the bottom all along the shore have. They've all been on the charts since I was a little girl."

"How are you going to be able to determine you've found those things?"

"Burt says he'll know. He was going to hire this salvage outfit in Wilmington, but now he's got a metal detector and he's talking about renting some high-tech sonar gear."

"Can he afford that?"

"He's paid off his boat. I guess he means to mortgage it again. He even talked about selling it."

Westman's cell phone jangled. He smiled, politely, and took it from his pocket.

"Westman."

A pause. "This is Admiral dePayse. Where are you?"

"Just a moment." He put his hand over the mouthpiece. "I think I'd better take this outside, if you don't mind."

She seemed surprised. "Sure."

He walked out to the parking lot, leaning back against the hood of his Grand Cherokee. "Hi."

"Hi yourself, Special Agent. Where the hell are you?"

"Just up the shore from Ocean City. I was at the police station there."

"Any developments?"

"The FBI lifted some good prints from the crime scene. I

think that by now they've traced a rental car and a driver's license to one of the bridge-case attackers. They should have a photo ID on him by now. I don't know if it's going to be distributed. I haven't checked with my friend in the task force yet."

"Why aren't you aboard the *Manteo*?"

"It was headed up the Delaware. I think the action's down here."

"But you're no longer part of the FBI task force."

"I don't know that I need to be."

There was a long silence. "I wonder if you ought to come back in."

"Headquarters in Arlington is not exactly where the action is."

"I mean back here—Buzzard's Point."

He had no immediate response to that. "Joan, what if I told you there was some nuclear ordnance lying in maybe thirty feet of water off Cape Henlopen."

"I've seen nothing about that in any reports. How have you come by this knowledge?"

"I've met the former C-130 pilot who jettisoned two of those things somewhere in that location back in the sixties. He's trying to find them."

"Air Force pilot?"

"Yes, ma'am."

"I think we'd better leave that to them."

"Those bombs are in coastal waters, Admiral. Our jurisdiction."

She gave a pronounced sigh of exasperation. "Erik. We have a very high-priority matter before us. How long did you say these bombs have been there—if they actually exist?"

"Forty years. A little less."

"They can wait a little while longer, don't you think? Get back on the bridge case, please. And until we can sort out your problem with the FBI, get back on the *Manteo*."

"Admiral, there's nothing going on up the Delaware."

"Consider that an order."

"Yes, ma'am."

"And report in more frequently, please."

"Yes, ma'am."

She clicked off.

Westman looked up to see Catherine come out from the restaurant. "This was supposed to be my treat."

"Next time," she said. "You saved me a lot of money today. I was afraid I was going to have to hock my car to raise bail." She briefly put her hand on his arm. "Thanks."

"I have to get back to my ship."

"I know that drill." She looked back to her Jeep. "Burt wants to head out to Deepkill as soon as we get back, but I'm going to make him wait until tomorrow. Let him get some sleep."

"What will you do?"

"Call my Navy lawyer and find out how much trouble I'm in."

"I wish I could help."

"You already have." She hesitated, then reached into her purse. She wrote something quickly on a piece of notepaper, then handed it to him. "Call me."

He pocketed the number. "I will."

"Tonight."

"All right."

She waved from her Wrangler. She had turned into the street and was speeding north by the time he got his Grand Cherokee started.

Turko had not wished to risk crossing the Delaware River at any of the Interstate bridges for fear the police might have established roadblocks or checkpoints—a strong possibility at the tollgates at the Delaware Memorial Bridge just south of Wilmington. He doubted they'd have any high-priority watch for the cheap stolen car he was driving, but it was a chance he shouldn't take.

He kept to the Pennsylvania side of the river all the way to Trenton, crossing on an old bridge north of the Interstate. There was a sign at the edge of the highway saying George Washington and his army had crossed the Delaware at this point en route to his victory there. They'd taken the drunken Hessians by surprise and slaughtered them. The British had looked upon the Americans as little better than terrorists. The Americans had wanted what the people of Chechnya wanted. Independence. Freedom.

Holding his speed to five miles an hour over the limit, he took Interstate 295 back down the river on the Jersey side, switching to Highway 49 at Penn's Grove and following it around a wide curve of the Delaware until the huge tapered towers of the Farmingdale nuclear power plant came into view.

Pulling off to the side, he went to the backseat to turn on the video camera he had bought that morning and placed it on the ledge at the rear window, adjusting a windbreaker jacket over it. Then he continued on.

Careful now to keep his speed exactly at the limit, Turko drove by the huge, sprawling complex with his eyes fixed on the road ahead of him. The highway did not come very near the plant, but some knowledge was better than none.

He'd read the report on nuclear power plant security Pec had given him, three times through. The anonymous testimony it contained from security guards never made clear which plants they were talking about, but he'd acquired a fair idea of their general plan and security arrangements. At several of them, perhaps even this one, guards were made to work twelve-hour shifts and there was a problem with sleepiness toward the end of the shift.

The guards had nine-millimeter automatics, shotguns, and semiautomatic civilian versions of the military M-16 rifle. The latter were kept in cases, however, and not instantly available.

At some of these sites, the guard force had been trained only to deal with small, single parties of intruders coming from one direction. The only reinforcements they could expect were local first responders—meaning small-town cops and state troopers. The people from the other twelve-hour shift were not allowed to take their weapons home with them.

This was possible. But with only four men?

He drove on to the next town, then made right turns until he was headed back on the highway again. Approaching the main gate, he on impulse hit the brakes and carefully pulled up to the guards' station. Two men in dark uniforms quickly came up to him.

"You can't stop here, sir," said one. He was wearing a side arm but it remained in his holster.

"I'm sorry," Turko said. "I'm trying to find Farmingdale Beach." He remembered the name from a long study of the road map.

"Go back the way you just came. At the next town, make a right and follow the road to the end."

"Thanks," said Turko, smiling. "Sorry to trouble you."

"That's all right. But in the future, get your directions somewhere else."

"Yes, sir." He drove away as instructed. Instead of making a right at the intersection, he went left, heading east cross-country until he came to a major north-south highway.

In Camden, New Jersey, he sought another bad neighborhood and pulled into a debris-strewn vacant lot. He had no idea whether they had had closed-circuit surveillance cameras at the power plant gate, but it was a worthwhile precaution to ditch this vehicle and obtain a new one. Taking out his shoulder bag and putting his video camera in it, he left the car in the lot, certain it would be stripped clean by morning. Unbothered by local residents this time, he walked some twenty blocks to a main street with an open gas station and called a taxicab to take him to Philadelphia.

Dropped off downtown on Broad Street, he found the side door of a big hotel and entered it, crossing the lobby to the pay phones.

He'd memorized the Bethesda number. He'd been told to use it only once. If necessary, he'd be given another one.

It was answered immediately. Turko realized it was probably manned full-time. Incoming calls would be patched to where they needed to be.

Turko gave his name—another name. He was told to wait. He was made to wait for more than ten minutes. One of the hotel bellmen began to watch him.

"Yes?" said a voice.

"I have news."

When he was done, Turko hurried out of the lobby through the main entrance and got into a waiting cab, ordering the driver to go to the Philadelphia airport, where he proceeded to one of the parking garages.

He searched the garage for a car with a parking stub on top of the dashboard. He found a fairly new Honda sedan, not a rental.

Turko was eating a cheeseburger and drinking vodka in a new motel in Wilmington within the hour. He turned the television set to an all-news cable channel, learning nothing new. When it was dark, he headed out on foot for the waterfront. It was always a good place to acquire things.

Bear Gergen was enjoying a beer in a Wilmington bar when he found himself joined by two African-American gentlemen from Philadelphia. The larger man, wearing sunglasses despite the night, a black shirt, and the shiniest gray suit Gergen had ever seen, took the empty stool to his left. The smaller one, wearing some sort of Afro shirt, took the right, after first suggesting to its occupant he might have business elsewhere.

Gergen had only just ordered a pitcher. They must have followed him to the bar, preferring to confront him in a place like this rather than going after him in the street or aboard his tug, where he'd have more advantage.

"Where's the shit?" said the larger one.

"Which particular shit is that?" Gergen took a cold gulp of his beer, keeping his eyes from either of them.

"The particular shit you promised to sell to us. That Mr. Diller paid you the motherfucking money for."

"I sent my cousin Leonard to tell you that the deal's off."

"He never showed. We ain't heard nothin'."

"Let me bring you up to date," said Bear. "Someone ripped off my stash and I've had a visit from Customs and the Coast Guard. So it works out like this. No deal. Not with you, not with anyone. I've nothing to deal. I'm probably being tailed. You're pretty fucking stupid to be sittin' here with me."

Stupid or no, they were sufficiently armed. The smaller gentleman put something large and heavy to Gergen's side and pushed hard. Bear could tell the caliber with his rib.

"You're the fucking stupid one," said the one with the gun.

Gergen couldn't argue with that. If he'd been smart, he wouldn't have been sitting here with his back to the door when they came in. He would have been out the back the second he saw them.

"Look," he said. "I'm going to take out my wallet here and show you a card. It's a snitch card. The Coast Guard gave it to me. Here. You see?"

The larger one took it gingerly, studied it a moment, then quickly handed it back, as though it were toxic.

"Let's go outside," the man said.

"No," said Bear.

"You want us to go outside and wait for you? Follow you

home? Blow up your boat? Blow your fuckin' head off when you're asleep?"

"Finish my beer," said Bear, reaching for the pitcher.

The smaller one attempted more rib surgery with the barrel of his automatic. Gergen refilled his glass and drank anyway.

"Okay," he said when he was done.

He led the way out to the street. There was a big black Lincoln Navigator SUV parked just up the block with another African leaning against the side. Bear's pickup truck was parked around the corner. He might be able to put the two from the bar out of commission long enough to get away, but not the backup guy by the Navigator.

So he stood there, arms folded, waiting.

"It's like this," said the smaller one, trying hard to get his face intimidatingly close to Bear's, but failing. "You lifted a big load off that boat. Not just marijuana, but big-time shit. We know that. Everybody knows that."

"Everybody ought to know that the Feds got that. All we took were some marijuana bags. The other stuff was underwater."

"People think you got it," the other man said. "They gonna come for you and maybe kill your ass, man. Mr. Diller's offerin' you your last chance to get rid of what you got—and more'n you're gonna get anywhere else."

It really would have been easy to smash their two heads together right then. But there was a smarter way. There was always a smarter way.

Gergen pushed his own face closer.

"It's not like that—'man,'" he said cheerily. "It's like this. I took a few bags of marijuana off that boat. Whatever else was aboard was underwater in the bilges where I couldn't get to it. The Customs guys have it now. I fucking well don't. The marijuana I stuck in an old half-sunk barge downriver from here and somebody ripped me off. So you and I got no business at any price. And it's no bullshit, man. I've probably got Feds watchin' everything I do—including standin' here talkin' to you."

The big pistol vanished. A finger jabbed toward Gergen's eye, but for emphasis, not in attack. "We ain't done, man."

"You're right," Gergen said. "I need to score a little."

"Say what?"

"A little something for the nose."

The two looked at each other.

"Whatever you can spare," Gergen said. "I got a hundred bucks."

Another look between them, and then glances to the shadows up and down the street, where half the DEA might well be lurking. A car was coming along rapidly, its headlight bouncing with the ruts and bumps and potholes.

They began walking away hurriedly. The man by the big SUV had the rear door open. Someone else had the motor running. It occurred to Gergen that their plans might now be to put a bullet in his brain in farewell.

But they seemed to have lost all interest in this place— and for the time being, in him. Gergen watched them drive off, then returned to the bar. He ordered another pitcher, went to the john, then stopped at the pay phone, pulling the Coast Guard snitch card from his pocket.

Agent Westman wasn't there, but someone else answered. Gergen left a brief message about the gentlemen from Philadelphia, their vehicle and its license plate, what they might be carrying, and the direction in which they were headed. There was the chance this crew could be traveling clean, but Gergen didn't think so. In any event, he'd warned them.

Whatever happened, maybe now they'd stay away.

He hung up the phone and turned to return to the bar. A man with a deep tan was standing in his way.

"Evenin'," said Bear, trying to step around him.

The man didn't budge. "Are you Gergen the tugboat captain?"

Bear just stood there, trying to decide if he was in trouble again.

"I want to talk to you," Turko said.

Chapter 18

It was late at night when Westman turned into Cat Mc-Grath's sandy little street. He had no wish to disturb her, but took the chance that she might be awake. The gamble was with happy result. Her living room windows were aglow with light.

He turned off his lights and killed the Cherokee's engine. As he approached the house, he could hear the television set. He listened carefully. A strong male voice spoke urgently, then a woman began crying.

Erik knocked, but there was no answer. He tried again, with no response. It was contrary to his sense of good manners, but he pushed open the door and stepped inside, drawn by the sounds of weeping.

She was seated on the floor, cross-legged, staring raptly at her television screen. On it was a black-and-white videotape of an aircraft carrier deck. A helicopter was hovering over the water just beyond.

The screen went dark.

"Is that the Kara Hultgreen mishap tape?" he asked.

She said nothing, ignoring his presence, taking a drink of what looked to be whiskey, as the scene was repeated—an F-14 on the base leg of approach, then turning on final, coming head-on toward the carrier deck and the camera. A single trail of thin smoke came from the rear of the aircraft. The big jet was crabbed, canting over toward its port side. The strong male voice of the air controller spoke again: "Wave off! Wave off!" The plane kept coming. "Pow-er. Pow-er! POWER!"

The aircraft veered left, away from the deck, and then began a slow roll over the sea. Just as it was turning belly-up, there were two nearly simultaneous flashes from the cockpit. Then the big jet plunged into the water, throwing up a huge curtain of spray.

She rubbed at her right eye, then took another drink. "It's mine. The official Navy videotape used by the board of inquiry and the evaluation board. But it could have been Kara's. It could have. They're almost exactly the same."

He didn't understand. All that was clear to him was that she was crying. He put his hand on her shoulder. The muscles there tensed, but she put her own hand over his, her eyes still fixed on the television screen, where the tape repeated the sequence once again.

At last the screen went blank. She leaned forward and turned off the set, then finished her drink and shakily got to her feet.

"If it upsets you so much," he said, "you shouldn't watch it."

She wiped at her eyes again. "I've watched it a thousand times, only now, for the first time, I see it. The same thing happened to her that happened to me. I see that now."

"What was that?"

"An engine stall induced by the aircraft's altitude. The angle of the aircraft in that crab—it shut off the air from the port engine. I caused that stall, like they said. I caused the accident." She took a deep breath. "I killed my weapons officer—my friend. I screwed up. Like Kara, I kept on flying. I wasn't going to let them beat me. Wasn't going to let anything beat me. I should have punched us out the instant I got a wave-off, but I kept on going. It was the wrong decision—the wrongest decision I could have made."

Westman could think of nothing to say—or do. Then she took a step forward and came into his arms and he held her close, her head against his shoulder, her blond hair soft against his cheek.

"Even if what you say is true, it wouldn't have happened if you'd had decent engines," he said. "You can't be blamed for a Pentagon foul-up."

"That doesn't matter." Her tears were wet against his neck.

"You shouldn't keep looking at that tape," he said.

"On that flight I took Burt on, we were replicating what happened to Burt when his engines went out—both on one side. The same thing as me, only he brought his plane back. He knew what he was doing. He knew what to do. I just kept flying. They were telling me, 'Call the ball. Call the ball.' But I was too far out of alignment to do that. Stupid. Stupid."

She was shivering. He held her closer still, and she began to cry in earnest, sobbing uncontrollably. Finally, the sound subsided.

Cat lifted her eyes to his. "Can you stay a while?"

"Yes. A while."

She turned away from him, going to the kitchen. She was wearing shorts and a T-shirt and her feet were bare. Her long blond hair was loose, falling to beneath her shoulders. "I'll get you some wine."

He seated himself on her couch uneasily. He'd picked a very bad time for this intrusion.

Cat returned with a glass of wine for him and another whiskey for herself. Sitting next to him, she handed him his glass.

"I have to tell you something." She looked down at her

feet. They were uncommonly narrow and uncommonly pretty. "I had a bad time of it, in the Navy, at the end. There was a guy. He was on my boat. A flier. My flight commander. I liked him. He took my side in the mishap investigation. But . . ."

Cat wiped her eye. He put his arm around her gently.

"He figured there was something in it for him. He figured that was me." She took a deep breath. "When I disagreed, he insisted. He was a big guy. It was horrible. The most horrible thing in my life, except for my losing that Tomcat."

Westman pulled her a little closer. She did not resist, but there was a stiffness to her.

"I hit him with something. A book. The sharp corner of the cover. He was a lieutenant commander. I filed charges against him and I was charged with striking a superior officer. It was my word against his word. And so I got bounced from the service. And that's why I'm here. I'm seeking a new hearing, and reinstatement, but it won't be easy."

"They don't like to admit mistakes."

She kept her eyes from him. "Erik. I can't sleep with you. Not with any man. Not yet." .

He stroked her cheek. There was nothing he needed to say.

She moved closer. "But I think I'm getting a little fond of you. Don't go away. Not just yet."

Seagulls awakened him. He had stayed the night, at her request, but spent it on her couch. Out the front window, there was the first light of morning.

He washed up in her bathroom, careful to make little noise. He was about to slip out her front door when he heard her enter the living room behind him.

"You weren't going to say good-bye?"

"I thought I'd let you sleep."

Cat seemed not quite awake. She gave him a fuzzy little smile. "Now I'm not so sad. I may even be happy."

"Then so am I."

"Coffee?"

"I should go."

"Duty."

"My job."

"I have to ask you something." She took a step closer. "This is embarrassing, but I feel I should know."

"Yes?"

"Are you married?"

Now he smiled. "No. Almost was, a couple of times."

"I won't ask you what happened."

"The first time, I think I was too much in love with the sea and not enough with the idea of home and hearth."

"And the second?"

"Simple enough. I was enlisted. She was an officer—with an excellent career track."

She had no answer to that. "I'm going to make you coffee."

He joined her in the kitchen, sitting at her table as he watched her at the stove.

"Is that a German name, Westman?" she asked.

"Icelandic."

"Icelandic?"

"On my father's side. My grandfather was from Iceland's Westman Islands. They were created by volcanoes."

"The McGraths are from all over. Navy. I was born up the bay in Wilmington, where my mother was from."

"So you've come home."

"My home's the Navy." She set down two steaming cups.

He sipped his. "Your bombs. They made me think of Palomares."

"Burt told me about that."

"It was a horrible mess."

"How did they find the bomb?"

"The admiral in charge said it was like using a flashlight to look for a bullet in a Grand Canyon filled with mud and water. It took forever, but the submersible they used—a

strange craft called 'Alvin'—finally discovered the track the
damned thing had made sliding down the slope to the sea
bottom. They followed that to the bomb. It broke loose on
them when they were bringing it up. But they found it again
and got it up on a ship. I think the job took seventy-five days
from start to finish."

"You seem to know a lot about it."

"I'm an admirer of Bob Ballard."

"The seagoing archeologist? Burt talks about him."

"The man who found the *Titanic*—and all sorts of other
famous wrecks. I went to hear him speak once."

"Too bad we can't hire him to find our bombs."

"It might interest him."

"No, it won't. Not any of them. Not anyone."

"It interests me." His cell phone rang. "Westman," he
said.

"This is Bilecki at headquarters."

Westman looked at his watch. "Something up?"

"You got a call from one of your snitches last night. He
was tipping you to some Philadelphia drug dealers who he
says may be connected to some drugs aboard a sailing yacht.
This make sense to you?"

"Yes. The snitch is a salvage-tug captain in Wilmington.
He brought in the yacht."

"He gave us a description of these guys, make of car, license. Said they had gone to Philadelphia. I called the
DEA."

"Good. I can't do anything with it. I'm working the
bridge bombing."

"They're putting us all on that."

"Are you coming out here?"

"No, we're working the west side of the bay."

"Good luck—and thanks." Westman clicked off the
phone, then finished his coffee. "I should go now."

They both rose. She kissed him. "At least you're not deploying to the Med."

"Just up and down the shore."

"I may see you out there."

"I'll wave."

"Do more than that."

As he went down Cat's front steps, Westman heard coughing from the house next door. Starting his engine, he heard it again as he drove away.

Bear Gergen sat in the wheelhouse of his tug, waiting for his crew and hoping no one else would show up. He knew very well that Enrique Diller would not be as easily intimidated as the mopes the drug dealer had sent down to threaten him—especially since Diller was more interested in Bear's imagined big marijuana haul than the trifling five thousand he was owed. Bear had spent the night aboard his vessel, sleeping with a .45 automatic at his side in the event Diller attempted further fellowship.

Bear also had little desire for a reunion with his other visitor the previous night—a Greek guy who gave his name as Nick Skouros. He'd been polite, and very respectful, but he gave Bear the creeps. There was something about him that set off every wary instinct Bear possessed. The fact that he had come to see Bear about buying a gun didn't help.

Gergen doubted he was any kind of Fed. He also doubted he was any kind of Greek. Bear had known a number of Greeks in the Navy, and had spent a lot of time in places like Piraeus in the Navy. This man's accent was off. He sounded kind of Russian.

All he'd asked for was a heavy-caliber piece. Bear had told him he'd see what he could turn up, though the order was easy to fill. Bear had a dozen handguns like that in a locker below.

Bear had asked for two thousand dollars. The alleged Greek had offered only one thousand, which was actually an acceptable street price for the low-quality arms Bear dealt in. Bear had told the man that he'd consider that price—depending on what kind of firearm he was able to produce. The one he had in mind had been used in a failed bank robbery in Baltimore. Bear had picked it up for fifty bucks off one of the gang members who'd been told to ditch the weapon in the harbor.

Bear was hoping the stranger would consider himself stiffed and not return. But if he did, Bear thought he might agree to the thousand-dollar price. He could give it to Diller as a down payment on the down payment.

Roy Creed, the chief deckhand and the meanest of Bear's crew as well as the largest, thumped down onto the tug's rear deck, dropping a heavy sack by the wheelhouse entrance.

He poked his large head into the wheelhouse. "I'm here like you said, Bear. Where we goin'?"

"It depends. If nothing interferes, I'm going to go find that guy who talked to me about an underwater recovery down by Cape Henlopen."

Roy considered this, but only briefly. "Okay. I'm goin' below. You want coffee?"

"Not yet."

Two other crew members showed up shortly afterward. Neither Leonard or Mary Lou made an appearance, but he hadn't asked for either to do so.

Bear looked at his watch, then rose from his captain's chair and went to start the engines. "Stand by fore and aft to cast off. Ready the forward bowline."

Turko had walked the length of the quay twice, observing everything and detecting nothing that might indicate the presence of law enforcement or any kind of trouble. It was a quiet day in a not-very-busy port.

He was dressed in blue jeans and white T-shirt, with a baseball cap pulled down low over his face. There were several men in the dockyard dressed much the same, though their clothes were dirtier. He would attend to that presently.

For safety's sake, he made one more trip along the dock. He had noted the location of the tug and seen crew members go aboard, but it still caught him by surprise when the vessel's engines started.

Looking to right and left, he hurried toward the boat. The large bearded man he had talked to the night before was in the wheelhouse and at the helm, his eyes on the deckhand who stood at the bow with a mooring line in his hands.

"Cast off the bowline," Gergen called out. "Stand by the stern."

The crewman efficiently did as commanded, allowing the bow to swing slowly into the current. Turko took a couple of running steps, and leapt aboard.

Bear snatched up the pistol he kept next to his binoculars to the side of his captain's chair, whirling as fast as his bulk would allow to face the intruder and scaring himself with how close he came to firing off a shot. When he saw who it was, he lowered the weapon and then took a deep breath before speaking.

"Mr. Skouros. You oughta find a better way to come aboard. Captains are kinda nervous these days, what with all these bombers on the loose. You could get yourself killed."

Skouros eyed him a moment before he spoke. "I'm sorry. But I saw you about to get under way. I wanted to conclude our business before you departed."

Bear returned the pistol to its place on the shelf next to the wheel. "Right. You said first thing in the morning. We're up to the second thing. Maybe even the third."

Something less amiable crept into the alleged Greek's voice. "Do you have it?"

"The piece?"

"Yes," said Skouras. "One automatic pistol. One thousand dollars."

"Sure, I got it. But . . ."

"Where are you going?"

"Down the bay, to Lewes."

"How long will it take?"

"Down and back? Till mid-afternoon. Maybe longer. I've gotta talk to a guy."

"May I come along?"

"Well . . ."

"I'll pay. And I'll stay out of the way."

"You just want to go for a boat ride?"

"I want to conclude our arrangement. And I want to talk to you about maybe future business."

"A hundred dollars," said Bear, feeling greedy. "That's the fare."

Skouros reached for his wallet. He did this so unhesitatingly, Bear wished he'd asked for more.

Gergen looked to the aft deckhand. "Cast off the stern line." When the tug was floating free, he engaged the engine and headed out into the channel, plowing the dirty gray-green water into a foamy furrow.

Dewey had just given an order to set a course for the north end of Delaware Bay when Westman came onto the bridge.

"There was a message from the DEA," said Dewey. "That salvage-tug skipper turned in a bona fide tip last night. They picked up three members of a Philly drug gang. Enough stuff in their SUV to charge them with possession with the intent to distribute."

"My office called me about it," Westman said. "I wasn't sure it would pay off. I'm surprised I never ran into that fellow before."

"Gergen? I don't think he's much of a Boy Scout. Probably prefers that he doesn't run into the likes of you."

"Can't say I want to go on a double date with him either. But maybe I can buy him a beer."

"Keep your hand on your wallet if you do," said DeGroot, watching the river ahead.

"What's today's mission?" Westman asked.

"We're at your disposal if you catch a case—or if you catch a part of the big case," said Dewey. "Otherwise, we patrol the bay. Bridge to the Cape."

"What about the shore below Henlopen?"

"Indian River's got a forty-seven out. But if something turns up . . ."

Westman said nothing. Dewey grinned.

Turko sat at the stern by himself. Gergen was in the wheelhouse with the deckhand named Creed. The other two crewmen were below. Gergen had let him use the binoculars, and Turko was making a point of looking at everything on both sides of the river with them, as well as at every boat and ship they passed.

Gergen came back to join him, leaving the big crewman at the helm. "I don't know what you've got in mind for that handgun you're buying off me, but I hope you're aware of how much heat there is around here because of that attack on the Bay Bridge. The Delmarva Peninsula's crawling with Feds from the Chesapeake and Delaware Canal down to Chincoteague."

"My friends and I just want some personal protection."

"I'm not a snitch, pal. I've stepped over the line selling you this stuff. I'm not going to bust your balls. I'm just offering friendly advice."

Turko lifted the glasses to look downriver at an approaching container ship.

"You've never seen ships before?" Gergen asked. "And you're from Greece?"

"Of course I've seen ships. I like them." He lowered the glasses.

"What do you really want that gun for?"

"We've got a job—a heist." He hoped he'd used the right word.

"Around here?"

"Philadelphia. That's all I'm going to tell you."

"A holdup?"

"No. The firearms are just in case."

"I don't want anything coming back to me."

"I know. It won't. I am grateful to you."

"Tell me again who put you onto me?"

"Guy in a bar. Face like a pig. Named Homer."

Bear nodded. "Okay." He looked down at the binoculars. "You still need these?"

"If you don't mind. There's so much to look at out here."

"Just don't drop them. They're Navy issue. Worth about twelve hundred bucks."

"I won't."

Bear took a step toward the wheelhouse.

"I need explosives."

Bear halted. "What?" he said.

"Got to blow a safe," said the alleged Mr. Skouras. "A vault. I need C-4. And a detonator."

"You know about C-4?"

"Yes."

Now Gergen was scared. He had Coast Guard and Customs sniffing around him, and now this. Was the alleged Skouras a Fed, and this a setup? Or was he the real thing? Either way, Bear wanted nothing more to do with him.

He came back and sat down next to the Greek, as though fearful someone on the river might hear him. "I don't deal in that shit, pal."

"That man Homer told me you deal in everything."

"He exaggerated. Anyway, this is no time to be trying to buy explosives. The FBI will be tracking every sale in four states after what happened on the Bay Bridge."

"That's why I came to you."

"Well, you made a mistake. Firearms. Maybe a little dope

on the side. Otherwise, I'm just an honest salvage man trying to make a buck on the sea."

"You know where explosive can be had, though, don't
you?"

Gergen searched the man's eyes, not liking what he
found. Whoever he was, he was not a cop or a Fed. He reminded Bear of someone he had known in the SEALs—a
man who had been on twenty-eight operations, and must
have killed that many people, mostly using his knife. It
wasn't that he enjoyed that kind of thing. It was that he
hadn't cared. All the same as swatting flies. He'd had no
friends. And didn't seem to want any.

"Maybe you'd better go back to Homer." Bear stood up.

"Think about it. I have money to pay."

"Sorry, pal. I'm in enough trouble. Let me get you that
piece."

The "Greek" lifted the binoculars again. "What's that?"

Bear squinted. "That's a nuclear power plant. Farmingdale. One of the biggest."

"I've not seen one this close before." Turko let the binoculars sag until he was looking at the waterline. There was a
sort of jetty and some sort of breakwater. A boat would not
be able to make a fast run-up directly to the perimeter.

A police boat was anchored just to the side of the jetty.
He lowered the glasses.

"It looks frightening," he said.

"You got that right."

Turko turned to look at the Delaware side of the river.
"What's over there?"

"Not much. I'll be in the wheelhouse."

DeGroot lowered his binoculars. "There's your tugboat
friend, Mr. Westman."

Erik borrowed the glasses. "I wonder where he's going.
The weather's good. You had any distress calls?"

"Negative," Dewey said.

DeGroot went out on the bridge wing and waved. He got a wave back from a figure stepping out of the tugboat's wheelhouse.

"Maybe he's headed out to sea and up the Jersey coast. You want to call him on the radio and thank him for the drug bust?"

"He'd probably not appreciate that—depending on who might be listening."

Dewey nodded, his attention turning from the tug to a small freighter dead ahead in the middle of the river.

The wind was off the land, southwest and running only five to ten knots, with seas only one to two feet beneath a sky of patchy sun and clouds. It was as good as they could ask for what Burt wanted to do, but after nearly three hours of trawling back and forth, they'd had no success. Looking over the chart, Burt had taken them over one of the wrecks that littered the bottom, just to make sure the sonar gear he'd rented was working.

It was. He had to assume they were looking in the wrong place.

Idling the engine, Burt called to Joe Whalleys to drop the bow anchor, and slumped in the captain's chair by the controls. For a moment, Cat was afraid he was going to fetch a bottle forth from one of his hiding places. He hadn't had a drop all that day and, eager about his task, hadn't seemed to mind that at all. Now, she feared, he was about to cave.

"I don't understand," he said. "We worked it all out."

"You can't expect to get it right with one flight in a Cessna 150," she said. "And the 1960's were a long time ago."

"No," he said. "I'm certain now. I should have reenacted that flight a long time ago. This is the place. The landmarks line up. It was like an epiphany. I just know it."

Cat took the chair opposite him. Amy was on the deck port-side, watching them both intently.

"I don't know what to do," Burt said. He rubbed his hands over his grizzled face, then turned to look at the cabinet in the control console.

"I think we're being kind of impatient, Burt," she said. "There's a lot of sea bottom here."

"I know." He lighted a cigarette, eyes to the horizon, then back to shore. "We'll keep looking."

She leaned back in her chair, her attention going to a flight of three gulls soaring obliquely overhead, tilted land-ward against the wind.

"How's the fuel?" she asked.

"About a quarter full."

"Why don't we give it another hour?" she said. "The weather's really good."

Calling to Whalleys to weigh anchor, Burt gentled the boat forward, creeping it up the slackening anchor line. When the anchor was aboard, he started to turn the wheel to port.

Cat's eyes were still fixed on the south.

"Wait," she said.

He ignored her, or didn't hear her.

"Burt! Wait!"

He idled the throttle, turning to her, perplexed.

"We've forgotten something very basic here," she said.

"And what is that?" he said, sounding as though he felt she was patronizing him.

"Velocity."

"Velocity?"

"Have you ever dropped bombs, Burt?"

"Only the two we're looking for."

"Well I have. GPS precision bombs. We guided them to target after deploying them."

"These weren't precision bombs."

"That's not the point. For all practical purposes, we flew

them down. When you're at speed, Burt, bombs don't drop straight down. They travel forward, depending on their velocity. I deployed some at targets twenty miles away."

"I wasn't flying a jet."

"You jettisoned them at close to two hundred miles an hour. Do you have a calculator?"

"There's one below," said Amy, who had come up to join them. "I'll get it."

Burt said nothing until she returned, and then he only grunted. Cat began making calculations. Making a mistake halfway through, she started over. Burt grunted again, impatient. The boat was turning sideways to the wind.

Cat extended her arm and thumb, sighting along the coast. "I want to go a mile down the shore."

Burt seemed reluctant to concede her point. He should have figured this out years before. "Even if you're right, they could be anywhere."

"Not anywhere. Somewhere. About a mile south. We'll work our way back up. Try it."

Cat took over the helm when they reached the waters she wanted. Sending Burt back to work his little sonar set, she cut the speed to near idle and then began a slow pattern, back and forth, creating a grid, starting at about fifteen feet of depth and working her way out to seventy-five feet. When she reached that outer limit, she changed the pattern, steering the *Roberta June* toward the shore and then out again, back and forth, over and over, filling a square.

She was just starting another outward-bound leg when she heard Burt call out to stop. Cat moved the throttle to neutral, then briefly into reverse, then back to neutral, ordering Joe Whalleys to drop anchor. He took his time about it and Cat feared they'd drift too far away.

But with the anchor set and the boat swinging back, held

shoreward by the incoming waves, Burt seemed still to have a target.

"Cat! Come back here!"

She did as commanded. "What did you find?"

"You found it. Take a look."

She stepped forward, leaning down close over the green-faced screen. "I see a long blob."

"Could be it."

"Could be anything."

"It's the right length."

"How can we make sure?"

"Have to go down and look."

She glanced at the depth finder. "Twenty-one feet. You could almost do it snorkeling."

"Burt! A boat!"

It was Amy, who was standing on the flying bridge, pointing to something off the port beam. With a flush, Cat turned, expecting to see the Coast Guard cutter. Her happiness faded at the sight of a large tug.

The big bearded man came aboard looking in a dark mood. "Looking for you all over, Captain Schilling."

"You should have called first, 'cause I'm afraid you've wasted your time coming all the way out here."

"What do you mean? Last time you were all set to sign a contract. Just had to get some money up, you said."

"I'm not going to need you after all. Sorry if you went to any trouble."

The bearded man looked over all of them, his eyes lingering on Cat. He turned back to Burt reluctantly. "You said you wanted to retrieve something from these waters. Something to do with the military."

"All I need to do now is find it."

"And have you?"

Burt shook his head. "No."

The bearded man swore, quietly but pointedly. Burt didn't want him to leave bitter. He got out some good whiskey, Jack Daniel's Black, and a bag of potato chips from the aft locker. The man looked as though he could consume the whole thing in two munches. Maybe one.

Bear Gergen passed on the chips, but took a coffee cup full of straight bourbon, downing a third of it in a single gulp.

"We had a deal," he said, punctuating the sentence with a belch.

"Not exactly true," Burt said. "You quoted me a price and I said it sounded okay. That was all. I didn't sign anything."

"A man's word. You were in the service. An officer and a gentleman, right? Just like me. You gave me your fucking word. The word was 'okay.' I turned down another job to take yours."

He looked around the deck of the *Roberta June*, as if to see if Burt had any weapons about. Amy was watching him like a cat.

"I said the price was okay," Burt said. "But now I don't need you."

"You're gonna do it yourself?"

"I have friends."

Another look to Cat. "I see."

Burt drained his glass. "Look, pal. It's nice of you to stop by, but I've got some stuff to do. So drink up, all right?"

Gergen took another large swallow of the whiskey, but left some in the cup, and didn't budge from the spot where he stood. "What is it you're looking for down there again?"

"I told you. Military relics."

"Yeah, but you never said just what they were. Just that they were big and heavy."

"Parts of an airplane I used to fly."

"You'd go through all this trouble to drag up some old airplane parts?"

"Historic value."

"Yeah, right. Come on, what's down there?"

"It's not a big deal, okay?"

"If it isn't a big deal, how come you talked to me about hiring my rig?"

"It was a mistake. I'm sorry."

"I need the work, Mr. Schilling. I can find whatever you're looking for. Find it fast. Give me a shot at it. You can take out a loan on your boat."

"No. I don't want to do that. Forget it. Now finish your drink."

"Tell you what. I'll do it contingent. For a cut of whatever you get. Your 'military relics' got to be worth some money, right? Or you wouldn't be doing this. What is it? A whole airplane? Something you can sell to a museum? Maybe some rich collector?"

Burt was feeling woozy again. He hoped he wasn't showing that. He didn't want to show this man any sense of weakness—or sign of age.

"They're bombs. They're not worth anything. Nobody wants them but me. And the Air Force."

"Bombs?"

"Very old bombs. Like fifty years old. I had to drop 'em in the water on a flight once when I was in the Air Force and now I want to get them out."

"What's in them?"

"High explosive," Burt said. "That's why I didn't tell you before. I was afraid you wouldn't take the job. But now there is no job. If I find them, I can get the Air Force to handle it."

Gergen stared at him, a measuring look in his eyes. "I don't believe you."

"Okay, pal. Enough's enough. Get off my boat now."

The bearded man's face twitched. He went to the bottle, refilled his cup, then poured the contents down his gullet in a few quick swallows. He belched again, wiped his mouth, and set the cup down.

"Thanks," he said, advancing to the rail. He stopped. "Sorry I got you at a bad time. But I still think we can do some business."

Amy came to Burt's side as he stood at the rail, watching the big man climb aboard his tug.

"Burt," she said. "I think you oughta call the cops."

"I don't need any cops."

Gergen went directly to his wheelhouse, swearing quietly. When his crew had cast off the tie-up lines, he spun the wheel to port and pushed forward the throttle, trying to calculate how much fuel he'd wasted on this trip. He'd forgotten all about the alleged Skouras, who stepped into the wheelhouse beside him.

"What did you want with those fishermen?"

Bear was not about to broach the subject of bombs with this guy. "We talked about a salvage job."

"You seem angry."

"He decided not to hire me."

"I'll hire you, if you'll get me some C-4."

"No, thanks, Mr. Skouras. Just find a seat somewhere and relax. We're going back to Wilmington."

Bear wondered if he should drop a dime on the man the way he had Diller's mopes. Watching Skouras make his way aft, he decided not to. He obviously wasn't attempting his Philadelphia "heist" alone. Bear doubted this guy had friends. But he undoubtedly had associates.

Westman called Special Agent Kelly three times during the day, each time having the same conversation. There were no new developments. They had picked up a photo of the suspect from the New Jersey motor vehicle department, but FBI headquarters in Washington was refusing to release it—

supposedly on orders from Justice. Same thinking. It was feared he'd go to ground if they did.

Erik was sure the man had already gone to ground, but said nothing further on the subject.

He got the call he'd been expecting just as the *Manteo* was clearing the Cape May inlet and entering the harbor. It was the admiral's secretary.

"You're to report here at Buzzard's Point ASAP."

"No matter how late?"

"Better not be late, Mr. Westman."

Chapter 19

Cat had fallen asleep waiting for Westman to call. Awakening in the near dark, she listened as though she thought she heard the phone ringing, but it was her groggy imagination. She had an impulse to phone him, but she fought it.

She'd thought long and hard about him. She'd had too many hasty relationships in the service, and here she was on the brink of another one, ignoring everything she supposedly had learned. Erik Westman was miles nicer than any of the macho carrier jocks she'd dated in the Navy, but she knew too little about him. Chiefest among his many mysteries was why a man with his background and education would have joined the Coast Guard as an enlisted man. Becoming a Naval officer like her father and uncle had meant everything to her.

The light of the day was almost gone. Feeling painfully lonely now, and wanting to talk to Burt about what he intended to do the next day, she went next door, surprised to find his house dark. There was no response to her knock or her calling out his name.

More than loneliness now, she felt a crushing sense of defeat. Westman, for whatever reason, had not called. Burt was probably off getting drunk somewhere, screwing up the end of his life much as he had the middle of it. Despite Westman's intercession, she was likely to get keelhauled by the FAA for her aerial reenactment the other morning. In which case she could forget about the flying job in Iowa and any hopes of reinstatement in the Navy.

It occurred to her that perhaps she should go back to the Caribbean, where she might be able to fly with a foreign certificate and get some kind of island-hopping job—maybe flying seaplanes. She might even like that.

She looked to her house, and then to the sea across the dune. Finally, she decided on a visit to the Lighthouse bar.

It was a pleasant walk, and a beautiful evening, but neither improved her mood. Two Johnnie Walker Reds were no help either. She nursed the last one, taking it out onto the deck by the river. Finishing the drink, she walked down the shore to the *Roberta June*'s mooring.

There were no lights. The gangplank had been pulled aboard, but it was a short hop from the dock to the deck.

She placed her hand on the boat's rail, and leapt, landing with a too loud thud. But if he was here at this hour, Burt was more likely to be passed out than simply asleep, and doubtless hadn't noticed.

Cat moved forward. The door to the main cabin was open, not locked as it would have been were Burt off the boat. She stepped inside. His sleeping cabin was down below. It was very dark, so she moved slowly, descending one careful step after another.

She heard the sound of snoring, and moved toward it. Pushing open the cabin door, she could see from the dim light through the porthole that the bunk was occupied.

"Burt?" she said, loudly enough to satisfy her conscience. She could tell herself she'd tried to wake him. "Burt, it's Cat."

She saw a head come up. The silhouette was all wrong.

"He's asleep," whispered a woman.

The voice was Amy's.

Cat didn't know what to say. She started to back away, but then there was another stirring, and Burt lifted his head.

"Who's there?" he asked.

"It's me, Burt. Cat. I was wondering if you were going out tomorrow. To take a closer look at that bomb."

This seemed to take him by surprise. "Sure. We need to get some scuba gear. The marine yard's got some. Do you want to go?"

Cat hesitated. "Yes."

"You're sure?"

"Yes. Sorry to have disturbed you." Without another word, she clambered back up the stairs, paused a moment on the deck, then put hand to rail again and jumped back to shore.

Bear Gergen sat in his pickup truck, sipping from a can of beer and keeping observant. The lights on the head boat moored on the other side of the parking lot had gone out long before, but the old bastard who owned it hadn't yet reappeared. Gergen's intention was to follow the man home, and continue their earlier conversation. He didn't want to go aboard the boat again. You were always at a disadvantage going onto another man's vessel. This guy was former military and had been on the water a long time. Gergen hadn't the slightest doubt he had a gun or two aboard the *Roberta June*. Schilling would know where they were, and Gergen wouldn't.

Schilling's little female first mate, or whatever that small, dark-haired witch was, had been aboard all day and still hadn't come off. Maybe she slept there now. But why? To guard something?

Now things got even curiouser. The tall blond woman

he'd seen on Schilling's boat suddenly appeared from the shadows, stood by the boat's rail a moment, then vaulted over it onto the deck. No light came on. Within five minutes, she reappeared, hopped the rail again, and started walking across the parking lot, coming obliquely toward Gergen's truck.

He leaned to the left as much as he could to reduce his silhouette. She passed by, absorbed by her own thoughts, and didn't glance his way once. Reaching the street, she turned up it, on foot. A fine-looking woman. Much too classy to be hanging out with an old derelict like that.

Schilling lived in that direction, over by the beach. Was she headed there? Did she know what was going on? It could be as interesting talking to her as talking to Schilling—and maybe more productive. She wouldn't be packing a piece.

She had left by way of the paved road that led to the bay. Gergen struck out in an obliquely different direction, cutting across a field of marshy grass. He reached Schilling's house well ahead of her, and found himself a hiding place in the darkness between it and one adjoining.

He'd wait until she was inside, depriving her of a means of retreat.

It was fairly noisy on this street. There was a party going on in one of the houses up the block, and a television set was playing loudly in one nearer. Whoever it was had a Bruce Willis movie on.

The television had distracted him—always a mistake. The blond had turned in one house short of Schilling's and was already at the door. Gergen started to move toward her when he saw the bouncing light of headlights coming down the sandy street. It was a large car with a smooth engine, a Jeep Grand Cherokee.

Pressing back into the bushes, Bear waited for it to pass, but it didn't. Instead, it slowed and turned up onto the patchy lawn of the woman's house. She stood at the door, taking a step forward as a man got out of the Cherokee. Gergen

didn't recognize him until he came up to her and the yellow
glow of the porch light. It was the Coast Guard detective.

They embraced, taking forever to go inside. When the
door finally closed behind them, Bear took off running.

"I can't stay," Westman said. "I have to go back to Washington."

"Orders?"

"A request. They want me to report in person—on the
bridge investigation."

"Sounds like an order to me."

"It didn't come through my director."

She moved farther down the hall, turning on a light. "You
have to make this report tonight?"

"0700 hours. At Buzzard's Point. The Homeland Security
Secretary will be there. The top boss."

"Like me going before the Secretary of Defense."

"Not so scary as that."

She proceeded to the kitchen, turning on that light.
"Would you like a drink?"

"Shouldn't."

"Are you on duty?"

"No, but it's a long drive."

"A glass of wine won't hurt. I'd appreciate your company
for a bit. I'm going down tomorrow."

"Down?"

"We found what could be the bomb. I'm going to take a
look at it in scuba gear."

"Why you?"

"Burt certainly can't do it. I've dived all over the Caribbean. Went to the brink of the Cayman Trench."

"How deep is this thing?"

"Not so deep. Twenty or thirty feet. I used to do that in
snorkel gear at Grand Cayman—a shipwreck there, right off

Cactus Jack's bar outside of Georgetown. What bothers me is what I'm going to find."

She took a bottle of white wine from the refrigerator, pouring two glasses.

"You shouldn't be doing this yourselves," he said. "You should leave it to the military."

"We've got to make sure what we've got down there first. It won't do the program much good if they dismiss Burt as a nutcase because all that comes to hand is an old ship container or something."

"And if it's more than that?"

"Then Burt can go to the Air Force."

"I'd be happy to talk to someone about it while I'm in Washington. It's our jurisdiction, after all."

She sipped her wine, then shook her head. "It's Burt's show." She sighed. "I'm just helping him."

"Don't get yourself in any more trouble."

She smiled. "And don't you get yourself in trouble on my account."

Westman stayed only a few minutes more, but left her in a much-improved mood.

Turko had too little time now to be particular—which was to say, to be overly cautious—about his source of explosive. If they'd been allowed to bring their own in, everything would have been much easier. Certainly the Canadian border was no great problem.

But that would have violated Pec's very firm rule. All the weapons to be used against the United States had to come from inside the United States. Knife, gun, or bomb. And Pec would be wanting to know about his preparations very soon. He likely had someone watching Turko's every move.

Homer had only three customers in his filthy, waterfront bar—a drunk who lay snoring over a tabletop and an elderly couple nearly as inebriated but still wakeful, seated on stools pulled close together as they made amorous noises.

Turko moved down to the other end of the bar, ordering a vodka on ice.

"How'd you make out?" said Homer as he set down the drink.

"Not so good."

"Didn't have a piece? He's got a trunk full."

"I need more than that."

"More guns?"

"Yes. Automatic weapons. And explosive. C-4. Got to have that. You know someone else?"

Homer paused. Turko took a hundred-dollar bill and put it atop the bar.

"How many automatic weapons?"

"Four."

"How much C-4?"

Turko thought on this. "Two pounds."

"Okay. I know someone."

"I need it tomorrow," Turko said.

"Tomorrow?"

"Yes."

"You got a lot of money?"

"Enough."

Homer pursed his blotchy, slightly mangled lips—souvenirs from dock fights in his previous life as a long-shoreman, then nodded, waddling down the bar and going over to a pay phone in the corner. A rat that had apparently been loitering there darted across the room.

Turko was amused. He had read in the American papers how the Justice Department and the FBI were turning away from dealing with ordinary crime to undertake their important new antiterrorism mission. Here he was using a very ordinary criminal.

The bartender returned at the same slow speed. "Twenty grand."

"Grand?"

"Thousand."

"Very well."

"You don't want to haggle?"

"No."

"Okay. I'll call them back and set it up."

Turko took a large swallow of his vodka. He wanted to get out of the place. "Where shall I go?"

"Come back here. Maybe a little before noon."

"And the material?"

"I'll have it out back."

Turko drove down Highway 1 all the way to Dover before pulling off into a gas station to make his call. The phone was answered by someone with a strange Middle Eastern accent.

Turko identified himself, then said, "I'm ready. Meet me tomorrow at the Dover Slots. Next to the racetrack. At Dover. Tomorrow. Two o'clock. Just inside the entrance."

"How will you know us?"

"I'll know you."

He hung up, then made another call—to the special number.

Chapter 20

Because of delays getting back across the Bay Bridge, Westman did not reach his Old Town Alexandria town house until well after midnight, and managed less than six hours' sleep before rising to prepare for his ordeal with officialdom.

To be summoned before a cabinet secretary to report on a criminal investigation was extraordinary. Admiral dePayse was the highest rank he'd ever had to deal with so directly, and that was a hell of a different circumstance.

He'd been asked to wear his dress uniform. It was still in the plastic bag from the cleaners, having not been worn for more than a year. He could not recall what that occasion had been.

Upon arriving, Westman was relieved to discover he would not be the star of this little show. Waiting outside the Buzzard's Point conference room were two officials from Coast Guard intelligence, a man from Customs, another from Immigration, and two investigators from the Transportation Security Agency, though to Westman's knowledge, no public conveyance had been involved in the bridge incident.

Nodding to the others, he seated himself and prepared to take his turn. It was more than an hour before he was summoned.

Cabinet secretaries went nowhere without a dozen aides, it seemed. The conference room was crowded with them and various high-ranking Coast Guard personnel, including Admiral dePayse. Westman stood before the table, as he might before any superior officer, but the Homeland Secretary motioned to him to sit down.

The man had a friendly but lined and weary face. He smiled at Westman, then consulted a paper someone had apparently prepared for him.

"It says here you were onto this Bertolucci fellow before the FBI," he said, looking up. "Is that true?"

"I just got lucky interviewing a waitress, sir."

"The FBI claims they made the identification."

"I can't say that they didn't, sir. We share information. Everything I told them I put in my report to Coast Guard headquarters—and vice versa."

The secretary read further. "It says the special agent in charge of the joint task force asked for you to be reassigned."

This was not the way Westman had hoped to begin his day.

"His privilege, sir."

"But you're still on the case."

"We often work alone, sir. There's not a jurisdiction problem. The waters around the Delmarva Peninsula are Coast Guard territory."

"We all have to get along with the FBI, Westman, just as I have to get along with the Attorney General. We're all in this together."

"Yes, sir. That would be my wish as well, sir." Westman could feel Joan dePayse's eyes burning into him.

The secretary leaned back in his chair. He wore a regulation Washington pinstriped suit, which was slightly too big for him.

"What do you make of these subsequent killings out there? They're definitely tied to the bombing?"

"Yes, sir. I think there was a fairly large group of these people, and for whatever reason, there's been a falling out."

The TSA man leaned forward to ask a question. "This Bertolucci, or whatever his real name is, do you suppose he's still alive?"

"None of the bodies that have been recovered was his."

"What would they have a falling out over?"

"Failure to accomplish the mission. The President's adviser is still alive. The Bay Bridge is still standing. It's all the same as the first attempt on the World Trade Center in 1993."

The TSA man leaned back. His name was also dePayse. He'd been a legal officer in the Coast Guard before turning civilian.

"You think they're still out there?"

"Yes, sir. Not far."

The Homeland Security Secretary frowned and leaned forward, resuming his proprietorship of the proceeding.

"On this side of the bay, do you think?" he asked.

"Probably not, sir. Washington has the most serious security in the country. These people tend to avoid hard targets."

"But what can they hit out on the Eastern Shore? Bean fields? Beach boardwalks?"

"I wish I knew, sir."

The secretary came forward again, resting his elbows on the table. He looked to either side of him. "Anyone else have any questions?" There was a shaking of heads. "Anything else you want to tell us, Westman?"

Here was an opportunity that would not be repeated. Perhaps he could spare Lieutenant McGrath her ordeal with a few simple words.

"I don't believe this is a major concern, sir," Westman said. "But it should be looked into. The captain of a fishing boat out in Delaware claims there are two jettisoned hydrogen bombs underwater southeast of Cape Henlopen and that one of them may have a nuclear core in it. He's been trying to locate them."

The secretary became fully alert. "Hydrogen bombs? I didn't know they still made those things."

"The mishap apparently happened back in the 1960's. An Air Force cargo plane lost two engines and had to jettison its load. The fishing boat captain was the pilot."

"And he waited until now to do something about it?"

"Yes, sir. He was worried about nuclear material being that close to shore. And he thinks one of these weapons can be detonated."

"Didn't he report it to anyone?"

"Yes, sir. The Air Force. By letter. Several times."

The secretary's facial muscles relaxed. A smile followed. "Well, then. We should leave the matter to them. Of all the agencies in Homeland Security, yours is the only one that's part of the military, Mr. Westman, but let's not take that too seriously."

"Yes, sir."

"Thank you." He was dismissed.

Stunned by the swiftness of his failure, Westman turned to leave. Admiral dePayse's suddenly metal-hard voice stayed him. "Warrant Officer Westman, I would like to speak to you after this meeting. Would you please wait outside?"

"Yes, ma'am."

She was only a few minutes more in the meeting. When she emerged, she nodded to him without speaking, indicating he was to follow her. It was not until they were seated in the cafeteria downstairs, coffee in hand, that she broke her silence.

"Why in hell did you bring up those damned bombs?"

she asked, glancing quickly to make certain no one could hear her.

"It's something I think should be looked into."

"It's crazy."

"No crazier than anything else going on over there."

"Erik. I'm trying to get us a seat at the table in this thing. We rightfully should be part of this. Wild tales about mysterious bombs no one's seen for forty years are no help. The secretary will think that boob of an FBI agent was right to separate you from the task force. You'll have our people back doing pollution patrols."

"That's supposed to be part of the job too."

Her gray eyes appeared to darken. "These terrorists are our top priority. We have auxiliarists to handle the rest."

"We've been making good progress. We have an ID on the one guy."

"We don't have the one guy. And until we do get him, I want no more nonsense about old hydrogen bombs, do you understand?"

Rank was rank. Westman nodded.

"Who are those hydrogen bomb people anyway? How did you get mixed up with them?" she asked.

"We stopped a head boat that was anchored offshore. The old pilot's. He and his people were looking for the bombs."

"With what?"

"Some sort of underwater metal detector."

"Who else is involved?"

"The head boat captain has a sort of crew on the boat, a couple of kids. And a Navy woman who helps out."

"Navy woman?"

"Ex-Navy. She used to fly Tomcats off a carrier."

"A woman carrier pilot, and she's working on a head boat?"

Westman glanced about the room. No one was paying much attention to them. "I don't know that much about it."

She sighed. "All right. We all have to get back to work.

The Homeland Security Secretary's going to meet with the President today. Perhaps we'll get an honorable mention."

The admiral finished her coffee. Westman did the same. He noticed her husband approaching. "What would you like me to do?" he asked.

"Get back on the case. I'll try to get you hooked up with the FBI again."

"All right. I'll head back for Cape May."

He started to get up, but the look in her eyes stayed him. "I don't want you on a boat anymore, Erik. I want you on land where the bad guys are."

"Very well."

"Do you need help?"

He shook his head. "There are police and FBI agents all over the Eastern Shore."

Her husband was standing at the table. "I thought that went well," he said, smiling down at his wife.

She smiled back. "Hope so." She stood up, prompting Westman to do the same.

"Good morning, Mr. dePayse," Westman said.

Her husband nodded in reply. "Good work out there."

"Thank you, sir."

DePayse took his wife's arm. "Ready?"

"Yes." She looked to Westman. "I'd like a report from you tonight. Do you have my cell phone number?"

Erik hesitated, but not too long. "Yes, ma'am."

The *Roberta June* lay listlessly at anchor off the south end of Deepkill Slough. It was mid-morning on what had become a muggy day and Cat was feeling the heat, and her own trepidation. But there was no longer any avoiding it. The time had come to take the plunge.

It seemed quite a different prospect now that it was at hand, and Cat didn't like it much. She'd come to realize she didn't want to be near a nuclear device—not staring it in the face, not coming within a mile of it—no matter how old it was.

But she'd promised. There was nothing for it.

She had marked the spot where they'd detected the underwater metal, using a Global Positioning System device Burt had rented to get an exact satellite reference. From here on, they could never lose their place.

Underwater, though, things might not be so neat and easy.

Cat went belowdecks to remove her shorts and bathing-suit top and put on her wet suit. The air temperature was in the eighties, with humidity to match. But the seawater at depth would be cool, even cold, and that would wear on her if she was working any length of time.

Amy Costa helped her get into the suit.

"You have a nice bod," she said.

"Thanks." Compliments like that from women made Cat uncomfortable. Her bosom was modest, proportionate to her slender form. Though small, Amy was very buxom.

Cat hurried the completion of her task. She had run water through the inside of the wet suit to ease her way into it, but the top was still a tight go. It caught at her hair, painfully, as she pulled it on.

"You have nice hair too," Amy said.

Cat ran her fingers through it, combing it free. "Such as there remains of it after that."

"Burt likes you, you know."

"I like him too."

"I mean, he likes the way you look."

Cat strapped on her weight belt. "Burt is kind of what my father was to me, except my father didn't drink so much."

"I don't think that's the way Burt looks at it."

"However he looks at it—and me—that's the way it is."

"Why are you doing this for him then?"

"What do you mean?"

"I thought—I mean, like you two are neighbors, and you spend so much time together."

"That's all we are. Neighbors, good friends. I'm doing this for Burt so he won't have to spend so much money finding what he's looking for."

"That's all?"

"Amy, I think Burt's pretty sick."

"He's been talking like that ever since I went to work for him. And that's been two years now."

She tugged Cat's weight belt around.

"I think it's a bit more serious now," Cat said. "Anyway, I don't want him wasting money on some high-priced salvage crew that could be better spent on medical care. I also think he shouldn't sell this boat."

"Same here."

"Amy, if Burt does get really sick, could you and Joe Whalleys run the boat on your own? Till he gets well. Or . . ."

"Sure. Burt doesn't like to think so, but I can handle the boat easy."

"It may come to that. You'd get more money. I'd see to that."

"Sure."

Cat was fiercely hot inside the wet suit. "Okay, let's get on with this."

"You know, I suppose it really could be kinda dangerous down there."

"In spots. I'm not exactly a neophyte."

"A what?"

"I know what I'm doing."

That could turn out to be a lie.

Tumbling backward off the aft rail of the *Roberta June* was quite like jumping into night.

In the Caymans—when the sun was high—there was enough light along the reefs to read by a hundred feet down. You could look in any direction and within a few minutes count a thousand kinds of sea life around you.

Here in northern Delaware, this far out from the shore, only twenty feet down, she could see not a single creature. She had a handheld light and another on her head affixed to her mask strap, but neither penetrated much beyond a few feet. Whatever it might be like along the beach, the water here at Deepkill Shoal and Slough was filthy—a dark murk like a bad fog.

Floating just above bottom, turning ever so slowly from side to side to gain a true picture of the underwater topography, Cat thought hard upon the matter and decided the project might still be doable—somehow. It had to be.

On the screen aboard the *Roberta June*, the metal object had been showing clearly. Down here—nothing, no matter where she looked.

A remotely operated undersea vehicle with high-intensity lights and a pinger-locator system would be really nice to have. Unfortunately, she had nothing of the kind at her disposal—only Burt's small magnetometer and the sonar device, which she'd left waiting up on the *Roberta June* until she first reconnoitered the area a little.

She urged herself on. She could see the huge dark shadow of the *Roberta June* right enough, just over her shoulder, as well as its anchor line, running from leeward down to the bottom. It was a little past low tide. If she followed the anchor line forward toward the top of the shoal, the water should get shallower.

With a kick, she began slowly moving ahead through the dark green gloom. Kick, float, pause. Kick, float, pause. Keeping the handheld lamp steady, she moved her head slowly from side to side, scanning the murk. Slightly below her, she glimpsed the shadowy silhouettes of three or four fish, then two more. Then there was nothing. Suddenly, a grotesque shape darted before her eyes, staring hard at her, then vanishing.

Her brain overcame the adrenaline. It was only a sea robin, its small size amplified by proximity. The little thing had spooked her, Cat McGrath, who had swum with barracuda and sharks when she was only a ten-year-old kid. She was losing her nerve.

The ocean bottom was now rising in grade, the dim light becoming a trifle brighter as she followed the upward slope.

There was something ahead and to the right in the sand, something metal. She could see the faint gleam—a sharp angle.

For the briefest imaginable fraction of a moment, she permitted herself the exhilarating rush of idiotic optimism, tantalizingly harboring the wish-fueled assumption that this could be one of the bombs, that their labored calculations had been spot on, that they were the deserving recipients of extraordinary good luck. She imagined herself saying years afterward, "Think of it. We found one of the bombs first time down and not a hundred feet from the boat."

She pushed herself nearer.

Foolish, foolish girl. The metallic object was nothing but a goddamned lawn chair! What kind of people lived here, dumping trash like that into the water? She could just imagine a big fat tubby motor cruiser, captained by some big fat tubby suburbanite with too much money. One of his deck chairs collapses under his weight and so he angrily tosses it overboard. In the Caymans, try something like that near a fragile offshore reef, and they'd run you into the nick.

Cat kicked still closer, reached down, and tried to lift the chair, discovering it was in large part imbedded in the sand. Trying again, she felt something rip across the side of her hand. A big fish lure. The chair frame was cluttered with snagged tackle.

Abandoning it, she moved away and back onto her intended path along the sea bottom, which continued upward. Finally, it leveled off.

She needed to orient herself. Kicking her way to the surface, she turned slowly around, spotting the boat standing off maybe a hundred feet from her. Amy and Burt were on the bridge. He was looking elsewhere, but Amy saw her, perhaps having noticed the splash Cat made rising.

Cat waved.

"You okay?" Amy called.

Burt had lifted his head in Cat's direction, but said nothing.

"Fine!" said Cat, after removing her mouthpiece, sounding like someone who'd gone for a dip at summer camp.

She had to get on with this. She waved a last time to the boat, reinserted her mouthpiece, then reluctantly returned to the water.

The bottom began to slip away from her now as she proceeded, a gentle grade at first—sloping down about ten feet, then more steeply. Swimming boldly into the darker area, she followed the decline to twenty-five or thirty feet, where the sea bottom leveled. Swiveling her lamp, she saw that she was on an apron. Bearing left, she moved to its edge, noting a very steep drop. She did not want to be there.

But she had come to look, to search. There was an investment here in time and risk that she must amortize.

The lamplight helped guide her a little, but with no certainty. She turned again, and this time she saw it—a long metallic object, maybe fifteen or sixteen feet. It had to be what they'd seen on the sonar screen. At last.

Kicking hard, she propelled herself to it, reaching to touch its hard edge. But there was something wrong—too many straight lines and sharp angles. Nothing round or cylindrical.

It was a boat! A skiff from the look of it. Sunk and overturned—fairly recently. Parts of the metal gleamed, even in this murk.

She was about to cry. She swore instead.

Her head burst above the surface, this time with a very large splash. The *Roberta June* was directly in front of her.

She headed toward home. It infuriated her that their

prospects now seemed so overwhelmingly hopeless, that the sea had betrayed them so teasingly. She feared she was losing her courage. Terrified by a sea robin. How the macho men on the carrier would have laughed over that.

Amy was standing on the platform aft, and helped her swing aboard and up to the main deck. Removing her belt and web gear and tank, pulling off the mask, and then her flippers, Cat sat down on the deck and leaned back against the rail, closing her eyes.

"How'd it go?" Amy asked.

"Not so good."

She took a few deep breaths. Next thing she knew, Burt had come down from the bridge and was leaning over her.

"What'd you find?"

"A lawn chair. And a rowboat."

Turko, playing a slot machine that faced the entrance to the Dover Downs racetrack casino, spotted the new men almost immediately. Two of them entered together, dressed almost identically in blue jeans and short-sleeved shirts. They came a few steps inside, then stood there, waiting, until the third joined them. He was wearing shorts and a bowling shirt. All had on sunglasses.

Having won twice, after losing only a little of his original ten-dollar stake, Turko had to put an inconveniently large amount of quarters into his pockets. He did so quickly, leaving the empty cardboard bucket on the machine. Careful to show no haste, he made his way to the entrance, leaning to whisper one word in Arabic to the man in shorts, whom he took to be Middle Eastern. Then he proceeded outside and from there to the parking lot.

He kept on until he was deep into the cars. Glancing back to make certain they were following, he found a space between a van and what the Americans called a sport utility vehicle and slipped into it. The three appeared shortly after.

The two in blue jeans were Uzbeks, and from the same tribe and village. The man in shorts was an Iraqi, a former member of the Fedayeen Saddam. The Uzbeks fortunately spoke Russian; the Iraqi, English. Turko could only wonder how the three of them had communicated with each other, but he was content that he could at least make himself understood with each.

Turko opened the sliding side door to the van, which he had stolen the night before in Newark, Delaware. Motioning the others to enter, he went around to the driver's side and got behind the wheel. He had decided on this vehicle because it looked so innocent; something a man with a young family might drive. It later occurred to him that the lack of such a family in so docile an automobile would make him and his passengers stand out. He commanded the others to stay down.

When they were on the wide, limited-access highway that led north toward Philadelphia, he allowed them to sit up.

"Where were you staying?" he asked.

"Nearby," said the Iraqi.

A careful fellow. Turko was pleased.

Chapter 21

Westman returned to his apartment to change into civilian clothes and check in by telephone with his CGIS director, who was intensely curious about his experience that morning with the cabinet secretary who ruled them all. Erik made a point of mentioning his intrusion of the subject of the hydrogen bombs and the Homeland Security Secretary's indifferent response.

"He's right," said the director. "It's an Air Force issue. If they ask for our assistance, we should provide it. Otherwise, we've enough to do."

"The bombs are in coastal waters, sir. The *Manteo* patrols by there regularly."

"Let's stay on target, Erik. If we miss something important on the bridge case because you're involved with some underwater exploration, the commandant will be all over us. Are you still reporting directly to Admiral dePayse?"

"Yes, I'm afraid I am."

"Strange she hasn't asked for any of the other investigators."

"We worked together—years ago. In Puerto Rico."

"Even so."

A silence followed.

"I'll check in with you later, sir," Westman said.

"Yes. Well, good luck."

Next, Westman called the cell phone of Special Agent Kelly.

"Nothing new to tell you," Kelly said, speaking quietly. "Except we moved our command post to Ocean City."

"What for?"

"Payne thinks the bad guys are still out here."

"Plotting what? Sabotaging the amusement park?"

"As a matter of fact, he thinks that's a possibility. He talked to the mayor here and got the place closed. Weren't many customers anyway."

"Any word yet on distributing the suspect's picture?"

"Still have a hold on that."

"That's crazy, Leon."

"They don't want this guy to bolt."

"If you ran his photo on the evening news, you'd have a few million people helping you look for him. Do you remember the D.C. sniper case? The only reason they caught those two creeps was that a cop broke orders and leaked the car description and plate numbers to a television station. It was a passing truck driver who nailed those bastards, not law enforcement."

"I'm told we raised that point, but the big boys are kind of stubborn on the subject. They still think that releasing the picture would drive the terrorist gang underground. Maybe make them leave the country."

"And if they try something again?"

"Catch 'em in the open."

"Crazy. If the 'open' looks like Ground Zero at the World Trade Center."

"Orders. Where're you working today, Erik?"

"I think I'll head out your way."

"Why?"

"Special Agent Payne may actually be right. Maybe they are after the Ferris wheel."

Westman made one more call before leaving, but Cat Mc-Grath didn't answer. It was curious she hadn't an answering machine.

Turko stole an old Mitsubishi station wagon in Chester, Pennsylvania, picked up his crew, and headed south toward the nuclear power plant. All of them were armed with handguns, but Turko put them in the back in the spare tire well, then piled all their fishing gear on top of that. Police were stopping cars with some frequency, seemingly at random.

He allowed himself one slow pass by the main gate of the power plant, having turned the rearview mirror sideways so he could observe the entrance carefully without turning his head. He took note of two guards stationed outside the gate and saw a third walking across the grounds. There would be many others posted around the site, but it was encouraging that there were so few at this location.

The Iraqi was not so encouraged. "We do this? Only four of us?"

"Yes. Two in a truck. Two in a boat."

"To blow up a big plant like this?"

"I told you. Not the plant. Just one of the spent-fuel storage bunkers. Very easy to get to. Just beyond the fence."

"And where do we go afterward?"

"To a car we'll have hidden nearby."

"And then?"

"We rendezvous with your Uzbek friends and head south."

"Why south?"

"Because the winds will be blowing the radioactivity north."

"How do you know that?"

"Because we won't do this until the winds are blowing from the south."

The Iraqi rubbed his face, thinking. Turko straightened the rearview mirror. The Uzbeks were listening intently, though they could not understand a word.

"We need to practice," the Iraqi said.

Turko shook his head. "Practicing will be noticed. We need to acquire more weapons and the explosives. And a truck. Then we move quickly, as soon as the wind turns."

"And now we go fishing?"

"We go to the water side of the plant. And pretend to fish. I've explained all this."

"I only want to understand."

He was a small man with a hooked nose and large black eyes. Turko supposed he used to have a mustache.

"What did you do before you joined us?" Turko asked.

The Iraqi stared straight ahead. "I help run narcotics through central Africa. I fought in a war in Nigeria—against the Christians in the north."

"I mean when you lived in Iraq."

"I was a kind of soldier. A bodyguard for important officials. Before the Americans came."

"Did you ever kill anyone?"

"Oh, yes. Many. Once I kill a disloyal general with a blowtorch."

They had anchored the *Roberta June* in waters on the edge of the grid they had laid out on the chart, having worked the area thoroughly all morning.

Burt was drinking a beer, his first of the day. He'd been behaving himself during this effort, as he had not always when he had fishing parties aboard, but his hangover was getting the better of him.

Cat was feeling a little fuzzy herself, but it wasn't from booze. Her nerves were not happy with this work.

She took a seat next to Burt's. Declining a beer, she accepted a Diet Coke. Amy was forward, checking the anchor chain. Joe Whalleys was aft, drowsing by the empty bait box.

Cat nodded toward Amy. "What's going on with you two?" she said quietly.

Burt replied with a blurry grin. "What's going on with you and that Coastie?"

"He seems a nice guy. And he wants to help us."

"Oh, yeah? What's he done for us lately?"

"Need I remind you that he got us out of the OC slammer? Couldn't do a lot of bomb hunting from in there, could we?"

Schilling took a deep drink of his Heinekens. "Not doing much better out here."

It was a muggy day with low clouds lying in the haze. The wind had dropped and the grayish water looked flaccid and uninviting. "Don't give up hope now," she said. "We're just beginning."

"What do you think we should do?" He squinted at the horizon.

"Keep looking."

"But where? We've worked that grid good. If your calculations are right . . ." He finished his beer in two more gulps.

"Let's move the grid to the south."

Burt squinted in that direction. "Doesn't look right."

"Let's just try it."

Westman had a Coast Guard radio under his dashboard that he kept tuned to the operations frequency. He turned it on as he crossed the Bay Bridge, listening to what sounded like normal chatter. An HH-60 Jayhawk chopper was approaching from the south on a standard LE patrol. A forty-one-footer had found something off Tilghman Island and had summoned a forty-seven to assist. A suspected oil spill had been detected across the bay up by Aberdeen.

It might have been an ordinary summer's day, were it not

for those terrible people out there. Perhaps there was only one left, the one they were calling Bertolucci. Westman desperately hoped so. A man alone couldn't do so much harm. And wouldn't put up so much of a fight if finally cornered.

But it was likely there were more of them. The murders at those two Ocean City apartment buildings indicated that.

The bridge descended toward the Eastern Shore. Westman glanced at the dashboard clock and decided to stop off on Kent Island for lunch, turning off Highway 50 at the first exit and doubling back to the restaurant on the water where the Bertolucci suspect had dined while waiting for the bridge to blow.

Westman took a table out on the deck, near to where the waitress had told him Bertolucci had sat. The view was the same that Bertolucci had had, except for the bright daylight. He could not comprehend the mind of a man who could sit in such a place watching a thousand or more people driving along the span, waiting and hoping for their doom. How could anything like that relate to religion, or politics?

He was being naïve. There had been men like that through the centuries. An endless parade of them.

He'd lost his appetite, but he ate anyway, idly listening to the television set in the main dining room behind him. When the news came on, he became more slightly attentive, but there was nothing much of interest. The set was tuned to a Baltimore station and the stories had to do with the city council and some minor crimes. There had been a rash of auto thefts from garages and parking lots in the Baltimore, Philadelphia, and Wilmington areas—twice the normal number. Police were also investigating an attempted break-in at an art museum, and the murders of two teenage boys in North Baltimore. A woman jogger had been attacked on the waterfront.

Except for the spike in auto thefts, it sounded like an ordinary day in Baltimore.

He paid for his lunch, inquiring after the waitress who had told him about the Bertolucci man. He was informed she had quit her job.

Following Highway 50 from Kent Island onto the Delmarva Peninsula, he considered heading for Bethany or Lewes, but decided to stick to his decision to visit Ocean City instead—though not to call upon the new FBI command center. He'd go to the local police headquarters, where there was a fairly elaborate computer system.

He'd need that. It had suddenly occurred to him that it might be well worth his while to check out all those stolen car reports.

The first marina Turko had gone to rented only small bass boats, which would be difficult to operate in choppy weather. The two Uzbeks looked to be poor mariners and might well swamp or capsize such a craft before they got near the power plant. The smallness did offer the advantage of a low profile in the water when they approached the plant security fence, but Turko was not interested in that. Whether they realized it or not, the Uzbeks' role in this enterprise was diversion. He wanted them to draw as many guards and as much fire as possible. The higher the silhouette and the noisier the engines the better.

Farther downriver was a marina that rented large pontoon boats. The young woman on duty in the small shack of an office hardly gave Turko a glance as she took his driver's license, a new one in the name of Skouras, and a two-hundred-dollar deposit. The youth with her watched him sign the rental form, but said nothing.

He led Turko and his party down to the dock. Explaining the workings of the rectangular-shaped pleasure craft and the rules for its use, he stood by as they took their fishing gear aboard and then cast off the lines after Turko started its

big outboard engine. Waving good-bye, Turko headed the
boat downriver first, dropping anchor close offshore and instructing the others to cast their fishing lines into the water.

He had filled two large thermos bottles—one with tea for
them and another containing vodka and a little orange juice
for him. He poured himself a plastic cupful of the latter, then
sat at the helm, calmly watching the river traffic while they
fished.

The Iraqi knew what he was doing, but the Uzbeks had
neither ability or interest, and were content to let their lines
drift in the current. When the bait of one was taken by a fish,
the daydreaming miscreant let the rod slip out of his hands
and into the water. Turko finished his drink and restarted the
engines, taking the boat out into the main ship channel and
then turning upstream.

"We're going too fast," said Cat to Burt, who sat slumped in
his chair at the *Roberta June*'s helm as they made another
pass over the new grid.

"What do you mean?"

She stepped closer.

"You're going too fast for the sonar. You're getting impatient, Burt. I don't know if it's to get this done or if you just
can't wait to get to the bar. But you've been going too damn
fast for the sonar and the magnetometer. We'll never find
anything this way."

He put the engine into neutral. "I'm not in a hurry for the
next drink," he said. He squinted, as he often did when feeling belligerent, then opened a side storage compartment and
pulled out a pint of Jim Beam, taking a large slug of it.

Cat's impulse was to fling the bottle into the sea, but she
restrained herself—barely. "Do you want me to help you
with this?"

"I'm the captain here—Lieutenant."

"And I'm the one who's going into that deep, dark water."

He wiped his mouth with the back of his hand. The veins were very prominent. She stiffened as he put his arm around her waist. "I'm sorry, Cat. I just don't have very long, you know."

"You're not going to die tomorrow, Burt. We've only just started. This could take weeks. Now, come on." She moved from his grasp, but then gave him an affectionate pat on the shoulder. "You have time enough to do this last row on the grid again, Cap'n. Slowly this time."

Burt put the bottle back into the storage bin. "Okeydoke," he said, engaging the engine and moving the throttle ever so slowly forward. The *Roberta June* shuddered and turned back onto the course they had just finished. The big boat seemed as reluctant as her skipper.

Westman and his Ocean City police captain friend went into the department's computer section, intruding upon a sergeant who was sitting back in his chair, eating a sandwich.

"Yes, sir," said the man, still chewing.

"The Coast Guard here says there's been a spike in auto thefts in the area—Philly, Wilmington, Baltimore, maybe Delmarva too. Can you get me some numbers?"

"Yes, sir. What's going on?"

"I think the bridge terrorists may be responsible for some of them," Westman said. "I'd like to map the locations, and I'm particularly interested in where the most recent ones took place."

"It'll take a while," the sergeant said.

"An hour?"

"Maybe."

"I'll go for a drive."

Turko had forgotten the exact distance from the power plant that passing vessels were required to stay under the new

Homeland Security rules now in force. He estimated what might be a half mile and decided to stick to that, approaching the facility on a parallel course from the south and maintaining his speed, so it would not seem he was making a reconnaissance.

"It looks so big from the water," the Iraqi said.

"It is big," said Turko.

"How can we do this?"

"It will be easy. Easier than knocking down the World Trade Center."

"Those men died."

"We won't."

Turko had made the Uzbeks sit on the side of the pontoon boat facing the shore, so they could look at the plant without seeming to be paying it particular attention. He asked them if they noticed the little jetty poking from the shore and the chain-link fence on top of it that extended far out into the water. A small motorboat with a low profile was sitting just to the left of this obstruction.

"If you come up fast to the right of that fence, you'll have them at a disadvantage," he said, speaking in Russian. "They'll have to come all the way around it to get at you—and you can get them when they do."

One of them nodded. The other merely stared.

"I'm going to teach you how to run this boat now," Turko said to the Uzbek he considered the brighter. "It's really very simple."

The man nodded again, then got up to take the controls from Turko.

Westman came upon three Sun and Fun stores during his drive and stopped in each, showing clerks his badge and ID and then the facsimile of Bertolucci's driver's license photo. He got recognition from the manager of the third store, a young man barely out of his teens who needed a shave.

"Yeah, I remember him. He spent a lot of time picking out clothes and sunglasses."

"What kind of clothes?"

"Not cool." He pointed to a rack with brightly patterned T-shirts.

"Do you remember anything specific?"

"No, sir. Just that he looked kinda like a dork, only he didn't."

"He did or he didn't?"

"Like his clothes didn't go with his face. He had a kinda mean face, like someone you wouldn't want to mess with."

"Did he pay with a credit card?"

"Don't think so. No, with cash."

"Thank you."

No one at the liquor store nearest the murder scene here remembered Bertolucci or his purchase of two half-gallons of vodka. Westman left them a snitch card in case the suspect came by again.

Lieutenant Dewey leaned back against the bulkhead on the *Manteo*'s bridge, leaving command to Lieutenant J.G. Kelleter as they made their way back down Delaware Bay from the Memorial Bridge.

It had been a dull day. They'd picked a couple of incoming ships at random to board and inspect, finding nothing. Dewey seldom bothered with small pleasure craft as long as they were operating legally and obeying the new emergency regulations. But he'd stopped several of those as well, keeping in mind the stash of narcotics found aboard the salvaged motor-sailor—keeping in mind the dead face of the girl washed up on the beach south of Henlopen.

There had been nothing amiss with any of the small craft, except for some excessive drinking aboard a cabin cruiser. The bos'n in charge of the boarding party had written out a citation, much to the crusier skipper's annoyance.

Now Dewey was tired, and interested mostly in getting back to port and his wife. As none of the craft he encountered on the homeward leg were exhibiting suspicious behavior, he left them unmolested.

"That's a funny place to be fishing," Kelleter said. DeGroot came up beside him.

Dewey looked up and then to where their attention was focused—noting a white pontoon boat with a green awning standing off the Jersey shoreline in deep water. The lieutenant moved to the port side of the bridge, raising his binoculars.

"They have to stay clear of that power plant—a thousand yards," said Dewey.

"But they're not going to catch any fish out there in the channel. They oughta head downstream and find a place to get close to shore where the rocks and fish holes are."

A burst of white water appeared at the stern of the pontoon boat.

"He must have heard you," said Dewey. He lowered the glasses and hung them back on their hook. "I wonder what Westman's up to today."

Bear Gergen watched Railroad Bob shuffle along the wharf, thinking the black man was simply passing by on one of his mysterious missions. He was an old fellow who had been a longshoreman until a crane had dropped a crate on him. He had had a cheekbone bashed in and a leg broken so badly that, two decades later, he still walked with the limb dragging behind him, giving him something of a snail's gait. Improbably, he earned his living—paid sometimes in money and sometimes in drink—running errands along the waterfront.

He slept in the railroad yards—no one was ever sure where—and spent his days hanging around waterfront bars. It was there that he got his assignments and there where he spent his income.

To Gergen's surprise, Bob turned at the steps leading down to the dock where Gergen's tug was moored, descending them sideways. He stopped at the stern, waiting, not wishing to come aboard.

Shaking his head, Bear got up from his chair and went aft, pausing only to snatch up a can of beer for Bob. The man accepted it thankfully and thirstily, popping the top and gurgling down several big swallows before speaking.

"What's happenin', Bob?"

"You know Homer?"

"Sure I know Homer."

"He wants to see you."

"Why did he send you? Why didn't he come himself?"

"He wants to see you where no one can see him seein' you."

"And where's that?"

"You know that big Dumpster down the alley from his place, the one beside the railroad embankment?"

"Yeah. I used to think you lived in that thing."

Railroad Bob had a bad eye with a lid that drooped over it. He had beer froth on his lip, which was bisected by a scar that continued down his chin. Gergen looked away.

"Some nights I does," said Bob. "Homer, he wants you to come talk with him behind that Dumpster."

"When?"

"He's waitin' now."

Westman took a seat at a vacant desk in the police station squad room, spreading out the computer printout the sergeant had made for him and opening a road atlas beside it.

He eliminated the thefts where the vehicle had not been recovered—usually a sign that the thieves were professional and that the cars had gone directly to chop shops. He also ignored those that bore signs of teens joyriding, including beer cans and the remains of marijuana joints.

Cases in which the vehicle had been recovered in a reasonably clean and intact state he circled. He numbered them in chronological order. Transferring the information to the road map, he sat a long while pondering the pattern that had emerged, then reached for the phone.

Agent Kelly answered his cell phone on the fourth ring, just before the message recorder would have kicked in.

"Yeah?"

"It's Westman. Are you still in Ocean City?"

"No. I'm way the hell over in Cambridge, Maryland. Payne got a tip, but it didn't pan out."

"Well, I am in Ocean City, at the police station, and I've got something better than a tip."

"A lead on Bertolucci?"

"Of a sort. There's been a jump in auto thefts in Philadelphia, Wilmington, and Baltimore. I've had a compilation made. When you eliminate the probable chop shop and youthful offender jobs, there's a pattern. In several cases, the abandoned car was found near the location of a subsequent theft."

"What makes you think it was Bertolucci?"

"Hunch mostly," Westman said. "But there's logic to it."

"Have they made a fingerprint match with the car we recovered from the OC murder scene?"

"No. Maybe you guys can do that."

There was a pause. "I'll need Payne's okay. And, once again, I'd better not bring you into it."

"Don't. I'll have the Ocean City police call Payne and suggest it."

"Good idea."

"You may want to move your command center."

"Why?"

"The most recent thefts were in Philadelphia and Wilmington."

"Delaware River."

"Right."

"Think they may be after the Memorial Bridge?"

"It's something to worry about."

Homer was using the privacy afforded by the Dumpster to relieve himself. Gergen waited for the bar owner to finish before approaching.

"What do you want, Homer?"

The other paused to zip up his pants, looked around the edge of the Dumpster to make certain they were alone, then turned to face Gergen.

"I got a buyer for some C-4," Homer said.

"I know," said Gergen. "I sent him to you."

"Why? You keep a shitload of that stuff."

"I don't like that guy. He gives me the creeps. I don't think he's going to use it for some bank job. I want nothing to do with him."

"But I don't know where else I can get it. Not as quick as he wants."

"Sorry," said Gergen. "No, thanks."

"I'll split my cut with you."

Gergen shook his head and turned to go.

"Wait," said Homer. "I got an idea."

"What's that?"

"He don't need to know where I got it."

"What do you mean?"

"Let me take it from you and tell him I got it from somebody else."

Gergen screwed up his face in thought. "How much are you asking?"

"A few thousand."

"I want five thousand. More if you can get it."

"Okay."

"Just like that?"

"I don't like him either. I just want him to go away."

Gergen nodded. "All right. I'll have Roy Creed drop off a

package. Leave it in your alley. Five A.M. You put the money out back in the usual place."

"I won't have the money until I give him the C-4."

Gergen thought again. "Yeah, okay. You get it to me as soon as he's gone."

"Right."

"And let me know if he tells you what he's going to do with it."

"It's a deal."

Gergen was not about to shake hands with him. "Later."

Homer stopped him again. "The guy wants something else, Bear."

"And just what the fuck is that?"

"Automatic weapons."

Gergen shook his head, and moved on. "See you around, Homer."

The sun was sinking into the thick yellow haze in the west, suffusing everything with a golden glow. They were at last heading home. Cat was at the helm, as she had been for most of the afternoon's search. Burt sat hunched over the sonar screen, moving so little she feared he might have fallen asleep.

They'd gone over the second grid as carefully as Cat could manage. She'd had to double back a few times because of the drift, but she was sure she'd covered a good square mile of water.

The sonar had detected nothing—no lawn chairs, no rowboats, no anything. At the end of the last run, she'd idled the engine and they'd talked it over. There was little to be gained in trying to cover any more ground at that hour. They'd have to come back the next day no matter what. Burt had nodded glumly, giving Cat the feeling he wasn't sure of that at all. As she shifted gear into forward again, she was all of a sudden gripped with the strange idea that they might not come back at all.

Her calculations had been off. They must have been. So had his. Repeating their folly would gain them nothing. She was wasting his time and hers by encouraging him. She should get on to Iowa, FAA permitting, and be done with it.

Steering the *Roberta June* out to sea a little, she took a bearing to the right of the Henlopen light to avoid Chicken Shoals. She held the speed slow, keeping down the wake.

"What are you doing, Cat?" Burt said, lifting his head from his sonar screen.

"Just keep your eyes glued to that thing until we're past Deepkill," she said. "No reason to waste this last pass over it."

She kept her own attention fixed dead ahead. There were a couple of fishing boats approaching from the north, heading down the shore to spend the night at work. A container ship, low in the water, was steaming in from the east, its forecastle turning yellow-gold as it made its slow turn toward the mouth of Delaware Bay.

Cat wondered if Westman had called her house. She had meant to buy a new answering machine but had put it off to save money. They'd be back in time for dinner, if he was nearby. She restrained an impulse to push the throttle up to full speed.

When they had passed the Deepkill shoal on the seaward side, she did just that, only to have Burt shout at her.

"Cut the engines!"

She did so instantly. "What's wrong?"

"Nothing's wrong."

"Then why . . ."

"I think we've found it."

For a long moment, Cat did not and could not speak. His words had stunned her like a blow to the head.

He had spoken them carefully, deliberately, without excitement, but with grave certainty.

Yelling to Joe Whalleys to drop anchor, Cat went to look at Burt's sonar. She leaned close to the screen, her neck hurting from the angle. The bright silhouette seemed just the right shape and dimension. Cat began to wish it didn't.

Returning to her chair, she gazed at him somberly. "What do you want to do?"

"It's late. We can probably get a good fix on this position and come back tomorrow."

"Did we get a reading on the magnetometer?"

He checked the paper roll in the device. "Yes, ma'am. Nice sharp spike in the pattern."

Turning back to the steering console, she checked the depth finder. "Forty feet of water, Burt."

"Almost into Deepkill Slough." He lighted a cigarette.

Cat could sense Amy's eyes upon her. "All right. Let's take a look. If it seems promising, we'll come back tomorrow for a longer visit."

"You sure?"

"I want to get this done, Burt."

"We could get help. Maybe that Coast Guard friend of yours."

The sun was setting. "Let's just do it."

Westman's next contact with local law enforcement occurred on Highway 1 between Bethany and Rehoboth. He was driving well over the fifty-five-mile-an-hour limit when a Delaware state cop pulled him over just north of Savage's Ditch Road. Summertime was when the otherwise tax-free state government refilled its coffers with traffic-citation revenue. With the bridge incident reducing the tourist flow so sharply, the highway cops were hungry for victims. Westman's speeding would cost him time.

He had his license, registration, and Coast Guard Investigative Service badge and ID card in hand by the time the trooper reached his open window.

"You're law enforcement?" the trooper asked, surprised.

"Yes. I've been working with units from your department for several days now."

"Working on what?"

"The Bay Bridge case. And the three homicides who turned up on the beach."

The trooper examined the identification card carefully. "Just wait in your car, please."

He went back to his own vehicle, calling the situation in. He soon returned, handing back the items.

"You working those cases now?" the trooper asked, remaining by the window.

"Yes."

"You don't have emergency lights you can turn on?"

Westman restrained his irritation. "That would kind of defeat the purpose. I have a dashboard light, but I reserve that for making actual arrests."

"Well, you know you're setting a bad example here."

Westman took a deep breath. "Yes. Sorry."

"Okay. You're free to go."

Pulling back into traffic, Westman watched the police cruiser cross the median strip and head back south. When the car was out of sight, Westman moved the Cherokee back up to sixty-five.

He left Highway 1 at the Lewes turnoff. There were no vehicles in front of either Cat's house or her neighbor Burt's. Westman's knock at her door went unanswered. He returned to his car, sat a long moment, then drove back to the highway, heading for Wilmington.

In relating the exploits of his hero, undersea archaeologist Bob Ballard, Westman had told Cat about the shoes.

Tannic acid made leather resistant to the sea life that consumed the bodies and bones and clothing of those who went to watery graves. As a consequence, the last surviving vestige of many a human fallen to the sea bottom was his or her shoes. Westman said they were numerous in the eerie debris field extending outward from the sunken *Titanic*—a pair here, a pair there; women's shoes, children's shoes, lying neatly together where their owners had come to their final rest.

"That's all that was left of them," Westman said. "The shoes of the dead."

The image had haunted her ever since.

She had it in mind as she slipped into the water off the *Roberta June*'s aft ladder, holding her legs close together. Cat carried three sources of illumination—her headlamp, a handheld light she had clipped to her belt, and a portable, battery-powered flood lamp she intended to set down off to the side to create a backlight and a sense of dimension.

Reaching bottom, she moved quickly to place the flood lamp, then turned to orient herself.

It was then she saw the pair of shoes, just in front of her. They looked to be hiking boots or workman's shoes. One lay on its side. The other, curiously, was set as though its owner was standing in it. She shuddered to think what might have happened to him. The shoes were close together. They hadn't just been dropped. They might have been there since World War II, when German submarines were sinking merchant vessels all up and down this coast.

She shuddered. Perhaps the shoes' owner had died unconscious, terribly injured. Perhaps he'd been already dead.

Hundreds, even thousands, had perished in these waters over the centuries. The Dutch and British had fought a nasty little war here over possession of Lewes in the 18th century. If one believed in ghosts, one could imagine many of them down here.

When she had gone diving in the Caribbean and the Gulf of Mexico, it was in warm, clean, impossibly clear water. Whether scuba diving or snorkeling, she'd always had the sensation of flying—more of one sometimes than she had behind the controls of an airplane.

Not so now. This was like burrowing, crawling in darkness—as good as being underground, as being buried.

Keeping to the sandy bottom, she slowly advanced, her eyes focused downward but seeing little, finding her way as much with her feet as with her eyes. It occurred to her she was adopting the ways of deep-sea creatures.

She groped along for about fifty feet, as far as the line she was tied to would permit. Looking up, she could barely make out the shape of the *Roberta June* above her. The boat's anchor chain, at the other end, was totally obscured.

Turning back toward the slack of her lifeline, she moved along the bottom a little faster, again going to the length of the rope. Finding nothing, she wondered at her next course, then began making a slow circle, like a yard dog on its tether, keeping the line taut.

Again nothing.

Having no better idea, she commenced an aimless wandering of the area within the circle, discovering, of all things, another lawn chair.

Finally, she came back to the shoes. She began to cry, the salt from the tears irritating her eyes beneath her face mask. Unable to rub them clear, she began to curse.

Three tugs on the line was the signal for them to haul her back aboard. Cat moved closer to the boat to obtain sufficient slack. Her second step brought sharp pain. She looked down, turning both headlamp and handheld light on the cause.

There was a sizable length of old metal visible in the sand, clearly only a portion of a larger bulk that lay beneath. The metal was oddly corroded. Looking very close, she saw that it had grown a thin layer of metal fur. When she touched it, there was a stinging sensation. She yanked her hand back.

Cat had brought a long, plastic-handled fishing knife

down with her. Taking it from its sheath, she knelt close to the strange, large metal object and began scraping sand away. She couldn't tell which end of the thing she was moving toward, but she kept on. Within a few minutes, she'd exposed four or five feet more of metal, which she found smoother now. After another minute or so, the knife blade struck a sharp edge, perpendicular to the longer piece. Scraping at it, she exposed what appeared to be a flange. Cleaning off more, she realized she had come upon some sort of tail assembly.

Then she realized what it was. The most destructive weapon ever devised by man—contained in this simple metal tube.

She'd done her job. This was all she had needed to do. She could leave now. She wouldn't ever have to go near this thing again. But there was one more task to deal with before she surfaced.

Scraping away more sand, she uncovered a bar that ran from one tail fin to another. Detaching the line from her belt, she tied one end tightly to the tail assembly. Pushing herself away, she removed her weight belt and let it fall to the sand. With a few kicks, she began to ascend. Cat was amazed how much light was gone from the sky when she reached the surface.

Joe Whalleys, with surprising strength, helped her up the ladder and onto the boat. Burt was watching her intently, a grin frozen on his face.

"Well?"

She grinned wearily. "It's there."

"You're sure?"

"Damn sure. I touched it. I attached my lifeline to it." She turned, looking to where the rope was tied to the aft winch. "Do you have a float of some kind?"

Amy stepped forward. "There's an old mooring can below."

"That'll do splendidly." Cat went aft and undid the knot, removing the line from the winch. She tied it strongly to the round metal float, which she then lowered over the side. It didn't sink.

"Won't that look suspicious?" Burt was observing from the rail.

"I doubt anyone's going to notice it this far out. They won't know what it's for, even if they do. Anyway, the tide's low. High tide, it'll be below the surface."

"Maybe you're right."

"Damn straight I'm right." Still in her gear, Cat sat down upon the deck, leaning wearily back against the rail. She felt now incapable of taking a single further step.

Burt's grin broadened. "Less than a week."

"What?"

"We've done it in less than a week. It's a miracle."

"You don't think my superb piloting and navigation skills had anything to do with it?"

Burt went to the storage compartment and took out his pint bottle, this time with two plastic cups, which he set out on the control console and filled. Then he took out two bottles of Heineken from the cooler, giving Amy and Joe each one. When everyone had a drink in hand, he raised his cup to the sea.

Cat looked at him over the rim of her cup as she drank.

"It's a miracle," he said.

Chapter 22

They tied up in twilight. Lewes, strangely, was thronged now with summer tourists moving along the embankment, though Cat had no notion of where they might have come from. Perhaps they'd been reassured by the police reports claiming that nearly all the bombing suspects had been killed.

After turning off the *Roberta June*'s engine, she could hear the visitors' laughter coming from the outdoor restaurants upriver. As they made fast the aft line, a couple of overweight men in T-shirts and baseball caps approached, asking if the boat would be taking out fishermen the next day.

"Sorry," said Burt. "Not tomorrow. There are some good head boats up by the Savannah Street bridge, though."

He shook his head after the two had gone. "Don't know when I'm going fishing again." He brightened. "You want to celebrate, Cat? A dinner at the Buttery?"

It was the finest restaurant in the town, comparable to what one might find in New York—with prices to match.

"All four of us?" asked Amy, stepping near Burt in assertive fashion.

"Hell, yes," Burt said. "And it's on me."

"I need a long shower, after all that time in the wet suit," Cat said. "I'll meet you there—if you can get a table."

"You all right, kid? You don't look so happy."

"I'm fine. Just a little beat. Let me freshen up and I'll be Miss Congeniality again."

She drove the Wrangler back to her house as fast as she dared, but for no good reason. There was no Grand Cherokee in her yard or on the street, and no note stuck in her door. Opening it, she looked through the mail that had been pushed through the slot, finding no note there either.

There was a letter, though, very official. Her heart leapt a little as she saw it was from the Navy. Her immediate fear was that the Federal Aviation Administration had tipped them to her misadventure involving theft of aircraft and multiple violations of flight regs. The admirals would be informing her that her request for a reinstatement hearing had been rejected out of hand.

She read the letter with great amazement. They were giving her a hearing.

Dropping the letter on the hall table, she went into her kitchen, dug out the home telephone number of her lawyer from a drawer full of various notes and scraps of paper, and hastily called him—overjoyed to find him home.

"I got a copy," he said. "It looks good."

"How's that?" Cat asked. She was feeling a little dizzy.

"Your flight commander attacked another female Naval officer."

"Anyone I know? A pilot?"

"No. She was a ship's officer. It was a case of date rape, much like yours, only this time there were witnesses. He tried for an Article 15, but he's going to get a court-martial. You may even be called as a witness."

"Roger that."

"We need to get together on your hearing. As soon as you can."

Cat stared blankly through the window at the small pine tree in the backyard. A small bird burst from it, flying high.

"I need a couple of days."

"Catherine. We need to call some witnesses ourselves. That woman who joined your squadron the same time you did. She's a lieutenant commander now."

"I'll get you some names. But I've got to stay out here at least another day."

"You're sure?"

"I'm helping a friend of my father's with something. It's important."

"Okay. I guess. Catherine?"

"Yes?"

"You've not gotten into any trouble since your discharge?"

She decided on an oblique defense. "No one's informed me of any officially."

He paused. "Let's keep it that way. And until this is over, no dates with Naval officers."

"How about Coast Guard?"

"What?"

"A joke."

"Not a laughing matter, Catherine."

"One more thing. If we win, will I get to fly again?"

The lawyer hesitated. "That's not the issue."

"It is with me."

"This hearing is about your reinstatement in the Navy."

"I think my flight commander's the one who had me grounded for that mishap."

"That mishap has been investigated and findings made. It's not the issue here, Catherine."

"Do you mean they won't let me fly?"

"Let's wait until we get you reinstated before we start worrying about that."

"Okay."

"If you can be in my office the day after tomorrow, that would be good."

"Okay."

After hanging up, she stood in the middle of the room for a long while, overwhelmed by her uncertainty. To her surprise, tears came into her eyes. She wiped them away and went upstairs, turning the shower as hot as she could stand it.

Utterly clean, she pulled on a pale-blue blouse and khaki skirt, slipped back into her Top-siders, and drove back to the river, stopping first at the Lighthouse Restaurant.

It was quite full, but there was no tanned, gray-haired Coast Guardsman to be seen. She stopped the cocktail waitress and asked after Erik, but he apparently had not been in.

Thanking the woman, Cat went back outside, crossing over the drawbridge and heading for the cheerful Victorian house that housed the Buttery Restaurant.

Westman was a complete stranger to the Wilmington police force, but they welcomed him to their headquarters as just another cop "on the job" when he showed them his ID. The lieutenant serving as watch commander this time was particularly friendly after Westman explained he was working on the bridge-bombing case. He was a dark-haired Irishman named Connelly, who said he'd been a military policeman in the Army. Always glad to help out the Coast Guard, he said.

Erik showed him the computer-generated image of Bertolucci. "This is our only suspect."

Connelly examined the image carefully. "How come the FBI hasn't put this out?"

"Wrong-headedness. They're afraid the guy will flee the country if his picture was out."

"May I make a copy?"

"You bet."

Connelly gave it to a sergeant to take to the copier. "Mind if we scan it into the computer system?"

Westman thought on that. The immediate result would be the FBI's learning that the picture had been disseminated—without authorization. The police lieutenant would have no choice but to tell the Bureau where he got it. Westman would be in big trouble.

He didn't work for the Justice Department. He could probably count on Joan dePayse to run interference for him. As should please her, this had nothing to do with hydrogen bombs.

"Go ahead," Westman said. "What's worrisome is that the perp doesn't seem to have left the area. The Bureau got his prints off a rental car he abandoned down in Ocean City, and a hour or so ago I was told that they made a match with some prints taken off a stolen car they recovered a few days ago in Philadelphia."

He showed the lieutenant his computer printout on area auto thefts and the accompanying map.

"I think there's a pattern here," Westman said. "If this is the same guy, he's been busy. He's hasn't fled the area and he hasn't gone deep underground. My fear is that he's up to something, and that he may not be alone."

Connelly was scanning the list. "A couple of Wilmington cars in here."

"That's why I'm here."

The lieutenant looked up. "Have a seat. Can I get you a cup of coffee?"

Gergen had been expecting the late-night visit. He wasn't certain if Enrique Diller himself was among the visitors, but he hoped so.

You could drive up to the section of dock where Gergen moored his tug, but you couldn't drive by. Not close up, at any rate, because the parallel street was way back from the water. An intruder had to turn into a large yard, proceed down a lane invariably bordered by ship's containers, conduct his business, and then make a sharp U-turn to effect his escape.

If Diller's people had been smart, they would have sought a different time and place for an attack—say, when Bear was in a bar or down at the marine dock refueling his boat. They would have used sharpshooters' rifles to make certain of a hit.

But these clowns were not smart. Like so many in the drug trade, they relied simply on firepower, indulging themselves with a big show. Gergen had done ambushes all over the world. These guys would be easy meat.

Ever since phoning in his tip on the goodwill ambassadors Diller had sent to join him in that bar, Bear had kept a lookout by the street at all times and, at night, stationed a second man among the containers near his tug. Everybody had a cell phone and an automatic pistol.

He could have used a couple more troops—including especially his cousin. Leonard had declined to help out that night, using the entirely plausible excuse that he was too stoned to walk straight, let alone drive his motorcycle all the way up from Ocean City.

Gergen's cell phone rang at 9:47 P.M. He looked at his watch as he reached to answer it.

"It's Roy," said Creed, who was in the pickup truck. "Got a big black SUV comin' your way fast. No lights."

Bear grabbed his Glock and a boat whistle, which he blew on three times in quick succession. Then, still in his skivvies, he clambered topside and flung himself on the dock, taking cover behind some large coils of hawser line.

The vehicle made the turn too fast, skidding a little as it bumped onto the rougher pavement of the cargo yard. Straightening, it headed straight for the tug, its engine noise reverberating off the metal sides of the containers.

Gergen had instructed his men well. The first thing was to take out the driver. What followed could be considered mopping up.

Mickey Ambrose, the man he'd stationed by the containers, caught the driver with a head shot just as he was slowing to make his U-turn by the edge of the dock. One of the gunmen on the right side of the SUV was leaning out the window, preparing to rake the tug with automatic fire. Bear popped him with two body shots.

The big vehicle swerved, and for a moment Bear feared it was going to do a roll right off the dock and onto his boat, which hadn't been part of his plan. Instead, it careened around in a circle and piled head-on into the container opposite. One of the Diller guys in the backseat was thrown forward. His head hit something and he snapped back, then stopped moving. The fourth and last clown made a break for it, pausing to fire off a quick burst in an aimless way at the tug, breaking some glass. Then he ran. Roy Creed picked him off from the truck.

Bear hurried to the SUV—a big Lincoln Navigator like the last one. The guy in the back was still alive. Gergen put a round in him and then he wasn't.

"What do you want to do, Bear?" asked Ambrose.

Gergen thought, quickly, as he waited for Creed to come up.

"That last one dead?" Bear asked.

"Real dead."

"We've got to get them out of here. Port security's going to be here in a minute and the cops won't be long after."

Bear looked to the side of the man he had just shot. There was what looked to be a Mac-10 or an Uzi on the seat and two more and some extra clips on the floor. The man next to the driver had one of the weapons as well.

He turned to Ambrose. "Get all these weapons and get them aboard the tug. You know those body bags I stole from the Navy?"

These had come in handy. Some of the wrecks Gergen had salvaged had had corpses aboard.

"Yeah. They're in the forward bin with the foul-weather gear."

"Put the guns in one of 'em. Get a line around it. Tie it to the aft ladder and drop it overboard. Fast!"

He moved to follow orders without another word. Bear turned to Creed. "Put that stiff in here with the others and drive them the hell out of here. Fast. You know that abandoned wharf downriver? Past the refinery?"

"Sure."

"How deep's the water off that thing?"

"Fifteen feet at least."

"I want this SUV on the bottom. Leave the windows open so it'll sink fast and the fishes get a chance for some dinner." He turned to his remaining crewman, Benny Adamouskas. "You follow him in the pickup truck. Don't come back here until morning. Now move!"

Connelly had Westman sit next to him as he made a computer check for auto thefts in the Philadelphia-Wilmington-Camden area for that day. There were several, but nothing that fit Westman's profile. Making statewide checks, he found something of interest in the New Jersey report and pointed to an entry on the screen.

"This might be something."

Westman leaned close. "A Mitsubishi was recovered in Atlantic City."

"Stolen from the Amtrak parking lot a day ago. But look at this."

Two brand-new entries, both from Atlantic City. "They recovered two other stolen vehicles there?"

"No, sir," said the lieutenant. "Two vehicles were stolen from there. Just an hour ago. Not long after they found that Mitsubishi."

Westman squinted at the screen. Auto thefts were not his forte.

"A Dodge minivan and a Subaru Forester—taken within fifteen minutes of each other."

"How far from the Mitsubishi?"

"Can't be more'n a few blocks. AC isn't that big."

"If it is him, he's moved to New Jersey."

"And he has friends now. At least one. Can't drive both cars at once."

Westman leaned back. "What's in South Jersey? Aside from the other end of the Delaware Memorial Bridge."

"A lot of chemical plants. A couple of nuclear power plants. And Atlantic City."

"Those casinos are more secure than the White House."

"Maybe the Boardwalk." Connelly shrugged. "Maybe these auto heists have nothing to do with your Mr. Bertolucci."

A uniformed officer stuck his head through the doorway. "Excuse me, Lieutenant. We got a report of shots fired down at the wharf."

Connelly grinned. "Second time this week."

"Not just a couple, Lieutenant. Many shots."

"Are you okay, Cat? You having problems from the water pressure?"

She raised her eyes from her wine, from which she had only taken a small sip. "I have a little headache. I'm all right."

Burt was seated on the opposite side of the table from her, with Amy on his right. It wasn't the best part of the restaurant, but they hadn't had a reservation, and counted themselves lucky. Burt was eating with a better appetite than she had seen in all her time in Lewes, though Joe Whalleys was outdoing everyone in the volume of food consumed. He'd even asked for a second serving of mashed potatoes.

She took another sip of her wine, which was delicious.

This dinner would cost her entire food budget for a month. She supposed Burt could afford this one indulgence. She hoped so.

He and Amy were holding hands under the table. Cat was happy for them, but not really happy.

"I'm sorry," she said, pushing back her chair. "I'm going to the head. Be right back."

Burt nodded, his concern still evident.

Slipping carefully out the front door, she ran the block to the river and then over the bridge, not slowing until she was in the gravel parking lot of the Lighthouse. Collecting herself, catching her breath, fighting back a bit of dizziness, she walked the rest of the way to the front door.

He still wasn't there. She looked into all the rooms and out on the deck. It was too humiliating to ask the cocktail waitress again if he'd been by.

There were four cop cars at the crime scene by the time Lieutenant Connelly and Westman got to the docks—but very little evidence of crime. Someone was playing a heavy-duty flashlight along the side of the tug. A window had been shot out.

Bear Gergen was talking to one of the uniformed policemen. Noticing Westman and Connelly, he came over.

"I'm sure glad to see you guys. Damn druggies. Like to have killed me." He squinted at Westman. "You're the Coast Guard man, right? Hard to see. You remember I dropped a dime on these guys from Philly? Well, they came down for some payback."

"You know for certain it was them?" Westman asked.

"No, I don't. But who else could it have been? They tried a drive-by, but it was a little hard with all these ship containers. I'm lucky."

"Nobody's hurt?" Connelly asked.

"No. We were all below. Three of us."

"You fire back?" Connelly asked.

"I'm not going to break the law, Lieutenant."

"Not even in self-defense?"

Bear folded his arms. "I've got a .38-caliber Smith and Wesson in the pilothouse, Lieutenant. Perfectly legal. You can examine it. Didn't fire a shot. I told you. We were below."

"Where'd they go?"

"North, I think. Up the street. Real fast. I'm surprised you didn't bump into them."

"What kind of car?"

"Black Lincoln Navigator. Just like the one they came calling on me in the last time."

"Automatic weapons?"

"Yeah. Sounded like AK-47's."

"How do you know that?"

"Twelve years in the Navy. Nine in the SEALs."

"Why didn't you call the police?"

"I did. I called it in." He took a step closer. "You gonna give me some protection? They could come back."

"I'll ask," said Connelly, making a few quick notes himself. "You're sure nobody's hurt?"

Gergen nodded. "You gonna go arrest Diller? Go to Philly?"

Connelly shook his head. "My authority stops at the state line. I'll inform Philly PD, though."

"How about you, Coast Guard?"

"Already have a case," said Westman.

Joe Whalleys, who had two desserts, drove home to his father's farm outside Georgetown in his beaten-up old Toyota pickup. Cat took Burt—which also meant Amy now—home in her Wrangler, declining his invitation for a nightcap.

She put the letter from the Navy in a desk drawer and then went into her living room. Inserting a Miles Davis CD in her old stereo, she then sank slouching into her favorite old chair by the open window. When the CD finished, she closed her eyes, listening to the sea.

Cat was just beginning to slip into sleep when she heard the knocking at her door.

She ignored it. She did not want to join in Burt and Amy's little party, or talk about the bomb, or even think about what had to be done the next day.

But the knocking came again. Finally, she rose and went to the door, prepared to fling it open and communicate to Burt that, this night at least, she would very much like to be left alone.

Instead, she opened it slowly, carefully, suddenly fearful that it might not be Burt at all.

It wasn't.

"I'm sorry to be so late," Westman said. "There were developments in my case. I was up in Wilmington."

"I don't mind." She opened the door fully.

Chapter 23

Westman awoke to the cool air and slanted sunlight of early morning, and the sounds of seagulls and the horn blasts of the first Lewes-Cape May ferry of the day. It was a pleasant way to return to consciousness, made all the more so by his memories and the presence of the beautiful, troubled woman lying next to him.

But then he realized she wasn't there. She had spent much of the night pressed warmly against his side, her head on his shoulder and her long blond hair flung across his chest. Now she was gone. He reached and touched the sheet, and found it cold.

Turning, he saw her seated in a chair by the window, a blanket around her shoulders.

"Are you all right?" he asked.

"Yes," she said quietly.

"Did I . . . ?"

"No, Erik. You have been wonderful. It's just that . . ."

"You have regrets."

"No. I had a dream about the bomb."

Westman sat up, his gaze steady upon her. "I guess that's not surprising."

"All that death, Erik, in such a small package. It's almost Biblical."

"I think they said something like that when they tested the first atom bomb at Los Alamos."

"I don't want to go down there again, Erik. I don't want to touch that thing again."

"You won't have to. Now that you've found it, the military will take over."

"They damn well better." She thought upon this a moment, then gave him a warmer look, then rose and came back to the bed, pulling the sheet over her long body and turning to face him. "Do you have to leave?"

"Soon."

"Not so soon," she said, moving closer.

Captain Baldessari wanted nothing more than to go for a run on Pickering Beach, which was what he usually wanted to do when he was working. He ran in the morning before reporting for duty, ran during his lunch hour, ran before going home, ran in the evening, and sometimes he ran late at night.

It was just past nine in the morning. Baldessari had two file folders on the desk in front of him—a slim one containing three typewritten letters and a thick and very musty one containing some very old and recently declassified reports. He decided to make a single file of it all, putting the three letters on top of the reports. Then he called Colonel Baker.

The colonel's desk was home to an array of grown-up toys, some of them electronic gizmos from the Sharper Image, some of them museum souvenirs, a few of them models of Air Force aircraft. Most prominent among these was a large-scale model of a B-1 bomber.

Baker had been a B-1 pilot. As far as nonpilot Baldessari had been able to determine, the B-1 was the least efficacious aircraft the Air Force had ever put on line. Brought in during the Reagan era at a price of $300 million a copy, the B-1 was supposed to have replaced the half-century-old B-52 as the service's main strategic bomber. There'd been crashes from the git-go. On a demonstration flight for members of Congress over Northern Virginia, a B-1 had lost two of its doors. The aircraft finally saw service in Kosovo, Afghanistan, and the Iraq War, but as an infantry weapon. They used it to kill tanks—a task at which A-10 Warthogs were far superior.

Baldessari remembered working a Pentagon news conference once at which a two-star general had been asked what the B-1, which had cost the taxpayers more than thirty billion dollars for the entire fleet, had been good for. Without hesitation, the general had said: "Deterence." Also without hesitation, an aviation writer had added: "The concept worked. The Russians were deterred from building anything like it."

Baldessari had not been surprised to learn that Baker had been a B-1 pilot.

"Captain," said the colonel as Baldessari approached his desk. "Is this really worth the bother?"

"Think so, sir."

Baker frowned.

"Okay. Have a seat. But make it short—and sweet."

Baldessari sat, set the thick file folder on the desktop, opened it, and started to hand the colonel one of the three letters. Baker waved it off.

"Just tell me," he said.

"I already did, I think, sir. The retired C-130 pilot who dropped a couple of H-bombs off Delaware Bay?"

"What?"

"Back in the sixties."

Baker had started to come forward in his chair. At the

word "sixties," he sank back again. "Oh, yeah. That guy. He wrote another letter?"

Baldessari held it up. "Yes, sir."

Because he had been a pilot, Baker would make general someday. Baldessari was a public affairs officer who wore glasses and had last flown an aircraft as a cadet in the Civil Air Patrol. He would be lucky to make lieutenant colonel.

"This makes three," Baldessari added.

"So what does he say this time?"

The colonel had picked up one of his Sharper Image toys—a handheld game that gave off tiny beeps.

"More or less the same thing. That he has reason to believe that one of two bombs he jettisoned off the mouth of Delaware Bay was armed—fitted with a plutonium core and trigger device."

"What do all those official files say?"

Baldessari pulled out the one that had arrested his attention.

"They say it was impossible for that to be the case. Those were Mark 28's. They were never armed during transport. The cores were shipped separately."

"Two bombs?"

"Yes."

"And how many cores arrived in Germany?"

Baldessari flipped through the pages.

"Doesn't say," he said.

"Does it say if anyone checked?" Baker was getting irritable.

"It says no information available, sir."

The little beeps ceased. "That's all?"

"Yes, sir."

"And they just let this go?"

Baldessari shrugged. "Apparently so."

"You got the guy's 201 file?"

"Yes, sir. Good record—up until the incident. Subsequent to that, he was grounded. Then separated from active duty."

"You mean pilot error was involved in that thing?"

"No, sir. Flight surgeon took him off the duty roster after the incident. He left the service a few months later."

Baker pursed his lips. "Booze?"

"Partly. They lost a member of the crew in that thing. The flight engineer."

The colonel sighed and set down his handheld game. "So what do you think?"

"I think we ought to listen to him. He called again this morning. Said he's found one of the bombs."

"You're kidding."

Baldessari shrugged. "I'm not, sir. If he's a nutcase, he didn't sound like it. He wants us to recover the object."

"We don't do that. The Navy does that." The colonel frowned. "How do you think it would go down with the public—and the Congress—our pulling up half-century-old H-bombs that could have been leaking radioactivity into seafood all this time?"

"They'd be nervous. Somebody in Congress would hold hearings."

"The chief of staff would be on my ass if that happened."

Baldessari wished the man would stop thinking aloud.

"Those files are classified?" Baker asked.

"Ours are. The pilot's aren't."

The colonel swiveled around to stare out his window. There was a gigantic C-17 rising slowly into the sky.

"Well, it really isn't a concern for this base, is it?"

"That C-130 was based here, sir."

The colonel swiveled back, picking up one of his model airplanes by its stand. "What do you think we ought to do?"

"I think we should talk to him, sir."

"Where is he?"

"Just down in Lewes."

Baker pressed his lips together hard, swiveling a few inches back and forth in his chair. "Can't we just send this file on to the Pentagon?"

"That's where it came from, Colonel—minus Captain Schilling's letters."

Baker came forward in his chair, opening a leather-bound appointment book. Baldessari knew the colonel had a golf game with the general in the afternoon and lunch with his wife just before that.

"Right," Baker said. "Do you suppose he could get up here by eleven?"

"I suppose so. He seemed anxious to see us."

"Then see to it. I don't have a lot of time to spare for this."

Bear Gergen walked in through the front door of Homer's grungy saloon with Roy Creed following behind him. The bar was empty except for a lone drunk still slumbering in a corner from the night before, but the two tugboat men made the place almost seem crowded. Homer was surprised to see them.

"Breakfast?" he asked.

Bear nodded. Homer poured two shots of whiskey, and then set out two steins of beer. Fetching two eggs from the refrigerator, he cracked them into the two steins and pushed the lot across the bar. Gergen sipped his whiskey, but Creed poured his shot into the beer and then drank the entire mix down, asking Homer for another but nixing a second egg.

"What're you doing here, Bear?" Homer asked.

"Changing my mind." He drank again, wrinkling his nose. The bar smelled of equal parts of spilled beer, vomit, urine, and ammonia.

"About what?"

"About your request, on behalf of your, uh, client."

"Yeah? So?"

"You put your garbage out last night."

"Yeah. Maybe this week they'll collect it."

"There's an extra bag out there. You might want to check it out." He finished the whiskey. "It's kinda heavy."

Homer pursed his lips, then nodded, understanding. "That's good."

"See if you can get more money."

"Okay."

"I want it at the boat by midnight. Send Railroad Bob with it."

"You got it."

Cat and Westman were having coffee in her kitchen when Burt came up the front steps and entered without knocking. Westman was dressed, but Cat was not. Giving Schilling a dark look as she pulled a dish towel around her, she went quickly upstairs, returning in shorts and T-shirt.

"If you're not careful, Captain Schilling, somebody's going to think you're a dirty old man."

Schilling had taken a seat and a cup of coffee for himself. "I'm sorry, Cat. I've got news. The Air Force wants to see us."

"Us?"

"Me. But you've got to come with me. You identified the thing. They might look at me as some sort of crazy man, but if you're along—anyway. It's just up in Dover. And . . ."

Cat smiled. "Calm down, Burt. Of course I'll go with you. This is what we've been waiting for, isn't it?"

"I hope so."

"When?"

"Today. Eleven o'clock."

She glanced at Westman, who was looking upon her amiably. "I'll go with you," Westman said.

Cat was surprised. "But you're on duty."

"Dover's on the way to Wilmington."

"I appreciate this," Burt said.

There was the slam of a screen door. In a moment, Amy appeared at Cat's front steps.

* * *

Turko had taken two rooms at the Atlantic City hotel—one for himself and the other for the two Uzbeks and the Iraqi. It was on the cheap side, but had a casino and a sort of night-club and there was cable television that included the Weather Channel among its offerings. Every ten minutes, they gave the local weather, a detailed forecast for the next two days, and a more general one for the week.

The winds were currently from the northeast, owing to a high-pressure center lingering over Washington. This was predicted to slide slowly eastward, changing the wind direction and raising temperatures above their summer norms. The change could occur within the next twenty-four hours.

If he was to go through with this, it would have to be now. Pec would be onto him with guns blazing if he let this opportunity slide.

Turko needed his weapons and explosives. It was an hour's drive to Wilmington and the bar where he hoped they would be waiting. He didn't want to drive there—didn't want to expose himself to either the U.S. authorities or Pec for that length of time before attempting the mission. But he didn't dare send any of his crew. The Uzbeks would get lost and end up in Perth Amboy.

He finished his vodka and Pepsi Cola, then mixed another. When that was gone, he would go.

The conference room was predictably utilitarian—gray metal-top table, blue-gray metal-frame chairs, walls painted a lighter shade of blue-gray, the only decoration a large, framed painting of a B-1 bomber in flight. Slatted blinds had been partially drawn against the sun. Though there was air-conditioning and the windows were tightly closed, aircraft engines were making a distracting noise.

The three visitors had been given seats along one side of the table. Colonel Baker and Captain Baldessari sat opposite them. An Air Force major from the Pentagon had taken a chair in the corner, which clearly bothered Schilling, the old C-130 pilot. He kept glancing over at the man, who was wearing aviator-style sunglasses indoors. The major had a shiny pair of pilot's wings on his chest, and his uniform was very sharply pressed, unlike either of the other officers.

Baker had the very thick, complete file on the bomb matter in front of him. He opened it and read something on the cover page, then sat back and eyed Schilling as he might a pile of rancid Brussels sprouts. Then, abruptly, he smiled. Your friendly neighborhood brass hat, extending hospitality to some of the nice citizens who paid his wages.

"I can't tell you anything new, Captain Schilling," he said, deciding not to treat the old man as a civilian, but as a military person of inferior rank. "This is a very old business, and nothing's changed, has it? This is just jettisoned ordnance. Ocean's full of it. Nothing in the record to indicate any danger or threat. Hasn't caused any kind of problem in nearly forty years. Everything's fine."

Burt opened his own file folder to its few contents. On top was a Xerox copy of the letter from his deceased copilot. He shoved it across the table. "Not fine. Sir."

Baker briefly studied it, then pushed it back.

"Right," he said. "You referred to this man in your other letters."

"My copilot, and he says the last bomb to go out had the plutonium core in it."

"He waited a long time to write you this."

"Yes, he did, but that doesn't change anything."

"And now he's dead."

"Yes, he is."

Baker leaned back in his chair. "You say you've found one of these bombs? Just off Cape Henlopen?"

"To the southeast of it. We've had it marked with a float. You can come and get it."

"You have a picture?" the major asked.

Cat cursed herself. It would have been easy to have taken

a photograph. A simple little detail she'd overlooked. And now it might cost them the Air Force's help.

"No, sir," she said. "Not yet."

The colonel's eyebrows lifted. "Do you have it marked on a chart?"

"Yes, sir. It's near Deepkill Slough."

"And you're sure this is the bomb that has the plutonium core?"

Burt shook his head. "Haven't gotten to the nose housing—yet. It's hard to tell."

Baker glanced at Cat, his eyes lingering.

"And you were the one who found the bomb?"

"Yes, sir."

He glanced at the visitor list Baldessari had given him. "Just who are you, Miss, er, McGrath?"

"She's my neighbor," Schilling said. "She's been helping me. She's a former Navy Tomcat pilot."

Baker seemed interested—too much so. Cat wished Burt hadn't brought that up.

"You a professional diver, miss?" said the major in the corner.

"No," said Cat. "It's just something I used to do."

"What do you do for a living?"

"I fly advertising banners along the beach. I may be taking a job with an airline in the Midwest."

"And you?" he asked Westman, taking an interest in him for the first time.

Westmant met the man's gaze. "I'm a friend."

"It says here you're with the Coast Guard."

"Coast Guard Investigative Service."

"You have jurisdiction in this case?"

"I'm just here as a friend. Nothing official. But I have some knowledge in the field of sea-bottom recovery and their contention sounds entirely reasonable. It's hardly the first time nuclear weaponry has gone into the ocean."

"Is that so?" the colonel said.

"And I can vouch for these people. They've been assisting me with a case I'm working on."

"And what is that, Warrant Officer Westman?"

"The attack on the Bay Bridge."

There was a silence. "Are you saying there's a connection?" the colonel asked.

"No, sir. But if there's a chance there could be in the future, I'd like to do everything possible to prevent that from happening."

Baker leaned back. "All right, Captain Schilling, what is it you'd like us to do?"

"You mean you'll help us?"

"Didn't say that. Don't know if I can. Tell me what you think we can do."

Burt scowled. "Like I said in all my letters. Get the goddamn thing out of the water. Help me find the other one and get that out too. We had no choice when we dropped them into the bay, but they shouldn't have been left there."

"Have you been in contact with the Navy?" said the major in the corner.

Burt scowled at him. "No."

Baker ignored Schilling's folder. "Our records indicate there's no problem. You say no one removed the trigger housing. All you have is a letter from a dead man, who had a hard-on against the Air Force for years." He grinned, but with no friendliness. "Just like you, Captain."

"Look, Colonel. That bomb came from this base. I flew it out of here. It's up to the base to get it back. It's up to you."

"Maybe if you could establish there's a nuclear core."

"You'd want me to come back here with a couple pounds of fissionable plutonium and dump it on your desk?"

"Captain, it's time to face facts. There is no plutonium. The Air Force would not have left these bombs down there if there was."

"You were going to leave a bomb with plutonium in it in the water at Palomares."

"I don't know anything about that," said the colonel. "Long before my time."

Burt gripped the edge of the table a moment, as if fighting back pain. Then wiped his eyes and turned them back on the colonel. "What if I were to go to the Wilmington paper with this?"

Baker colored. Before he could speak, the major in the corner intruded again.

"They'd call this base to check it out, being a responsible publication," the major said, "and we'd tell them that you're being treated at the Veterans Hospital for an alcohol-related medical condition."

Burt swore.

"It's true," the major said to Baker. "It's all in the records."

Cat stood up, putting her hand on Schilling's shoulder.

"Come on, Burt," she said. "This isn't getting us anywhere."

The colonel rose, relieved that the conversation seemed to be over. He'd try to leave them happy, or at least happier.

"Look, Captain. I understand your concern. I appreciate it. You're worried about the welfare of the local community, and so are we at this base. So is the entire Air Force."

Burt got to his feet, shoving his chair back. Westman was still seated.

"All right," Baker said. "I'll do this for you. I'll take it up with my boss. If he says okay, we'll make another check of the records."

"Records? You don't need records. Check out the bomb."

"Let us follow proper procedure, okay? Go through channels. This is the military, remember, Captain?"

Schilling just turned his back and started for the door.

"The papers in the file," said the major. "Those are originals?"

"Copies," snarled Burt, going through the door.

*　*　*

When the visitors had gone, the major came around to Baker's side of the table, taking up the file folder Captain Schilling had left.

"I'd better take that," he said. He nodded toward the thicker folder Baldessari had in front of him. "That one too."

Baldessari slid it to the other man carefully. It didn't matter. Following habit, he'd made copies of everything. Never once in his military career had he ever gotten chewed out for losing something.

"What next?" Baker asked.

"Nothing next," said the major. "Not for you. We'll take over from here. As far as this base is concerned, it's a dead issue. Case closed."

"But that guy's been hassling us for months. He's not going to stop."

"Colonel. We checked his records. He hasn't got long to live."

Chapter 24

Westman said good-bye to Cat and Schilling at the main gate of the base and drove north toward the Memorial Bridge, using his cell phone to call Dewey on the *Manteo*.

"Where are you?" he asked when the lieutenant came on the line. The connection was bad.

"Corson's Inlet," Dewey said.

"That's up the Jersey shore by Sea Isle City."

"Right."

"Something going on?"

"Rescue."

"Sorry. I shouldn't be bothering you when you're busy."

"Not busy. We recovered the boaters. Everybody survived."

"Where are you headed? I'd like to come aboard. I think our bad guys may hit something up Delaware Bay. The Wilmington police think so too."

Dewey hesitated. "Buzzard's Point was looking for you. They flashed me a few minutes ago."

"Who at Buzzard's Point?"

"Admiral dePayse."

"Did she say what's up?"

"No. Just that it's important."

Westman pulled off to the side of the road. "Thank you, Tim. Talk to you soon."

"Roger that."

Erik sat there, unwilling to make the call, for many minutes. But this was cowardice as bad as flinching under fire. Finally, irritably, he punched in the number, grateful when there was no answer.

Checking his own messages, he found two from Joan dePayse and a later one from his director.

The CGIS chief answered after only one ring. "Erik. I've been trying to reach you."

"That's why I'm calling, sir."

"You're being transferred."

"Sir?"

"TDY. To Portsmouth."

"What? Why?"

"Cargo-container case. Fifth District headquarters'll give you a fill."

"Where does this order come from?"

There was a pause as the director looked for something. "Admiral dePayse," he said.

When he called the lady again, her secretary answered. He was very blunt in his request.

Cat heard her phone ringing in the house as she turned off the Wrangler's engine. She ignored it for a moment, then leapt out of the car and bounded up her wooden steps—thankful for once that her caller was persistent. She answered after the sixth ring.

Her happiness at hearing Westman's voice did not last long. She spoke with him briefly, then returned the phone to its hook clumsily. Going to the door, she called to Schilling to come in. When he had taken a seat on the couch, she slumped down next to him, taking a deep breath before speaking. "I don't know how to tell you this, Burt. But the Air Force isn't going to help us."

"What are you talking about? We only just left them. They couldn't get through to the right people in the Pentagon in this short a time."

"That was Erik. They phoned the Coast Guard to check on his bona fides and the call got kicked up to this woman admiral who seems to rule his life. She told them the bomb story was fraudulent. She said we were crackpots who had hoodwinked him and that they shouldn't listen to us. Said we'd both been kicked out of the service and were trying to get back at the powers that be. And she's had him transferred to Portsmouth to work a case that has nothing to do with our bombs or even the bridge case or anything at all of any real consequence."

Burt mouthed an obscenity, sinking back, his sense of defeat overwhelming him completely. He seemed too weary even to speak.

"I'm sorry, Burt. He didn't make this up."

Schilling remained silent, his eyes turning to the kitchen, but lacking the will even to ask for a drink.

"Do you want a whiskey?" she asked. She rose, anticipating an affirmative answer.

"No. Not now." He recalled his manners. "Thanks, though."

She went to her front window. "What are you going to do?"

"We don't need them, Cat. All we have to do is get the thing to the surface. The water's not that deep. It's . . ."

"I'm not going back down there, Burt. Not for anything. I hate to say that. I don't want to make you any unhappier than you are now. But I just can't handle it. Landing F-14's on boats, that I think I can go back to. But hugging hydrogen bombs, I'm afraid not."

"You're sure?"

"As sure as death."

She wished she hadn't chosen those words, but appreciated their effect. He ceased further argument.

"I'll hire that salvage outfit. I can still sell the boat."

"You neither like nor trust that guy."

"Yeah. Well."

"What about you and Amy?"

"What do you mean?" He was becoming animated now—the color of life returning to his face.

"Aren't you two going to get married?"

"I said that?"

"You needn't have. It's seemed pretty clear to me you would." She put a hand on his arm. "I think it's great. But live or die, Burt, you've got to provide a means of support. And that's the *Roberta June*. Amy runs that boat better than you do. Certainly better than I do. Leave it to her, and she's got a chance. Otherwise, she'll be cutting bait the rest of her life. Maybe, if she's lucky, she might get a job waitressing. The Bridgeville diner or something." She shook his shoulder gently. "Burt, you can't sell your boat."

"And you won't help me. So what do I do?"

"You found the bomb. You told the Air Force where it is. You've done your job."

"Saying that won't get the damn thing off the sea bottom."

"Maybe that's the best place for it."

"I don't think you understand, Cat."

"Maybe not. But right now I've got a fight on my hands getting back into the Navy, and I may have another trying to keep my pilot's license. And I've got to get a job that will actually put food on the table. To put it simply, Burton Schilling, I've got better things to do." She stood up. "I'll get you that drink now."

"He's the guy who fucked this up, you know. Your pal Westman. Hadn't been for him, we might have gotten somewhere with those Air Force people."

"Not in a million years, Burt. They were just indulging you." She went into the kitchen.

"That Colonel Baker is a pilot. You and I are pilots. He would have helped us. Your friend Westman is what put him off—him and that lady admiral."

"He was trying to help you, Burt. Let's leave it at that."

She filled a glass half-full of bourbon, then added water from her tap. He never used ice.

He nodded thanks, then stood contemplating this refreshment, as though it played a role in some momentous decision. Then, to her amazement, he set that glass down on the counter.

"Later maybe," he said. "I appreciate it, Cat. Everything." He moved toward the door.

"Where are you going?" she asked.

"See a man about fishing nets."

Orders were orders, whoever gave them. With reluctance that bordered on a painful affliction, Westman drove the coast road back down to Ocean City, following a route that would take him to the southern end of the Delmarva Peninsula and across the mouth of Chesapeake Bay via the long bridge and tunnel. He'd be in Portsmouth in an hour.

He knew the commander there—a man he'd worked with in the Caribbean on drug cases years before. The container case he'd been assigned to now involved drugs as well. It was as routine as anything the Coast Guard had ever handled. The shipper of the containership was legitimate and respectable, well known to U.S. Customs. The drug shipment, nearly a million dollars' worth of coccaine, had obviously been placed in the container by someone else. It had turned up in a random search.

The investigation was to discover the intended recipient of the shipment, a discovery that Westman doubted would ever be made. Portsmouth could easily handle the case without him. It was a pointless misdirection of CGIS resources. It was an exile.

Coming to a familiar crossroads, he on impulse turned off the main highway onto an access road that led across the small Verrazano Bridge and the causeway to Assateague Island. Once on the other side, he drove past the Maryland state park that occupied the northern end of the long barrier-reef island. The state facility banned dogs, a prohibition that had long annoyed him. The National Park Service's Assateague Island National Seashore just to the south welcomed them. He continued on to the entrance to that substantial holding, pulling into a parking lot near the dune and beach.

There were few people in attendance, and only two dogs. Curiously, three of the wild ponies who inhabited the island had come down to the beach and settled down in the sand near the farthest reach of the waves, looking for all the world like vacationers. Westman smiled, the first time he had done so since talking to his director.

Moving down the beach a bit, he seated himself in the sand, drawing up his knees and resting his chin on his folded arms as he contemplated the sea—and his dilemma.

His relationships with Catherine McGrath and Joan de-Payse were simple matters. He was not going to let the Navy lady slip out of his life and he was not going to let Joan interfere with that—no matter what.

The question he had to resolve was his relationship with the Coast Guard, which he loved as well. He had never knowingly disobeyed an order in all his time in service. But the Coast Guard Investigative Service was conceived as an independent agency, and its investigators were properly not subject to outside orders. The transgression here was Admiral dePayse's. It was she who had crossed a line.

But it was she who could cause him and his agency considerable pain and suffering. Westman had to do what he thought best and right, but somehow without directly violating dePayse's instructions. He rang back his director, using his cell phone.

"You owe me thirty days leave, sir," he said. "I'd like to take it."

"Erik, you can't do that. Not now."

"Two weeks ago, you all but ordered me to do that—because I hadn't taken leave due me last year at all."

"Yes, but with this Bay Bridge attack, everything's changed. We're on a stop-loss order. Every available man and woman is on this terrorist case."

"Except me, remember? Sending me down to Portsmouth is as good as letting me take leave. Worse actually—because you're sending me out of the area. On leave, I'll be here in Delaware, handy to everything."

"Your plan would be to work the bridge case in that event?"

"Sir, should I come upon any information while on leave that would be helpful in that investigation, I would of course contact you immediately."

The director sighed. A brief silence followed. Westman listened to the man's breathing. "Send me your request for leave in writing—by e-mail," he said finally. "While I'm considering whether to grant it, you'll be exempt from having to go to Portsmouth."

"How many days do you think I'll have before you come to a decision?"

"Enough. Erik, are you really onto something?"

"I believe so, sir." Westman told him of the stolen-car reports.

"I'll alert the Delaware River units. You carry on. I'll see to it all your orders come directly from me."

"Thank you, sir."

"We'll get through this, Erik. And we'll get those people."

Chapter 25

Westman was relieved to see the white Wrangler parked in front of her house. When there was no response to his knock, he opened the screen door and stepped inside, calling her name.

She was at her kitchen table, a cup of coffee in front of her. All he got from her was a glance.

He took the chair opposite. "You don't seem particularly pleased to see me."

"Normally, I would be, but you've done an unfortunate thing. I was sitting here trying to make up my mind about something. By turning up now, you've done it for me."

"I don't understand."

"I told Burt I wasn't going to help him with this anymore—not if it involves diving underwater to wrestle bare-handed with the bomb. He took it badly. I feel crummy doing this to him. But there it is."

"Yes."

"Maybe you could take my place."

"Cat, I'm already in trouble with my chain of command. We're onto something with the Bay Bridge case. I'm happy to help you as much as I can, but I can't devote full-time to Burt's quest. I know you got a raw deal from the Air Force— and my admiral. I'm terribly sorry about that. But I can't cut loose from this terrorist thing."

"I know that, Erik. I was in the Navy. First things first."

"How have I helped you make up your mind?"

"You can't take the time to do the dive for Burt. I don't want to. So that's that."

He could not tell if she was being facetious or just brutally frank. There was a very great deal about this woman he had yet to learn.

"Let me think about it," he said. "Let's see what happens today."

"Let's go see what Burt's up to."

They pulled the Wrangler to a stop just forward of the *Roberta June*'s bow. Despite the season, it was a clammy day, with the temperature hovering around sixty. The river mist was thick, and looked persistent.

Amy was up on the flying bridge, seated by the controls and drinking from a disposable container of coffee.

"Burt's below—sleeping," she said. "He's had a hard night of it."

"Drinking?" Cat asked.

"No. Working. Come aft. I'll show you."

Descending the ladder as they stepped aboard, she led them to the aft deck. A large piece of machinery had been installed where the soft-drink cooler had been.

"What in hell is that?" Cat asked.

Amy patted the thing as she might a pet. "Can't you tell, Navy? It's a winch."

"It's all beaten up and rusty."

"It's the original that used to be on this boat. Burt sold it to a commercial fisherman upriver when he turned the *Roberta June* into a head boat. The guy got a new one a couple of years ago but he still had this sitting out back. Burt got it back cheap."

"Does it run?" Westman asked.

"Yup. We tested it twice. Got a hundred fifty feet of heavy-duty line on it, plus some cable and shackle. We're good to go."

She turned to Cat, a hint of challenge in her voice as she said, "You coming?"

Cat looked at Westman, expressing nothing.

"Yes," he said. "Both of us."

After a remarkably enjoyable evening of drinking and fellowship with his cousin-in-law, Gergen had taken his crew back aboard the tug and cast off a little past midnight. They were anchored now well out into Delaware Bay near the Roosevelt Inlet. The fog was heavy, but he had good radar.

Nothing much was moving on the water. Two large inbound ships had entered the estuary and anchored. Otherwise, the screen was blank. None of the fishing vessels that usually worked this end of the bay appeared to be out.

He'd wait.

Mary Lou entered the pilothouse, carrying two beers. "Morning." Her voice was a little dreamy.

"Does Leonard know where you are?"

"He probably thinks I'm on the Moon. Or would, if he knew there was a Moon."

"I'll be out on the water a while."

"That's all right. I like it here." She handed him one of the beers, and took a big swallow from the other.

"When we're done here, I'll run you down home to Ocean City."

"Isn't this tug too big for the bay down there? People Leonard rents to even run aground on those Jet Skis."

"The channel's deep enough. Anyway, I want to talk to Leonard about something."

She gave him a quick, nervous glance, then returned her attention to her beer.

"You think he'll still be stoned?" Bear asked.

She shrugged. "I never know."

An unexpected swell rocked the tug a little, causing her to reach out to him for support.

"It'll be a while, getting down to OC from here," she said.

He grinned. "I know."

There was a flicker on the radar screen, hard by the line marking the coast. It showed again, a sizable boat emerging from the inlet. With an unhappy look at Mary Lou, Bear called to Roy Creed to start the engines.

Burt had stirred from his bunk, looking as bleary from his night's work as if he had been on a bender. Amy was at the helm, her eyes on the radar. They were heading out to sea at a careful ten knots.

"Any traffic?" Burt asked.

"All behind us," she said.

"Okay, you keep the helm." Amy gave every indication that she would in no way be willing to relinquish it.

Burt looked to Cat and Westman, smiling, not quite understanding why they were there, but glad of it. Oddly, in that moment, his old handsomeness returned. Cat could imagine him in some pilots' hangout, a half century before, catching every lady's eye.

Then he ruined it by taking a coffee mug and going over to a storage compartment on the other side, taking out a full bottle of Jim Beam.

"Is this the right time for that, Burt?"

"Didn't touch a drop last night. Time to celebrate."

"Again," she said.

Westman observed the old pilot carefully. He sensed that the girl at the controls was very competent and that there would be no problem as long as Schilling stayed away from them. Were he officially on duty, he'd be compelled to make the man turn back, and possibly place him under arrest. But he was on leave.

Cat went to the windscreen, looking forward. They were moving into a perpetual curtain of whitish gray that after a moment began to hypnotize her. She turned away, her eyes on Westman. She was wearing shorts, a T-shirt, and a Navy windbreaker—willing to assist but making no preparations to go into the water. Holding Burt to his word.

After finishing his whiskey, Burt went to stand behind Amy, holding on to the back of her chair, observing the radar screen as intently as she was. He remained that way until they had rounded Cape Henlopen—largely invisible in the mist. He then went to the navigation gear, unrolling a plastic-covered chart and consulting both the GPS and his Loran readings.

"South by southeast, five points off the bow," he said.

She responded with precision. Westman thought that, in their strange way, they'd make a good team. He briefly pondered the notion of Catherine McGrath and himself working a boat in the future. There were worse ways to spend a life.

They proceeded perhaps a mile in this fashion, then Burt called for full stop. At his command, Joe Whalleys deployed the anchor. The shackle and chain rattled unpleasantly through the cleat; then quiet returned as the hemp line ran through and stopped. Whalleys bent over to make it fast around the cleat as the *Roberta June* began to swing stern-first to the shore, the bow pointing seaward.

He searched the sea surface in all directions. They all did. Without success.

"It's only an hour off low tide," Burt said. "That float ought to be showing."

"Maybe it sank," said Amy. "Coulda been leaky."

"I should have bought a new one," Burt said.

"Maybe we're off the mark," said Cat, staring ahead. "With this ground fog, it could be fifty yards away and we'd miss it."

"Visibility's better than that, Catherine," Burt said. "Give us a break."

No one spoke; the tension slowly abated.

"Someone could have run over it," Westman said. "There are all manner of explanations."

Schilling lost his balance momentarily as another large swell moved the boat. Grasping for support, he flung himself into the seat opposite the controls. "So what do we do now?" he asked after taking a few deep breaths. "Make another search of the grid?"

Westman eyed the small inflatable dinghy tied to the bulkhead just aft of the flying bridge. "You have a motor for that?"

"Yeah."

"Let me use it—and the magnetometer."

"Look, Westman, this is my . . ."

"Burt! Chill! We're all after the same thing here," said Cat.

"I thought you said you were out of it."

"One more time. Today. Then all bets are off."

She went out with Westman, acting out of an impulse she couldn't quite explain to herself, keeping the metal detector's float clear of the outboard's prop wash. Westman steered the inflatable in a slow, careful zigzag pattern out to the front of the *Roberta June*, stopping when the big boat became enveloped in mist behind them.

He idled the engine. "Let's look to the south."

Another zigzag pattern, equally without success.

"The other side?" she asked.

He nodded, then moved the throttle forward, crossing behind the *Roberta June*'s stern. She bent over her instrument. He observed her happily a moment: the tan, trim but muscular arms, a few strands of her long blond hair falling over her face. Then, noting that the big boat had disappeared from view again, he corrected his course, heading closer.

"Wait!" she said. "Stop!"

Before he could move the throttle back into neutral, he heard a loud "Bopff" as the bow of the inflatable struck the metal float.

"We're stern to," said Burt. "This is perfect. We'll just come aft another fifty yards and re-anchor. Then the winch can do all the work."

"It's stuck fast in the sand," Cat said. "You'll need more power than that winch engine to shake her loose."

"What do you suggest?"

She gestured at the control console. "Forget the winch. Use the *Roberta June*."

Schilling thought upon this. "Okay. We'll wind the cable around a couple of the stanchions and then haul it out like a horse team pulling a stump."

Leaving Schilling and Joe Whalleys to attend to that task, Westman went below to get into diving gear. He was strapping on a weight belt when he sensed someone behind him, and turned to see Cat standing completely naked.

But she was pulling on a wet suit.

"I thought you didn't want any more of what's down there," he said.

"It's different, working with two. Working with you."

"The bomb's no different."

"I'll help you. I just don't want to touch it."

"Okay."

"Do you mind?"

"I mind like hell, but let's just do it."

They heard someone coming down the stairs from above deck.

"Are you guys ready?" Amy asked.

Cat really wasn't. She doubted she would ever be. But it was like her first carrier landing. The trick was to get into the air. Then she could worry about getting down again.

"Yes," she said.

Westman stood aside. "After you."

Bear Gergen was tired of watching the radar screen and the motionless blip that was the head boat. The old pilot was either fishing—which seemed doubtful—or going after his bomb, if there really was one.

If there was, and its nomenclature was what Bear figured, it would be one fucking valuable hunk of metal—to someone. The Pentagon had spent millions recovering these things in the past. Maybe they'd be happy to spring for one or two now to get this back. That was surely what the C-130 pilot had in mind—a little nest egg for his retirement, enough to keep that little dark-haired broad happy. Otherwise, he would have told the Feds about the bomb long before.

Who the eventual buyer might be was something Bear could work out later. The recovery was a trickier business. If these head boat people couldn't manage it, Bear's crew would do it. And if Schilling's crew did accomplish it by themselves—well, Bear's work would be all the easier.

He'd marked their location on his chart. Hovering this close any longer was a bad idea. Checking his onboard computer, which he'd clicked to the National Weather Service website, he saw that it was clearing to the west.

Bear gave the helm to Roy Creed. "Take her up the shore maybe a mile. But keep that head boat on the radar screen."

"Okay, Bear."

Going below, he found Mary Lou on a bunk, wearing nothing and smoking a joint. She eyed him through the smoke.

"Working," he said, going by. Opening his arms locker, he took inventory: seven handguns, all automatics; a short-barreled .22-caliber rifle; and an M-16 that had left the service with him, along with much else. He stuck an eleven-millimeter Sig Sauer in his belt under his T-shirt, then went back to Mary Lou. Removing the joint from her hand, he took a long drag from it, then squashed it out on the deck with his shoe. "Get some sleep. You'll need it."

"I thought you were taking me home."

"I am, but we got some business first."

With the anchor weighed, Amy backed the *Roberta June* to within fifty feet of the float, and dropped anchor again. Once they were underwater, the plan was to have Cat and Westman yank three times on the float line when they had located the exposed rear section of the bomb, at which time Burt was to lower the winch cable and wait for them to attach the hook. When that was accomplished, they were to yank three times on the float again and then surface. What happened next was to be up to Burt.

He stood watching Westman and Cat, his coffee mug in hand. Cat kept her eyes elsewhere.

Westman smiled at her before pulling on his mask, but he seemed very serious. She touched his arm, to show she was still willing. When both were fully ready, she took hold of his hand as they got onto the aft platform, and both went backward into the water. Like thrown-back fish, they headed for the depths immediately.

The murk oppressed her as before. She followed Erik as he moved forward over the bottom sand, though she had little idea of what direction they were following. Looking up, she vaguely perceived a long shadow she presumed to be the *Roberta June*'s hull, but it was hardly comforting.

Westman turned on his light, prompting her to do the same. The effect was to render the murk to complete darkness but for the cones of illumination, but they could see clearly a few feet ahead. Zigzagging slightly, then lunging to the right, Westman stopped, pulling free of her hand.

She looked around him, seeing first the float line and then following it down to the strange shape on the sea bottom. Westman crouched by the tail of the bomb, feeling as much as looking. He began scraping sand away with his hands, removing enough to reveal the angle at which the weapon lay imbedded. He stepped back, studying the thing further, then reached and yanked on the line three times.

He took her by the arm and they began backing away.

The hook, shackle, and winch cable came down in a silent whoosh, stirring bubbles and then sand as the hook struck bottom. The uncoiling line followed quickly. Burt apparently wasn't too deep into his whiskey, for the line halted in its descent only a few seconds after. Westman moved toward it, his headlamp swinging from side to side.

Cat hurried after, not wanting to lose sight of him. With work now to be done, she pushed her fear aside. She was tired of being afraid. She now saw a point to all this. The several and sundry imbeciles and idiots they had dealt with had to be shown they were wrong. You couldn't just leave a great lump of nuclear material on the sea bottom and treat it as an inconvenience to be ignored or forgotten. They weren't going to let it be forgotten, whatever the cost.

She went to Westman's side. He had taken the big heavy hook into hand and dragged the shackle and cable forward as he returned to the bomb. Kneeling beside him, she took hold of the cable while he worked the hook through the opening between the tail flange and the metal bar connecting the fins. When it seemed secure, he stood up. Without instruction, she began backing up, keeping tension on the hook and preventing the line from looping. It was heavy and bristly against the flesh of her palms, but she persevered, her eyes fixed on Erik through her increasingly cloudy mask.

He motioned to her to continue backing, and she did, though a moment later he disappeared from view. In another moment, the slack in the heavy cable vanished and it pulled taut. She saw him coming at her, as fast as he could manage. He flung an arm across her chest, pulling her away, making her drop the cable.

They heard the boat's engine increase in RPMs, causing a whirl of bubbles. The shadow above began to move. The cable was only vaguely visible in the propeller wash. The hook appeared to be holding. They could see waves and flurries of sand spreading out to either side of the bomb's midsection from the stress of the pull.

Reflexively, Westman hunched down, and she did the same, wondering what might occur should the shackle or tail frame break. A swoop of chain link in the face? Or would the bomb pull apart, exposing its devilish innards to the seawater?

Too late for such worries, at all events. Whatever was going to happen was going to in a very few seconds.

The RPMs and the clouds of bubbles increased. The boat's engine made an irritable, protesting sound. Its anger accumulated. Westman could hear then a second noise—a chordlike reverberation, and then a sort of groan.

The bomb moved. Another two or three feet of metal became suddenly exposed. But then the movement ceased.

Was Amy easing off? Had she accidentally shoved the gears into idle? The line seemed a little slack now. The head boat's propeller had stopped. Then, suddenly, it began whirring like mad—stirring a blizzard of bubbles and aeration. Westman could feel the force of it. There was a wrenching clang and thunk.

Amy had put the motor in idle, but only in preparation to

slam it back into gear and produce a sudden yank on the chain. A jerk pull. There was an enormous wail and moan. With everything engaged, the engine was churning at maximum RPM.

Sand whirled everywhere about. The bomb shook and shuddered, then came heaving forth, growing in size as it emerged from the sea bottom, looking like some monstrous evil monster being freed from its prison. Its nose emerged from the sand battered and crumpled, ugly and malevolent.

The boat's engine stopped. Westman kicked forward, staying close to the bottom, inching his way toward the nose of the bomb.

What had Robert Oppenheimer said at the first atomic test at Los Alamos? "I am become death."

Here was death again. They had pulled it out of the bottom of the sea. They could never get it back into the sandy bottom.

He examined the nose as carefully as he could. It was crumpled and flattened, like the fender of a car in a smashup. If there was a plutonium trigger housing, it had become lost in the metal mush.

The stirring above resumed. Pushing himself back up on his feet, Westman looked wildly about for Cat. Something heavy struck the back of his head and he went forward and down—into the sand. Then something hard and abrasive scraped along the side of his leg, burning where it touched.

He felt a hand take hold of his other ankle and pull, dragging him away. He turned over on his back, looking up through a gray-green fog at a blizzard of bubbles and great heaving shapes. There was a screeching groan, continuing relentlessly.

He saw Cat's masked face, moving by, felt her hands as she removed his weight belt. Then he was floating upward, ever upward, arriving at the surface just as he heard a great clanking and clatter, and then an enormous crunch.

Cat came up beside him, letting her mouthpiece fall free.

The inflatable was upside down and Joe Whalleys was swimming toward the *Roberta June*.

They started swimming toward it as well, heading for the stern platform. It was covered with twisted metal. The aft rail had been pulled over the stern as though with an enormous pair of pliers. One of the stanchions had been broken off and the other was severely bent. A portion of the hull seemed to be cracked, or at least badly scraped. Hanging perpendicular to this wreckage, looking like some huge landed game fish, was the bomb, still dark and malevolent in this eerie, misty light.

Chapter 26

Turko had been watching the Weather Channel for hours. The conditions and forecast had changed significantly, but never the wind direction, which was always from the north or northwest, when it was blowing at all.

Finally, when he could not stand another "Local on the Eights," he turned to the other channels in search of a newscast—finding one quickly. They were reporting the recovery of a sport utility vehicle full of bodies that had gone into the Delaware River. For a moment, Turko wondered if the dead might be from another cell that Pec had decided to eliminate, but the reporter eventually revealed that the victims were all African American, and that the murders appeared to be part of a drug-related Philadelphia gang war.

When the weather forecast finally came on, it was the same as the Weather Channel's.

Turko decided he had been sitting there too long and had been drinking too much vodka. He set down his glass, clicked off the television set, and went into the next room.

"We go tonight," he said, repeating himself in Russian for

the benefit of the Uzbeks. They seemed elated. The Iraqi, whose name was actually Hussein, frowned.

"The wind is right?" he asked.

"It will be."

"I saw a weather forecast. It said light winds—and from the north."

"And northwest. That will be good. Radioactive cloud over Atlantic City. A place of sin," said Turko. "No better symbol of American values. Greed and sin. Promiscuous women."

"But Atlantic City is to the east of the power plant."

"It will not escape. And even if the radioactivity should go elsewhere, it doesn't matter. The mere fact of the blast will panic the nation. Immobilize it. A gigantic blow."

"But not like the World Trade Center," said Hussein.

"Nothing will be like the World Trade Center. No one will be that effective again."

The Iraqi was still doubtful. "The man said it is going to rain."

Turko had paid no attention to that, concerned only about the wind direction. "Rain is good."

"Why is rain good?"

"Security guards do not like to stand in the rain. They do not like to go out into the rain. They cannot see very far in the rain."

"What about us?"

"We know where we're going." Turko drained his glass. "Now let us go. We need to rent the pontoon boat and pre-pare the cars."

The Iraqi looked at him for an uncomfortably long time. "We must not squander this opportunity."

"And we will not. Come now. Please. We must hurry."

With the stern rendered unusable by the bomb and rail wreckage, Joe Whalleys hooked the metal ladder over the

starboard side. Cat was weighed down by her oxygen tank
and days of fatigue, but managed to get aboard with Joe
pulling her up over the rail. The Coast Guardsman managed
by himself.

Amy remained at the controls. Schilling was standing by
the damaged stern, examining the bomb. His eyes had a
slightly maniacal cast, as though he had found the corpse of
an old enemy.

"This is it," he said finally. "One of 'em, anyway." He
turned to Cat. "They'll believe us now."

She removed her mask and her oxygen gear, letting it fall
to the deck with a loud clank. She wanted to get out of her wet
suit. "How do we get it to them? You can't sail up to Dover
Air Force Base. Or do you plan to go around the Delmarva
and up the Potomac—maybe drop it off at the Pentagon?"

"Can't," Burt said, as though taking her seriously. "The
Roberta June won't fit under Memorial Bridge."

"The *Roberta June*'s not going anywhere," said Amy.
"Has nobody noticed that the engine's stopped?"

"I thought you'd turned it off," Westman said.

"Nope. It stalled out because something's caught in the
propeller—the line from the float, I'm guessing. Bet it's
wound tight around."

Burt looked over the twisted railing. "Shit," he muttered.

"We're going nowhere," Amy repeated.

Cat swore as well. Not caring that anyone could see her
naked breasts, she peeled off the top of her wet suit, flung it
on the deck, and then went below.

Westman went to the remains of the aft rail. Amy was
right. "All right. We're a vessel in distress. I'll call the Coast
Guard."

"I thought you were the Coast Guard," Amy said.

"I'm not a Coast Guard cutter." He pulled off the top of
his own wet suit and went below as well, finding Cat in the
equipment cabin, where they had left their clothes. She had
not yet dressed, and was toweling the seawater and perspira-

tion off her long body. He reached to take the towel, to help her. She snapped it away.

"Leave me be," she said.

"Cat. We've done it. You've done it. I'm going to call the Cape May Coast Guard station. They'll come and take the bomb off our hands. It's over, Cat. You should be happy."

She shook her head, as though he were muttering nonsense. "Haven't you seen the disaster area we've made of the stern? It's a sign. This whole crazy enterprise of ours is cursed. We've wrecked the *Roberta June* and we may well have doomed ourselves with radioactive poisoning as well."

"There's no indication of that. I'll call the *Manteo* and she'll come down and take care of everything. It's all over, Cat. We've won."

"They won't do a thing. The U.S. military isn't going to lift a finger to help with this. They've made that clear. Coast Guard. Air Force. U.S. Navy. It doesn't matter. We're stuck."

He put his hands on her bare moist shoulders, but she twisted away, going to the shelf where she had left her blouse. She put it on, buttoning it quickly, then pulled on her shorts.

With effort, he removed the lower part of his wet suit. She paid his nakedness no mind. Instead, as he began to dress, she hurried back up the companionway to the main deck.

When he came up himself she was seated at the bow, as far as she could be from the bomb. The mist was thinning. They could see to the vague outline of the shore and the breaking surf.

"I'm calling my cutter," Westman said to Schilling.

The old pilot shrugged.

Erik used his cell phone. There were four rings, and then Dewey's voice mail came on the line. Westman left a message for the lieutenant to call as soon as possible, then clicked off.

"Homeland Security," Cat said derisively.

Amy sat slumped at the controls, looking unhappy. Joe Whalleys was staring at the bomb. "Can't believe it," he said. "I can't believe we just pulled up an A-bomb."

"H-bomb," corrected Amy.

Westman tried Dewey again, with the same result. Leaving no message this time, he called Leon Kelly, who answered directly.

"Are you still in Ocean City?" Westman asked.

"Wilmington."

"Why there?"

There was a pause. Westman sensed that Kelly was moving around again. "We got some new intelligence," Kelly said finally. "They've had a shooting on the docks up here. You know about the big upturn in stolen cars. Payne figures they may try for the Memorial Bridge, or maybe the Walt Whitman up by Philly. They say they may raise the threat level to red again."

"Scare the hell out of the people in Fargo because of something happening in the East."

"Now you know why the terrorists like to come here."

"Leon, I may need your help."

"You got a new lead?"

Westman spoke very carefully now. "We've come upon some nuclear material."

"What? Where are you? Who's 'we'?"

"On a fishing boat just south of Cape Henlopen. I'm with some former military people."

The agent seemed to be walking still farther. In a moment, Westman heard automobile traffic. "Look," said Kelly. "I'm at the Wilmington police station with Payne. We're trying to set up a command center. I can't talk much longer. Now what kind of nuclear material is this? I mean, is it radioactive? What's it in?"

"It's protected. It's inside an old bomb. It's a long, complicated story, but we've recovered a Mark-28 H-bomb from the ocean bottom at an underwater ravine called Deepkill.

But we damaged the boat in the process and are immobilized. We're at anchor, maybe two hundred, three hundred yards offshore. We need a tow and someone to take possession of this nuclear weapon."

"Jeez, Erik. Sounds like a big fucking deal. But there's nothing this task force can do about it. We're deployed up here and . . ."

"Can you call the field office?"

"Sure, but why don't you? It's routine. Tell 'em you caught a case and you're turning it over to them as primary."

"This isn't routine. And it will be more effective if they hear it from you. At all events, I'm not supposed to be here."

"I thought you guys could go wherever you wanted."

"I work for the federal government too, Leon."

"All right. I'll give them a call. But they've probably got their hands full too. This alert . . ."

"I appreciate it, Leon. You're the best they've got."

"Why aren't you up here, Erik? You'd think . . ."

"I'm supposed to be in Portsmouth."

"Is something happening in Portsmouth?"

"No."

"Gotta go, Erik. There's Payne."

Westman thanked the agent again, then stood staring at the cell phone. Calling Dewey one more time, with more disappointment, he said: "I'll try them on the radio."

"No," said Schilling. "I don't want to turn this over to the Coast Guard. And the damned FBI'll just arrest us all as suspected terrorists."

"What do you want to do, Burt?" Amy said. "What can we do?"

Schilling was looking to the shore. "Get a truck."

Cat shook her head.

Burt ignored this. "I've got a friend with a garage over near Georgetown. He's got a flatbed truck that he uses to haul his stock cars to the Dover Speedway and some other tracks. It has a winch rig because he makes side money hauling fisherman's cars out of the sand when they get stuck on the state beaches."

"Does this truck float?" Cat asked.

"Won't need to." Schilling explained his idea. They'd tow the *Roberta June* close to shore with the inflatable and ground her. Then they'd go borrow the truck and wait for low tide. They'd be able to run a line from the truck winch to the bomb and drag it ashore and onto the truck bed. Then they could take it anywhere.

Cat had come back to the main deck. "It'll take an hour or more to walk from here to Lewes to get a car. By the time you get back from Georgetown with that truck, it'll be after dark."

"Low tide's just after eleven," Schilling said. The times of the tides were doubtless the chief facts he kept in mind every day. "I've got enough lights. We can probably get that fouled cable off the propeller at the same time."

Amy was smiling at him. "You never told me you were so smart, Burt."

He grinned in reply. It occurred to Cat there was something more between them than Amy's willingness to go to bed with the old guy. Probably had been for some time, even though he hadn't realized it.

Cat studied the bomb. "You don't think this thing is killing us with radioactivity as we speak?"

"It looks more or less just like it did when we loaded it forty years ago. Don't think there're any metal fractures or perforations. Except for Mikulski, none of my crew died of anything. Nobody got radiation sickness."

"Okay, Burt," Cat said. "I'll help you. I don't exactly have a heavy date tonight."

"This is about as heavy a date as you'll ever have," Westman said.

Cat eyed him coldly, then sighed, giving him a friendly punch on the arm. "Let's get to work."

"You'll stick with us?" Schilling asked Westman.

"It's probably the most useful thing I can be doing at this moment."

"What about Portsmouth, and your admiral?" Cat asked.

"We're trained to act on our own initiative."

"That won't stop them from kicking you out of the service."

"We're also trained to take risks."

Amy did her job well, steering the *Roberta June* at an angle as Cat hauled it shoreward with the inflatable, so the head boat would slide up easily into the shallow water rather than have the bow plow into the bottom sand.

When this was accomplished and the anchor dropped again, Joe Whalleys ferried Cat, Schilling, and the Coast Guardsman to the beach, and then brought the inflatable back, tying it fast to the railing on the starboard side where he'd put the ladder.

"They're going to be gone a long time," he said, dropping into the seat next to Amy's.

"Yeah? So?"

"Well, would you mind if I got myself another beer?"

"No, not so long as it doesn't give you ideas."

"Got no ideas, Amy. Just thirsty."

"Then bring me one too."

She leaned back in the chair, swiveling to the right to watch the three trudge along the beach, heading north. Cat and the Coastie walked close together, with Burt following just behind, but dragging a little.

That morning, he'd promised Amy that "if anything happened" to him, the boat would be hers. A year or two from this foggy, nasty day, she could be captain—one of the Lewes head-boat captains.

And she'd do a damn sight better job of it than Burt had been doing.

He was falling behind the other two now. Cat took note of that and stopped, waiting for Burt to catch up. He was nuts about her. Amy had long been well aware of that. But he liked Amy too. And she liked him. And was very, very nice to him. Cat was all wrapped up in problems. Except for the work with the bomb and a belt or two together, she'd have no time for Burt. Not with that Coast Guard guy around.

Amy's life was in order, and looking good, as it never really had been before. She felt happy. She had a future. She was safe.

The mist was shifting—rising to landward, closing from seaward, opening wide to the north. She thought for a moment she saw the outline of another boat in that direction—a squat silhouette too large to be another fishing craft. But the veil of mist descended again and it was lost to her.

She turned again toward the shore. The fog had lifted there enough for her to see the horizon, and something she hadn't expected—a great, dark wall of threatening cloud that seemed to rise ever heavenward as it moved toward her. If there were winds to match its evil look, the *Roberta June* would be in for a hell of a knocking. The weather report had predicted only rain. This looked to be a damned lot more than that.

Joe set down her beer and resumed his seat. "Do you think we'll get some extra money out of this?"

"Yeah. Probably. But do you think that's what this is about?"

He puzzled over this. "Seems to me, what this is about is that Burt's kinda like a little nuts."

"I used to think that myself," she said, swiveling her chair to face the stern. "But look at that damned thing. No way Burt's nuts."

It began to rain.

Chapter 27

"We're going through a protected wildlife habitat," Cat said. "Nesting ground for shore birds."

They walked huddled together, arm in arm, against the rain that had appeared from nowhere and was falling relentlessly. Burt walked apart from them, lost in his own thoughts, but was keeping up the pace.

They had reached the point of the cape, and were now following the curving shore of the bay beyond. A sign warned them that these were nesting grounds. Westman, whom she'd thought such a straight arrow, ignored it.

"Cat. When we get to your house, I think you should just get into your Jeep and head for Washington. Burt and I can handle everything."

"That's a two-thousand-pound bomb hanging on the back of his boat."

"We have the winch—and there's Joe Whalleys. You need to be at your lawyer's office in the morning."

She hunched her shoulders against the downpour. "We'll see."

Westman's cell phone began ringing. He was going to ignore it, but remembered the message he had left Tim Dewey. He took the device from his pocket, shielding it from the rain. The lady or the tiger. In this case, Admiral dePayse was the tiger. He clicked it on.

"Erik? It's Tim Dewey. Sorry to get back to you so late. I left my cell in my cabin, and we've got our hands full here. What's up?"

"Hands full with what?"

"Major alert. The FBI expects a strike against one of the Delaware River bridges. We're patrolling locked and loaded."

"They give any reason?"

"No. What did you call about?"

Westman hesitated. "I'm with some civilians who have recovered a 1960's nuclear weapon from the sea bottom south of Henlopen. They're looking for help transporting it to a place of safety."

"Nuclear weapon?"

"That's what it appears to be."

"It's out of the water?"

"On the stern of their boat, but the propeller's fouled and they can't get under way. I was requesting assistance."

A pause. "Erik, with this alert, I can't go anywhere without orders from the District. Why don't you try for one of the forty-sevens at Indian River?"

"Roger that."

"Check in later. Maybe we'll be standing down."

Before Westman could reply, Schilling reached and took hold of the cell phone, clicking it off. He returned it to Westman. "I don't want the Coast Guard. I told you that. We'll do it ourselves."

"Just trying to help."

"I know. I respect that. But this'll work. You'll see."

* * *

Dewey stared at his now-silent cell phone a moment, then clipped it back on his belt. "I talked to Westman," he said to DeGroot. "What a wild story."

The master chief's eyes were focused ahead, where the twin spans of the Delaware Memorial Bridge had come into view. "How wild?"

"He says he's with some civilians who pulled a nuclear bomb out of the ocean."

"What strength line were they using?" DeGroot grunted, his form of laughter.

"Actually, he sounded pretty serious. If it weren't for this alert, I might go down the shore for a look-see. I gather these are the head-boat people we ran into before."

The rain increased, lowering visibility still further. DeGroot could see only one of the bridge towers now. "Including maybe that tall blond."

"Probably so."

"That guy gets nothing but trouble out of his women."

Dewey thought of his Sally, who had never in any way been trouble for him. "Thing about Erik," Dewey said. "I think he likes trouble."

"Well, he's got the job for it."

A small motorboat appeared abruptly out of the fog bank to port, coming across the *Manteo*'s bow.

"What the hell is he up to?" DeGroot asked.

"Let's find out," said Dewey, sounding his horn in rapid succession as a signal to heave to. When the smaller craft did not, he ordered a sharp turn to starboard to pursue.

Leaving the Uzbeks by the main highway in the rental truck he'd stolen, Turko drove with the Iraqi down the road to the marina in his latest acquisition—a Toyota sedan. Two cars were parked outside the office shack—a sign they were open for business, though the rain was pelting down hard.

There were three pontoon boats at the dock, all with canvas canopies up and in place. Turko supposed it would not be too wet underneath, at least if the wind remained light.

The sliding door opened, and they went into the office, finding no one behind the counter. They waited quietly for several minutes, with the Iraqi looking at some pictures of sport fishermen and their catches that had been tacked to one wall.

Finally, Turko heard some stirring in a room to the rear he took to be used for storage. He could see piles of life preservers through the partially opened door.

"Hello!" he said.

"We're closed," came a female voice he presumed to be that of the woman they had rented the boat from previously.

"Your door is open," he replied. "We need a boat."

"We're closed!"

"You have three pontoon boats. We want to rent one. We want to go fishing."

A male voice responded now. "You can't go fishing in this weather. Now get the hell out of here. We're closed!"

"It's those weird foreign guys," Turko heard the girl say, more quietly.

A decision was required, and very soon. They could just as easily steal one of the boats, but the couple would report them and the police or Coast Guard would then be looking for them. Alternatively, they could tie up and gag the couple and put them in the back of the rental truck—maybe deposited in some woods along the way.

The Iraqi made Turko's decision for him. Taking out the automatic pistol Turko had given him, he went behind the counter and stepped through the open door.

The two had made a sort of bed with life preservers on the floor and were lying upon it, both completely naked, obviously waiting for Turko and his friends to go. The girl attempted to cover herself with one of the life jackets.

"Who the fuck are . . ." began the boy.

The Iraqi shot him through the face. The girl attempted to

worm herself away under the life preservers. It took three shots—two in the back and one below—before she stopped moving.

"You like doing that, don't you?" Turko said.

"You object?"

He was in no position to object. He left the office and started toward the dock, leaving the Iraqi to bring down the two Uzbeks.

Bear Gergen had been watching Schilling's head boat on the radar as it did absolutely nothing for nearly an hour. It had moved shoreward, so close in it had to have run aground, and then sat there, stuck. It would likely have to go through the entire tide cycle before floating again.

All that was obvious. What perplexed Gergen was why they had done this. A logical answer was that they wanted to go ashore. But they could have done that with the inflatable he'd seen aboard.

He figured there was something they wanted to unload on the beach. He was oddly put in mind of the books he had read as a kid—pirates carrying chests of loot and treasure ashore.

Maybe that's what they were doing, only with something far more valuable than a box of gold coins. He couldn't wait any longer. If they'd all left the boat, he could claim salvage. If someone was still aboard, he would be within his rights to investigate. Either way, he meant to find out if they had on board what he thought they did.

"Head for that boat," he said to Roy Creed. "But keep an eye on the depth finder."

Schilling insisted on driving his pickup truck to George-town. It had a bench seat, and Cat rode between the two men, sitting closest to Westman.

"You all right?" he asked.

"Yeah. Sure. I've made carrier traps in weather like this."

"You didn't have to mess with the bombs yourself."

"I guess that's the difference between Navy and civilian life."

Schilling laughed. He thought that over a moment, then laughed even harder, his face a picture of supreme content in the flare of headlights of oncoming cars. This had become a very strange journey. She hoped she'd be able to see it through to the end.

Westman put his arm around her. She rested her head against his shoulder. "Are you okay?" she asked.

"What do you mean?" he asked.

"You're putting your career on the line here."

"I'm doing my job."

Turko had the Uzbeks carry the bodies, the clothing, and the bloodstained life jackets to one of the pontoon boats, and then had them douse the pile of flesh and cloth with gasoline from the dockside fuel pump.

"You'll go out in the third boat with these two in tow," he said in Russian. "When you get out mid-river, you light this flare, throw it into the boat with the bodies, and then cast them off."

"Why?"

"It will catch fire and float downstream. A lot of people will see it and call the Coast Guard. Their attention will be drawn to it—and away from what you're going to do at the power plant."

The smarter Uzbek began chewing his lip. "It's raining."

"Yes. It is raining."

"It will put out the fire."

"It won't put out the flare when you throw it and it will not put out the gasoline explosion."

"This will not kill us?"

"Not if you do it right."

Turko had promised the Iraqi and the Uzbeks something no one else in Pec's group had been offered—a chance not to die for Allah. They were to make their attack, then head upriver to the marshy landing that was to be their rendezvous point. Turko had little interest in being there to greet them, even if able. But they had no idea of that.

"Hurry now," he said.

He helped them start the big outboard engine. "When you cut loose the other boat, come close to shore and stay there until it's time."

"We will," said the smarter Uzbek. The other was staring at the bodies.

"Go," said Turko.

He hopped back on the deck and cast them off. Their departure was clumsy, but they managed to keep the other two pontoon boats in train. He watched them until they disappeared into the rain and mist, waiting. Perhaps fifteen minutes later, there was a sudden flare. Its glow continued. Turko hurried to the Toyota. When he returned to the main road, he was half-surprised to find the Iraqi and the rental truck still there.

The distress call broke into the other marine radio chatter like an uninvited guest. Fire on the water was the worst possible search-and-rescue mission situation. Dewey knew they'd not be relieved from his bridge patrol to attend to the call, but he went through the calculations of how long it would take them to reach the stricken vessel nonetheless. The coal-freighter skipper who'd called in the sighting had described the boat as small and fully aflame.

It was hopeless. There would likely be nothing but charred flotsam by the time he got there.

There was a chopper at Cape May. Dewey radioed in a request for a search-and-assist. The reply was affirmative.

DeGroot was observing him.

"Something wrong, Master Chief?"

"What kind of fire do you get in a downpour like this?" DeGroot said. "Who would be out in the river in this weather?"

"Seems a little strange, doesn't it?"

"Yes. I would like to know the answer."

"I've got my orders, Hugo. Maintain the patrol."

DeGroot made a face, then nodded. "The people aboard those boats, they must be dead by now."

The rain abated just as they were turning onto the road to Lewes, and stopped altogether by the time they reached their neighboring houses. Cat, who had driven Burt's pickup from Georgetown, parked it in front of Schilling's place. Then they joined him in the big flatbed truck he'd borrowed.

He gunned the engine. "Let's go."

"Do you think this rig is going to make it over all that wet sand?"

"Sure," Burt said. "How do you think all those trucks got off the beach at Normandy?"

She smiled. "Wasn't around for Normandy. And this isn't an Army deuce-and-a-half."

"It has a better gear ratio. Anyway, if we get stuck, we can winch her out."

Cat looked to Westman, but he offered no counsel. "The only good way into that stretch of shoreline from here is through the State Park," she said.

"The gate extends only across the road," Burt said. "Plenty of space to drive around it."

"There must be a half-dozen park rangers who live around there. And they patrol it regularly, looking for kids and pot parties."

"They won't be expecting intruders on a night like this," Westman offered.

Burt nodded. "We'll kill the headlights. I know that access road. We'll make it." He tossed his cigarette end out the window. "Look, Cat. We don't have any choice. Amy and Joe are out there waiting for us. Sit here much longer, and we'll lose the low tide."

Westman was deferring to Cat on this. "Okay," she said, "but let's take the Wrangler too. There's all kinds of trouble we can get into over there, Burt. It could come in handy. Four-wheel drive."

He lighted another cigarette. "I'm not objecting. You take the lead."

She had forgotten to put up her side curtains. The seats were wet and there were a couple of inches of water on the floor. She removed her shoes and got in. Westman climbed in beside her, making no complaint.

They had trouble getting the truck over a deep sandy rise, accomplishing this feat only with a tow from the Wrangler. But once down on the tidal flat of the beach, they rolled along smoothly. In the lightening sky, the *Roberta June* was clearly visible, sitting canted over to one side very close to the shore.

Cat stopped the Wrangler just short of the furthest reach of wave. Burt pulled the big truck up behind her, turning it toward the sea. He flashed the headlights on and off three times.

There was no response from the boat. Cat turned off her engine and stepped out on the sand. Westman, and then Burt, came up beside her.

Burt tried shouting, but his whiskey-and-smoke-damaged voice wasn't up to it. Cat managed better, calling Amy's name twice.

No answer.

"Maybe they're asleep," Burt said.

Cat and Westman both shouted for Amy, with the same result.

"Maybe they got tired of waiting and came ashore," Burt said.

"Amy wouldn't do that," said Cat. "And I don't see the inflatable."

"It's almost shallow enough to wade out there," Burt said.

"I'll do that," Westman said. He pulled off his shirt and shoes and set his wallet and pistol on top of them.

Cat removed her shoes and moved into the water ahead of him. "Let me go first. I know the boat."

Westman hesitated, then retrieved his pistol. "Lead on."

The ladder was still in place at the port side. The *Roberta June* was leaning in that direction and the climb was difficult. Cat scraped her calf getting over the rail. Westman came up silently behind her.

There was something very wrong. Cat thought at first it was a trick of the eye in the night's darkness, but it wasn't. She had excellent night vision. What she saw was fact.

The bomb was gone. She could not imagine how it had been removed. It was as though the hand of God had reached down and taken the evil thing. It was as though it had never existed, and was only a wild imagining.

"Look aft," she said to Westman.

"I see."

"Amy!" Cat realized she sounded angry. She was.

Again no reply.

The deck was deserted. With Westman following, Cat moved into the main cabin, finding nothing untoward.

She said it again, more gently now. "Amy?"

Only the surf responded. "Erik?"

"Right behind you."

She started up the companionway, the metal cold against her bare feet.

Good pilots could tell when something was amiss before it registered on their instruments. Cat had that feeling now.

Everything seemed normal up on the flying bridge, until she noticed the dark form beneath the captain's chair. Burt kept a flashlight in the bin to the side. Cat groped for it and turned it on. With sudden reluctance, she pointed the beam at the motionless shape on the deck.

It was Amy, facing away and utterly still, as though in deep sleep. She'd been wearing a white T-shirt. Now it was red, except for the right shoulder.

"Amy? Are you all right?"

The question was absurd. She was speaking to someone who could not ever answer. Cat looked down at a face still contorted with surprise and fear and shock. There was an odd suggestion of a grin, but that came not from Amy's mouth. Her throat had been cut in a thick crimson line running all the way to her ear.

Cat realized she was standing in the poor girl's blood.

She backed away, incautiously, almost slipping on the steps. "Erik?"

He took a while to answer. "I'm down below."

"Have you found Joe Whalleys?"

Another hesitation. "Yes."

Her head reeling, she somehow got back down the steps to the main deck, but could go no farther. "Is he alive?" she asked.

"No."

An instant later, the lower cabin lights came on. "Amy's dead," she said. "They cut her throat." She tried to speak matter-of-factly, but could not keep the fear and anguish out of her voice.

Nothing from him. For a moment, she feared something might have just happened to Erik as well. And might be about to happen to her.

"Erik?"

"Cat. Get off the boat. Now! Get ashore!"

"What?"

"Hurry! Get off the boat!"

She heard him coming up the stairs, fast. Perplexed, she stepped toward the rail. He was suddenly beside her.

"Cat. Please! Now!"

When, confused, she still remained in place, he took her by the waist and lifted her over the rail. He hit the water not two seconds after she did.

"Hurry!" he said. "Get ashore!"

They swam several quick strokes and then, touching bottom, lunged forward on foot. She had just stepped onto the beach when a hissing roar split the silence and a great, bright heat enveloped her. She was flying, propelled through the air as though by magic, then slammed down viciously hard against the sand.

Chapter 28

Turko pulled the rental truck over onto the shoulder of the road perhaps half a mile short of the main gate to the power plant. Then, to the Iraqi's dismay, he got out.

"Move over," he said. "You will drive."

"Why?"

"Because, if you do not drive, the truck will stay here and will be of no use."

"What about you?"

"I'm going to go ahead on foot."

"Why do that?"

"To provide suppressing fire so that when you crash through the fence, they will not be able to kill you. I will be killing them."

The Iraqi showed no sign of moving. "Why don't I do that and you drive?"

Turko had a trump card—the best there was. "Because Pec put me in charge of this and if it fails because you would not cooperate, Pec will be unhappy. Have you had experience with Pec when he is unhappy?"

"It is not in the plan, what you propose to do."

"I have changed the plan."

"I do not want to die."

"And I do not want to die. That's why I have changed the plan. The Uzbeks will attract the main fire. They should draw most of the guards to that side of the compound. But there may be others. If they turn to fire on you, I need to be in a position to take them out. That I would not be if I were driving the truck or riding in the truck on the passenger side. I would simply be a target."

"So what is the new plan?"

"It is much like the other, only I will position myself to provide covering fire so that you can break through the fence and set off the explosive without harm coming to you."

"Break through the fence where?"

"Where I showed you. Just to the left of the gate. Drive as fast as you can and hit it as hard as you can. That should get you through both the outer and inner fence. Then you run about two hundred feet to the nearest spent-fuel bunker, pull the lanyard on the satchel, and run back. Then we go through the woods to where we left the car."

"If it works, there will be radiation."

Turko looked behind him. "The wind's from the west. We will be driving north. We will be fine."

"And the Uzbeks?"

"I think that they will be killed."

"We won't wait for them?"

"No. If we do that, we will die."

The Iraqi opened his door and got out. Cars were passing but none of their occupants seemed to take any special note of them. Turko kept his face turned away from the flare of their headlights.

"Pec does not want us to live," said the Iraqi.

"He wants this job done. If it works, it won't matter that we live."

"Okay."

"You will do this, Hussein?"

"Yes."

Turko consulted his watch. "We have eighteen minutes before the Uzbeks are to start their run. Listen for it, then wait a few minutes for the guard force to engage. When they are fully committed, move. Move fast."

"Okay."

There was another flare of headlights, which made a sweep, that began to slow. The vehicle stopped, freezing the rental truck in brightness. Turko was unhappy to see that it was a police car.

Westman had hit the sand hard on his right shoulder, rolling over onto his back and throwing his arm over his eyes to shield them against the writhing curtain of flame flung into the air by the explosion. All manner of debris rained down afterward, including a burning life jacket that landed not three feet from him. When the concussion, heat, and debris subsided, he sat up, hurting in a dozen different places. Brushing the sand from his eyes, he looked about frantically for Cat.

She was near him, off to the right, lying motionless. He went to her at a crouch, as he had done the previous year aiding a fellow investigator when they had come under fire in Colombia. There'd been no shooting here, just the explosive package, which he had triggered entering the cabin where he'd found Joe Whalleys, putting tension on a cord that pulled the lanyard of a delayed-fuse satchel charge. He was amazed they had both gotten off the boat in time.

She was very still, but conscious. He lifted her gently and turned her in his arms. Her blue-gray eyes were staring, but not at him.

"Cat. Cat. Can you hear me?"

"Yes."

"Are you hurt?"

"Not sure. Are you?"

"Not really. Can you move?"

She extended her arm, and then her fingers, and then her other arm. "Yes. I'm fine. Do I still have hair? I had this fear the bomb had burned off my hair."

He stroked her head, lifting long strands of her silky hair in front of her eyes. "Your hair is very much intact."

She craned her neck, looking for Burt. The old pilot was on his knees, staring at the burning wreckage on the water. He was sobbing and swearing, hurling the words "sons of bitches" at the night sky, his fury aimed at the perpetrators of this atrocity and at every son of a bitch who had had a hand in making a botch of his military career and his life.

Westman held Cat close. She was shivering, though the night was still warm.

"I flew seven missions in Iraq," she said. "They were just high-altitude, dumb patrols, but once I got painted by a Ba'athist Iraqi radar. I followed SOP and dropped a precision-guided GBU on the radar unit that targeted me, but I don't know what I hit. The bomb-damage assessment credited me with a score. I scrammed. I was scared I might get shot down and I was afraid of what they might do to me if I was. Nothing happened. I made it back to the boat. It was a routine trap. Now, all these years later, here in my home state, the bastards come at me again. They almost killed me. Almost killed you."

He kissed her, then got to his feet and helped her up carefully. Burt was still on his knees, ranting at his fate.

"Now it's our turn again," he said.

Cat turned and looked up the beach. "Someone's coming."

The policeman was a New Jersey state trooper. He got out of his patrol car slowly, a flashlight held high in his left hand, his right hand kept near his holstered automatic.

Turko was standing by the left rear tire. As the policeman

approached, he looked down at it, inserting a finger in the tread. Then he stood erect.

"Do you have a problem, sir?" said the policeman, who was as large as he was young.

"This wheel was making a noise," said Turko. "I think maybe it was just a stone caught in the tread."

"What do you have in there?"

"Nothing yet. We are moving furniture in the morning."

The policeman remained in place. "Would you open the rear doors, please?"

Turko shrugged. The satchel charge they'd prepared for this was in the right front seat. He went to the doors in back and pulled on the handle. They swung open with a slight screech of hinge.

The cargo area was empty, but for two submachine guns Turko had placed under a tarpaulin. The policeman played the light over it. "What's under there?"

"Nothing," said Turko. "I told you. We're moving tomorrow."

The young cop looked at him with great seriousness, leaning close. "May I see your license and registration?"

Turko reached for his wallet. The Iraqi reached for a pistol and shot the policeman twice in the back. The gunfire was loud and carried, but by then the Uzbeks had started their attack.

The senior ranger on duty at the State Park was an older, gruff man, with close-cropped hair and a weather-beaten face. He stared at Westman's CGIS identification for a long time after it was handed to him, as though there was something he could not quite make out. Finally, studying Westman just as thoroughly, he returned it.

"And what brings the Coast Guard to this state park?"

"These people were helping me with an investigation,"

Westman said. "Their boat ran aground and I was trying to help them get it under way again."

The ranger turned his attention to the sea. There were still flames flickering on floating debris. "That explosion rattled my windows. What was it, bilge fumes?"

Schilling was standing up, but looked dead. "Wasn't bilge fumes, damn it. Someone blew up my boat."

"Who did?"

"Don't know. But I'm going to find out."

The ranger turned back to Westman. "What investigation are you talking about?"

"The Bay Bridge bombing. This is Burt Schilling, captain of the *Roberta June*—or what little remains of her."

"Goddamn bastards," said Burt, still staring at the wreckage.

"You brought these vehicles onto the beach after hours," said the ranger, nodding at the flatbed. "You want to explain why you disobeyed park regulations?"

There were three other rangers with the man—two men and a young woman. They appeared to have no idea what to do, except stand there and listen to their leader.

"We were in a hurry to get the boat afloat," Westman said. "We were going to haul some heavy equipment off her with the winch and put it on the truck, but she blew up before we could even get a line out."

"You could have stopped by my quarters on the way in and asked permission."

Westman was wearying of this. "Look. I don't have time to discuss the matter any further. We have two fatalities—crew members. They were aboard the boat when she went up. I have to report this to the Cape May Coast Guard station and the state police as well. So, if you'll excuse me . . ."

He turned his back on the senior ranger and took out his cell phone. Cat limped over to Schilling to comfort him, ignoring the rangers as well.

Dewey answered immediately, very businesslike. "This is the Coast Guard cutter *Manteo,* Lieutenant Dewey speaking."

"Tim, it's Erik. I've got a bad situation here. The *Roberta June*'s been sabotaged, we've got two dead. The local park rangers are trying to arrest us for trespassing. I need some assistance on the scene."

"Can't assist anyone," Dewey replied. "The Farmingdale Nuclear Power Plant's taking automatic-weapons fire from the river. We're en route—full speed."

"I don't understand. The power plant's under attack?"

"Affirmative. From the water side. We've got everything that floats under way."

Westman's place now was up the Delaware at the attack scene. Orders, suspensions, the chain of command, none of that mattered. With the Coast Guard's limited resources, the first responsibility of any officer or seaman was deciding priorities. This one was obvious.

But he could be two hours getting to the New Jersey side of the river—if he could ever get free of these park rangers.

Westman took a step closer to the chief ranger, and used his cell phone again, calling the Delaware State Police.

"This is Special Agent Erik Westman of the Coast Guard Investigative Service," he said, loudly enough for all the rangers to hear. "I am in Henlopen State Park, on the beach approximately one and a half miles south of the cape. There has been an explosion aboard a boat that ran aground and homicide is suspected. We have two fatalities. I'm requesting assistance. All available Coast Guard personnel are responding to an incident at the Farmingdale Nuclear Power Plant in New Jersey."

"Stand by, please." The detective was checking him out. She came back on the phone in less than a minute. "You're the investigator who worked the three drownings with us?"

"Affirmative. I have orders to proceed to the power plant. The local park rangers are detaining us. Your assistance is requested."

"Got a unit on Highway 1 now. Will divert."

"Thank you."

"Do you think your case is connected to Farmingdale?"

It would be a useful lie. "Affirmative."

Concluding his cell phone conversation, Westman returned the instrument to his pocket and went to stand intimidatingly close to the senior park ranger, who was several inches shorter than he.

"I have alerted the Coast Guard and summoned the state police," he said. "They should be here shortly. There has been a terrorist attack on the Farmingdale nuclear plant in New Jersey. I've been ordered to get up there. I want you to secure this crime scene until the state police arrive."

The senior ranger was standing his ground. "Mister, all I know is that you've come sneaking in here at night and somehow a big boat gets blown up. You're not going anywhere until this is straightened out."

It was then that Westman noticed that the ranger had a holstered revolver. What law enforcement officer carried those anymore?

He leaned even closer. "I have identified myself as an agent of the Coast Guard Investigative Service. We have a major emergency. I am taking these people and leaving now. If you interfere with us any further, I am going to file charges against you for obstructing a federal investigation."

The ranger took out his pistol. "I'm following SOP, mister. You're staying here until the state police arrive."

Westman shook his head, then called to Cat and Schilling. "We're leaving now."

"What about Amy and Joe?" Schilling asked.

"They're dead, Burt," said Cat. "We saw them."

"We can't just leave them."

Cat glanced back at the rangers, who hadn't moved an inch. "These people will take care of them."

* * *

Turko considered the situation carefully. The security guards would fire on the truck. They wouldn't shoot at the police cruiser. He changed the plan again.

"I will take the police car," he said. "I can get in much closer with it before they start shooting. It will be better for you."

They lifted the policeman's body inside the rental truck and closed the doors. Turko gripped the Iraqi's shoulder in encouragement, then got into the police vehicle, searching for the light and siren switches as he waited for his colleague to start the truck. They would have to hurry, as the Uzbeks were probably dead by now.

The truck lights came on. Turko started his engine and hit the switches. Thumping onto the hard pavement, he held his speed down until the Iraqi was able to attain some momentum with his heavier vehicle. Then he began to accelerate.

The truck's headlights were bouncing and sliding back and forth in Turko's rearview mirror. The Iraqi was following too closely. They needed more of an interval when they reached the gate.

Turko slammed on his brakes. The rental truck skidded, its headlights growing large. When Turko stomped the accelerator to the floor, they receded.

The gate was just ahead. He could see men standing by it, looking his way. Keeping his siren whooping, Turko hit the brakes hard again, slewing sideways and then skidding off toward the other side of the road.

There were only two security guards at the gate. Turko had expected an army of them. They stared at him, but didn't raise their weapons. Then they did, looking up the road and at the rental truck that was careening toward them along it.

The Iraqi didn't hesitate, but aimed straight for the fence.

The wrenching squeal of snapping, stressed metal took Turko by surprise with the violence of its sound as the truck smashed through both fence lines almost without pause. The

Iraqi swerved from side to side briefly, then caught sight of the spent-fuel bunker and headed for it.

One of the security guards opened fire with his automatic weapon, but he hadn't a clear shot at the Iraqi. Turko watched amazed as Hussein leapt out of the truck and ran the short distance to the bunker, satchel in hand. Coming to a stop, he busied himself with the explosive package for a moment, then broke into a mad run back toward the hole he'd made in the fence.

He was hit several times and twisted as he fell. Slamming the police cruiser into reverse, Turko backed swiftly around and then ground into forward gear, roaring with squealing tires back up the road. A few seconds later, the darkness behind him flashed bright with a tremendous boom.

Other cars zoomed by in the oncoming lane, including another state police car. The uniformed officer behind the wheel seemed to pay Turko no mind, intent on his destination. It was several miles up the road.

Reaching the side road where he had hidden another car—a rusty Pontiac two-door sedan he'd stolen the day before—Turko drove the police car well into the bushes before getting out. He soon had the Pontiac heading north, hoping that was not yet the direction of the wind.

Lieutenant Dewey had stationed lookouts fore and aft, port and starboard, and had assigned a man full time to the radar. He had a searchlight at the bow and another atop the radar mast playing back and forth over the waters to forward.

It was the lookout to port who first caught sight of the pontoon boat, which was heading downriver with outboard full out, making a large, visible wake off the cutter's port beam. It had to be the intruder they'd been alerted to. No one else would be out in these waters at this hour, behaving this way. There was always the possibility it was a drunken fisherman, trying to avoid a citation. But Dewey meant to stop the boat, no matter what.

The *Manteo* was keeping pace with the smaller craft, but Dewey needed to overtake it, blocking its path. He needed to get close enough to fire a telling shot.

"Hugo," said Dewey to DeGroot. "We need to use the inflatable. I'll slow for the launch, but not for long. Take the .50-caliber sniper rifle and a good man for the helm. Call me on the intercom when you're ready."

"Aye, aye, Captain."

Dewey hadn't heard that from the master chief in a long time. "Shoot the motors, Hugo. Not the fugitives."

DeGroot merely nodded this time, then exited fast.

Dewey turned the cutter beam to the wind, providing DeGroot some shelter for the launch. When the faster inflatable was under way, white froth kicking up behind it, he ordered the *Manteo* back to full speed ahead, aiming for the barely discernible wake of the retreating pontoon boat.

Kelleter, Dewey's No. 2, came onto the bridge, having helped with the inflatable.

"Get someone on the machine gun," Dewey said. "I want periodic bursts. Get their attention and keep it."

"You got it."

The officer clambered noisily back down the ladder. Dewey looked to the computer projection of the Delaware River chart on his video screen. There was a wide bend in the river coming up. If they could keep herding the fugitive craft to port, there was a chance of forcing it to the shore.

Dewey went out onto the bridge wing. "Keep it on 'em," he shouted to the man working the forward searchlight. "We don't want to run him over when they stop him."

There were pinpricks of orange light from the fleeing boat. The wretches were shooting back. Dewey knew he could end it all with his twenty-five millimeter deck gun. He was sorely tempted.

The radio was crackling with official chatter. Coast

Guard and police vessels of all sorts were swarming over the river, seeking the terrorists everywhere. One police boat had run bow-first into the muck at the north end of Fort Delaware's island. In his haste, Dewey had failed to report his sighting and pursuit.

But he didn't want to take his eyes off his quarry. He called to a seaman standing at the window. "Get on the horn and inform all units of our location. Tell them we have suspects in sight and are pursuing."

The young man moved to the radio. Peering ahead, Dewey noted that the cone of illumination from the searchlight was sliding farther to port. Suddenly, the boat vanished into the darkness.

He'd turned, hard, to port. For a moment, Dewey feared the bastard was doubling back on them. With his shorter turning radius, he might get in the clear. Dewey stepped back inside and called DeGroot on the handheld radio.

"This is Dewey. Have we lost them?"

"Negative. I'm on him. He's running for the shore."

"Have you a shot at their motor?"

"Not if you want them alive."

"Stick with 'em. I'm following." He ordered a course change to due east, going now to the radar. He didn't want to pile the *Manteo* into the riverbank.

The quartermaster was calling to him from the helm. The searchlight had caught the fugitive boat again. Just as DeGroot had said, he was headed straight for the darker line of the horizon.

There were more gunfire flashes. The bad guys were shooting at DeGroot, who apparently was maneuvering off the pontoon boat's stern quarter. Dewey called out a reduction in speed. The shallow water was coming up fast.

Too fast. Dewey ordered a sharp turn to starboard and full stop. He crossed to the other side of the bridge. There were three more bursts of gunfire, then silence. The searchlight found the boat, which was now motionless.

DeGroot came onto the handheld. "We got 'em."
"Got the boat?" Dewey asked.
"Affirmative. And two suspects."
"Alive?"
"One dead. One alive."

Chapter 29

Leaving the uncertain park rangers behind, Westman, Cat, and Schilling departed Henlopen State Park by driving south along the beach toward Rehoboth instead of back through the park's main entrance, where the state police would be arriving. If this made them fugitives, Westman didn't care.

He drove the flatbed truck. Cat followed in the Wrangler, with a shell-shocked Burt beside her.

Once in Rehoboth and on hard pavement, they used the back streets of the town, passing by Silver Lake and rejoining Highway 1 at Dewey Beach. In the darkness of the Delaware State Seashore beyond, there were state cops to be seen on the highway, a couple whizzing by with rooftop lights whirling. But none bothered them. Everyone's attention was to the north. New Jersey. The possibility of radioactive clouds.

Westman rented a double room for them in a motel at the north end of Ocean City, just across the Maryland line from Fenwick Island, Delaware. Burt collapsed on one of the beds, asking for whiskey.

Cat sighed. "Is that really necessary, Captain Schilling?"

"Yes, ma'am. Can't think of anything more necessary."

He'd more or less lost everything of any importance to him that night. He had something coming. She hoped it would make him go to sleep.

"Do you think it's safe to go back out?" she asked Westman. They had parked the truck and the Wrangler behind the motel, by a Dumpster.

"Yes. I think we're a pretty low priority for law enforcement at the moment. But I want to look at you."

"Erik . . ."

"Let's not take any chances." He had her stand in the light so he could examine her face. The pupils of her eyes seemed normal. Apparently she'd suffered no concussion. But there was a nasty abrasion along her left cheekbone and cuts on her forehead and hand, plus a bloody scrape along her knee and shinbone.

"You must hurt like hell," he said.

"You don't look like a finalist in the Miss America contest yourself." She clung to him a moment, resting her head against his shoulder. "I'm not sure I'm up for what comes next."

"I'm not either—though I've no idea what it will be."

"You don't look unsure. You look like some Viking action hero."

"That's just Icelandic stoicism. I'm completely at a loss here."

"So what do we do?"

"I live in the belief that we'll know when the time comes." He kissed her forehead. "But right now, I'm going to try to get some help." He took out his cell phone.

"I'll be back in ten minutes," she said.

When she returned, he was watching the news on television. She took the fifth of Jack Daniel's from its brown paper bag and poured some of the whiskey into a cheap plastic cup, bringing it to Schilling as she might medicine to a sick child. "Here's your bourbon, Burt. Now sit up."

He'd been lying with his face to the wall. Slowly, he turned over and looked up at her. "You should get out of here," he said.

"No such luck," she said, handing him the cup. "Only one way out of this now."

She rose and went to Westman. "Where do we stand?"

"Help will be a while in coming."

The television networks were providing continuous live coverage of what seemed to be mass panic everywhere. Atlantic City was being evacuated—a massive traffic jam on the causeway leading to the mainland the result. People were fleeing Philadelphia for Bucks County.

"Are we all going to die of radiation?" she asked. "The people in the liquor store didn't seem to give a damn."

"Someone from the Nuclear Regulatory Commission came on to say there was no danger. A lot of people apparently think he's lying."

She sat down next to him. "Imagine the federal government doing that. Did you find anyone to help us?"

"I've called the Wilmington police, who haven't an officer to spare, and the Coast Guard. I hope to hear from my friend Tim Dewey on the *Manteo* again. But he has his hands full. More than anyone. He captured a terrorist suspect. They haven't identified him. Speaks a strange language. Something like Afghan."

"And now?"

"I'm going to walk over to the shore."

"It looks like rain."

"I need the sea."

They strolled an empty street hand in hand, coming finally to a beach just as deserted. The windows of the high-rises that stretched to the south were mostly dark.

She sat down in the sand and he joined her, putting his arm around her. Rough weather was sliding along the northern horizon again, darkening the night. A moment later, it was illuminated by a flash of lightning.

Westman listened to the following thunder. "It's a good ten miles away."

"You're good at that."

"Spent some time at sea."

"So did I."

"You Naval aviators are contemptuous of the sea. You call a ship a boat and the bow the sharp end."

She leaned closer, resting her head on his shoulder. "We're only contemptuous of people who don't fly."

He said nothing.

"Not you," she said. Her hand went to his.

The lightning became more general. Orange streaks darted from cloud to sea all along the line of storm.

"It looks like a battle," he said.

"Or a nuclear power plant turning into an apocalyptic disaster."

He squeezed her hand. "I don't think that's a worry. If there was a radioactive leak, you wouldn't have TV crews lined up outside the plant."

She shivered. "There's another worry."

"We'll get back the bomb."

Cat laughed. "A sick old drunk. A washed-up Navy flyer. And a Coast Guard cop who's in trouble with his own people."

"We'll get help."

"No, we won't. I don't know how it's been for you in your service, Warrant Officer Four, but if you haven't noticed yet, when the military wants to be stupid, it gets stupid from the top four-star down to E-1. That Air Force colonel at Dover could have ended this whole mess with a single phone call. So could that lady admiral of yours. Instead, they treat us like crazy people. There's a nuclear weapon somewhere along this coastline and another underwater right off the beach and they act like we're talking about flying saucers. I just hate them now. The Navy was everything to me. Like it was for my father. Now I hate it."

He kissed her forehead. "As I said before, you should take your Wrangler and go to Washington. Now. Tonight."

"No."

"You've got a shot, Cat. You were in the right. Now they know that. Take the chance."

"No. This is going to come first."

"What would your dad think?"

"I'm sorry you couldn't have known my dad. He'd be sitting right here with us. He did crazier things. I don't know how he stayed a commander."

Westman released her hand and got to his feet. "Very well, Lieutenant. We'll carry on."

Six or seven stabs of orange struck the sea in succession to the northeast, followed by a blue-white flare of light. In the brightness, they could see the distant silhouette of a ship.

She got up, facing the storm. "What do we do now, Erik? Let's figure that out."

"That's easy. Sleep. We're going to need it."

Encountering heavy traffic on Highway 49, Turko cut inland, turning to back roads and making his way by dead reckoning. The car radio was full of news, but much of it was contradictory. For some reason, there was no weather report. But the winds had been from the northwest just before he and his team had gone after the power plant. He'd have to gamble they'd stay that way.

All the bars he passed were closed. Finally, near a town called Mullica Hill, he found one with lights on. The bartender and three men dressed in jeans and T-shirts were staring fixedly at the television screen, which showed a blond woman with a microphone standing in front of a police car.

She was quoting unnamed federal officials as saying the attack on the Farmingdale plant had been successfully repulsed and there was no danger of radiation.

Turko had seen the explosion. The amazing little Iraqi had detonated the package inside the fence.

He ordered a double vodka and Coca-Cola, paying for it immediately. The bartender hardly glanced at him, returning quickly to the television set.

"Fuckin' rag-heads," said one of the men in jeans. "How many times do we gotta go over there and kick their ass?"

"They're tryin' to nuke us. We oughta drop a couple nukes on them," said another of the men. "End this shit."

The bartender gestured at them to be quiet as the network anchorman came on the screen. He had a bulletin. "The New Jersey State Police report that a suspect has been apprehended."

This was impossible. Turko had seen the Iraqi die.

"He has not been identified. He is being flown by helicopter to Washington. Police say he has been injured but we don't know the extent of his injuries. The police also say they have identified another suspect."

Turko ordered and paid for a second drink. He was nearly done with it when an image came on the screen that chilled him to the bone. It was his own picture, taken from the driver's license he had used. He was identified as Anthony Bertolucci.

Dewey got a radio call from the Lewes pilot boat station that an inbound vessel was headed into the bay. Immediately after the power plant explosion the Homeland Security Department had ordered the Delaware River closed to all maritime traffic except military and law enforcement, and the pilot station assumed that applied to Delaware Bay as well.

"Only to the river north of Bombay Hook," Dewey said, "but thanks for the heads-up. What type vessel?"

"Looks like a big tug."

"That's the one I'm looking for. Thanks again."

He went to the radar screen. The tug was still out of range. "Prepare a boarding party, Master Chief," he said. "And I want a man on the twenty-millimeter and the fifty-caliber."

Turko stopped at a convenience store and went directly to a pay telephone. He knew the number indelibly though he had only used it twice before.

"I need to talk to him," he said to the voice that answered.

"You'll have to wait."

"I understand. But I must talk to him."

"Wait."

"I will."

While he did, he continued to talk. Behind the counter were a teenage boy and a dark-skinned Asian woman who, having nothing else to do, were watching him.

He kept his face turned away.

"Why are you calling?" A different, gruffer voice.

"My picture is on television. The name Bertolucci too."

"Could not be helped."

"You promised."

"Could not be helped."

Turko hesitated. "The job is done. I want to leave now."

"No. The job is not done. You must do what you promised."

"What do you mean?"

"You know what I mean. Deliver the goods."

"I'm not sure that will be possible."

"It better be." The line went dead.

The cutter came out of the misty darkness fast, turning on its forward searchlight and flooding Bear Gergen's wheelhouse with an incapacitating brightness. Bear hove to, idling his engines. He'd picked up the approaching ship on his radar, but hadn't realized it was Coast Guard.

He'd prepared for that possibility, though. All of his explosives and firearms had been taken off and left with his cousin Leonard. The only thing illegal on the tug was the pint of Jim Beam in his back pocket. He tossed that over the side.

The Coast Guard vessel pulled close alongside and an officer came out on the bridge wing with a loud-hailer.

"Stand by to receive boarders!" he commanded.

Bear went out on deck and waved, signaling his acquiescence. He stood in the wheelhouse door as the cutter lowered an inflatable and four men clambered into it. When they came alongside, Bear recognized the cutter skipper, Lieutenant Dewey, and his master chief, Hugo DeGroot. All of the Coast Guardsman were wearing side arms.

"What's up, Lieutenant?" Gergen asked as Dewey came aboard.

The lieutenant adjusted his belt and uniform, then stepped forward, peering into the wheelhouse. "Don't you keep your radio on?" he said. "There was a terrorist attack on the Farmingdale nuclear power plant. The river's been closed from Bombay Hook to Trenton."

Bear's surprise was not feigned. He'd not been paying attention to anything but the task he'd had at hand. "I heard a lot of emergency chatter on the radio, but wasn't sure what it was."

"That's interesting," said Dewey. "Emergencies are your business, Gergen."

"I listen for distress calls."

"Right. What are you doing out here tonight—if you weren't responding to a distress call?"

"Taking some equipment down to my cousin's place in Ocean City." Once again, the best lie was the truth.

Dewey took a flashlight off his belt. Master Chief De-

Groot already had his in hand. "I'm going to have to search your boat, Gergen. Stand aside, please."

"Sure," Bear said, obeying. "How come?"

"Searching all vessels—because of the attack."

Gergen followed Dewey as he went into the wheelhouse. "What happened? Did they blow up the reactor?"

"They were going for one of the spent-fuel bunkers," said Dewey, leafing through Bear's logbook. "Might have done it if the perps had set the charge properly. It exploded in the yard. The perp was killed and the bunker's intact."

"Second time they fucked up."

"They've got the whole country in an uproar." Dewey pointed to a locked wooden cabinet. "Open that, please."

It contained legal papers from a number of salvage jobs, plus a collection of coastal charts. Everything was in order.

They went through the boat from bow to stern, tossing everything—turning bunk mattresses over and even checking out the bilges.

"Is this necessary, Captain?" Gergen asked when they'd returned topside again. "You guys know me. I've tipped you to a lot of bad guys. Why're you giving me a hard time?"

Dewey flashed his light around the deck. Something caught his eye and he went over to the starboard rail. It was scraped and bent. The wood below was marred and splintery. "What happened here?" he asked.

"I brought in a freighter a few days ago. She rode up on her towline."

"I don't recall seeing that when we visited you in Wilmington."

Gergen grinned. "As I remember that day, Lieutenant, my cousin's wife was aboard. You may have been distracted."

"We're not supposed to get distracted." Dewey made some entries in his notebook, then shoved it into a pocket. He stepped near Gergen. The former SEAL was slightly taller than him, and considerably wider.

"There was an incident down the shore from Cape Henlopen," Dewey said. "A head boat from Lewes blew up with two of the crew aboard. It's down as a suspected arson and homicide. You were in those waters tonight."

Master Chief DeGroot had his hand on his holstered automatic.

"I came alongside 'em—close as I could. They'd run aground on a falling tide. I asked if they wanted assistance, but they declined. As long as someone's aboard, I can't do anything on my own, unless they ask me to lay a line on a vessel. I knew that guy—Schilling. Former Air Force. We had a business deal. Anyway, I thought we had a deal, but he bailed out of it. Is he all right? He wasn't aboard when I came by. Some girl had charge of the boat."

"Schilling's alive. She's dead."

"Well, I don't know anything about any explosion. When did it happen?"

"Around ten o'clock."

"Hell, I was passing the Fenwick Island light by then."

Dewey snapped his notebook shut. "The Delaware State Police will be taking over the case," he said. "They'll likely be coming around to talk to you."

"Always happy to help, Lieutenant."

Dewey moved toward the rail. "You're forbidden north of Bombay Hook until this alert is lifted."

"Yes, sir."

When they were back aboard the *Manteo*, Dewey turned to DeGroot. "What do you think, Hugo?"

"I think that man's a bad actor."

"I haven't sufficient reason to take him into custody. But that tugboat could stand a going-over by a forensics team."

"I'll radio the Wilmington police."

Bear stood in his wheelhouse, watching the Coast Guard cutter slip off the radar screen, heading south.

"Start the engines," he said to Roy Creed.

"Where we going?" Creed responded. "He said the river's closed."

"Fuck it."

Westman awakened to early light and, once again, a ringing of his cell phone. Without disturbing Cat, he rose and went to the chair by the window of the motel room.

If it was dePayse, he would click off. This would be a form of insubordination, but he was past worrying about that.

It was Dewey.

"Sorry to get back to you so late. We've had a busy night."

"You get any more terrorists?" Westman asked, speaking softly.

"There was a dead one. We put him ashore in New Jersey. The live one was taken by helo to the Federal Detention Center in Alexandria. What's your situation?"

"We're in a motel at the north end of Ocean City. Was there a state police report on the *Roberta June*?"

Cat had awakened. She made a face and rolled over on her back, looking up at the grubby ceiling. He'd heard her crying during the night, but that was gone now.

"They've opened a homicide investigation," Dewey said. "They're trying to identify the two victims. They recovered the remains."

"Amy Costa and Joseph Whalleys," Erik said. "Attribute that to other Lewes mariners."

"Roger that." Dewey paused to give an order to a crewman, then quickly came back on. "We stopped Gergen's tug last night. Made a thorough search. Found nothing—and I mean nothing."

"It's pretty hard to hide a two-thousand-pound hydrogen bomb."

"The starboard rail and bulkhead showed some damage. Could have come from a very heavy object."

"Where did you encounter him?"

"In Delaware Bay—four miles south of Bombay Hook."

"Coming from the south?"

"Affirmative."

Cat was watching him intently now. "Could he have been up the Jersey coast?"

"Maybe. But he said he had stopped by the *Roberta June*. Found the boat run aground. He said he offered assistance but it was declined."

"So he was coming from the south and had been below Cape Henlopen?"

"Affirmative."

Westman pondered the view out the window, which was of the alley and—over a flat rooftop—a glimpse of Assawoman Bay. "I have no map or chart here. How far south could he go last night and still be back to Delaware Bay in time to run into your patrol?"

"Stand by."

Westman watched Cat rise and stretch. She unhappily surveyed their quarters.

"He could get no farther than Assateague Island," Dewey said.

"But he could make the cut into Isle of Wight Bay at the south end of Ocean City."

Dewey paused. "Sure. Easy. But that's mighty shallow water for an oceangoing tug."

"Not in the Intracoastal. That channel runs close in shore."

"Right along the waterfront."

"Tim, can you get down here?"

"We have orders to maintain patrols until sixteen hundred hours."

"And after sixteen hundred?"

"They may let us stand down. The Justice Department thinks they have all the tangos." "Tango" was the phonetic alphabet for "T"—as in "terrorist."

"Except for Anthony Bertolucci."

"Washington says there were only three in the attack. They have two killed, one in custody. He wasn't among them."

"Would you attack a nuclear power plant with three men?"

"They destroyed the World Trade Center and part of the Pentagon with only nineteen."

"There is a hydrogen bomb somewhere out there, Tim. And someone took it off the *Roberta June*."

"I believe you. But I'm under orders."

"I could really use your help down here."

"I can respond to situations." Dewey hesitated. "Admiral dePayse had half the Coast Guard looking for you last night. Before the attack on Farmingdale. I don't know how to put this, but our orders include locating you and having you brought back to Buzzard's Point."

"I hope you're not going to declare me found."

"This is a very unofficial conversation. I'll check in later." He was gone.

Cat was looking through the gym bag they had brought in from the Wrangler. "We have a revolver, two automatics, and no clean clothes." She stood up straight, looking at herself in the wall mirror with great disapproval. "No toothbrush. No comb. And, more to the point, no food."

"I'll go to an ATM machine. We'll resupply."

Burt was snoring. "I'll go with you," Cat said.

Creed called back to Gergen from the bow. "Got a welcoming committee, Bear."

"I see 'em."

Some uniformed police and two men in civilian clothes were standing at Gergen's dock. He kept the tug moving toward them.

"You think they mean to arrest us?"

"If they were going to do that, they would have come out after us. Just be cool."

The group on the dock did and said nothing as Bear's crew completed the tie-up. When Bear finally stepped out of the wheelhouse, Customs Agent Elward came aboard, followed by a man in a sport coat Bear presumed to be a local police detective.

"Good morning, Mr. Elward. What can I do for you?"

"Few things happened last night I'd like to talk to you about," Elward said, seating himself on the rail.

"Yeah, I heard there was an attack on the Farmingdale power plant. But I don't know anything about that."

"We don't suppose you did. The perps are dead or in custody, though we're also looking for another suspect." He took out a four-by-five police print of a driver's license and photo, the license made out to an Anthony Bertolucci. "You come across this guy anywhere?"

Bear studied the picture of the man he knew as Skouras carefully. He might buy a little extra consideration for himself if he told what he knew about the fellow. But he'd implicate himself in illegal gun sales and worse. And he'd screw up his big score.

"Sorry," Bear said, handing back the photo. "Nobody I know."

"They came within an inch of blowing open one of those spent-fuel bunkers. Any idea how many people might have died?"

Bear edged backward a little, not liking the way his visitors had him encircled. "Haven't a clue. Was this Bertolucci guy involved in it?"

"He's wanted in connection with the Bay Bridge attack,"

said the detective. "But it's a good guess this is all the same terrorist gang we're dealing with."

"You said 'a few things' happened last night," Bear said.

"That's right. Which is why we'd like you to come with us."

"Come with you where?"

"To police headquarters," said the detective.

"Just to talk," Elward said.

They'd bought some new shirts and shorts, and then a breakfast of doughnuts and coffee, bringing an ample amount of both back for Burt.

He awoke grudgingly.

"Good morning, Burt," said Cat. "We're going to go looking for the bomb."

Schilling rubbed his eyes. "What? Where?"

"Here, in Ocean City," said Westman. "One of our cutters stopped your friend Gergen's tug and searched it. Except for a broken railing that I think was damaged taking the bomb aboard, they found nothing. He had to put it somewhere. He couldn't get much farther south than Ocean City. Either he dropped it back in the water, or put it ashore. A tug that size couldn't get close in to a beach. We think he used the Intracoastal channel and took it to Ocean City."

Sitting up, Schilling blinked, as though unsure of his surroundings. "Where in hell would they put a two-thousand-pound bomb in Ocean City?"

"We're going to take a look."

"We brought you doughnuts and coffee," Cat said.

Schilling took note of them. "Okay. You go ahead. I need to think." He rubbed his chin. "Got to shave."

They left him to his morning. Theirs took them down every side street the length of Ocean City, from 145th Street down to First. The bay side of the town had many, many harbors, but only a half dozen or so reached by a deep-water channel.

Below Seventh Street, however, the channel ran parallel to the shore and close to it. Driving by every dock and mooring in that far section of the city, they encountered only what they had along the northern reaches of the resort town—charter fishing boats, runabouts, pontoon boats, and Jet-Skis and other "personal watercraft" as the industry called them.

Westman parked at the end of the Coastal Highway, near the amusement park and the causeway leading west across Isle of Wight Bay to the mainland.

Across the cut to the south was the north end of Assateague Island.

"You were crying last night," he said.

"No. I'm done with that. That was Burt."

Bear's crew was invited to come along to police headquarters as well. Roy Creed was taken to a separate interrogation room while the others were made to wait. Bear got special treatment. Elward, the detective, and two men Bear took to be federal agents gathered around him at a table in the main chamber.

"Wilmington police recovered a vehicle from the Delaware River," Elward said. "There were four dead men inside. They were shot to death."

"Sorry to hear."

"The vehicle was a black Lincoln SUV that matched the description you gave us in your drive-by shooting complaint."

"Well, I'm glad you got the bastards."

"You don't know how they got into the river?"

"If it's the same SUV, all I know is that they came and went. That's what they do in drive-bys."

"They were shot up pretty good," said the detective.

Bear shrugged.

"They were identified as associates of Enrique Diller," said Elward. "We had agents call on Mr. Diller in Philadel-

phia. He was not at home but they found several bags of
high-grade marijuana and cocaine. They're a perfect match
with the packages we took off the motor-sailor."

"We've been over that," Gergen said. "I brought in that
vessel. I didn't mess with any dope. When I ran into these
guys in a bar, I called in a tip and you people made a bust."

One of the other cops, apparently a narc, leaned in. "How
did you run into these guys in a bar?"

Bear sighed. "I was having a beer and they came in. They
asked me about the dope on the boat."

"And?"

"I told them I knew nothing about it."

"And?"

"They gave me a hard time. When they left, I dropped a
dime on them. Then they came around for their nasty visit,
and now someone has ended their drug sales careers. Happy
ending."

The homicide detective resumed control of the conversation. "Do you know a Homer Grunz?"

"Guy that runs a bar?"

"Yes."

"I drink there every once in a while. I never knew his last
name."

"He was found in a Dumpster near his tavern. He was
shot to death."

Bear was startled, but worked to keep his cool. "That's a
bad neighborhood."

"He had a lot of money on him. Several thousand dollars."

"Must be working something on the side."

"The money was still on him," said the detective. "That's
not what you expect when someone gets rolled in a neighborhood like that."

Bear shrugged again.

"You've been making a lot of trips up and down the
river," Elward said.

"I work the coast. Only way to get there."

"Did you notice anything suspicious around the Farming-dale power plant?"

Gergen shook his head. "What's up with that? Did I sail through radiation?"

"The National Nuclear Security Administration has the case. They say there's no danger."

Bear shifted in his chair, though his discomfort had nothing to do with his position. "When are you guys going to catch those ratfuckers?"

"We'll ask the questions, Gergen," said Elward. "But since you ask, the Coast Guard took one in custody. Two others turned up dead. We're looking for this Anthony Bertolucci."

"Don't know him. Can I go now?"

"There's another small matter," Elward said. "A fishing boat out of Lewes blew up last night south of Cape Henlopen. You were on the scene just prior."

"I've already explained that to the Coast Guard. The boat had gone aground. I know the owner, Burt Schilling. I came alongside to offer assistance."

"Or take it under tow as salvage," said Elward.

Gergen nodded. "That too. But there was crew aboard. They wanted nothing to do with me. They hadn't even made a distress call."

"They're dead."

"Yeah, I know. It's really too bad. She was a nice-looking kid."

Every eye on the room was on him hard. Judgments were being made—by experts.

"Look," Bear said. "I'm known to you guys. I've helped out law enforcement for years. I'm ex-military. Why are you hassling me?"

Elward smiled. "We're just looking for a little more help, Mr. Gergen."

"What were you doing down below Cape Henlopen?" the homicide detective asked.

"I told the Coast Guard. Moving some equipment down to Ocean City."

"What kind of equipment?"

"Welding tools. Acetylene. Some grapples and hooks. My cousin Leonard has a boat rental down there. He's got some repairs to make."

"You couldn't drive? You have a pickup truck."

"We've had severe weather. Never know when a salvage job'll turn up. Thought I had one with that head boat."

The policemen fell silent. Bear sensed this was over.

"I expect we'll want to talk to you again, Mr. Gergen," said Elward. "Don't go on any long voyages."

Roy Creed rode in the cab of the pickup truck with Bear. His other two crew members sat in back. It was a short drive back to the docks.

"How much you think they know, Bear?" Creed asked.

Gergen turned to spit out the window, then wiped his mouth on the back of his hand. "I think they suspect we're mixed up with the whack job on the four in the SUV, but that's all. I don't think they're going to push it. If you're going to be in our line of work, Roy, it pays to be a snitch. Legal bribery, if you know what I mean."

Creed nodded. "What now?"

"We go into the military surplus business."

Bear dropped Creed and the two other crew members at the main gate to the dockyard, then continued down the street to a convenience store, where he stopped to pick up two twelve-packs of Budweiser.

He took his time. When he finally returned to the docks and parked near his tug, he paused to retrieve a black plastic trash bag from behind a container. Inside was a Beretta nine-millimeter, which he removed.

Climbing aboard, he went immediately below, handgun pointing the way. The man at the foot of the stairs, a pistol in his own hand, stood frozen in place.

"Mr. Skouras," said Bear. "We gotta talk."

Chapter 30

Colonel Baker had gone to a meeting on base recreation, which Captain Baldessari took to mean he was getting in a morning round of golf. That left Baldessari more than ample time to ponder the decision he was about to make, but—as matters developed—he didn't need much time at all.

He sat watching CNN replay footage from the New Jersey power plant attack, sipping coffee as he calculated the distance from there to Dover Air Force Base. He figured something like twenty miles as the crow flies—and the radioactive particles drifted—but it wouldn't have mattered if it had been fifty miles. If the terrorists had succeeded—a few feet closer, a different wind direction—*finito*.

If they were actually to acquire a useful amount of nuclear material to take where they wished . . .

So there was only one decision to make after all.

He finished his coffee, then opened the right-hand lower drawer of his desk. Removing a stack of old Air Force news releases he'd put there, he took out the file he'd hidden beneath.

It was thick. He'd made a copy of everything, including the service records of Schilling and the Navy woman. Placing them in a large, padded mailer, he sealed it and affixed an address label, filling it out by hand. Then he went to his office closet, stripped to his underwear, and pulled on a pair of jogging shorts.

"Going for a run," he said to the sergeant at the desk outside.

"Yes, sir," said the man, barely taking notice. Baldessari was always going for runs.

His route took him out the main gate of the base and up Highway 113 to the State Capitol complex—a mere three miles. The post office was not much farther. Pausing to cool off before entering, he reconsidered his plan, but could think of no alternative.

"I'd like to send this Express Mail," he said to the woman postal clerk behind the counter.

"You'll need to fill out an Express Mail label," she said. He felt stupid as he completed the one she gave him. What he was, though, was rattled. Baker would cut him orders for Thule, Greenland, if he ever learned what Baldessari was about to do.

But it had to be done. He returned the package to the woman. After she had affixed postage and collected money from him, she dropped it in a canvas bin. He left the post office without looking back at it.

When he returned to his office after stopping at the BOQ for a shower, he felt good—as he always did after a run.

Pec sat at the kitchen table, sipping from a cup of hot, strong tea while he cleaned his pistol, pausing also from time to time to glance irritably at the wall clock. They were late, and then later. Finally, the screen door from the rear porch and three men came in. He had been expecting four.

"Is he dead?" Pec asked.

The first man through the door slumped into the chair opposite, yawning. Then he shook his head. "Don't know."

Pec slammed the receiver of his automatic closed. "You were to have followed him throughout, and taken him afterward."

The other man, an Albanian named Kucove with a pleasant face and a close-cut beard, now shrugged. "We waited by the car—where he left it—but he never came back for it."

"Did he have another car?"

"No. Just the Toyota and the rental truck. The only other car we saw on the road was a police car. It sped away after the explosion."

Pec set down his pistol and took a larger swallow of tea. "Was he killed in the explosion then?"

"It is strongly possible. The man with him was found dead by the security fence. Turko was to lay the charge himself. Perhaps, to make certain it did what we wished, he gave his life for the cause."

"They said nothing about a fourth man on the television news."

"Perhaps his body was completely destroyed. It was a large explosion."

Pec pondered this, slowly finishing his tea. Kucove patiently waited. The other two had gone into the living room of the shabby apartment and now could be heard snoring. "I would not expect Turko to do anything like that," Pec finally said.

"Perhaps you misjudge him."

Pec gave the Albanian a sharp look. The effect was the same as a slap. "If I misjudged men like Turko, I would be dead now."

A vaguely pained expression came over Kucove's face. He gave every indication of wanting to join the other two in the living room. "Are you angry that he failed?"

"He was more successful than I thought he would be. I had doubts that he would even try. I thought he would run."

Another yawn. "But now he is dead—probably. We are done with him."

"He is not dead."

Kucove became more alert. "How can you know that?"

"You said the police car sped away from the power plant."

"Yes."

"Police cars would be speeding toward the plant, you idiot. That was Turko. He drove right by you."

"How would he get a police car?"

"He is a smart man." Pec stood, putting the pistol into his pocket. "Come. We must leave this place now."

The instant Turko saw the gun in Gergen's hand, he knew he had made a serious miscalculation. He should have been suspicious when he found the tugboat at its mooring with no one aboard or about, yet with the wheelhouse doors and aft hatch standing open. He had been waiting with his pistol ready, but had completely lost the advantage.

"Is your crew with you?" Turko asked.

Gergen nodded, taking a step forward. "If you look up at that open hatch above you, you'll see a large firearm pointed at your head. Another man is behind the door to your right. A third is waiting on the deck to cut short any attempt at a departure."

Turko lowered his own weapon. "Is it your intention to kill me?"

"If I was going to do that, I would have done that. I want to talk to you."

The door to Turko's right opened and a crewman as large as Gergen entered, carrying a baseball bat. Turko had been tortured by Russians. These Americans didn't seem any more benevolent.

"What do you want to know?" Turko asked. "Are you working for the police?"

Gergen came close and snatched away Turko's pistol, then motioned to the Chechen to sit down on the flooring, as he seated himself on a nearby bunk. The large crewman stood just behind Turko, brandishing the bat.

"You killed Homer?" Gergen asked.

Turko doubted the two were close friends. "An associate did that. He has a compulsion. If it is consolation, he is now dead."

"This was so he wouldn't be able to identify you as the man he sold explosives to?" Another nod. "And you came here because you thought I supplied that C-4 to Homer?"

"You were the most likely source of it. That tavern keeper would have trouble laying hands on firecrackers."

"And you were going to kill me too?"

"No. I wanted to join forces. My associates are all dead. I need a refuge."

"You're a cautious man."

"I'm still alive."

"For guys who like to still be alive, I may not be the best choice for a pal."

"I don't have a lot of choices."

Gergen studied the man's face, leaning forward on his knees. "I want to talk to you about a business proposition—involving a more interesting kind of explosive."

"What could be more interesting than C-4?"

Bear assumed an unnatural calm, which only increased Turko's nervousness. "A nuclear weapon."

Turko looked at him incomprehensibly. "We have no nuclear weapons."

Gergen grinned, relaxing a little, letting the barrel of his pistol swing slightly away from Turko. "I know that. What I have in mind is a way for you to take care of that lack."

"You're offering to provide us with a nuclear weapon?" For a fleeting moment, he thought Gergen might be insane. But, except for his bizarre offer, he showed no sign whatsoever of that.

"I believe that operative word is 'sell.'" Gergen grinned again, more widely.

Not insane at all. "What sort of nuclear weapon?" Turko asked. "A missile—something like that? It would be no use to us."

Gergen shook his head. This "Skouras," or whatever his real name was, was no military man. "It's not a missile. It's a forty-year-old Mark-28 hydrogen bomb. Detonated according to the manual, set it for an airburst at, say, two thousand feet, you could wipe out a pretty good-sized city— Baltimore, Washington—even Philly. But that's not any good to you. You guys probably don't have a bomber, do you? And even if you did, you'd still never get near 'em. The Air Force has combat air patrols over pretty much any place with traffic lights."

"Then what . . ."

Gergen raised his hand. "What you want is what's inside. Plutonium. All kinds of nasty things you can do with that."

Turko stared, thinking. "What proof have you that you have this bomb?"

Gergen pulled up the left leg of his jeans and tugged something out of the lining of his boot. He handed it over to Turko.

It was a Polaroid photograph of the stern of a large boat. A long cylindrical object hung in what appeared to be a basket. Holding it closer, Turko saw that it was the twisted wreckage of the aft rail. The bomb, if that's what it was, appeared to be heavy. The boat leaned to one side.

"How do I know this is a nuclear bomb?"

"What else could it be? You ever see a conventional bomb like that?"

"They used big strange bombs in Afghanistan and Iraq. Also in Iran. 'Bunker Busters,' they call them."

"This is no mere Bunker Buster. This is a genuine Cold War H-bomb, designed to be dropped by B-52's. The guy who owned this boat? He was the pilot of the cargo plane that jettisoned the bomb and another just like it into the Atlantic. Engine failure or something. He let them sit there on the bottom all this time. Now, for some reason, he's pulled it up again. Maybe he plans to sell it. Or maybe use it to shake the government down for something he wants. Anyway, I have it now."

Turko held the photo very close. "There is someone lying on that upper deck. What do you call it?"

"The bridge. The flying bridge."

"The person seems dead."

"The person is. There was an explosion. The boat is kaput. *Finito*."

"This picture was taken before that."

"Obviously."

"But you have the bomb?"

"I do."

Turko handed the bent photo back to the bearded man. "You said 'sell,' Mr. Gergen."

Bear liked the "Mister." "I did indeed. You have associates left, Skouras? Superiors? Someone up the food chain?"

"I cannot speak for them."

"But you can speak to them. That is what I want you to do—as soon as possible."

"I'm not sure."

Bear nodded to Roy Creed, who grabbed Turko by the collar and dragged him close to where Gergen sat on the bunk. "Here's what you can be sure of, Skouras. I have to get rid of this thing fast. Thanks to you shitheads, there are Feds from every agency in the book swarming all over the place, including the Coast Guard. They're the biggest problem of all." He leaned down, his face not a foot from Turko's. "I want a million dollars in cash."

"That much? You're crazy."

"Maybe so. But I like the sound of it. A million. Very nice and neat. That's what I want. When I turn you loose, you will have twenty-four hours to do the deal. You will need an oceangoing boat and—did I mention it?—a million dollars in cash."

"This is ridiculous. Impossible." Turko felt the end of the baseball bat come to rest at the back of his neck.

"Nothing is impossible for you guys. Look at all you've accomplished. Nineteen guys with plastic box cutters knocking down the World Trade Center. You got the U.S. to go to war in the Mideast—and we still have people getting killed over there. Look at what's happened since. Jeez, these last few days, a handful of you just about shut down five states and the District of Columbia, even though you blew your missions."

"A million dollars. We have nothing like that."

Gergen shook his head. "Sure you do. A cell phone call to Saudi Arabia. That ought to do it."

"I am not an Arab."

Gear made a face. "I'm an ex-Naval officer, pal. I've been dealing with you pricks for years. I know exactly where your money comes from. It's time you recycled a little of it, don't you think? Anyway, that's my offer. A million dollars. You get the bomb. You bring a vessel that can handle it. You do all this within twenty-four hours. If not—well, I'll go elsewhere."

"How will I contact you?"

"I'll give you the number of my cell phone. I'll expect your call before midnight. Later 'n that, you can forget it. I'm going elsewhere." Bear nodded to Roy Creed, who pressed down with the baseball bat until Turko's head was against the flooring. "I want you to know something else, Skouras. You're a little too homicidal for my liking. I was in the Navy eleven years. Navy SEALs. All that time, I don't think I've killed as many people as you have in the last couple of weeks."

He put his foot on Turko's head. "I kinda liked Homer. Really pissed me off, your whacking him like that. I want you to put it out of your mind that you might try doing that to

me. That's not how this is going to end. If I even have a
dream about your trying that, you're all dead. I'm better than
you. My crew, we're all better than you. We're all ex-
military. You understand?"

"Yes."

Bear nodded to Creed again. The foot and the bat were removed. Turko sat up. "You're going to let me go?" he said.

"Twenty-four hours. My guys will give you a ride to
wherever you need to go."

Harpoon Hannah's was a waterfront restaurant and bar that
sat on the busy channel connecting Assawoman Bay with
Little Assawoman Bay just south of the bridge that carried
Highway 54 from Fenwick Island to the mainland. In normal
times on such a warm and pleasant summer evening, it
would have been jam-packed, but on this nervous night
fewer than half the tables were taken.

The outdoor Tiki bar was a little livelier than the restaurant, and closer to the water. Cat and Westman found an
empty open-air booth with a view up and down the channel.
The adjoining rental operation had some pontoon boats and
a couple of runabouts tied up along its dock, but appeared to
be closed. The channel otherwise was surprisingly busy with
traffic.

A breathless, harried waitress appeared suddenly beside
them. Westman ordered a glass of red wine and Cat a gin
and tonic.

"Do you want to eat in the restaurant?" he asked.

Cat shook her head, a strand of blond hair falling across
her eye. She brushed it back. "Out here is fine. I'm not too
hungry. They have a good crab dip."

The sun was near setting and had slipped into the west-
ward haze, suffusing everything with a pinkish glow. On the
water, a pontoon boat with two elderly couples on it was
heading upstream toward the bridge. Behind it, a Boston

Whaler was following close—a young man in cap and T-shirt at the wheel, his girlfriend, similarly dressed, riding up front at the bow.

High in the eastern sky, a faint circle of moon was emerging in the darkening blue. Cat's eyes were on the wooden table. He touched her hand.

"You holding up?"

She gave him the weakest of smiles. "Not really. How could I be?"

"Can you make it?"

"Sure. As you put it, to the end."

Their drinks came. She withdrew her hand. Westman ordered their food, then leaned back, looking down the channel.

"I wish I knew how to get from here to there," he said.

"To where?"

"The end."

She took a large swallow of the gin and tonic. "We'll think of something."

"The bomb has to be in Ocean City—unless they moved it inland."

"There's no place where that big tug could get close enough to the shore. No deep-water dock. We looked at every inch of that bay front today."

"I know."

The water in the channel had turned a luminescent turquoise. It would be gone in a few minutes, but it made the moment magical.

"Romantic," he said.

"What?"

"It's romantic here."

She sighed. "I'm sorry. That's not exactly where I have my thoughts right now."

He sipped his wine, watching the distant running lights of another boat coming up the channel. "Whatever we do," he said, "we're going to need Burt. Do you think he's up to this?"

"If he got some sleep today. That, a decent meal, and a couple of shots of Jim Beam, he'll be up to it. Whatever 'it' is going to be." She looked at her watch. "Your Coast Guard mates said they might be free to help us after 1600 hours. It's almost eight o'clock."

"He said he'd call when he was clear. I don't want to bother him again."

The approaching vessel was fully in view now—a pontoon boat, with a green-and-white-striped canopy. There was a large party aboard—every seat taken—yet the big pontoons kept it high above water.

"Poor Coast Guard," she said, "stuck in the Homeland Security Department—the only federal agency more screwed up than the Pentagon."

The boat went by—its passengers looking happy, snatches of music audible over the noise of the outboard.

"Erik. Are you all right?"

He took out his cell phone, quickly punching in a number.

"I thought you said you weren't going to bother Dewey," she said.

"I'm not calling him," Westman said. "I just now realized where they've put the bomb."

Chapter 31

Once free of Gergen's man, Turko walked to the parking lot of Wilmington's Amtrak station and a Volkswagen Jetta. He had become so good at this form of theft that, if he could somehow extricate himself from his dangerous situation, he supposed he might go to New York, Chicago, or Los Angeles and take it up as a profession. They weren't going to let him practice law in this country.

Using a circuitous route, he drove to the parking area on the Delaware River opposite the Farmingdale plant. He'd no idea whether Pec had tried to follow his movements since their last encounter, but he'd done his best to throw off the Kosovar's people. Presuming he'd succeeded, he put this car in place well before he made his telephone call, using Pec's special number. The conversation took only a few seconds.

Within an hour, a van came down the entry road to the park, pulling off to the side well before the parking lot.

Turko was not in the Volkswagen but hiding in bushes on

a sandy bluff that had a view of the entry road. He watched intently as the vehicle stopped well short of the parking lot. Its headlamps went out and four men emerged, moving swiftly and silently toward the river. When they were past him, he crept down the sandy slope, and moved back up the road toward the van, keeping to the deepest shadows.

Circling around behind the van, he snapped open the passenger-side door, sticking the barrel of his pistol into Pec's neck.

"Get out."

Pec hesitated, then did as instructed. Turko slid open the rear door with his left hand, then used the gun to urge Pec into the rear seat, and then to the far side of it. Keeping the pistol aimed at the other's chest, he climbed in afterward, pulling the door shut and locking it.

"They will be coming back," Pec said.

"Yes. But not right away. When they discover my car is empty, they will take cover, not knowing where I am. Then they will go looking for me. It will be several minutes before they realize I'm not there."

Pec glanced away, down the road. "What do you want?"

"Simply to talk to you—without being killed."

"Be quick."

"I have something very important to offer you."

"And what can that be? You have managed to accomplish nothing important. Your photograph is being shown on television. The explosion on the bridge caused no real harm and the nuclear power plant attack was a failure. Things have gone very badly, and it is all your fault."

"That doesn't matter. What I have to offer would make even my success irrelevant."

"Out with it. I don't like being teased."

"I have a nuclear bomb."

Pec's head snapped around. He studied Turko's face as best he could in the darkness. "This is the first joke I have ever heard you make, Turko."

"It is not a joke." He related Gergen's story and proposition.

"Do you believe this man?"

"Yes. He showed me a photograph of this bomb. It can be nothing else."

"There are police—federal investigators—everywhere here. How could someone hide anything so big as that?"

"It will fit on a truck," Turko said. "Or on a boat. What you want is what's inside. The plutonium core. You possess that plutonium, and the uranium that's also inside, and the world is yours. Our failures here—my failures—will be forgotten. They will honor you. Reward you."

"He asks a price?"

"A million dollars."

Pec swore in his native language. "You know that is impossible. It is crazy."

"Yes, but . . ."

"How can you trust a man who is so foolish that he thinks we can produce one million dollars in American money by tomorrow noon?"

"I don't trust him. But I believe his claim that he has this bomb. He pretends to be a simple salvage operator. He is a professional criminal. He would not dare lie or cheat about this. He knows it would mean his life."

"I must see this bomb before we talk about money."

"He wants it the other way around."

"No. We do it my way. We will look at this bomb and then decide."

They sat silently. Pec's men were approaching the van. Another of them suddenly appeared at the window next to Turko, an automatic weapon pressed against the glass—aimed at the center of Turko's head. Were he to fire, Turko would die instantly, but Pec might be killed as well. Turko pretended to ignore him.

"You don't mean to pay him anything for this, do you?" Turko said.

"That I decide later," Pec said. "I want to see this bomb."

"We are to meet him tomorrow. At noon. He gave me an address. In Ocean City."

"Ocean City? Can that be safe for us now?"

"It's where the bomb is."

Pec thought. "You have an address?"

"Yes."

"Okay, then. We go now."

"Now?"

"Now. To Ocean City. Now."

Leon Kelly responded to Westman's request within fifteen minutes. "Got Gergen's military 201 file," the FBI agent said. "And the VICAP database has entries from Customs and you guys as well."

"What connections does he have in Ocean City, Maryland?" Westman asked.

"Stand by," Kelly said. "I'm on my laptop. We've got all his associates listed here."

Westman waited. They were back at the motel. Burt had gone out, leaving no explanation. Cat was lying on the plastic-covered couch, gazing up at the ceiling.

"One of his crew is from there," Kelly said. "Used to live there anyway. Wait a minute." Westman could hear the clicking of keys. "Here's another guy. Leonard Ruger. Cousin. Operates a boat rental—pontoon boats, runabouts, personal watercraft. Dope dealer on the side. Local narcs and the DEA have left him alone because Gergen is on so many snitch lists."

"Can you give me the address of the boat rental?"

"You bet." The FBI man consulted his computer again and then gave Westman a location at the southern end of Ocean City—where the Intracoastal channel ran close to the shore.

"Thank you, Leon," Westman said. "It's exactly what I was looking for."

"You need an assist?"

"Is Payne about to help me?"

"If you got a line on the terrorists."

"Got to be straight with you, Leon. This has to do with the missing hydrogen bomb."

"I bring that up with Payne again and I'm going to be reassigned to our Des Moines office."

"Thought as much. Maybe I can still get some help from my guys."

"Find me a terrorist link. I'll pass it on to headquarters and maybe we can work up another joint task force."

"If there's a terrorist link to this bomb, then we may be too late."

"Call me back." Kelly killed his phone.

Cat stretched out her legs and turned her head toward Westman. "Any luck?"

"Yes. An address. South end of Ocean City."

She sat up, rubbing her left elbow. "You and me—we take this on all by ourselves?"

"I just want to determine that the bomb is there. Once we've identified it, maybe we'll get reinforcements."

"We should wait for Burt."

"Why?"

"To bring the truck."

"If we get help, we won't need it."

"Erik, we're going to need everything we can lay our hands on—with or without your 'reinforcements.' "

Westman's cell phone began to ring.

Dewey went out on the bridge wing, holding his phone tightly close to his ear. They were moving at top speed down Delaware Bay's main channel, between Joe Flogger and Miah Maull Shoals—forty feet of water beneath them but only thirteen feet to the port side and twenty-one feet to starboard.

"Erik," he said. "We got a break. I've been authorized to run a patrol down the shore. They said to the Delaware state line, but I can extend the area if there's anything suspicious."

"Can you come down as far as the OC Inlet?"

Dewey considered this. "Did you find your bomb?"

"I think so, but I haven't confirmed it. You willing to take a chance on me? With Admiral dePayse breathing so much fire, that could be taking quite a chance."

"As a matter of fact, there's a district-wide order for your apprehension and transport to headquarters in Washington," Dewey said.

"That's not where I want to be."

"Who does?" Dewey looked to the water outside. "I'm not sure how much latitude I have. Can you rendezvous? Where?"

"If you could proceed to the inlet, I'll call you with an exact location. Soon as I determine it."

"All right. Will do. Good luck."

"You too." Westman clicked off. When they went out to the Wrangler, they found Burt waiting for them—sitting on the back of the flatbed truck and eating a cheeseburger.

"Where have you been?" Cat asked.

Gergen took care to keep to Delaware's fifty-mile-an-hour speed limit, well aware of the penchant of the local police in the high tourist season for ticketing motorists driving one mile an hour above it.

Conversations with state troopers were not high on Gergen's list of personal desires at the moment.

"You think Skouras is following us?" Creed asked.

"You tell me. I'm driving."

Creed looked back through the rear window. Their other two crew members were lying down in the back of the truck. They had automatic weapons hidden beneath a tarpaulin between them.

"Can't tell."

"Doesn't matter. I gave him Leonard's address for the meet tomorrow," Bear said.

"You must trust the son of a bitch pretty good."

"Trust a river rat more. But with you three guys and Leonard, we should be able to handle him and his friends."

"We don't know how many friends he's got."

"I was in the SEALs, remember? Don't sweat it."

"You think the rag-heads can come up with the money this quick?"

"Probably not. But their appetite will be whetted. I think we'll get a good chunk of change."

"Wetted?"

"Never mind. We'll be talking with these people. Right now, I want to get down to Leonard's."

Westman drove Cat's Wrangler, letting Cat rest in the front passenger seat. Burt was following in the flatbed truck about a block behind.

Cat tilted her head back and looked out the side, where a few stars were visible above the horizon despite the haze and ground light.

"Did I ever tell you I was the best pilot in my squadron?" she said.

"I've no doubt."

"I'm serious. Do you know about 'greenie boards'?"

"Not in the Coast Guard lexicon."

"Every trap—every landing—on a carrier is observed, evaluated, and graded, with the data fed permanently into a computer and the grades posted on a board they call the 'greenie board.' The best landings get a green. Average landings get a yellow. Below-average landings get a white. Bad traps can get you a 'down'—and too many 'downs' can get you grounded. Two of my traps were yellows, but all the rest were greens. I was ahead of everybody. There were better pilots than I was—than I am—especially at combat tactics. But nobody could land a Tomcat as well as I could. Some jerk started a rumor that I had to be shacking up with the squadron commander or the air boss to get such good grades, but that was crap. I nailed the landings. Nearly every one."

"Too many jerks get into the military. There are times when I wonder if they don't go out and deliberately recruit them."

She turned to look behind them. Reassured, though Westman could not tell why, she looked to the front again.

"I was just now thinking how far I've fallen since I was the best on the 'greenie board,'" she continued. "I mean, look at me. But it's all my own fault. When I was making that bad landing—when I made that sloppy turn onto final and caused that compressor stall trying to get back in the groove—all I could think of was what they'd put on the 'greenie board.' And when I lost it, when I was headed straight for a ramp strike, I just wouldn't let go. I wouldn't let myself punch out and put that big wonderful airplane into the water. It wasn't just the 'down.' I knew they'd go after me then. They'd run me off the ship. So I just kept trying to reach the deck."

He took her hand and held it tightly, letting go only to downshift as they came to a red light. "You have more courage than I could ever imagine finding in myself."

"That's nonsense, Erik. If you didn't have guts, you wouldn't be here. And if I thought you were a candy-ass, I wouldn't be here."

"Thank you, ma'am."

She reached into the gym bag on the floorboard in front of her, taking out one of the pistols and checking its load. "You ever kill anyone, Viking man?"

He thought of La Perla, of a night when he and Joan de-Payse were firing handguns from behind great black chunks of rock, of the sparks their enemy's bullets made as they struck around them, of the look of a human body as the blood drained out of it.

"Yes," he said.

"I'm not sure I did. That Iraqi radar site. I still don't know if I hit anyone."

"That's something you probably don't want to know."

She sighed. "And now there's tonight."

Gergen went two blocks past the street leading to Leonard's dock, made a left, headed north again, then headed for the boat-rental facility from the east.

He slammed on his brakes just shy of the place.

Creed's head hit the sun visor. "What the fuck's wrong?"

"Another one of those big black Lincoln Navigators. Diller must buy them by the fleet."

Creed squinted. "You think they're a reception committee?"

"If they were making a hit, they wouldn't be parked out in the open like that. You can't be that stupid and run a drug ring."

"So what are they doin' there?"

"Maybe just looking around." Bear shoved the truck into gear and made a U-turn, retreating up the street and parking in the shadows. "We'll just wait."

They did so, for more than ten minutes.

"They're sure taking a long time lookin' around," Creed said.

"No, they're moving out now. Get down."

There was a flare of headlights. Three headlights. Pressing back against the door, Gergen watched through the rear window as a motorcycle, followed by the black SUV, turned from the side street onto Philadelphia Avenue, heading south.

"They're going to Leonard's house," he said.

"How can you tell?"

"That was Leonard on that Harley."

"Expensive-lookin' machine."

"Top of the line, Roy. Cousin Leonard must have won the lottery."

After proceeding down the length of the Delaware shore to Ocean City at flank speed, Dewey ordered the *Manteo* slowed as the town's amusement pier came into view. Just beyond it was the tower that marked the southern end of the peninsula.

Despite the late hour and lack of tourists, there was abundant traffic and lights shining from buildings. It was the most improbable hiding place for a two-thousand-pound nuclear weapon Dewey could imagine.

He called Westman on his cell phone—the third time he had done so in the last fifteen minutes. This time, there was an answer.

"Westman." The CGIS man's voice was almost a whisper.

"Did you find it?" Dewey asked.

"Pretty sure. I think it may be stored on a pontoon boat over on the bay side."

"What is your location?"

"The municipal parking lot next to the tower."

"How many subjects are we dealing with?"

"Unknown."

"And how many are you?"

"Three."

"You mean the blond and the old man?"

"Both ex-military."

"I read you. Have you tried the Ocean City Coast Guard station? They're by the Highway 50 bridge."

"I tried them by phone. They have orders to apprehend me. All the stations do."

"Me too," said Dewey.

"You do what you think best, Tim."

"I've got to follow orders—even if this is only dePayse taking things out on you. But maybe there's a way. I'm going to heave to off the mouth of the inlet and come in by inflatable. I have an M-60 on the gun mount and we'll bring the .50-caliber rifle. This needn't have anything to do with you."

"This could be tricky."

"We've got to deal with it."

"If you don't take me in, you could lose yourself a command. Maybe more."

"I'll see if I can work something out."

"How many will you be?"

Dewey looked about the bridge. "Four."

"We'll be waiting for you."

"Do my best." Dewey clicked off, turning toward De-Groot. "You want to join me in a shore party?"

"You're asking for volunteers?"

"I'm not sure this little operation is authorized."

"I'm with you."

"Pick two good men."

"Dourai and Lamia."

Machinist Mate Aboud Dourai was a Lebanese-American and an Arabic speaker, a skill that might prove useful. Petty Officer Third Valerie Lamia was only in her third year with the Coast Guard, but, like Dourai, one of the best aboard the *Manteo*.

"Okay. Get some side arms from the arms locker and join me on the foredeck. We're taking the fast inflatable."

"Aye, aye, Captain." DeGroot's formality was intended as a compliment.

Dewey picked up the cutter's intercom mike. "Lieutenant Kelleter, lay to on the quarter deck."

A moment later, the other officer burst onto the bridge. "Tim?"

"I'm taking a party ashore. I want you to take command of the *Manteo* until we get back. Stay on station here at the entrance to the inlet. Prepare to come to our assistance if called. I'm taking one of the handheld radios. We'll be in constant communication."

"Yes, sir. How long will you be ashore?"

"I wish I knew."

Chapter 32

Westman parked the Wrangler in a largely deserted lot three blocks from the address Leon Kelly had given him. Schilling pulled the flatbed up beside him.

"This is it?" Schilling asked.

Westman shook his head. "It's on the bay. We should walk there." Schilling looked somewhat wobbly. "Can you manage?"

The old pilot took a swig from his pint bottle of whiskey. "I'll keep up."

Westman led them across to the bay shore, then along the docks and the forest of masts and bridge canopies.

The boat rental was where Kelly had said—among several others along this stretch of shoreline at a dock Westman and Cat had passed by in the morning. A half-dozen personal watercraft were tied up in the shallow water, and there were two pontoon boats at the end of the short dock. The one farthest out was riding low in the water.

"Burt," Westman said. "You stay here as lookout."

Schilling nodded.

Cat had brought her pistol. "Will you back me up?" Westman asked.

"That's why I'm here."

Westman moved at a crouch to the foot of the dock, then knelt, waiting and watching, not moving farther even as Cat joined him.

Nothing stirred. The rental shack was dark and appeared to be locked. Aside from the distant traffic, the only sound to be heard was the gentle slosh of water.

"Keep low," he said. Taking out his own automatic, he stepped onto the dock, then crept along to the first pontoon boat.

Its deck was empty. Glancing back to make certain Cat was with him, he then moved on to the second.

There was a tarpaulin stretched rail to rail over the boat's deck, running almost its entire length. Westman swung onto the outside of the rail, then untied one of the lines holding the canvas fast. Moving farther along the boat's side, he undid another knot and then flipped back about six feet of the tarpaulin, waiting for Cat and helping her aboard.

"Why haven't they left a guard?" she whispered.

"Maybe they thought that would look suspicious. Draw attention. Be thankful."

He loosened yet another line, folding back the canvas still more. There was little light, but the long, dark form was unmistakable. Westman touched the cold, rough surface, as though to make sure it was real.

Cat did the same. "All right. Here it is, like you said. Now what?"

"We put the tarpaulin back in place and get the hell out of here. I want to wait for Dewey before we do anything more."

"Well, it's not like we can just pick it up and put it in the back of the Jeep."

Westman thought of the big truck. "Or even get it off the boat onto the dock." He reached for the edge of the canvas.

"Why don't we just take the boat?" Cat said.

"And take it where?"

"To your Coast Guard cutter."

"That would be theft."

"Erik . . ."

"I'm not sure Dewey would go along with that."

"That's crazy."

"He likes to follow procedure."

Carrying a baseball bat and an automatic pistol, Gergen led his crew toward Leonard's ratty little house on foot. Leonard's shiny new motorcycle was standing in the driveway. The Lincoln Navigator was parked in the sandy street. Bear could see the silhouette of a human head through the rear window. Someone was in the driver's seat, waiting.

He whispered a command to Creed, who crouched down as much as his big body would permit and moved to the right side of the vehicle. Bear did the same on the left, halting just to the rear of the driver's-side door. Both let a few seconds pass; then Creed rapped gently on the passenger-side window.

The driver leaned to his right. Assuming the man had a gun, Bear yanked the driver's-side door open swiftly and in almost the same motion grabbed the man by his collar, pulling him back and out of the SUV and flinging him to the ground. His next move was to stomp on the poor devil's neck. A gurgling sound followed, then ceased. He didn't need the ball bat.

Not yet.

Bear motioned the rest of his crew forward. They put their heads together on the street side of the SUV. He thought of Mary Lou. "I don't want any shooting."

Creed gave him a questioning look.

"If we can help it," Bear said.

*   *   *

DEEPKILL 365

Turko sat uneasily in the rearmost seat of Pec's fully loaded eight-passenger van, just behind the Kosovar. There was no way Turko could exit the vehicle without crawling over Pec and the man next to him, a Saudi named Ibn. He'd be dead within two seconds of initiating the attempt.

Turko wondered if the six men Pec now had with him were the last of his supply of troops. Sleeper cells survived because no one knew about them until they were called into action. So it had been with Turko's. There could be more of them here on the East Coast, just waiting for Pec's summons. But Turko didn't think so. He desperately hoped not.

The Kosovar was obviously very interested in acquiring this bomb. His head was on the chopping block as well. The weapon would be as much of a lifeline for him as it was for Turko.

But Turko's lifeline was short. He'd told Pec about the bomb and where to find it. He had nothing left to barter. He'd be useful in negotiating with the tugboat man, but after that, he'd be expendable, just as Gergen would be expendable once Pec had acquired the bomb.

As Turko now knew, but Pec might not realize, Gergen was an unusually intelligent man. In this fact lay Turko's only real chance of survival.

"I suggest that we haggle with them over the price," Turko said. "And question how we might remove the bomb from wherever they have it. Work the one thing against the other."

Pec said nothing. When he finally spoke, it was about something else. "How did you get away so easily in New Jersey?"

"I prepared carefully," Turko said.

"It's always escape with you. Are you afraid to die, Turko?"

"Not afraid. There is more that I would like to do."

Turko sensed Pec's grin. "The time comes when that is no longer of any consequence."

The driver slowed. "This is the street," he said.

* * *

Hearing the sound of a large, outboard engine, Westman used the flashlight from the Wrangler to signal the craft, trusting it was Dewey and his inflatable. He sent a simple message, in Morse code: "CG, CG, CG."

The outboard droned on. The boat had gone far past them when at last a light blinked on in reply, flashing the same message. Westman then clicked the flashlight fully on.

The inflatable altered course and headed directly for Westman and his friends, slowing as it approached the concrete seawall. One of the crew threw Westman a line. He made it fast to a metal post and, a moment later, Dewey and DeGroot clambered ashore.

"What's the situation?" Dewey asked.

"As of a few minutes ago," Westman replied, "the bomb was on the boat and completely unguarded."

"Not very bright, these guys," said Dewey.

"Bright enough to steal the thing," DeGroot countered.

"And kill two nice kids," said Cat.

Dewey took note of her presence and Schilling's with a friendly nod. "Well, I think we should call in the Ocean City police. As Miss McGrath says, there are homicides involved."

"We'd have to go up through channels to get a warrant," DeGroot said. "Justice Department gets involved and you know what that means."

"We could simply inform the police that there are illegal explosives aboard that boat," Westman said. "They'll be down here quick enough."

Dewey frowned. "They will need a warrant."

"Why?" Cat asked.

"Procedure." Dewey turned back to Westman. "The bomb was covered by a tarp when you went aboard?"

"Yes."

"Then you should have had a warrant. It involves a search."

"Tim . . ."

"Lieutenant, this is a goddamn hydrogen bomb!" interjected Schilling. "It's sitting on a boat tied up three blocks from here! We're in Ocean City, Maryland. Thousands of people here. And we're just a hundred thirty miles from Washington."

"He means to sell it and we don't know who to," Westman said.

"It's a night we should throw away the book, Skipper," DeGroot added.

If Dewey threw away the book, if he blew any successful prosecution of this case, he could be throwing away his next assignment as commander of the *Sentinel*—along with his career.

"So what do you propose?" Dewey asked.

Westman looked to DeGroot. They had worked together in the Caribbean. "We take the boat. We take it out to the *Manteo* and haul the bomb aboard. We bring it down to Norfolk, and turn it over to the U.S. Navy."

Cat shivered. "Why are we standing around talking?"

Dewey made a face. "What do you think, Hugo?"

"Easy enough to do, Lieutenant. If you're willing."

Schilling stepped forward. "It's there. On the goddamn boat. Forty years it's been under the sea and now it's right there. What's the problem?"

Dewey stood a little straighter. "The problem, Captain, is that we've had two terrorist attacks in less than two weeks and I'm responsible for patrolling a very important waterway where one of them took place. I'm under orders. I am well acquainted with Chief Warrant Officer Westman here, but I don't know you very well, and it's your word we're all relying on that this is an operational weapon. Mr. Westman told me your belief is based on a deathbed letter you received from a former crew member."

"I haven't any doubt, Tim," Westman said. "None. I've seen it."

Dewey sighed. "Erik, I've got to get authority for this.

One quick official call. From the *Manteo*. As per standing orders."

Westman shook his head. "You go up the operations food chain and you'll run right into Admiral dePayse."

"Erik. You've been a Coastie a hell of a lot longer than I have. You know I have to do this."

Cat turned in disgust and started walking away.

Gergen had Creed and one of the other crew members go to the rear of Leonard's house. He kept his fourth guy, Valdi Pinski, with him at the front. Roy was to move first, making a lot of noise as he attacked the door.

Watching through the front window, Bear waited for Roy's attack, then saw Leonard get up from the couch and, taking up a pistol, disappear through a doorway. A black man rose from a chair, pulling out an automatic but not taking a step. Bear guessed there might be more of these guys in the house, but even so, now was the time to move.

He kicked in the front door, quickly, with one jolt. He had his own .44 out. Seeing it, the black man who had gotten to his feet dropped his weapon, but in his peripheral vision Bear caught sight of another African man to the left, rising from a chair and reaching within his coat.

Now Bear had no choice. He swung his gun left and squeezed off one round. His aim was a little off. Instead of hitting the man squarely in the stomach, the bullet went left, taking out his liver. He dropped fast.

Gergen moved his pistol back to the first black man. "You get facedown on the floor right now and don't move one inch." He nodded to Pinski. "See to that."

Then he went to where Leonard had gone.

Pec had his man at the wheel drive past the address Turko had given him and pull up across the street.

"I think I heard a gunshot," said one of the men up front.

"Fired at us?" Pec asked.

"I do not think so."

Pec turned around to fix Turko with an accusing stare. "Would he know we were coming tonight?"

"No. It was very specifically agreed. Noon tomorrow. To give us time to acquire the money."

Another of the men laughed.

"Where could he have this bomb?" Pec said. "Not in that little house."

"No. But near. He is a tugboat man. Maybe it is on a boat."

A convertible full of noisy young men and women came down the street, its radio blaring strange American music. They rolled by without pause or notice, turning at the next corner.

"This is very clumsy. I am not certain it is worth the risk. We have never taken such risks."

"I think it is worth the risk."

Pec considered this. "We wait. If there is another gunshot, we leave."

Turko knew full well that, in that event, he would quickly leave this life.

Gergen dragged his cousin into the living room. He had been careful only to whack Leonard in the leg with the baseball bat, though his inclination had been to knock his head off.

Nodding to Roy Creed to stand behind Leonard, Gergen went over to the still-prone black man, who did not appear to have moved even an eyelid. "Enrique Diller sent you guys, right?"

"No. We came with him."

"Came? Where is he?"

"Over there. You have killed him."

Gergen swore. He had questions for Diller. "What're you doing down here?"

"Business."

"With my cousin here?"

The eyes moved to Leonard, then back to Bear. Easy choice. "Yes. With him."

"He sold you bastards my stash of drugs off that yacht, right?"

"He did."

"And what was he fixing to sell you now?"

"I am not sure."

"Something he had on one of his boats? That why you sons of bitches were down by his dock?"

The man did not reply. Bear kicked him in the ribs. "Yes."

"What would a bunch of dumb druggie bastards like you do with something like that?"

"Your cousin said there were people who would pay a lot of money for it."

"How much were you going to pay him?"

"Five. Ten. I don't know."

Gergen went over to Leonard, hulking over him, bringing his face down to his cousin's as he might an aimed heavy weapon. Leonard had been doping, but he seemed now very alert.

"I'm sorry, Bear."

"You're what?"

"Sorry."

Gergen stood up straight, smiling. "You're sorry, all right, you sorry-assed bastard. Only you're going to be sorrier."

"Please, Bear. I got a wife."

"Yeah, I know." Gergen went to an armchair he guessed to be the one Leonard used, as it was directly in front of the television set. "Get me a beer, Roy. He'll have beer. And some for you guys."

"Okay, Bear."

Seating himself, Gergen leaned back carefully, then raised his pistol to aim it at Leonard's James Dean nose. "You know what you are, Leonard? A fucking traitor to your country—trying to sell something like this to the enemy."

"Enrique Diller's an American, Bear. Least he was."

"Well, who the hell did you think he was going to sell it to, the Daughters of the American Revolution?"

"Who?"

"Never mind."

"What about you, Bear? You're tryin' to sell it to the fucking rag-heads!"

"You dumb shit. Once we had the money I was going to drop a dime on them. You think I'd leave a nuke with a bunch of murderous pricks like that? I'm ex-Navy. I voted for both Bushes—twice each. I was going to call the Coast Guard the second we were clear of these guys."

Bear heard a click and turned to see the front door open.

Chapter 33

Westman led the way back to the dock, halting in the shadows at the near end behind a storage shack. Cat knelt beside him. "Something wrong? Is someone there?"

"No, I don't think so. I'm wondering where we should go with the boat."

"Out to the cutter."

He shook his head. "I know Dewey. I think he's spooked by our having become outlaws."

"If we go out there and confront him with it, he'll have no choice."

"We can't count on that. He may well have gotten new orders by now. With the terrorist flag up, they like to keep everybody in motion."

"So what do we do?"

Westman made a map in his mind. "We should go south. On the Intracoastal behind Assateague Island. Where they can't find us. There are coves back there, and islands."

"How far?"

"I don't know. Follow the Intracoastal channel down Sinepuxent Bay."

"You want to go to Wallops Island," she said.

"It's an idea. Federal facility. NASA. We could turn the bomb over to them."

"There's a Navy installation there," she said. "Some sort of test site."

He nodded. "Yes."

"Is your friend Dewey up for promotion?"

Westman nodded again. "A bigger boat."

She swore. "Your Coast Guard's no better than the Navy."

A car was moving slowly along the waterfront.

"No more talk," said Burt. "Time to go. Move it or lose it."

Bear lowered his pistol when he saw it was Mary Lou coming through the door. Upon seeing Leonard and the dead man, she stopped cold, fear creeping into her eyes when they returned to Gergen.

"Where the hell were you?" he asked.

"I went out for a couple of beers. Leonard said he had some business and that I should get lost for a while."

"You didn't know what was goin' on here?"

She shrugged. "Some kind of drug deal?"

Bear swore. "Your husband was ripping me off—again!" He pointed to the still-bleeding corpse. "That's Enrique Diller, out of Philly. Leonard wasn't selling him marijuana this time. He was selling him my bomb."

"I don't want to know anything about that." She went to a chair, slumping into it, putting her hand to her forehead but opening her fingers to keep both Bear and Leonard in view.

"Mary Lou . . ." Leonard mumbled.

"Shut up." Bear went over to the surviving black man, still lying facedown on the floor. "Sorry." He fired a single shot into the man's head, causing him to flatten.

Mary Lou gave a little shriek, but caught herself. Bear took out the clip from the gun, emptied its remaining rounds into his pocket, wiped the handgrip and trigger, and then brought it over to Leonard.

"Here," he said. When Leonard only stared blankly, Bear thrust the weapon receiver-first into his belly. Finally understanding what he was supposed to do, Leonard took hold of the gun. "Congratulations," Bear said. "You are now an official murderer."

His cousin dropped the gun. That would do him no good. Bear went to retrieve his baseball bat, then returned to stand before Leonard. "Turn your head, Mary Lou."

"You can't do that!" she said.

"No choice." He swung the bat back as though preparing to hit a three-bagger. He paused to wonder just how far Leonard's handsome head could be hit by a baseball bat.

Bear had waited too long. Mary Lou had left the front door slightly ajar behind her. Now it swung open and against the wall with a bang. In walked Skouras and some of the nastiest-looking people Bear had ever seen in two decades of hunting down or doing business with the scum of the earth.

Leonard smiled at his reprieve. He'd live—for the two or three minutes Bear figured *he* had left to live.

"I said noon tomorrow," Gergen said.

"Be quiet," Turko said in a voice as cold as winter. "Go sit next to the woman."

Dewey went hurriedly to the cutter's bridge, DeGroot following after.

"Any incidents?" Dewey asked Kelleter, going to one of the forward windows. The *Manteo* was pointing out to sea, the bright lights of Ocean City spreading away to port; the dark, soft shape of the north end of Assateague visible to starboard.

"Nothing."

"Radio messages?"

"Activities Baltimore. Cape May. Both asking our position and status."

"No orders?"

"Just to keep them advised of our position."

"Nothing else?"

"Telephone call from Buzzard's Point."

"And?"

"Admiral dePayse."

"For Chief Warrant Officer Westman?"

"For you. She wants you to apprehend Chief Warrant Officer Westman and hold him. She thinks you know where he is."

DeGroot shook his head. Dewey went to the chart table. "Prepare to get under way," he said.

Westman and Cat untied the tarpaulin from the rails of the pontoon boat so they'd have room to move about, but left the canvas covering the bomb. The slowly moving car had moved on, turning back toward the main thoroughfare. Westman waited until he was sure there was no other nearby traffic before attempting to start the big outboard.

He went to the control console. He'd had considerable experience with boat theft in his time and had become thoroughly acquainted with hot-wiring techniques. But the cowling over the engine controls was made of thick fiberglass and of a piece with the hull. In the darkness, he could find no way to get at the wiring. In not anticipating this obstacle, he had been singularly dumb.

"Burt," he said, looking aft. "I can't get at the wires. Any ideas?"

Schilling came over and squatted beside the controls. "Cat," he said. "Check beneath the rear seat. See if there isn't a toolbox by the battery."

She moved quickly. "Screwdriver, pliers, and wrench. And a grappling hook."

"Bring it all."

Burt used the screwdriver to punch out the ignition core, then lifted it and the wiring with the pliers. When they caught and refused to budge farther, he inserted the end of the hook in the opening and, jerking it hard, broke the casing wide, making a noise almost as loud as a gunshot.

In a moment, he had the wires clear of the ignition-lock core, and a moment after that, with a brief shower of sparks, connected the right pair. The engine commenced a throbbing rumble.

"Stand by the lines," he said.

Pec had left it to Turko to take the lead in negotiating with Gergen, presuming on his abilities as a lawyer with long experience dealing with criminals.

Their goal was to determine the location of the bomb and acquire the means to remove it, so they might then eliminate Gergen and his people and move on. Gergen wanted the money and to escape—and to be rid of the bomb, which would be a hazard for anyone to possess. Turko decided the best initial approach was to be friendly.

"We could not stay where we were," Turko said to Gergen. "There are police and government agents everywhere up there. We wish to leave the area as soon as possible."

"How did you plan to take the bomb with you?" Gergen asked. "In a suitcase?"

"By truck. We have a rental truck waiting not far from here."

Gergen pondered this, wondering where and how they might make the transfer. "I don't suppose you brought the money," he said.

Turko looked to Pec, who gave a quick nod. "We brought some money," Turko said. "All we have at our disposal."

"We can give you one hundred thousand dollars," said Pec. "We have it in our vehicle."

"But you must tell us where you have the bomb," Turko said. "We want to see it. Now."

Bear contemplated the two dead men on the floor. Diller was staring at him with one eye. The inescapable fact was that they all had to get out of Ocean City as soon as possible. There was no time for dickering.

He hadn't checked on the amount, but there had to be a very large reward for this terrorist crew. What he needed most was for the Tangos to be on the road with the bomb so he could call the Feds to interdict them.

"All right," he said. "I'll take the hundred grand. And I'll help you get the bomb aboard your truck."

"No. We will do that. Just tell us where it is."

Gergen shook his head. "Sorry. My way or no way."

Pec spoke to Ibn the Saudi in Arabic, saying, "Kill him." He was looking at Leonard Ruger.

Ibn got up and went to Leonard, putting the gun to his head. "Tell us." Gergen began to laugh. Turko was puzzled. "He is your cousin," Turko said.

"I was about to do that myself when you came in," Bear said.

Turko aimed his pistol at Mary Lou.

"She's his wife," Gergen said, laughing some more, regretting the dark look he got from her. He stood up, much like a giant Kodiak rising on its hind legs. "We're not going to let you kill us and take off with the bomb. That's what would happen if I told you where it is, but it's not going to happen, pal. I'll show you the merchandise. But we'll all go together, with my people backing me up. You're going to need us anyway. You won't be able to pull this off without us."

Pec nodded to Ibn, who quickly fired a shot through Leonard's head, splattering the top of the couch and the wall beyond with blood and something worse. Pec appeared pleased.

The woman began sobbing. Gergen was smiling.

"That changes nothing," he said. "In fact, you helped me out. I owe you."

Pec was now irritated—his more normal state—but appeared not to know what to do. "What are you suggesting?" Turko asked Gergen.

"I'm not suggesting," he said. "I'm telling you what's going to happen. Me and my crew are going to get into the big Lincoln Navigator outside. You follow us, and we'll take you to the bomb. We'll help you get it onto your truck. You'll give us the hundred thousand. Then you go your way and we'll go ours. The cops'll be after all of us, you know. We have as much reason to get the hell out of here as you do."

Pec and Turko communicated with silent glances. "Very well," said Turko.

Bear went over to his dead cousin, who no longer looked like Jimmy Dean. He reached into the right front pocket of the man's jeans. "We'll need his keys," he said. Finding them, he jangled them a moment, then confronted Turko again, assuming command. "There's a dead body out by the street, in case you haven't noticed. We need to bring him in here."

With Schilling at the controls of the heavily laden pontoon boat, they moved down the channel as quietly as possible, passing under the Harry Kelly Bridge, which led to the mainland, and heading for the lighted buoy that marked the intersection with the channel that connected with the inlet. Schilling started to increase their speed a little, then abruptly pushed the control handle into idle.

"What's wrong?" Westman asked.

"Just thought of something." Burt looked back. "Cat, would you check the fuel tank?"

Cat went aft. There was just enough light from the city

and its amusement park to see by, and what she found was not a happy sight.

"Nearly empty, Burt," she called out.

"There's not an auxiliary tank?"

"None that I can find."

He leaned back in the seat, letting the boat drift in the gentle swells. "We'll never make it to Wallops. Not anywhere near."

"Can't we stop for fuel someplace?" she asked.

"There's a campground marina eight or nine miles down the bay, but I don't think it's open at night and I'm not sure we can make it."

Westman looked up the shore toward the bridge. "We better not go back there."

"That pretty well leaves us without anywhere to go," Schilling said. He lighted a cigarette, then took out his pint bottle.

"No, it doesn't," said Cat, moving closer to Schilling. "Ocean City Airport's just two or three miles down, just at the first narrows."

"How am I going to get gasoline there?"

"You're not. There's a marsh with a good two feet of water all alongside it—and a long, narrow cut that runs from the bay all the way up to the parking lot. You can run this boat right up to the end and be within a few feet of the truck, if we can get it there. Then we can do what we were going to do at the beach south of Henlopen. Drag the bomb ashore with a winch. Get it on the truck. We can drive to Wallops."

Burt took another whiskey swig. "How're we going to do that? The truck's back in Ocean City."

"We'll have to put to shore and go get the truck. One of us can drive it around to the airport."

"I think that's our only chance," Westman said.

"Cat, you come with me," Burt said. "I don't know that airport, and we'll have to drive through it without lights."

She wanted to stay with Westman. "Can you handle this boat without us?"

"Coast Guard, ma'am."

"Right. Sorry. Take the helm then, and put us ashore by the parking lot where we had that chat with your Mr. Dewey."

Westman waited as Burt unsteadily removed himself from his seat and let Erik take his place.

"You going to make it, Burt?" Cat asked.

"You bet." He sat down on the seat opposite, holding to its back. "You better drive the truck, though."

At the terrorists' strong suggestion, Bear and Mary Lou rode in the rearmost seat of the van, while two of the terrorists rode in the Lincoln Navigator with Roy Creed and the rest of Bear's crew. Creed was driving and leading the way.

Gergen didn't mind so much because it gave him an opportunity to move the transaction along.

"You said you had the money in the car," he said as they got under way.

None of the Tangos spoke.

"If it is in here, I'd like to see it," Bear said, feeling inexplicably bold. Maybe it was having Mary Lou sitting next to him. "If I don't get to, I'm not showing you the bomb."

"Your man in the other car is doing that."

"No, he isn't. He's taking you to the docks. He won't show you where the bomb is unless I tell him to."

He felt Mary Lou stiffen. He supposed he was making her nervous with this bravado.

The man who called himself Skouras leaned close to the one Bear took to be the boss, speaking in a foreign language Bear didn't recognize.

"Okay," said the boss. He had the man in the front seat hand over a backpack Unzipping it, he thrust it toward Bear's face.

Bear took it, peering inside. There were many paper-bound stacks of hundred-dollar bills. It looked right.

He handed it back. "Good. We're almost there."

When they'd parked, he suggested everyone stay in the cars, except for Creed, the alleged Skouras, and one of the other Tangos. Mary Lou got out on her own accord and no one stopped her.

"It's on a boat," Bear said. "The best way to handle it is to get it across the bay to one of the boat ramps over there on the other side and get it on a trailer you can run into the water. Then you can load it onto your truck from that."

The alleged Skouras nodded. "A good idea."

"Come on then," Bear said. He began walking out on the dock, passing the line of personal watercraft and then the empty pontoon boat. He went all the way out to the end and stood looking out at the lights across the bay.

"There's nothing on this pontoon boat," Skouras said.

"I know. It's not on that boat."

"What boat is it on then?"

Bear took a deep breath, and then exhaled, slowly, his eyes still fixed on the distant reach of night-dark water. "On a boat out there."

Chapter 34

Cat killed the truck's headlights as she turned off Stephen Decatur Highway onto Airport Road. After passing through several thick groves of trees, they finally came to a wide clear space and the airport itself. There were a few lights on here and there among the buildings, though she assumed the facility was closed, except for military use.

She could see the two Hercules C-130's still parked at the west side of the field. She presumed they were being guarded, but she wasn't going anywhere near the cumbersome-looking aircraft and she didn't expect a sentry to abandon his post to investigate anything happening elsewhere on the field.

Holding the truck at low speed, she quietly proceeded into the long rectangular parking lot, turning left toward the east end of it. There were a half-dozen or so cars parked near the small terminal building, but she guessed they had been left overnight. Cat recognized a couple of them as having been there for more than a week.

She pulled to a creaking halt just at the edge of the lot, the watery cut visible as a long glimmer leading from the edge of the parking lot out to the bay through the marshland.

"Do you think Erik can find us?" she asked Burt.

He was smoking another cigarette, his haggard face looking a bit macabre in its glow. "Coast Guard. He'd better."

"I don't know the tides tonight."

He consulted his watch. "High tide was more than an hour ago. It's falling."

"Damn."

"We got one lucky break. They laid the bomb onto the pontoon boat with the rear end toward the bow. He can come in prow-first and we can just yank it right off of there."

"There's all that railing up front. It'll be in the way."

"It's aluminum. We'll use the winch to pull it off and then hook up the bomb."

She was still gripping the steering wheel, though the truck was not moving. "Do you realize how crazy this is?"

"Nothing's crazier than building one of those things in the first place." He opened the door and carefully stepped down to the pavement in old-man fashion. "Come on, I'll help you back the truck around."

Westman proceeded slowly, keeping the outboard engine noise low and avoiding making a wake. He steered as near as he could to the western shore of the bay, rumbling along in the manner of a trolling fisherman and bearing in mind the shallowness of the water. The marshland beside him was alive with sounds—frogs, insects in profusion, night birds calling—but not quite enough to cover the noise of his passing. Sounds carried far at night over water.

While passing the inlet, he'd caught sight of the departing *Manteo,* stern to the land and heading out to sea. There was nothing else moving along the channel; nothing at all visible or audible ahead of him in the bay. He was alone on this long, long stretch of water.

Then, in a slowly gathering awareness, he sensed that he

wasn't. He could hear somewhere in the vagueness behind
him a faint buzz. Within a minute or two, it became the familiar whine of a personal watercraft. The machine was
quickly joined by others. He hated the obnoxious craft in the
best of times. Now they'd become objects of dread.

Westman had his Coast Guard-issue Beretta with him, but
no extra clip. Like the FBI, the CGIS trained its agents not to
take on adversaries unless they had superior numbers and
firepower. The H-bomb at his feet, he supposed, didn't
count.

He felt very vulnerable all by himself, but was immensely relieved that Cat and Burt Schilling were now out
of danger. If there was gunfire, he trusted they would take it
as a sign to get the hell out as fast as possible.

Gergen had taken all six of Leonard's water-going motorcy-
cles, putting Creed and his two other guys aboard three of
them and giving the others to Skouras's people, while taking
the pontoon boat himself. One of the Tangos had fallen off
his PWC almost immediately, making too tight a turn. But
they'd hauled him out and righted the watercraft quickly
enough. The little flotilla was moving line-abreast down the
bay, with the pontoon boat he was driving serving as flag-
ship. If their prey was on this waterway, they'd catch them.
No doubt about it.

Sitting hunched over the controls, Bear tried to keep what
the Navy called "situational awareness" while surrounded
by these foreign bastards. The man called Skouras—and
Bear now was absolutely certain that was not his name—was
on his boat, sitting in the side seat just ahead of him. The
head Tango was across the deck from Skouras and the
largest of these foreigners was sitting right behind Bear. He
was thankful that at least they'd allowed Mary Lou aboard.
She was in the seat opposite him, with arms folded tightly
across her chest and her head hanging down. She might have

been someone awaiting execution. Were it not for the fact that the alleged Skouras and his mean-looking master needed them to retrieve the bomb and get it aboard some sort of transport, execution might have been the order of the night.

Bear figured it still might—if he wasn't very, very careful and very, very smart.

Smarter than them anyway. The idiots had left the backpack with the money in the van.

Bear considered the mission orders he'd issued himself that night:

Get the nuclear device into the hands of the Tangos.

Separate himself, Mary Lou, and his crew from them as quickly as possible.

Contact the Feds and make them understand and respond to what was going down with the nuclear device.

Retrieve the money from the Tangos' vehicle and hide it—fast.

"Discover" the bodies at Leonard's place and inform the local cops and the Feds about that.

Bear had been given more difficult assignments in his time. In the first Gulf War, he and his team had snatched an Iraqi colonel from occupied Kuwait before the launch of the ground war, suffering no casualties and inflicting fifteen on the enemy.

The easiest part of this job would be taking out the old pilot and the blond. The two other crew members who'd been on the head boat were extremely dead, and Bear couldn't imagine how they'd pick up reinforcements down here in Leonard Land. Maybe the gray-haired Coast Guard agent had joined them, but there was no sign of any other Coasties. No sign of police interest thus far.

The alleged Skouras leaned close to speak over the engine noise.

"You think they've gone south?"

"No other place for them," Bear said. "No place for them

to hide from us on the upper bay. No place to off-load the bomb—unless they get their hands on a boat trailer, and I don't think they've had time to do that. They can't go out to sea with a load like that on a boat like that. No other place to go but south."

"What would be down there?"

"Not much. The bay runs thirty-seven miles down to Chincoteague. Unless they took time to top off the tanks, I don't think they can even get that far."

The alleged Skouras leaned closer, nodding toward his boss. "I think he is becoming impatient."

"Too fucking bad. We have to find these people first."

The alleged Skouras sat back. "Find them fast."

Westman rumbled on along past an extensive stand of trees to his right. At the end of them was a stretch of swampy meadow, and then he could see the lights of the airport. The water to starboard suddenly widened into a fair-sized cove. Cat had warned him not to turn here but to continue on to the next and more narrow opening, which would be the cut.

She was wrong. Rounding a flat peninsula, he came to another wide bay that gave little evidence of a waterway leading inland. Westman put the throttle in neutral and let the boat drift a little, keeping his eyes on the shoreline.

Then he saw it—a sharp depression in the distant marsh. Slowly edging the throttle forward, he steered the boat toward it, mindful of the buzzing of the PWCs in the open water behind him. He really needed a flashlight, but that would mean the end of everything.

A slap in the water to his left startled him. A fish. The buzzing of the PWCs began to fade.

With the alleged Skouras's permission, Gergen had Mary Lou take the helm while he went forward to the bow. One of the Tangos raised a pistol—as though presuming Bear was about to jump overboard in an ill-considered attempt to escape. That was not the plan. That was death.

Still nothing on the horizon. The only lights were those on the channel markers. Far to the south, Bear could now see the span of the Verrazano Bridge—the northernmost of the only two road connections to Assateague. The other was down at Chincoteague, many miles away.

He sensed his little navy had gone too far. He'd been running at speed. The old pilot's boat had not. If he had, Bear would have heard the sound or seen the wake.

Returning to the control console, he gestured to Mary Lou to keep her seat and reached past her for the flashlight in the storage bin. Going forward again, he signaled to Creed and the others on the PWCs to heave to. His mate responded immediately. The others followed suit—the Tangos getting the idea last.

"I think we passed them," Bear said to Creed as he brought the PWC near. "I want to double back. Fan out and keep an eye to the shore."

"You got it, Bear." The PWC's engine burbled back into life.

Westman's boat slid into the cut much like a foot into a shoe. The waterway was narrower than he'd expected. The weeds and marsh grass seemed to press in equally on both sides.

He held the wheel with great care, steering almost by feel but taking his bearing on one of the airport lights. Cat had said the parking lot was on the north side of the field. Everything seemed to be lining up.

Westman had been in this situation before, taking a small motorboat into a mangrove swamp along Grand Cayman Island's North Sound on a moonless night. Then he'd been after some narcotics traffickers who'd just made a substantial deposit at one of the tiny island's five hundred banks.

Then, as he'd penetrated the thick undergrowth, he'd been moving ever nearer some exceedingly dangerous bad guys. Here, at least, he was moving away from them—toward friends.

Like that of an annoying insect, the noise made by his pursuers returned. They were coming back up the bay, bent on retrieving something they'd lost. Him.

He'd kept his eye on the watery path ahead, but the sound of the PWCs broke his concentration. There was a sudden "bonk!" and the pontoon boat came to a halt, its engine shuddering as it skewed to starboard. He quickly put the craft in neutral, wondering what he'd struck. He was a hundred yards or more from the airport grounds.

Burt had activated the mechanism that tilted the truck's bed to the ground—a grinding crunch signifying the completion of the movement. He pushed the lever back and quiet returned.

No light came on at the airport. Nothing moved. There was a sound that might have been a voice calling out, coming from the direction of the two military cargo planes, but Burt wasn't sure.

"You hear that?" he asked Cat.

She was looking down the cut. "I think I see him. Yes. He's about halfway along."

Cat had fighter pilot's vision. Burt's had been diminished by age. Finally, he made out Westman's boat, noting the rectangular shape of its canopy. They might soon be out of this place, with the bomb secured. "He's moving real slow," Burt said.

She went to the edge of the grass that separated the parking lot pavement from the marsh. "No, Burt. He's not moving at all."

* * *

Gergen's little fleet prowled back up the bay. He began to worry that he'd paid too little attention to the Assateague side of the channel and steered closer to that. The water was too shallow in most places along that dark shoreline, but back up by the north end of the island and the inlet it ran deep close in—five feet or more even at low tide.

The old pilot's people might dump the bomb somewhere along that stretch to be retrieved later—just as they had plucked it from the ocean bottom by Cape Henlopen. Their main interest this night would be keeping it out of the hands of Bear and his crew.

But they couldn't dispose of the pontoon boat they'd stolen so easily. It had to be somewhere.

Bear skirted the curving shore at the north end of Assateague, turning into the inlet with the accompanying PWCs trailing behind. Proceeding all the way to the open sea, fighting the heaving swells where outgoing tide collided with incoming waves, he kept on until he had a view down the ocean side of Assateague. Easing back the throttle, steering to keep the waves on the starboard quarter of the clumsy boat, he looked hard to the southern horizon, seeking the telltale rectangular silhouette of the craft.

There was nothing. Only the winking light of two fishing boats working far out in deep water.

"We go back," he said.

Making the turn back into the inlet in the cross-currents of tide and surf required all the mariner's skills he'd acquired in his years at sea. He had to time the maneuver perfectly, spinning the wheel to port on the backside of one wave and gunning the engine hard to get the stern on to the next.

The motor proved too sluggish. They were all but beam to when the following wave rolled into them, lifting the starboard pontoon and heeling the craft over so severely the alleged Skouras came out of his seat, sliding to his boss's feet.

"Damn it, Bear, you're going to drown us!" Mary Lou shouted.

He ignored her. The wave passed on, the boat thumped back down, and he was able to complete the turn easily in the ensuing trough. Holding the throttle full forward, he plunged on back into the inlet.

"Now we go back to the dock," said the alleged Skouras, who had exchanged words with his chief.

"No, you don't want to do that," Bear argued.

"He does. My boss. Now."

"You don't want to let this slip through your hands just because you went through a little rough water."

"You have searched up and down that bay and found nothing. You are wasting our time."

"There's a stretch of shoreline down there I didn't search. Not carefully. It's worth a second look."

The alleged Skouras had an exchange with the chief in a language Bear did not recognize. "Okay," said the alleged Skouras. "A last look."

Cat got to Westman in water that reached to her breasts. He was struggling with something beneath the surface and didn't notice her approach, twisting around with some violence when she touched his shoulder and nearly clipping her with his elbow.

"Sorry," he said upon recognizing her. "Jumpy business tonight."

"What's wrong?"

"Hit a log. Anyway, a big branch on a log. It's stuck on the bottom of the hull."

There was splashing behind them. Burt had come out. Westman repeated his explanation of his predicament.

Schilling went to the bow and submerged himself up to his neck, feeling around the craft's port pontoon. Then he moved around to the side of the boat, exploring the length of the log. "We're in luck," he said.

"If this is luck . . ." Cat began.

"It's afloat—not a bottom snag," Schilling said. "Help me get aboard the boat." They did so. Westman was struck by how light the old man was. "Okay," Schilling continued. "Just give me a minute."

He seated himself at the controls, listening to the still-rumbling engine.

"Can we help?" Westman asked.

"Not yet." Leaving the gear in neutral, Schilling pushed the throttle forward until the rumble became a roar. "Stand back!"

Westman put his arm around Cat as they retreated a few feet back up the cut. She pulled very close to him as they waited. A moment later, Schilling jammed the gearshift into reverse. The outboard's propeller churned up a huge froth of water. There was a long squealing sound, and then a loud bang as the boat sprang free, lunging backward into the marsh until Burt was able to get the shift back into neutral.

The log bobbed up with a splash, a thick, broken branch sticking up like a mast.

"Okay," said Westman. "Home free." He took hold of the branch and used it to push and steer the log into the marsh on the other side of the cut. The pontoon boat now had a clear channel to move in. Westman signaled Burt to come forward, then turned to join Cat in wading to shore.

Turko could tell from Pec's silence and icy demeanor that the Kosovar would like to kill him and the salvage-tug men at the very first opportunity. This trolling up and down the bay was accomplishing nothing but increasing their risk of getting caught. The likelihood of their coming away from this folly with a two-thousand-pound nuclear weapon was diminishing proportionately. The only thing staying Pec's hand, Turko supposed, was the presence of Gergen's three armed crewmen on the PWCs—as nasty a gang as any of the homicidal Chechen rebels Turko had fought with. They would not respond kindly to a gunshot or two aboard this pontoon boat. If Pec tried to use a knife on the big, bearded American, Turko had no doubt who would win that fight.

So Pec sat stiffly silent, waiting. Turko guessed he would try to kill them when everyone returned to the Ocean City dock. Surely they would do that soon, as this folly of a search would soon be over.

Traveling at a slow speed, Bear heard the snap and bang of injured metal over the noise of his engine. He idled it quickly, concentrating on the direction of the sudden sound. It had come from ahead and to the right—exactly where he was intending to go—the marshy shoreline fronting the local airport. He wasn't sure how they could get the bomb onshore there; but if they could, and had a vehicle that could carry it, they'd be long gone before Bear and the Tangos could do anything about it.

Gergen turned his craft toward the patch of open water where the bang had come from, easing the throttle forward. Steering with one hand, he took up the flashlight and quickly signaled to the PWCs on either side to join him.

Spotting a long cut running through the marsh, he idled the engine again. Like all Navy SEALs, he had excellent night vision. He couldn't quite make out any people, but the other pontoon boat was about two hundred yards ahead.

"What is it?" the Tango chief asked.

"Quiet," Bear whispered. He leaned close. "It's them. They have the boat. They're bringing the bomb onto shore at that airport."

The chief and the alleged Skouras stared into the darkness, probably not able to discern much.

"I see them," said the alleged Skouras. "Why are they going to that airport?"

"I'm guessing they have a vehicle—or know where they can get one."

"Then we must stop them at once," said the chief Tango.

"We'll take them out soon enough," Bear said. "I want to see how many they are—and where they are. And if they do have a truck or whatever, I want to wait until they get the bomb on it."

"That is crazy," said the chief.

"No. It'll save us a lot of trouble. You can drive the bomb away on it."

"Easy as that," said the alleged Skouras.

"Maybe easier. I was a Navy SEAL, Mr. Skouras. My crew are all ex-military. We know what we're doing."

"Okay, so what will you do?"

Schilling mushed the bow-heavy pontoon boat against the grassy shore, coming forward to gather up the anchor and its line from a storage bin. Tossing it to Westman, he affixed his end of the line to a stanchion as the Coast Guardsman dug the anchor blade into the earth.

"We have to bust off this forward railing," Burt said. "We'll use the winch."

"That will make too much noise," Westman said. "Do you have a crowbar on the truck?"

"A big tire iron."

"Let's use that."

Cat froze. "Quiet."

"What is it?" Burt asked.

"Shhh. I think there's something out there."

All three of them listened. Insects and birds, and a strengthening breeze.

"We have to keep moving," Westman said. "We have to get this done."

"Right." Burt went to the truck.

"We heard those PWCs go by," Cat said.

"They came back again."

"Nobody rents those things out at night. They're dangerous enough in broad daylight. And there were a lot of them."

Westman took out his Beretta and checked the clip. "Do you still have your pistol?" he asked.

"Yes. Survival-kit issue."

"Do you have any extra ammunition?"

She shook her head.

Burt returned with the crowbar. Westman took it from him and climbed aboard the pontoon boat. The right-hand portion of the front railing opened as a gate. There was a post in the center, and then another on the port side where the railing connected. He'd need to uproot only the center one.

As best he could tell in the dim light from the high lamps farther along the parking lot, the posts were bolted to the fiberglass decking. He worked the angled blade of the tire iron underneath the flanged base of the post, then pushed down hard.

There was a squeaking sound in response, but the flange barely budged. He worked the blade in again, then turned the main bar of the tire iron parallel to the deck and jumped on it.

The iron went flying and he barely managed to keep it from going overboard. But the opening between flange and deck had substantially increased. Inserting the blade once more, he shoved it deep. Positioning the rod with care, he set one foot on it, then stepped squarely on its full length.

This time it gave. He needed only two or three more quick pries to loosen it completely. The railing itself moved an inch or more when he pushed on it, but no farther.

"Burt. We'll need the winch after all. It shouldn't take long."

"Okay. You'll have to carry off the line. I'll put the winch in neutral."

A hundred feet of rope and cable, plus chain and hook, proved a sizable weight, but Westman managed, slowly unspooling the line until he had brought it to the water's edge. His muscles were shaking from the effort when he bent to affix the hook to the boat railing's lower bar.

Climbing to the other side, Erik backed up, then signaled to Burt to start the winch. Schilling did so with a loud clank, and then an increasing roar as the machine struggled with the fixed aluminum. Slowly, the winch began to win the tug-of-war. The rail began to bend backward, then with another, louder bang, jerked completely forward—its mounting on the port side broken completely.

Schilling stopped the winch with a rasping shudder. The front of the boat was completely open, the rear of the bomb waiting, reminding Westman oddly of a bull hesitating at the gate of a *corrida*.

He retrieved the hook and returned to the boat, as Burt paid out more slack. Examining the bomb's tail assembly carefully before deciding upon the best placement for the hook, Erik set it on a steel cross member, then asked Burt to slowly pull the line taut. It was inch-thick line, plus twenty or so feet of cable. This would be something of a gamble.

Burt said nothing. At Westman's signal, he put the winch into gear.

The bomb moved freely forward along the deck. It was so long that there was no dipping of the tail as it came out over the edge of the bow. Coming onto the ground, however, it dug into the earth. Burt's attempt to pull it free only dug it in deeper.

"You're going to have to back up the truck."

"It's soft ground for this kind of load," Burt said.

Westman looked to the bay. "We have no choice," he said.

Bear waited impatiently for the Tangos and his own crew to get into position. He'd had to explain his plan to the chief and the alleged Skouras twice. Their idea of an ambush was to cut a target vehicle off on a road and spray it with automatic-weapons fire—or simply blow it up with a remote-control bomb. Blowing up things was out of the question here. And you didn't want to shoot up the vehicle.

What was called for here was a basic U.S. military ambush—an attacking force and a blocking force. The first would drive the adversary into the guns of the second. It was standard practice for U.S. special operations units and it almost always worked.

The Tangos understood the attacking-force part, and happily assumed that role. The problem was coordinating their effort with the blocking force, which was Roy Creed and Bear's other two crewmen. He had sent them ashore to set up in the trees by the airport access road, presuming their targets would try to exit the situation by that route. It was the only way they could get the heavy bomb out of there.

Bear had wanted to go with Creed, but the Tango chief wouldn't permit that, demanding that Bear and Mary Lou stay aboard the pontoon boat—hostages to who knows what. Failure? Maybe success. Once the bomb was secured, he and Mary Lou could be fish food.

Maybe not. Roy Creed and the other guys would still be out there. They were tougher customers than any of the Tangos. And Bear had a pistol in his belt as well. It was part of the plan. A shot from it was supposed to be the signal to execute the ambush.

"We've got to move closer," Bear said.

"They will see us," said the alleged Skouras.

"By the time they do it will be too late." Bear put the boat once again into forward gear and let the near-idle carry it forward.

Cat and Westman positioned themselves at either side of the truck as Burt raised its bed to clear the ground, then walked backward with the huge vehicle as he proceeded in reverse, ready to call out if the wheels looked to slip into unmanageable terrain. Schilling inched the vehicle rearward, halting twice without their warning.

"Sorry," he said. "Just being careful."

He ground it into gear again, and crept on. The tires were digging channels in the earth, but the truck kept moving. Westman called out to Burt to stop.

"We're there?"

"Close enough for government work."

Cat stiffened. "I hear boat engines again."

"Then let's be quick."

The end of the truck bed came down, settling on the moist earth a foot from the bomb's tail assembly. Westman placed the hook, holding the line taut until Burt had descended from the truck's cab and activated the winch. It clanked and clattered. The line became taut, and then the bomb began to move, still digging into the ground, but then rising up onto the steel plating of the truck bed. With scrapes and screeches, it continued up the incline. Westman feared it might roll off to the side, but the line and cable held it straight.

There'd be no such stability rounding highway curves.

"We've got to tie it down," Westman said.

"Wait till I lift the truck bed into position." Burt worked another lever. The truck bed began to straighten.

Westman glanced over his shoulder in the direction Cat was looking. Of a sudden, out of the darkness, another pontoon boat emerged, heading straight for the stern of the one they'd stolen. Before either of them could move, there was the flash and bark of a gunshot. Then over to the right, the fireworks display of an automatic weapon. Then more.

Chapter 35

Cat flung herself to the ground at the first shot, pulling out her pistol as she pressed her head against the cool grass. Westman had done the same, but now raised his head and aimed his automatic to the right, where gunfire was coming in bursts. She could hear the bullets striking the truck. A slightly different sound indicated they were also hitting the bomb.

Westman fired one round just as the gunfire on the right ceased. Cat thought she heard a sort of scream. Then there was yet more shooting, coming from farther down the shore. One bullet sang by just above her head.

She'd spent time at rifle and pistol ranges going through officers' boot camp, and she'd undergone a survival course that included a few sessions on the use of side arms in situations like this. But she was in no way prepared for this gunfight. She was an F-14 shooter, firing air-to-air and air-to-ground missiles and precision-guided bombs. She had little idea what to do in this fix, except to keep low. One thing she had learned is that most people—especially nonmilitary—fired high. And with automatic weapons, the continuous recoils tended to throw the aim high and to the side.

That Westman may have hit one of the intruders with a single shot at a gun flash utterly mystified her. She fired off one round into the darkness herself, but she might as well have thrown a rose petal. There was no muffled scream in response to her shot—only more shooting coming their way. Sparks were flying everywhere from the strikes against the truck and bomb. She was stung on her leg by a piece of hot metal as flying bits of dirt sprayed against her arm and cheek. Life had been reduced to seconds. With a painful turn of the neck, she looked back to Burt, and saw him climbing into the cab of the truck.

"Go with him!" Westman said. "I'll give you covering fire!"

"What about you?"

"Give me your gun. I haven't enough ammo. But get in the truck. You and Burt, get out of here! Get the bomb away from them!"

"Erik . . ."

"I'll get scarce—real soon. Now go, Cat, please. Now!"

He might as well have said those were "orders." You don't question orders under fire. Warrant officer or no, he was tactical commander in the field. Still, she hesitated.

"Erik, where will I find you?"

"If you make it, go to your house. I'll meet you. Now go! Damn it, he's waiting for you!"

She slid Westman her pistol, then rolled and rolled again, finally crawling to the other side of the truck and making a lunge for the passenger-side door, opening it with a wild, banging swing. Burt reached to take her arm and pull her in.

With that door still hanging open, Schilling shoved the truck into gear and churned away, throwing up a spray of mud clots. The wheels spun helplessly, then found purchase. The truck lurched forward with a jerk, and began rolling.

Despite the continuing fire, Cat raised her head enough to look for Westman through the rear window. He had disappeared.

Erik crawled onto the ruined bow of the pontoon boat they had used, moving to where he was shielded by the seats and then on to the stern, satisfied at least that Schilling had gotten the truck away. Westman assumed Cat had gotten aboard unharmed. He would not allow himself to think anything else.

He turned his attention to the pontoon boat that had come up behind theirs, using the outboard engine cowling for cover. He found an argument in progress on the other craft. A burly, bearded figure he recognized as the salvage-tug captain had risen from the control console to face a smaller, thinner man who was shouting at him in some strange language. Another man, stockier, rose as well. A woman, in one of the side seats, ducked down.

Turko realized the moment of termination had come. He would not have an opportunity like this again. Pec could not be allowed to proceed any further. Whatever his instructions, Turko now had to act upon his instinct. And he had to do what was right.

The big tugboat captain's eyes were fully on Pec, but Turko could see that they were taking in much more as he lifted his own pistol and aimed it at Pec's head just behind his ear, the angle one that would send the exiting bullet into clear air.

Erik heard two gunshots. He was amazed to realize they were not fired at him. The smaller man went down, much like a marionette with its strings cut. Then, to Westman's further surprise, the two other men and the girl leapt into the water, heading for the darker marsh shore.

Westman swung himself onto the second boat, hoping to find more weapons. The small man, now dead, had dropped an automatic pistol. There was also what looked to be an AK-47 on the deck behind him. Sticking the handgun in his belt next to the one Cat had left him, Westman picked up the automatic rifle, moved to the rear of the boat, and waited. In short time, a PWC came sputtering up through shallow water, a large man in the seat.

In La Perla, in Puerto Rico, mindful of children playing in the street, Westman had hesitated too long when a druggie had charged his partner with an automatic weapon. The officer probably would have been killed if another task force member hadn't dropped the man with a burst from her own CQB automatic pistol.

Her name was Joan dePayse. Her fusillade killed the attacker.

Westman fired two quick shots at the man on the PWC. One hit the handlebars of the craft. The second hit the miscreant in the chest. He fell backward, the waterborne motorcycle spinning to the left and capsizing.

Erik heard another of the infernal machines coming, and one behind that. His training guided his movements. He quickly crawled back to the bow of the boat, taking the AK-47 with him.

The new intruder took one look at the capsized PWC and began firing, starting at the stern of the pontoon boat. Westman dropped him with a burst from the AK-47, then rolled off the deck into the water, wondering how much he had improved his odds.

The other PWC stopped. Westman heard a splash. This new adversary was smart, and not about to make himself an easy target. Westman kept his eyes fixed in that direction, but turned slightly to the side to pick up any movement with the periphery of his retina—the seat of night vision.

More automatic-weapons fire came from behind Erik, aimed too high but taking him by surprise. He plunged forward, diving into the underwater marsh grass. Another burst followed, better directed. A third firearm joined this chorus, three single shots fired in quick succession—these coming from his side. He was caught in a triangle of enemies.

Westman raised his head for a quick breath, then went underwater again, this time heading back in the direction from which he had come.

Schilling swerved the truck right, onto the airport access road.

"Careful, Burt! The damn bomb almost rolled off the truck!" She was kneeling on the seat, looking out the rear window. Schilling had given her his gun and she gripped it tightly.

"Careful later. We've got to get out of here!"

"They don't have a vehicle, Burt. They came by boat."

"They might steal one of those in the parking lot. We've got to move."

He drove bent low over the wheel. He'd not turned on the headlights, and was having trouble making out the road. Approaching the ninety-degree turn toward the highway, the truck slid off onto the grass, skidding, the bomb rolling this time to the right.

"Careful, damn it!"

All at once the shadowy tree line ahead was illuminated with flashes of gunfire. There were at least two shooters. Bullets thumped against the hood. Then the windshield exploded into a million pieces, several of them slashing across Cat's bare leg and arm.

She shoved herself down onto the floorboard, ignoring the stabs of pain. Head down, Burt spun the wheel, bouncing the truck across the roadway and onto the grass on the other side. Insanely, Cat leaned out the side window and fired two shots at their attackers.

"The damn bastards are everywhere!" she said.

Burt yanked the wheel again, trying to zigzag. It was pointless. The truck was too slow.

The rear window vanished. A shard cut Cat's arm again. She put her hand to the wound and it came away sticky with blood.

"Where are you going?!!" she screamed.

"Other side of the airport. Maybe there's another way out to the highway."

"There isn't. There's a golf course, but there's a creek in the way. And a fence. These sons of bitches may be there too."

"Okay, okay."

"It's not okay. We're going to have to ditch this fucking rig and run for it."

"No. Then they'll get the bomb."

There were loud sprangs of bullets hitting the truck frame.

"They'll get it fast enough if we get killed," she said. "Where the hell are the cops? All this noise. They ought to be here."

"I'm going to head for those C-130's. There have to be guards. Maybe they can help us."

"More likely they'll shoot us."

"Our only chance, Cat."

Her mind went to Westman, all alone in the muck, an untold number of bad guys trying to kill him. She wanted to scream. How had she let this happen? She felt as out of control as she had been careening in a Tomcat toward a ramp strike on the stern of the *Lincoln*.

The truck bumped up onto asphalt again. Schilling shifted into higher gear, heading for an opening between two hangars.

* * *

Westman plunged on underwater, swimming for the protection of the pontoon boats, maddened by the illogic of his pursuers' acute awareness of his location. Perhaps they were guessing, but all their bullets were coming close. Increasingly close. He was barely able to put his head above water.

Reaching the boat with a touch of hand against steel pontoon, he rose to take a quick breath of air. A moment later, there was more gunfire. It then became incessant, from several directions, tearing apart the boat's canopy and shattering a length of rail. Westman tried for the stern, but someone on the shore sent two rounds that way.

Underwater again. Abandoning the AK-47, he clung to the bottom muck, propelling himself forward with hands and feet, squeezing under the pontoon and proceeding to the next. His lungs were hurting but he willed himself to keep on, once again pressing his body between the steel and the mud. His belt caught as he started to emerge on the other side and he almost panicked, which would have meant taking in mouthfuls of water and drowning just a few inches from air.

Concentrating hard on survival, he reached back and pulled his belt off the obstruction. Another push and he was free. His head came up into the cool air. He gasped loudly several times, then calmed himself and turned toward his foe.

Roaring along the taxiway, with the airport buildings screening them from gunfire, Burt turned on the truck's headlights, wanting better to see what lay ahead of them. The two big cargo planes at the far end were sideways to him, the one mostly masking the other. There was movement beneath one wing—doubtless a guard. Burt could only hope he wasn't lining up a shot.

In case that was what the National Guardsman had in

mind, Burt began swerving the truck from one side of the taxiway to the other. He could hear the bomb rolling on the steel bed behind him, but took to turning to the other side just as it sounded about to fall off.

The soldier had gotten behind some equipment piled on the tarmac. Burt realized now that his speed and evasive action must seem threatening. He slowed, and ceased his frantic lurching from side to side.

"I can't believe it," he said.

"Can't believe what?"

"The back end of that 130 is open. They've got the ramp down."

"What are you thinking?"

"This truck'll fit in there. You can put a Bradley Infantry Fighting Vehicle in one of those."

Cat stared through the shattered windshield. "You want to hide the bomb inside that plane? Those bastards will be all over us in a few minutes. They know where we went."

"Not hide it. Fly it."

She looked at him hard. "You're crazy."

"No other way out, Cat. Your friend bought us some time. We've got to use it."

They were almost to the planes. The National Guardsman was standing up behind the equipment pile, an M-16 aimed at them.

"He isn't going to let us," she said.

Burt stopped the truck. "I'll talk to him."

"No. I will." She snapped open the door and jumped out, landing painfully. There was blood all over her leg.

Putting her pistol into the back of her shorts, she came around the truck and approached the soldier with arms held away from her sides.

"Halt!" The voice was strangely high.

"Lieutenant Catherine McGrath, U.S. Navy. This airport is under terrorist attack. We need your help."

"U.S. Navy?"

"I have identification." They had asked her to turn in her military ID when she was discharged, but she'd lied and said she'd lost it. Giving it up would have seemed a final surrender. She reached slowly for her wallet and pulled the laminated card from it. The Guardsman did not shoot.

"Come closer," the Guardsman commanded.

Cat did so, slowly, holding up the ID card as she advanced like some magic talisman.

"Stop there." Cat halted. "Set it down on the ground and step back." Cat obeyed.

The Guardsman came around the pile of equipment and into the lights of the truck, revealing herself to be female. Holding the M-16 with her right hand, she knelt to pick up the card, examining it as carefully as the poor illumination and her pronounced nervousness permitted.

Cat realized that, then and there, she had just thrown away whatever chance she might have had for a resumption of her Naval career. The National Guard lady had it all—name, rank, and serial number.

There was still gunfire coming from the bay, sounding louder—and maybe nearer.

"What do you want, Lieutenant?"

"Are you alone?" Cat asked.

The question spooked the young woman. Still clutching the ID card, she moved backward, glancing from Cat to the flashes of light along the shore. Cat took the continued shooting as a hopeful sign. Westman might still be alive, though she could not imagine how that could be.

"Got another airman with me. He went over to see what the gunfire was about. He told me to stay here."

"He won't like what he finds," Cat said. "Do you have a two-way?"

"I just called him, but he won't answer." Her nervousness was very evident now.

"What about your CP? Your relief? Your chain of command?"

"We're set up in Bethany Beach—at a National Guard compound."

Cat was running out of patience. "Didn't you call them?"

"My buddy did. He said they were on the way."

Cat calculated the time it would take for them to reach this place—tempted by the possibility that they might hold off these fiends until rescued by the cavalry in the form of a bunch of Air National Guardsmen.

It was far more time than she figured they were going to have. Now Burt, apparently run dry on patience, complicated matters by shifting into first and driving the flatbed past them, turning to go around the rear of the first Hercules.

"Where's he going?" the female airman asked, really afraid now.

"To get the truck out of sight. I told you. This is what the terrorists are after."

"What kind of terrorists?"

"The kind with guns—as you can plainly hear."

They both watched the shoreline. Cat then heard shouting back among the airport buildings. She could only hope it was the good guys.

"Hey!" The Guardsman saw that Burt was driving the truck up the ramp into the C-130. "He can't do that!"

"We have to. We have to keep that truck away from them."

"Away from them?"

"Get it away from here."

"You're going to fly it out?"

"Yes. We're both pilots."

"What's on that truck?"

"Highly specialized munitions."

"But you can't do that." The young woman, uncertain, looked back toward the bay—doubtless hoping to find her fellow Guardsman returning.

Cat strode forward, snatching back her ID with her right hand and then, with the woman's attention following the card, grabbing away the M-16 with her left.

"There," Cat said. "You're officially disarmed by an intruder and absolved from any responsibility. Now you can
stay at your post or go hide in one of those hangars until relief comes or you can come with us, which I'd strongly rec-
ommend. But choose now, because we're leaving."

"Are you really Navy?"

"Was. Not anymore." That was for damn sure.

By going underwater to the far side of the pontoon boat,
Westman had deprived his adversaries of a clear fix on his
location. This apparently confused and frustrated them, for
they began shooting randomly along the marsh in the hope
of killing or flushing him through chance. He was safe only
for the moment, as they were working their way toward him,
firing bursts as they came. If he broke away from the shelter
of the boat, they'd have a clear shot at him. If he stayed,
they'd have him trapped.

He had to throw them off balance. Moving to the bow, he
fired one shot wildly to attract their attention. Then he dove
again, pulling himself under the starboard side float and rising quietly in the space between the two pontoons.

One of the men called to the others. Then the sound of a
boat intruded, a quite different engine noise than that made
by pontoon boats or PWCs. Reinforcements possibly.

The next noise he heard was deafening—automatic-
weapons fire blasting the water just the other side of the pontoon. When the echoes faded, Westman heard someone
moving close through the water on that side.

As silently as he could manage, Westman returned to the
bow, slowly peering around the float at what proved to be a
man's broad back not four feet away.

Westman raised the automatic Cat had left with him,
slowly pulling the trigger. It clicked, with no report. He
yanked back the receiver to clear the chamber of the dud,

just as the man turned around, banging his weapon against the boat.

Erik's next trigger pull produced the desired result.

Burt had found chocks, cables, and hooks to secure the truck and was standing to the side of the big open hatch. After Cat had clambered aboard, he pointed to a lever.

"That raises the ramp, but I've got to release the safety locks from up there first," he said, pointing to the high flight deck up forward. "Wait till I start the engines, then push the lever. When the ramp and door close, we'll be out of here."

"Don't you need an external booster to start those big turboprops?" she asked, referring to the portable auxiliary power units that were used to provide ignition for the big engines of most cargo aircraft.

"This is a J model. Has an internal APU. You could start it up in a cornfield if you had to."

"You really flew these things?"

"Hercs first went into service in 1956. They're almost as old as the B-52."

He squeezed her shoulder, then started forward—to Cat's distress, dragging his right leg. She should have asked if he could have flown anything in his condition, but he moved resolutely on. One had to climb a ladder to reach the flight deck from the cargo hold. Burt took a painfully long time to complete the ascension, but managed it. In less than a minute, she heard a familiar whine of turboprop, then a few coughs and chuffs, and then the roar of the outboard port engine. Another soon joined in, and soon there was a full chorus.

There was also more gunfire—very near. Bullets began striking the fuselage. Burt took note of this. The big plane began to move.

Cat heard a horrendous scraping noise. The ramp was

dragging. She'd failed to move the lever. She did so. The scraping eased, then was gone.

Out of the shadows Cat saw someone running toward them. The C-130 was moving no faster than a walk and the runner was quickly closing the gap. Cat had given her pistol to Westman and now was glad of that. She stopped the ramp and leaned out over it to extend a hand to the young Air National Guard woman. Had Cat still been armed, she might have shot her.

The woman flung herself onto the partially raised ramp first, then reached to take Cat's hand. Rising, she gripped Cat's arm with both hands, mouthing the words "Thank you."

She never got to say more. Cat could barely hear the gunfire now in the racket from the engines, but the girl's body jolted twice and she released Cat's arm, falling to the steel plating of the ramp and then rolling off onto the taxiway.

"Burt!" Cat shouted. "Stop!"

"What?" He sounded so distant.

"STOP!"

He hit the brakes. The Hercules rolled a few yards more, then lurched to a halt. This was a big mistake. Before Cat could jump out to see to the Air National Guard woman, two figures emerged from the dark and leapt aboard the ramp—a slender, long-haired woman and a huge man Cat recognized all too easily.

Ducking back beneath the center of the pontoon boat, Westman began wading to the stern, wondering if he had made a big dumb mistake. If they discovered where he was, they could just keep blasting at the boat until they hit him or destroyed it. His best move now would be to remove himself from this location with all deliberate speed.

Reaching the stern, he made a quick reconnaissance of the waters beyond. They seemed clear, though the engine noise from a new boat that was approaching indicated it was near and coming on fast.

He had to get away. Pistol in hand, he took a deep breath and slipped beneath the surface, not rising for ten strokes.

They were not enough. As he sucked in air, splatters of bullets hit the water ahead and to the right and then behind him. He went under again, changing course, heading north parallel to the shoreline. When he surfaced once more, he saw this ruse had worked. The shooters were firing in frequent bursts, but they no longer had a focus.

And suddenly they had something else to occupy their attention. The approaching boat now swerved into view, trailing a wide, foaming wake. A searchlight came on at its orange-colored bow, sweeping toward the pontoon boats. Then Westman heard the delightful sound of a .50-caliber machine gun, which began working the water back and forth within the cone of light. Westman saw one of his adversaries drop, then another. His hopes that these were the last of them were dashed when return fire commenced farther down the shore.

The big, bearded man whacked Cat along the side of her head with the edge of his huge fist, dropping her to the hard steel deck in a painful blur. She stayed conscious, but barely, as he stepped over her and moved forward along the side of the secured flatbed, heading toward the flight deck. Cat tried to get up, or at least call out to Burt, but nothing much happened.

The big man spoke for himself. "Get down from there!" he shouted at Burt. "I'm taking this truck."

Schilling's response was to shove the throttles forward and resume taxiing, only at a much faster speed. Gergan gripped the truck bed to keep his balance, then groped his way forward, pistol in hand.

Cat rolled over onto her belly, then pushed herself to her knees, swaying from side to side. The bearded man was aiming his gun up at Burt. "Stop this fucking plane!" he shouted.

Burt ignored him. The C-130 continued to increase its speed, bumping along on its low-slung landing gear over the lumpy asphalt.

Swearing, Gergen swung up onto the ladder. Cat managed to get to her feet, but could think of no way to stop this man. Worse, the woman he'd brought aboard with him was moving toward the ladder herself. And Burt just sat there, like an airline captain preparing for some dull flight from Topeka to Sioux City. Did he mean to get them airborne, so the tugboat captain would be at a disadvantage? He'd be dead before they got off the ground.

There was a pry bar hooked to the bulkhead. Cat reached for it, slipped, then tried again. Working it loose, she struggled forward, far too late. The tugboat captain was halfway up the ladder and the woman was just below him.

Wearing a pair of cut-off blue jeans and a halter top, the lady was armed as well. She glanced back at Cat, but then chose to ignore her, aiming her revolver as though she wanted to shoot past Gergen at Burt. But from that angle, she could have no shot.

Actually, she did—a perfect shot—but at a different target. She fired twice, and Gergen dropped like a rock, hitting the deck with a thump louder than the four growling engines.

The woman kicked the bearded man in the head. "You fucking bastard. Why'd you let them kill Leonard?" She kicked him again. "Think I wanted you instead of him?" Another blow. "You fat fuck."

She then turned to Cat, who had come a few faltering steps closer. "Take me to the end of the runway!" the woman commanded.

"That's where we're going," Cat said.

"I want to get off there. I need to get to the highway." She aimed her pistol at Cat's belly.

Cat was more than willing to comply. "Burt! Stop when you get to the runway!"

There was no response.

"Burt! This woman needs to get off! She's okay! She helped us! She just took out Gergen."

When Schilling made no reply again, Cat willed herself out of her dizziness and exhaustion and began climbing the ladder. When she reached the top, she found Burt slumped in his seat and the C-130 only a few hundred feet from the end of the taxiway—the darkness beyond filled with every imaginable danger and disaster.

Flinging herself into the copilot's seat, she yanked back the throttles. When she could get her feet on the rudder pedals, she pushed down hard on the brakes.

The Hercules shuddered, slowing, but not fast enough. Desperately searching the cockpit for the propeller pitch control, she at last found it, skewing the big paddles blade-first into the wind and rendering them highly inefficient. At last, the aircraft stopped.

She looked back over the seat. "Okay. Go!"

"I had nothing to do with any of this," the woman said.

"Who are you?"

"Never mind. Just married into the wrong fucking family."

"Did you shoot that soldier?"

"No. Only one I shot is him."

"Get going then."

"Thanks. I owe you." The woman hurried down to the partially raised ramp and then leaped from it onto the tarmac.

Schilling raised his head, blinking. "Get us out of here, Cat." His voice was little more than a mutter.

"I've never flown anything this big."

"Just point it down the runway and give it full throttle. You know the drill."

"This runway's only four thousand feet."

"Hercs'll take off full load in three thousand—less than

two thousand empty. Back in '63, one of 'em landed and took off from a carrier."

"Jeez, Burt . . ."

He pushed himself up in the seat, wiping cold sweat from his brow and blinking some more.

"Are you okay?" she asked. Stupid question. He was no more okay than she was, and she was now becoming so woozy and frazzled she wondered if she was going to be able to stay in the chair.

"Fine, fine," he said. "Just feelin' my age a little." Pushing himself up still higher, he took her hand from the throttles, then pushed all four forward, pressing right rudder to turn the plane. When the bulbous nose was pointed down the runway, he turned on the landing lights.

"No preflight run-up," she said.

"No, ma'am."

He found the strength to put both feet on the brakes as he revved the engines to maximum RPM.

"Burt! The ramp's only partway up!"

He released the brakes and the C-130 lurched forward. "No time."

She saw what he meant. Orange dots flashing to either side of the runway a hundred yards ahead showed that once again they were coming under fire.

The swift-moving inflatable sped to within fifty yards of Westman, then slowed and briefly stopped—two of those aboard dropping quickly into the water. As the heavily armed craft moved away, the two started wading toward the shore. Westman recognized them even in the dark.

"Tim. Hugo. Over here."

Dewey and DeGroot turned and froze like wild animals sensing the presence of a predator. "Westman?" Dewey said, his voice strained between a whisper and a shout. He had a side arm in hand, pointing it vaguely.

" 'Service, integrity, justice,' " Westman replied. It was the CGIS's official motto—as few people, especially foreign terrorists, could possibly know.

Dewey started immediately toward him, DeGroot following behind.

"I thought you were headed back to Cape May," Westman said.

"I was, until I got orders from the deputy assistant commandant for operations to 'apprehend' you at once," Dewey said. "So I came back. I always follow orders."

"What's the situation?" said DeGroot, coming up to them.

"I got three of them. There's a fourth one down but he was shot by one of his own. Had an unknown number on the landward side of the marsh—I think you saw them. Don't know where they've gone, except I think they've moved to the south a bit."

"I sent the other inflatable that way," Dewey said. He studied the landscape between their position and the airport buildings as might a Naval gunnery officer. "I don't like this ground. It's too open."

"There's firing on the other side of the airport," DeGroot said.

"That's where they took the truck," said Westman.

"What truck?" asked Dewey.

"The truck that has the bomb on it."

"You saw it?"

"I helped them put it on the truck."

"Where are they now—your friends?"

"They were in the truck."

"All right," said Dewey. "Let's try to help them." Keeping low, they started wading to shore.

As Dewey and Westman prowled along the shoreline, the two Coast Guardsmen aboard the other inflatable flushed some gunfire and immediately engaged the shooters, the .50-caliber dominating. The exchange was so intense the flashes illuminated the marsh for hundreds of yards. Westman was reminded of the machine gun course at boot camp.

Moving at a crouch, he led Dewey and DeGroot in an encircling movement. They hurried across the parking lot and headed for the side of a hangar, flattening themselves against it.

There was more gunfire, but it was quickly drowned out by the sound of airplane engines—turboprops.

"What the hell's that?" DeGroot asked.

"Let's find out," Westman said.

Erik led the way, darting from the one hangar to the next, and then on to the one after that. Finally, there was nothing but open meadow. He turned the corner of the last hangar and ran in its shadow to the taxiway side. Looking to the end of the runway, he saw an enormous airplane with its landing lights on. It was moving toward them—very fast.

Westman noted two shooters running out onto the runway and firing at the oncoming aircraft. As it came closer, engines roaring, the gunmen quickly retreated to the side of the runway.

The big cargo plane lifted from the asphalt just shy of them, the engines beginning a high-pitched drone as the aircraft lumbered into the air. The bad guys kept firing at it as it continued to climb. Not wanting to miss, Westman emptied one pistol at the nearest of the shooters. The man jiggled and jolted his way to the ground. His companion stopped firing, dropping his weapon. "Okay, okay!"

"I was hoping we'd get some prisoners," Dewey said to Erik.

Westman watched the big airplane continue to rise slowly into the night sky, its navigation lights twinkling. He could only wonder who they were and where they were bound.

* * *

Cat saw Burt's head fall back and hands slip from the controls. She quickly gripped the wheel on the copilot's side, checking the airspeed indicator as an incipient stall alarm began to sound. There was too much drag from the ramp at this altitude. She pushed the control wheel forward, dropping the nose slightly. The airspeed crept up, but not enough.

Too near, the narrow bay passed beneath and they were over sandy Assateague, the ocean beckoning beyond. If she could not get more thrust out of this big clown of an aircraft, she'd be doomed to repeat Burt's experience of four decades before—only there was no way she could drop their cargo in time.

"Burt?"

His head was still tilted back, but he opened his eyes. "Cat."

"Can't get enough altitude, Burt. I'm afraid I'm going to stall."

"Gear up, Cat. Couldn't . . ."

She felt like an idiot, more so now because she'd no idea where the lever was that operated that hydraulic.

Burt raised his hand, pointing. She yanked it back quickly, letting out a long breath of air as she heard the multiwheeled tricycle gear rise into place. It wasn't quite like slipping a dog from a leash, but the Hercules began to climb much faster.

When she was over the sea, she put the plane in a slow bank and altered course to the north. The flight to Dover Air Force Base would be short. She didn't want to go there. Even if she were able to land this monster, it would mean the end of everything for her.

As if there was anything left.

But it would be the same wherever she went. Dover, at least, had a tremendously long runway. It gave them their best chance of avoiding the death that they had just now so narrowly escaped.

The lights of Ocean City were passing on the left. Ahead,

she could see the other shore towns all the way up the coast to Delaware Bay.

"Doin' fine, Cat."

"What's wrong with you, Burt? You keep passing out."

"Comes and goes."

"But what's wrong with you?"

"Too old."

"Can you help me fly this thing?"

"Yeah." He took a deep breath, then exhaled, and then did nothing.

"Burt?"

Nothing. She heard the noise of something scraping on metal, but it was not coming from him.

Cat leaned over her instruments. The readings all seemed normal. Fuel was low, but there was enough to get up to Dover. The aircraft was climbing. She adjusted the trim, then sat back again.

A moment later, large hands closed around her neck.

Chapter 36

The remaining gunman by the runway watched the receding airplane with raised hands.

"You hit?" DeGroot asked.

"No," said the man. Westman recognized him as a crewman off Gergen's salvage tug. "Where's your boss?"

"Don't know."

"Why did you throw in with terrorists?"

"You have to ask him."

"Take him to the terminal building and hold them," Dewey ordered DeGroot. "I'm going to check on the inflatable. It's gone quiet out there. I don't like that."

Westman was looking out to the bay. He took out his cell phone.

"You calling the local police?" Dewey asked. "They should have been here by now."

"Ocean City won't come out unless they're called to assist," Westman said. "This is Worcester County's jurisdiction."

"Are you calling the sheriff?"

"No. I'm following standard operating procedure."

Special Agent Leon Kelly answered on the fourth ring, yawning.

"It's Westman."

"Jeez, Erik. Where are you? We've got an advisory on you."

"An advisory."

"Request for assistance from the Coast Guard. You're AWOL or something."

Westman swore. "I'm at Ocean City Airport."

"What're you doing there?"

"I've got a case for you."

"A case?"

"I think you'll like it. We have some dead terrorists. Another live perp."

He explained the situation further. "Payne can take the credit."

"Payne's not here."

"Where'd he go?"

"Didn't say. But he left a good guy in charge."

"You'll be coming?"

"You bet."

Westman clicked off.

"You want to come with me?" Dewey said. "We've got to clean this up."

"You'll have plenty of help shortly. FBI. I'd like to get scarce."

"Am I supposed to let you do that?"

"Then you won't have to 'apprehend' me."

"Where're you going?"

"I want to take one of the pontoon boats and go back to Ocean City."

"What for?"

"Continue my investigation."

Dewey seemed dubious. "Those aren't your orders."

"They are tonight."

"And tomorrow? You're on a lot of bad paper, Erik."

"Deal with that then."

"How many years do you have in the service?"

"Sixteen."

"We'll get over there when we can."

Cat couldn't understand why she wasn't dead. The bearded man was strong enough to break her larynx with one hand. But he was also supposed to be dead. The woman in the cut-offs had shot him twice. His face had been covered in blood.

Yet here he was, a Lazarus, having found the strength and will to climb all the way up the ladder to the flight deck and attack her.

He was an idiot. Burt was passed out. She was flying the Hercules. The stupid bearded bastard would kill them all.

She was beginning to black out. In the passing seconds she'd been thinking these thoughts, she had not been breathing. Her neck was being crushed. Her head was tilted painfully against the back of the seat. The only parts of her that were functioning were her arms and hands, which were currently occupied with gripping the control wheel.

Cat managed one last thought. The son of a bitch was obviously in a weakened state, or she'd have been dead by now. There was only one opportunity left to her, and there was actually a chance that what she had in mind would work.

She yanked back on the yoke, making the cargo plane's strange clown nose commence to rise. Gergen removed one hand from her neck to take hold of the seat back in an effort to keep his footing despite the rising angle of the floor. She wondered how much he knew about flying. She wished she could recall their altitude. Last time she had looked they were climbing out of two heading for three.

Just as she took a quick, deep breath, he shifted his weight and put his forearm across her neck, gravity reinforcing his remaining strength in his effort to add Catherine Anne McGrath to the KIA list in this insane battle. The stall alarm commenced its raucous warning. A joyous sound. He appeared to have no idea what was happening—or what was about to.

The nose was pointed up at the stars now. An instant later, it dropped like a thrill ride. The windshield filled with the dark vision of the sea below as the Hercules assumed the flight characteristics of a boulder.

Gergen lost his grip, his footing, his balance. As he flung himself forward, trying to regain all three, she whacked him hard in the face with her elbow as hard as she could manage. He didn't cry out. He just vanished.

There was no time to worry about him. She had done more than a few stall recoveries in her time—most in practice, a few in deadly earnest. One time, over the Pacific, she had fought compressor stalls in both of her F-14's original lousy engines from eleven thousand feet all the way to the watery deck, restarting one only a few hundred feet above the sea.

She had no idea how this hulking airplane would behave in a recovery attempt, but she followed procedure. Pushing the yoke forward to regain flying airspeed in the dive, giving it a little left rudder to prevent the spin it was showing an interest in, she then pulled steadily back on the controls to resume level flight.

When the instruments showed she had accomplished that, she looked in disbelief at the altimeter. According to that most important of navaids, they had no altitude at all. She shoved the throttles all the way forward and pulled on full flaps, allowing herself finally a quick glance out the portside window. They were passing a row of town houses along the Fenwick Island beach. Some were lighted, and she could see into their windows.

Slowly, the big airplane began to ascend. By the time they had cleared the long stretch of empty Delaware State Seashore and were flying by Bethany Beach, she had managed to get the Hercules back up to a thousand feet. She retracted the flaps and the climb rate increased.

"I got it."

In flight training, when an instructor uttered those words, one instantly removed hands and feet from the controls. To do otherwise was such a major sin, one could get washed out of the program for the transgression. But Cat did not yield command.

"It's all right, Burt," she said, the words coming out in croaks. Her throat hurt enormously.

"No," he said. "I've got it. Find out what happened to that bastard."

"You've been passing out, Burt. I . . ."

"Damn it, I'm fine! I'm command pilot here and I've got the controls. Check him out!"

She undid her seat harness and warily rose, eyes first on Burt to confirm what he was claiming. Then she looked to the rear edge of the flight deck, where Gergen's foot was twisted in the angle of the ladder.

Peering over the edge, she saw him hanging upside down, making weak little efforts to grab hold of the ladder and pull himself upright again.

"His foot's caught," she said. "He's just hanging there."

Burt reached to his belt and handed her his automatic. "Shoot him."

She took the gun obediently, glad for its presence, but did nothing more.

"Damn it, Cat. Shoot him. He has it coming."

Amy Costa. Joe Whalleys. The young Air National Guard woman. And maybe, Chief Warrant Officer and Coast Guard Investigative Service Special Agent Erik Westman.

And who knows how many thousands or millions if he had succeeded in turning this bomb over to the fiends of fundamentalism.

"Can't do it, Burt," she said, sticking the side arm in her

belt. Urging the wounded man to grab hold of the ladder, she knelt and took hold of his boot. He groaned as she twisted his foot back toward her, freeing it from the ladder brace. But the boot came off in her hand. He fell the remaining distance to the cargo deck headfirst, the rest of his huge bulk coming down upon his neck and skull with a great crash.

She climbed back into her seat, catching her breath. "He's out of the picture," she said. "I can take over now."

"No. I've got it. I'm doing fine."

"You're sure?"

"Affirmative. How many jumps have you made in the Navy?"

Cat couldn't quite think of the total exactly. "I don't know. A couple dozen maybe. Why?"

"I want you to go down to the cargo hold and put on one of those parachutes you'll find hanging along the starboard bulkhead."

She glanced at the altimeter. They were back up to two thousand. There was still sufficient fuel. "Why?"

"You have a chance to get out of this, Cat. Nobody knows you're involved."

"The National Guard woman."

"She's dead, right? You told me they killed her."

"The woman who came aboard with Gergen. We let her go."

"You let her go. I would have blown her brains out. But she's not going to talk to anyone. Damn it, Cat. We've got the bomb. We're in the clear. You've done your bit. You've got your reinstatement hearing coming. Why fuck that up? Put that chute on and get the hell out of here!"

"But what about you?"

"Look at me. I'm flying the aircraft. I'm taking it to Dover."

"They'll crucify you."

"They've already done that."

"Burt . . ."

"You said you were my friend. Do it!"

Cat shook her head, hesitated, then rose and gave his shoulder a squeeze. "Okay, Captain."

She descended the ladder, still reluctant, stepping gingerly over the motionless form of the tugboat skipper.

The chute was a familiar fit but a painful one. There was no place on her body that didn't hurt.

With difficulty, she climbed back up the ladder to the flight deck. "I don't want to do this, Burt."

"Damn it, Cat, you're just complicating things. I don't want to have to worry about you, okay? Now get going. I'm fine. Thousands of hours in Hercs."

He took his right hand from the control wheel and reached back toward her. She put her hand over his.

"Love you, Cat."

"You too, Burt."

He squeezed her hand hard, then returned his to the controls. "I'm going to head over Cape Henlopen. With this wind, I'm going to drop you over the dunes so you don't miss the beach and end up in the water. You'll have to walk home."

"Okay."

"You've got to lower the ramp again. When you jump, take a running leap out the hatch so you'll clear the prop wash fast. Got it?"

"Got it." She took a step down the ladder, then halted. "I don't want to do this."

"Yes, you do."

He was right. "Good-bye, Burt."

"Good-bye, Cat. Hell of a time we've had."

"Yes."

"Hell of a good time."

"See you soon."

She descended to the cargo deck again. Moving back toward the hatch, she paused to look at the long dark shape of the bomb. Maybe one day, they would get rid of all these damned things.

But probably not. She shuddered, and moved on to the hydraulic lever by the door. The ramp lowered swiftly when she pushed it. She could see Bethany Beach receding in the distance behind them. Below was a thin strip of barrier reef that was also part of the Delaware State Seashore. As she was looking backward, the Atlantic was on her left, the wide expanse of Rehoboth Bay to her right. Then the lights of the Rehoboth Beach boardwalk suddenly appeared below.

She moved closer to the ramp, the flatbed truck just behind her. The garish boardwalk passed beneath, and then she could see house lights. Henlopen Acres. Houses in the woods belonging to rich people. A thin line that was the canal that linked Rehoboth with Lewes appeared just to the west.

The beach below widened, spreading back into rolling dunes. The time had come.

With what seemed the last strength left to her, she leaned back, then bolted forward, four quick steps taking her across the downward-angled ramp. Then she was a bird in flight. For a brief, crazed moment, she thought of spreading out her arms and sailing to earth and ending life in one final, perfect, extraordinary flight.

But she pulled the rip cord.

Burt could no longer see the instruments clearly. He hadn't told Cat, but he'd taken a round through the leg in the fracas at the airport. It hadn't hit bone. The leg still worked. But there'd been bleeding, and it hadn't stopped. He couldn't quite remember how many times he had gone under since. If he let it happen again, he and the bomb and this great big wonderful airplane were going into the drink.

He didn't want that to happen. More than anything in what life was left to him he didn't want that to happen. And so he wouldn't let it. Whatever it took, blurry-eyed or no, half-dead or no, he was going to Dover.

It wasn't that far—a flight measured in minutes. Straight

up the western shore of Delaware Bay and then a quick shallow turn to the left onto final. He could do it in his sleep. He had done it in his sleep in a thousand tortured dreams. He could almost see the runway lights. And then he actually could—twin strobes at the apron, parallel rows of amber lights running back from there. It was a wide runway and went on and on forever—built to handle the biggest jumbo cargo jets known to man.

Piece of cake.

Burt slapped himself hard. He had let the nose drop, gathering too much speed and losing too much altitude. Adjusting his trim, powering back the engines, he pulled on flaps, then moved his hand to the landing gear control.

He didn't think about what might happen to him—what was most certainly going to happen to him when his beloved U.S. military got their mitts on him. None of that mattered, except he wasn't too high on the idea of spending his last days and hours a lonely old man in some military prison hospital, expiring unvisited and unmourned.

He worried about Cat. She was all he worried about. He'd given her a chance. He thought it was a pretty good one—if she kept her mouth shut and went by the Navy book. She'd been done wrong by that flight leader and the Navy now recognized that. They'd become highly sensitive to sex cases in the years since Tailhook and the Naval Academy scandals.

But Cat had been through a lot—maybe too much. Like him, she'd lost pretty much everything—including, apparently, this Coast Guard man of hers, a pretty good guy, except that he wasn't a pilot.

She might blow it all with one little ill-timed, ill-directed, wrong-headed outburst.

There was nothing he could do about that. All he could do was land this big bird and deliver its strange, precious, monstrous cargo to where it belonged, as he had meant to do all those years before.

It was almost a giddy feeling, that he was doing this. That

he and a few good people had accomplished what the military had not and would not. He was completing a mission—as it occurred to him, the most important mission he had ever flown.

He lowered the gear, listening to it fall into place. Then he pulled on full flaps as he made his turn.

Things were very blurry now. He could barely make out the distant runway. He realized he had turned too soon, that he was not properly aligned. There was no chance for a go-around. He wasn't sure he could stay conscious that long. He had to make this landing.

He put on full power, slewing the Hercules to the right and crossing the approach flight path obliquely. Hitting left rudder hard, he turned back again, making yet one more turn to finally line himself up.

But he'd put on too much power. He was much too high and the runway was fast approaching. He cut power sharply, pointing the nose down. But that gave him too much speed. He was flying like an aviation cadet on his first solo.

Burt blinked and then rubbed his eyes, hard. He was fading fast. Seat of the pants. Get it down. Keep it straight. Get it down.

The sudden jerk of the opening chute caused Cat to lose her shoes. She was beyond laughing at anything, but suddenly found her stupidity vastly amusing. They'd be found by some beach walker who'd presume they'd been left by some careless swimmer. But they were Catherine McGrath's shoes. They'd be a monument to her. Maybe the only one she'd ever get.

She put them from her mind. There was something more important to attend to. Burt had warned she might drift back over the surf, but the wind and her momentum from the C-130's speed were carrying her north, toward Cape Henlopen itself and its narrow point. She needed to spill air and steer to stay over the beach. Otherwise she was going to get very wet.

Tugging hard on the canopy lines, she went into a slow spiral. At what she guessed was about five hundred feet, she let go of the lines and allowed the chute to resume its forward glide.

Her landing was hard. Her feet caught in a line of rope fencing that set the bird sanctuary apart from the public beach area, and she slammed down on her backside and elbow and rolled twice, the parachute shrouds tangling around her. Letting waves of pain rise and subside, she lay there for what seemed a very long time, then set to work extricating herself.

When finally clear, she dragged the chute and harness to the shallow, tidal water on the lee side of the cape, carrying it out to where the canopy could catch the wind. It didn't travel very far, collapsing a few yards farther, but it began moving out to sea.

Then she took a deep breath. It was a long walk. She was more exhausted than she had ever been in her life. But she wanted to be in that little house of hers more than anywhere she had ever wanted to be in her life.

As she started up the sandy trail that led to the road out of the state park, she heard a loud thump to the north.

It had to be thunder from an isolated thunderstorm. It had to be.

Chapter 37

Mary Lou walked all the way back to Highway 50 and then across the causeway and bridge to Ocean City. She was careful to avoid contact with anyone, ducking away when she could to stay out of the headlights of passing motorists, fearing especially the kind of person who would be interested in picking up a hitchhiker at such a late hour.

Instead of going directly to Leonard's dock, she walked the back streets to their little house, which seemed undisturbed from when they had left it. Opening the front door, she went directly to her husband's body. In the gloom, he seemed merely asleep, and the thought of that made tears come into her eyes.

But there was no time for that. She went to one pocket of his jeans, taking out his wallet and removing a sheaf of hundred-dollar bills. Returning the billfold, she dug into another pocket and took out his keys, quickly finding the one she sought.

Leonard had taught her how to drive a motorcycle years before. Starting the big engine of the Harley, she glided through the darkened town at low speed, keeping noise to a minimum.

To her surprise, there was no one at the dock. The terrorists' van was where they had left it.

The Harley had a big wrench in the tool kit at the back. She smashed the van's side window, grabbed up the backpack, taking a quick look inside to make sure the money had not been removed. Climbing back on the Harley, she sought again the back streets, turning frequently to make sure she wasn't being followed, then headed north on the main drag out of town, not stopping until she crossed the Delaware line at Fenwick Island.

Pulling behind an all-night gas station, she carefully examined the contents of the backpack.

The terrorist boss had lied to Bear. By her count, there was only about thirty-one thousand dollars in there. Still, it was a start. Along the way, she could pick up another ten, or maybe twenty, selling the Harley.

She knew exactly where she'd go—her favorite place in the whole damn country—Panama City, Florida. She'd stash her money somewhere and get a job waitressing—if not there, maybe down in Mexico Beach or Port St. Joe. She doubted anyone would come looking for her. Who'd pursue a murder warrant on her for killing the likes of Bear Gergen?

Gassing up the Harley, she continued north to Bethany, turning west on Highway 26 and following that road inland to the back roads out in the bean fields.

Maybe she'd get married again. She couldn't possibly do any worse than Leonard Ruger.

Westman figured that any survivors of the fight at the airport would go back to the dock from which they'd taken the pontoon boat and the personal watercraft. They'd have vehicles there and who knows what else. But instead he steered toward the concrete seawall by the parking lot where they'd left the Wrangler. He still had the keys. He needed to be very mobile.

The Wrangler was low on gas, but there was enough for the moment. Ultimately, he planned to drive to Cat's house and wait. What happened right now was completely beyond his control.

He wanted to make a pass by the rental-boat dock, if only to see what their adversaries might have left behind. Turning into the dead-end street, he killed his headlights, proceeding slowly without them.

There was a van badly parked at the near end of the dock. Stopping well short of it, Westman turned off his engine and stepped out of the Jeep.

The area looked deserted, but then he saw movement. Someone was in the rear of the van, looking for something. After several minutes, the figure backed out and opened the front door of the vehicle, searching under the seat there. It was a man, the same stocky man Westman had seen on the boat at the airport—the same who had killed his confederate and then fled. Bertolucci.

Stepping back from the van, he stood a moment, arms folded, head down, thinking.

Westman had no idea how the man had made his way back here, but he was clearly frustrated at not finding what he had come for. He slammed the van's door shut.

Moving quietly back to the Jeep, Westman hid behind it. If Bertolucci came by on foot, Erik would follow him walking. If he drove, Westman could in a moment be right behind him.

If the man chose to depart by boat, Westman would be out of luck. But he guessed the man had had his fill of boats.

There was the sound of an engine. Headlights came on and the van came rushing up the street. One of the windows had been broken open. Keeping the Wrangler's lights off, Erik moved out in pursuit.

* * *

Captain Baldessari heard what seemed to be his phone ringing. He squinted at his alarm clock, wondering if the hour was wrong or if the ringing of the phone was a hallucination. As the realization sunk in that neither could possibly be the case, he rose wearily and went to the telephone, sinking into a nearby armchair before finally picking up.

As he feared, it was Colonel Baker. "Baldessari?"

Who else would answer his phone? "Yes, sir."

"I just got a call from the general."

"Yes, sir."

"There was a mishap on the main runway tonight."

Had he heard sirens? "Yes, sir. Anything serious?"

"No explosion. Damn thing was nearly bone-dry on fuel. A C-130 they sent here as part of the National Guard contingent."

"Any fatalities?"

"Two dead. Don't know the details. Anyway, that's not why the general called. He wants me at the Pentagon at 10 A.M."

"The Pentagon?"

"Any idea why?"

"No, sir." As Baldessari thought upon it, that was a lie. He knew very well why they wanted Baker in Washington. "Maybe something to do with the terrorist attacks."

"Hmmm." A silence intruded.

"Do you want me to come with you, Colonel?"

"No. I'm supposed to come alone."

"Very well, sir."

Another pause. "You think this may have something to do with that old guy and his bomb?"

"Couldn't say, sir."

"They said the dead in the C-130 were civilians."

"Why would civilians be in a C-130?"

"Maybe that's what they want to know."

"I'm afraid I can't help you with this, Colonel."

"Okay, Baldessari. I'll talk to you when I get back."

"Yes, sir."

Baldessari hung up, then stretched out his legs, staring up at the ceiling. Some mornings were better than others. This was a lovely morning.

The van went up the main highway almost as far as Fenwick Island, then turned abruptly into the parking area of a cheap motel. Westman continued past a few blocks, then made a U-turn, returning to the motel but parking in front of a closed coin laundry next door.

There was no sign of Bertolucci. Westman assumed he had entered one of the rooms. There was only one with a light on—along the second-floor walkway.

"Sit down, Turko."

There were two of them in the room, Special Agent Payne and another man. They had brought containers of coffee, but none for Turko. As they were occupying the two chairs in the room, Payne motioned him to a seat on the bed. Turko declined, continuing to stand, a short distance from the door.

"Everything is over," Turko said. "They're all dead. It is the end of things."

"And Pec?" Payne asked.

"He is dead."

"What happened?"

"Pec got us mixed up with some American criminals. They said they had a hydrogen bomb that had been recovered from the sea bottom. We went to look at it and ran up against the U.S. Coast Guard."

"The Coast Guard?"

"Yes."

Payne shook his head. "The fucking Coast Guard." He looked to his companion, doubtless also an FBI agent, then back to Turko. "Pec was killed in a gunfight?"

"The beginning of one, yes."

"This was not supposed to happen, Mr. Turko. You were supposed to deliver him over to me. That was the agreement from the git-go. Otherwise, you'd have been in a cage at Guantanamo long time ago."

"The situation changed."

"All you had to do was call. Simple fucking phone call. No matter what the situation. I could have made the bust. We might have taken him alive. It would have been the most important terrorist arrest within the United States since 9/11. He had a lot to tell us, Turko. A hell of a lot."

"Couldn't be helped."

Payne rubbed his chin. "Why did you ask for this meet, Turko? I expected you to be halfway to Mexico by now."

"I did my job. I set the explosive charges so the attacks on the Bay Bridge and the nuclear plant didn't work. I prevented Pec from doing many bad things."

"But that wasn't the deal, Turko. That isn't why I took you in and kept you out of trouble. I wanted Pec. You were supposed to deliver him."

"There was no chance to call you. I'd have been shot if I tried. I did my job. I saved many lives. I would like my money. You promised me money and transport out of here."

"If you gave me Pec," Payne said. "But you didn't."

The other man shifted slightly in his chair, a move Turko read instantly. "How did Pec get killed?" the man said.

"I shot him." The remark was calculated. It would prompt them to do what they were doubtless intending to do no matter what, but it would stun them for a moment.

In that moment, Turko dropped to the floor, yanked out his own gun, and rolled.

* * *

Westman positioned himself at the bottom of the stairs, waiting. At the sound of a gunshot, he started up the steps, then froze. There were two more shots in rapid succession, then a fourth.

Moving to the top of the stairs, he all of a sudden saw Bertolucci coming along the gallery toward him, a pistol in his hand. Westman now had his automatic out as well. Both weapons were held to the fore, but neither fired.

The walkway was lighted. They could see each other's faces.

"You were at the Ocean City airport," Turko said. "You're one of the Coast Guard men."

"Yes. And you're Bertolucci."

A painfully long silence followed. Westman's pistol began to grow heavy in his hand. There was no round in the chamber. He'd have to slide back the receiver before he could fire.

"I mean to leave here alive," Turko said. "It would be wise to kill you first, but I think I don't need to do that."

"Why not?"

"Because you might kill me first."

"What I must do is arrest you."

"That is something you can't do now. I will not shoot you, but you must let me pass."

"I can't. There were gunshots up here."

"Yes. Room Number Nine. There are two dead men in there. I was working for them but they tried to kill me. Now, please, step aside and put away your weapon. I need to leave. Police will be coming."

"Who are the dead men?"

"Agents of the FBI. You have better ones."

Westman reacted with anger and bafflement. This man was working for the FBI?

He had put himself off guard. Bertolucci took a swift step forward and kneed Westman in the groin, quickly following that with a push down the stairs. Westman's head thumped painfully on four or five steps as he slid downward. His pistol slipped from his hand. Bertolucci picked it up and flung it across the parking lot, then stuck his own weapon in his belt and stepped over Erik, hesitating once he reached the stair below.

"Why are you letting me live now?" Westman asked.

"Because I want to tell you something. I am a friend to the U.S. I save the lives of thousands of your people that others were trying to kill. You tell that to your government."

With that, he ran down the remaining stairs and to his car. Westman had only just managed to sit up when the other turned from the parking lot onto the main coast road, squealing tires and heading north.

Chapter 38

Cat lay facedown in the water, watching a barracuda move along the reef, pursuing its murderous trade—the raison d'etre of all denizens of the deep.

It was late morning and the high sun was bright and hot upon her back. The water was warm and of an uncommon clarity. She felt rather like some unearthly angel hovering over the creatures of the reef below, as though the sea here were but another form of air.

There were more than ninety cays and major islands in the Caicos chain of the Turks and Caicos Islands. Except for Providenciales, Parrot Cay, and a couple of others, they were all uninhabited. The one lying a few hundred yards from where she floated had once been uninhabited, but it now was home to two visiting Americans—Americans who now found themselves happier than they had been in a very long time.

The barracuda was large—a four-foot length of gliding, sinuous silver with nasty mouth and flat, predatory eyes. It moved effortlessly, as though propelled solely by will, cruis-

ing along the coral rock. Other fish, innocent and strangely
unconcerned, darted and fluttered all around it, their myriad
brilliant hues—gold and royal blue and crimson, green and
yellow and mauve with black stripes—dazzling to the eye, a
marked contrast to the barracuda's obscuring paleness. The
big fish continued steadily on among them, as though shopping. Following a curve of reef, it came finally to a spot directly beneath Cat. There it halted. Then, with the merest
flick of edge of fin, it pivoted, tail going down, head rising,
its eyes fixed on hers.

She stared hard back through her snorkel mask, but had
nothing to say to it. She was observing its world, but keeping
out of it, the stillness of her body imparting this message.

The terrible fish seemed to understand. Head going
down, tail rising, it leveled itself and turned and glided close
to the caves and crannies of the reef, hesitating, then darting
into a patch of bright red weed. In two snaps, it consumed its
find—what had been life gone in an instant. Then it lifted
and moved on, leaving the stage. This was the daily business
of the beautiful reef. Killing. Eating. Hiding.

Cat altered her own position, lowering her legs and raising her head above water, lifting her mask to her brow, looking to seaward, where a small sailboat lay at anchor, its sail
neatly bundled on the tiny deck.

Westman sat by the tiller, content to wait for her, but
looking landward with unusual interest.

Decades before, the cay had been farmed after a fashion,
but had long since become derelict and was completely deserted but for them, though it was just three small islands
from Providenciales. The British government here, head-
quartered many miles away on Grand Turk, was allowing
them this habitation in the belief they were conducting a nat-
uralist's study of the indigenous iguanas and other wildlife.

It was a blissful place, not merely for the abundance of its
beauty but for the gentle rhythms of their life upon it. They
lived without electricity in the shelter of a large and very wa-

terproof tent, their possessions amounting to little more than some kerosene lamps, a battery-powered CD player, a few CDs, a large number of books, two cameras, sketch pads and watercolors, fishing rod, and some clothes—most of which remained packed.

She was naked. He wore a pair of shorts.

Westman's boat was a Laser, all of seventeen feet in length. It had a centerboard that allowed for easy beaching. The main wharf on Provo, as Providenciales was known locally, was only an hour or so away, depending on the weather. When in need of bottled water, kerosene for the lamps, or groceries, they'd go to Turtle Bay on Provo's seaward side. But these trips were infrequent and their stays there very brief.

They occasionally had visitors, for the most part stray tourists, but the nudity that had become their custom usually warded such people off. Cat wondered if his concern meant that more of these intruders had come.

Returning her mask to her face, she flattened out in the water again, drifting, observing the colorful tableau below disinterestedly now. Finally, she closed her eyes, withdrawing from all but the warmth of sun and sea and the gentle, limpid motion of the slight swells and breeze.

There was a snapping sound, and at once her head shot up. Westman had raised and sheeted his main, filling it with wind and steering toward her.

He hove to a few feet away, turning into the wind, causing the main to flap noisily.

"We have company," he said. "Not tourists. Do you want to greet them?"

She looked to the distant shore, making out vague figures standing on the beach. She had heard a motorboat earlier. It must have landed on the other side of the cay.

"No, thank you. I'll swim to shore."

"Go to the dune. I'll join you when it's clear."

He turned the boat into the wind, jolting forward. She

watched him take a single tack toward the island, then began swimming her shorter course to the nearer beach.

Coming ashore on a swift beam reach, point of sail, Westman pulled up the centerboard in time for the craft to slide far up the sand, then snapped loose the mainsheet and let the large sail flap free. Hopping over the side, he pulled the sailboat higher up onto the beach, lowering the mainsail and bending it over the boom. Securing the canvas with a length of dock line, he tied it fast, then went to meet his uninvited guests.

One he knew—Charlie Marantes, a fellow special agent in the Coast Guard Investigative Service who was assigned to the Southeast Region and based in San Juan. Marantes had been with Westman and dePayse in the La Perla action. Another Erik recognized was Thor Holm, with the Navy Criminal Investigative Service. The third visitor he had never seen before.

Marantes wore slacks and a polo shirt. The Navy man was dressed in a sport coat, slacks, and open-collared sport shirt. The mystery man was similarly garbed but was actually wearing a tie.

"Hello, Charlie," Westman said.

Marantes nodded. "Erik."

"Was it hard to find me?"

"No. Your lady friend attracted attention."

"Do you want to go to my tent?"

"No, thanks," said the Navy man. "Let's go find a shady tree."

As they walked to a nearby cluster of three palms, the mystery man still said nothing, even as they lowered themselves into a semicircle on the sand. He'd been wearing a Panama straw hat. He removed it, revealing little hair.

"Are you here to arrest us?" Westman said finally.

"No," said Marantes. "Not you, not her—though back in the States she'd probably get picked up for indecent exposure."

"This is not the States."

"We're here after some information," Marantes said. "You may have an idea what it is."

Marantes looked to the mystery man, who loosened his tie before speaking.

"We have gone through a great many files and a great deal of data," he said. "It now seems highly probable—in fact, almost certain—that Captain Schilling was correct in his conviction that one of the bombs he jettisoned back in the sixties contained its nuclear core and triggering device."

"He wouldn't have gone through all that he did if he wasn't sure," Westman said. "None of us would have."

"I appreciate that," said the mystery man. "But there's a problem. The bomb you recovered. The one that was pulled out of the wreck at Dover. It contained no plutonium, no nuclear trigger."

"Are you sure?" Erik was stunned.

"Sent it to Los Alamos. They're the experts. They said no."

"So it has to be in the other bomb," said Marantes. "The one that's still down there."

"You know our equipment," said Holm, the Navy man. "We're prepared to throw in all our resources to recover the other one."

"But we need a location, a starting point," said the mystery man. "We need to know where you found the one you pulled out of the sea."

"Did Schilling use a GPS?" Holm asked.

"Yes," said Westman. "Loran too. Every kind of navigational aid and every calculation he could. That's how he found it."

"He wrote this information down?" asked the mystery man.

"Yes."

"And you have it?"

"I know where it is."

"Well, then. That's what we'd like to know."

Westman watched a motor launch come around the side of the next cay. It had two black men forward, an older white man and two boys in the back—a tourist boat heading out to the flats to go bone fishing.

"Chief Warrant Officer Westman," said the mystery man. "You are still a serving member of the armed services of the United States. Please cooperate."

Erik picked up a handful of sand and let it pour through his fingers. "I would have thought my military status open to question," he said. "Certain breaches of discipline. Disobedience of standing orders—and direct orders."

Marantes grinned. "If that's what's worrying you, forget it. You're a certified hero now. So are Lieutenant Dewey and Master Chief DeGroot. The Homeland Security Secretary has so decreed."

"Those bad guys you bagged included a really big fish— Jozip Pec," said the mystery man. "We're sure it was his guys who were behind the Bay Bridge attack, and the one at the Farmingdale nuclear plant. The White House is very pleased with the way things turned out."

Westman ran a finger through the sand. "I was expecting a court-martial. And separation."

"You've never been taken off the active duty rolls," Marantes said. "There are no charges. DePayse's been after us to find you now so you can be flown back to Washington with the others for a medal ceremony. DePayse and Dewey are getting promotions out of this. DeGroot didn't want one."

"Promotion for you too," said Holm.

"I don't want one."

"He'd have to leave the CGIS," Marantes explained to the others.

A large brown pelican swooped and flapped overhead, then abruptly dived with a crash into the water, emerging a few seconds later with a large fish in its bill.

"So," said the mystery man. "Are you going to help us?"

Westman grimaced. "You know, you could have had the information you want in a trice—if someone in your vast, almighty military had just listened to Burt Schilling. He went to Dover and begged them to listen to him. There was a colonel there. . . ."

"Baker," said the mystery man. "He's now commanding a string of radar stations in Alaska."

"We haven't been following the news much down here," Erik said. "Does the general public know about the bomb?"

"No," said Marantes. "All that was released to the press was that there was a fight with terrorists and a hijacking of a C-130."

"Foiled by Captain Schilling," Holm added.

"And if the truth were to get out?" Westman asked.

"It won't," said the mystery man. "It's highly classified information."

Westman smiled, looking each one of them in the eye, then picking up another handful of sand. "There were two FBI agents killed, I think by one of the terrorists. Was he ever arrested?"

"Nope," Marantes said. "No one was ever arrested. It was written up as another terrorist strike. Do you know anything more about it?"

"That's not what you came down here to ask me about."

The three looked at each other, then back to Westman. "We need the coordinates, Westman," said Holm. "Schilling's charts. Do you have them?"

"I have them available."

"All right, Erik," said Marantes, getting the idea. "What do you want?"

Westman let go of all the sand. "We lost a Coast Guard crewman that night—Machinists Mate Aboud Dourai—and two Air National Guard people. They were killed in action fighting the terrorists. Saved the rest of us. I think that's worthy of Arlington, if their families wish."

"DOD already made arrangements for that," said Holm. "One of the families took them up on it."

"Schilling too," Erik said.

"That's another matter," said Holm. "According to his 201 file, he was run out of the service for being drunk on the flight line."

"I'd say he's redeemed himself."

"I'm sorry," said Holm. "The requirements for Arlington are pretty strict. You need your twenty years in, or to lose your life in the line of duty. Schilling qualifies for neither."

"There are waivers. I know of at least one son of a bitch with a phony military record who got a presidential waiver for Arlington because of the size of his campaign contribution."

"That was an anomaly," said Holm. "And they dug him up again."

"Come on, Erik," Marantes said. "Don't complicate things."

"It's all right," said the mystery man. "It can be arranged. No problem."

Westman nodded. "And then there's the matter of Lieutenant Catherine McGrath." He looked to Holm. "She deserves to be reinstated. She risked her life in this, from beginning to end. She flew carrier jets when she was on active duty. You've got officers putting in their twenty who never touched anything more lethal than a supply manifest."

"Her reinstatement was in the works," Holm said. "No reason the process can't be resumed, especially since all the evidence in that case now seems to favor her."

"I'm talking about her getting back into a Tomcat cockpit."

Holm shook his head. "The decision by the evaluation board to ground her was unanimous and irreversible. Those things never get overturned. There was demonstrable pilot error in that mishap. Her weapons officer was killed. Sorry. Can't be done."

The mystery man nodded.

Erik pondered this, staring at the sand before him. Then he got to his feet.

"Well?" said Marantes, rising also. The other two did the same.

"You're not going to stiff us, are you, Westman?" Holm asked. "You're not going to shake us down for something else?"

"Where are you staying?" Westman asked Marantes.

"On Provo. At the Ramada."

"Do you have a cell phone?"

"Of course. Regulation."

"Give me the number. I'll call you tomorrow morning."

The other two were eyeing him darkly. "You're not thinking of wandering away again?" Holm asked.

Westman shook his head. "I like it here. And my Laser isn't about to outrun you."

They turned to go. Erik stopped them. "There was a suspect we identified as an Anthony Bertolucci. Was he ever found?"

The mystery man shook his head. "No. He wasn't taken prisoner. He wasn't among the bodies."

"No trace of him? No word?"

"Nothing. You have something on him?"

Westman considered this. "No."

"Doesn't matter," Marantes said. "We've busted the whole operation."

"There've been no other incidents? No attacks?"

"None."

"I'll call tomorrow," Erik said.

They moved on down to the other side of the island, where a black man was lounging against the bow of a runabout hauled up on the sand. Westman remained at the top of the dune, watching them go. As they got under way, Marantes turned and waved.

* * *

Cat was lying on a towel in front of their tent, sipping a soft drink.

"They've gone," Westman said.

"Who were they?"

"Gentlemen from the federal government." He sat down beside her.

"You're frowning," she said. "Did they give you a hard time?"

"In a way."

"What did they want?"

"I don't know if you're ready to hear this, but there was no nuclear core in that bomb we recovered. It's in the other one."

She set down her drink and lay back on the towel, looking straight up at the limitless blue sky. "They want Burt's charts. The GPS coordinates."

"Right. I'm going to turn them over. I'm pretty sure they can find it, with the equipment they have today."

"What's going to happen to us?"

"If you can believe them—and I believe one of them— I'm being given back my career. And they're probably going to let you back in the Navy."

"How was this miracle achieved?"

"A brief negotiation."

"Back into Tomcats?"

He looked at her sadly. "No. Reinstatement, surface ships—I think they'll be happy to grease the skids for that. But no flying. They won't overturn a ruling by an evaluation board."

"That's for certain?"

"Yes, ma'am."

She rolled over again, looking at the sand. "I should have expected it. A lot of people feel something like that would poison the whole system—you undercut evaluators."

"There's no malice here. I think they're doing their best for us."

"I don't want reinstatement then, Erik."

"You're sure?"

"I did my best by my dad and my uncle. I gave it my best shot. But I'm a flier. I can't walk a deck or ride a desk. I'd go crazy. You know that."

"I guess I do."

"Besides, I like it down here. There are little Twin Otter and floatplane airlines all over these islands. I don't think it would be that hard for me to get a right-hand seat. A friend of my dad's used to run a seaplane line in the British Virgins. Maybe he's still around."

"Well, that makes things very simple for me."

"And how is that, my love?"

"They want me to go to Washington and take part in a medal ceremony. Dewey and me, the master chief, and Admiral dePayse, we're all to be honored for taking down the terrorists."

"Admiral dePayse."

"She owes me."

Cat turned to face him. They were very close to each other. "And how do you propose to collect?"

"I was thinking of asking for a transfer out of Washington. I'm pretty sure they'd give me any place I want—as things stand. Be happy to have me out of the way probably."

"And?"

He kissed her. "Now I know exactly where I want to go."

About the Author

Michael Kilian is a veteran Washington columnist and national security correspondent for the *Chicago Tribune* and the writer of the Dick Tracy comic strip. He is the author of twenty-five books, including Berkley's Harrison Raines Civil War Mystery series and Bedford Green Jazz Age Mystery series. A former pilot and longtime sailor, he is a captain in the U.S. Air Force Civil Air Patrol and a member of the U.S. Coast Guard Auxiliary. He served with the Eighth Army in Korea and the 82nd Airborne Division at Fort Bragg, North Carolina. He and his wife, Pamela, reside in McLean, Virginia, and Bethany Beach, Delaware.

MICHAEL KILIAN

**The Harrison Raines
Civil War Mystery series**

Based on actual events and extensive research, this innovative series follows U.S. Secret Service Agent Harrison Raines through the Civil War chronologically, battle-by-battle, using a specific historic battlefield as a setting for each novel.

MURDER AT MANASSAS
0-425-17743-2

A KILLING AT BALL'S BLUFF
0-425-18314-9

THE IRONCLAD ALIBI
0-425-18823-X

A GRAVE AT GLORIETA
0-425-19531-7

THE SHILOH SISTERS
0-425-20004-3

**Available wherever books are sold or at
www.penguin.com**

Michael Kilian

The Jazz Age Mystery Series

Set in the 1920s, this clever series takes readers
to the height of the Jazz Age. From speak-easies to the
bohemian scene, they'll follow Bedford Green, a
man-about-town who rubs elbows with famous
personalities, dabbles in art dealing,
and solves a few crimes.

"[Kilian] successfully combines the genre of
historical novel and murder mystery."
—*Booklist*

"Engaging." —*Denver Post*

"An absorbing period piece."
—*San Antonio Express-News*

The Weeping Woman

0-425-18001-8

The Uninvited Countess

0-425-18582-6

AVAILABLE WHEREVER BOOKS ARE SOLD OR AT
www.penguin.com